'TIL DARKNESS FALLS

Pearl Love

DSP PUBLICATIONS

Published by
DSP PUBLICATIONS

5032 Capital Circle SW, Suite 2, PMB# 279, Tallahassee, FL 32305-7886 USA
http://www.dsppublications.com/

'Til Darkness Falls
© 2015 Pearl Love.

Cover Art
© 2015 Paul Richmond.
http://www.paulrichmondstudio.com
Cover content is for illustrative purposes only and any person depicted on the cover is a model.

ISBN: 978-1-63476-056-0
Digital ISBN: 978-1-63476-057-7
Library of Congress Control Number: 2014959923
Second Edition July 2015
First Edition published by Dreamspinner Press, November 2010.

Printed in the United States of America
∞
This paper meets the requirements of
ANSI/NISO Z39.48-1992 (Permanence of Paper).

To my parents,
who always encouraged
me to scribble away.

PROLOGUE

Unto the ending of the world,
When darkness falls
And the sun shines no more,
My love shall never falter.

Tanis, Egypt
945 B.C.E.

PRINCE RAHOTEP, eldest son of the magnificent God-King Psusennes II, slammed out of the banquet hall, the false laughter of self-important old men ringing in his ears. His golden brown eyes sparked with anger and frustration as he strode down the hall, eager to reach his room and escape his fast-approaching fate.

Damn my father and his gods-blasted politics.

Tomorrow he would be forced to do his duty as the pharaoh's heir and forsake all personal ambitions and hopes in order to save the kingdom. The Libyans, their neighbors to the west, were a powerful and persistent lot. General Sheshonq I had long been a threat, striving to extend his reach from the arid soil of his land toward the lush country protected by the towering shadows of the mighty pyramids. After many years of increased bloodshed and the threat of war, Psusennes II had bowed beneath the pressure, unwilling to see his lands plundered and the mighty river stained red with blood. Sheshonq I had wanted to bind the pharaoh's vow of submission through marriage, and so Psusennes II had sacrificed his only son upon the altar of political expediency.

It was a shrewd maneuver, to be certain, but Rahotep could not find it in his heart to admire his father's cleverness. He was still a young man, barely eighteen, and he found it hard to accept that he was being forced into such a repugnant situation. The next rising of the sun would see him locked in matrimony to Sheshonq I's only daughter, the incomparable Hester, who had already taken the Egyptian name Hebeny as a sign of loyalty to her new country. She was soft in speech, graceful in manner, and her olive-skinned beauty was without equal.

Yet Rahotep had remained unmoved upon their first meeting several months before. Her dark eyes, subtly lined with kohl, had seemed to him lifeless and cold. Hebeny had struck him as a spoiled girl, calculating and mean of spirit. Rahotep wanted absolutely nothing to do with her, for how could he calmly accept this onerous duty when he already possessed everything he could possibly want?

The prince's step quickened as he at last reached his private chambers. His personal guard opened the ornately carved doors—resplendent with the symbols of the gods and his own royal status—and his rebellious discontent calmed instantly as his gaze fell eagerly upon a slender form.

"*Pa'sheri.*"

Tiye looked up at the quiet salutation and smiled, his soft brown eyes glowing in the candlelight as he looked upon his prince. The boy was slight in stature, though strong of limb from a lifetime of toil. His skin, which held the vibrant shades of rich, freshly turned soil—a legacy from his half-Nubian mother—reflected the flickering light of the tapers scattered about the opulent room. He had been born a slave and knew he would die as such. Yet his heart was not mired in sadness, for he knew the blissful joy of shared love.

"*Mery,*" Tiye replied. The endearment came easily to his lips, without causing a blush as it had oft done in the past. *Little one. Beloved.* Such were the names by which the prince and his slave were known only to each other. Tiye crossed the chamber, nimbly weaving his way among the rich furnishings, decorations, and objects of antique art that filled the room. He laughed as freely as any seventeen-year-old boy might, elated as his lover caught him up in a pair of strong arms.

Their lips met and clung, and Tiye pulled back reluctantly after the passage of several heavenly minutes. Excitement at his love's nearness quivered and hummed in his belly like the plucked string of an oud. Never did Rahotep fail to engender such a reaction within him, but as always, duty beckoned. Tiye grasped Rahotep's hand and led him into the bath chamber before turning his attention to the richly embroidered shirt and blue-dyed *kalasiris* that covered his prince's muscular form.

"How went the negotiations?" Tiye asked, keeping his tone neutral with effort. Hoping the familiar task might settle his nerves, he took care to fold the garments before placing them in the large cedar chest sitting in a corner of the room. Ever since he had heard the first whispered hints of the pharaoh's plans for placating the Libyan aggressors, his fretful gaze had been anxiously tracking Ra's fiery passage across the sky. When they had finally come, the general and his daughter, Tiye knew he and his lover were living on borrowed time.

"As well as my father hoped."

Rahotep sighed as he rubbed at tired eyes, the dark kohl lining them staining his fingertips. Glaring at the smudge in annoyance, he used his clean hand to dislodge the elaborate headdress from his long, silky black hair. His golden gaze tracked Tiye to the large, sunken tub that graced the center of the room, noticing the sudden stiffness in the youth's movements. Tiye knelt and poured a vial of fragrant sandalwood oil into the steaming hot water that filled the gold-lined depression. He had removed his modest cotton skirt in anticipation of bathing his master, and Rahotep was unable to resist the enticement of that sleek expanse of naked skin.

Tiye started when he was suddenly pulled flush against the prince's hard chest and harder manhood. The stiff length of flesh pressed into the furrow of his buttocks, seeking to become reacquainted with what had been so willingly offered time and again. Tiye allowed himself a moment's indulgence, pressing the curve of his ass against his lover's arousal. His own need rose eagerly in response. Groaning softly at the delicious tease, Rahotep leaned his cheek against Tiye's head and rubbed against the short nest of tight black curls before bending to press parted lips to the side of his long neck. Tiye closed his eyes and sighed as his hands fell to the arms wrapped around his waist, almost forgetting his duty as his prince sucked and nibbled at all of the sensitive spots he had spent the past few years charting.

Rahotep growled in disappointment when Tiye pulled away, a flush apparent even beneath the dusky hue of his skin. Tiye stepped into the water, and Rahotep resisted playfully for a moment when Tiye grabbed his hand to pull him into the tub, unconsciously seeking to lighten the mood between them. But heaviness crept back into the air even as he closed his eyes in gratitude when Tiye poured a generous measure of cleansing oil into his hair and began to work the long mass into a rich lather.

"And you are definitely to be wed tomorrow?"

The question caught in Tiye's throat, threatening to choke him, but he needed to know for certain. If he had learned anything during his life of servitude, it was that it did no good to ignore whatever Fate might bring. Tiye gently massaged Rahotep's scalp before shifting his attention to the tense muscles in his lover's shoulders. He was content for a while simply to trace his hands over Rahotep's powerful body, watching as the water sluiced from his bronzed skin. But when long minutes passed without an answer, Tiye reached out with a hand, the slightest of tremors betraying him, and lifted Rahotep's chin until he could look into his troubled eyes.

"Please tell me."

"Yes."

The succinct reply cut like a knife into Tiye's heart. He glanced away as tears stung his eyes, but he controlled them resolutely, unable to claim any surprise at the gut-wrenching answer. It had only been a matter of time before his beloved took a bride, as he must. For the past three years, he had been basking in a beautiful dream, but at last, the truth was no longer content to be neglected.

He had been a scared, lonely child when he found himself appointed to serve the pharaoh's son. When the pharaoh's servants had come to his mother's hovel in the slave village to take him away from her, his elder brother, and all he had ever known, he had wept bitter tears. Trembling with fear, he had gone to meet his new lord, but the prince's bright smile of welcome had dazzled him. The ogre he had so dreaded was nowhere to be found. Instead, the young prince was by turns playful and kind, teasing Tiye when he lost the battle against his clumsy growing limbs and giving him a warm chest against which to hide his tears when the absence of his family became too much to bear.

Tiye fell swiftly and irrevocably in love, swept away by the wonder that was his beautiful master. One night, not six months after he had come into the prince's service, Rahotep had caught him staring, his besotted expression unable to hide the adoration that had grown so quickly in his heart. But the prince showed no revulsion, despite their common gender. By the grace of the gods, Tiye had found his impossible love fully returned, and they had spent the ensuing days lost in a blur of tender happiness and blistering passion.

But now it was all to end. Tiye struggled desperately to hold himself together despite the shattering of his soul into a thousand pieces. Unable to speak, he turned away from Rahotep and moved to the edge of the tub. He tried to lift himself out of the water, but he was suddenly too weak. His prince would no longer be his alone. How would he survive knowing that his *mery* lay in the arms of another?

There was no warning save a low, rumbling growl and an agitated wave of water rushing toward him. Tiye gasped as a pair of muscular arms hauled him into a punishing grip. The prince's strong hands whirled him around until he was pinned by a fierce gaze that caused his heart to thunder in his chest. Tiye opened his mouth to speak, but whatever words he might have uttered were lost beneath the lips that descended upon his, devouring his will in a fervent kiss. Tiye moaned, his ribs creaking from the ferocious vise of Rahotep's arms, but he encircled the prince's neck just as desperately, pressing ever closer to his lover's tall body.

Rahotep pulled back only after Tiye had gone limp in his arms. When he opened his eyes, Rahotep fixed him with a turbulent stare, willing Tiye to heed him. "Do not doubt that I love you. Never doubt that!"

The prince's deep, commanding tone brooked no argument. For the first time, Tiye truly understood that this man, who had only ever filled his soul with joy and his body with sweet fire, would one day rule the most powerful kingdom in the known world. His blood sang with need as it rushed through his veins, sped by his pounding heart. So beautiful, his *mery*, his beloved prince. Rahotep's tawny skin glistened in the candlelight, the smoothly shifting muscles in the arms holding him so close, proclaiming his strength. Tiye knew he would die the day those golden eyes ceased to look upon him. And yet how could this closeness between them continue when confronted with the truth?

"I do not doubt it, but—" Tiye's voice dropped to a whisper as the elegant image of his lover's intended assailed him, taunting him with her cold perfection. "But we cannot continue on this way. You are to be wed, and I will have no further place in your life save as your devoted slave." Tiye pushed futilely against Rahotep's broad shoulders, voice cracking as his throat choked with unshed tears.

Rahotep's hold never slackened as Tiye struggled. He paid Tiye's logic no more heed than he would a damselfly flitting along the shores of the Nile. "Nothing will ever replace you in my heart, my beautiful *pa'sheri*. Not pharaoh nor country, and certainly not a bride for whom I hold not the slightest affection. I go to this union like a beast to slaughter, powerless except to rail against my fate. But you will be my salvation, as you have always been." With powerful grace, he lifted Tiye out of the water, holding him so they were eye-to-eye. "Not even the gods themselves can keep us apart. I will love you forever." Rahotep gazed lovingly into Tiye's shimmering eyes as he laid him against the cool golden tiles and slowly closed the distance between them. "And I will keep you here and make love to you until you accept this as truth or the gods damn our souls to the underworld."

Tiye parted his full lips in welcome at the questing thrust of a bold tongue, intoxicated by the sweetness of his prince. Powerful hips pushed forward, obliging him to spread his legs wide in accommodation. He moaned, his head falling back helplessly as Rahotep's heavy arousal found his own swollen shaft. His body flamed with a sudden rush of exquisite heat, the aching flesh between his thighs straining upward wantonly to meet its fellow. Gentle fingertips brushed across his lashes, and a warm palm tenderly cupped his cheek. Tiye's eyes blinked open to meet Rahotep's soft regard. For a long moment, they gazed at each other, the vast gulf of their disparate births reduced to nothing. With only the softly lapping water to bear witness, a promise was made, silent but no less solemn and binding for its quiet. If there were such a thing as Fate, if destiny truly did hold sway over the lives of men, then without question they were meant to be together. Surely not even death itself could separate them.

"Until the ending of the world," Rahotep murmured against Tiye's lips, urging him to finish the lines of the verse they had formed together one starry night on the banks of the great river.

"My love shall never falter."

Tiye gloried in his lover's strength as Rahotep lifted him and carried him to the soft hide stretched before the glowing hearth fire. Clever lips and a wicked tongue nuzzled and nipped at the brown nubs on his chest, coaxing them into sensitive points as he writhed helplessly beneath the tender caresses.

"*Mery*!" Tiye cried as Rahotep delved between his legs to reverently worship his weeping shaft. His voice swiftly grew hoarse in shouted appreciation of his master's skill. He reached down with frantic hands to bury his fingers in the soft hair that brushed against the skin of his inner thighs and draped teasingly over his belly and hips.

"No," Tiye moaned as his body shuddered. "Please, do not… yesss!"

Rahotep smiled at the breathy, contradictory pleas as Tiye's shaft pulsed desperately against his tongue. Tiye's moans sounded to his ears like the singing of Isis, which could drive men mad with its divine beauty. With a long finger, he probed the tender entrance revealed by the careless sprawl of Tiye's slender legs. Rahotep groaned, his own manhood throbbing in response as soft flesh fluttered and clenched around his finger.

Flashes of light sparked behind Tiye's shut lids as the finger deftly caressing his inner flesh withdrew and the wet heat of an intrepid tongue took its place. As though trying to escape from his overwrought body, he twisted his torso around and pressed his flushed face into the rug, grasping fitfully at the soft wool as Rahotep licked at his sensitive flesh. Strong thumbs pulled the smooth globes of his ass apart, and Tiye began to spout incoherent prayers for mercy as his lover's tongue swirled against his quivering ring before dipping inside to taste his hidden depths. A possessive hand took hold of his arousal, stroking it slowly with a sword-roughened palm. Desire pooled low in his belly before slowly spreading through his trembling limbs until his entire body was bathed in heat and sweat.

Lost in the taste of his beloved *pa'sheri*, Rahotep lingered as long as he dared, but his body soon clamored with the need to claim what was his. Bracing himself with arms that shivered with desperate weakness, he looked down at the boy stretched beneath him. Tiye's smooth, dark skin glistened with the sweat of passion, glowing in the candlelight. Honey-tinted eyes gazed at him adoringly, and soft, full lips parted with gentle pants, tempting him to partake of this sweet gift from the gods.

Tiye wrapped his slim legs around his prince's waist, drawing Rahotep forward into the cradle of his thighs. Rahotep's manhood touched Tiye's sacred place, and it lengthened and hardened as he sensed the nearness of his treasured goal. Rahotep buried his face in the sweet curve of Tiye's neck, inhaling the heady scent of clean sweat and heated arousal. He sucked gently at the long, vulnerable column, a primitive growl on his lips when he raised his head and saw the faint mark that he had made on the dark skin. Tiye's dazed gaze caressed his face, and Rahotep answered his wordless plea with a soft kiss.

"'Til darkness falls," Rahotep whispered.

Tiye's brown eyes warmed in understanding as Rahotep thrust himself forward into paradise.

Tiye clung to his prince throughout the long, passion-filled night, knowing it would be the last time they could be together so innocently. Tomorrow, his beloved would marry, and Rahotep's new bride would usurp his place in his lover's bed. As he slept in his prince's arms, anguished tears slid down his face and into the solid warmth pillowing his head.

"BASTARD! SON of a diseased whore! How dare he betray me?" The clatter of expensive trinkets hitting the stone floor filled the room as Hebeny cleared her dressing table with a violent swipe of her bangle-laden arm. "Am I not the daughter of the mighty Sheshonq? And he would set me aside for some unclean Nubian filth on the very eve of our wedding?"

Trella winced as the lines around her lady's mouth deepened, making her look far older than her seventeen years. She had been forced to be the bearer of the unwelcome tidings, and now she waited silently for her mistress's heated tirade to run its course, having learned that was always the most prudent option. What would inevitably follow, she knew from experience, would be far worse. Indeed, silence soon fell, and Hebeny sat quietly for a long moment. Her black eyes, lined extravagantly with kohl, flashed with hatred as she gazed upon the cruelly beautiful reflection looking back at her from a sheet of beaten metal. A shudder racked Trella's frail body when the girl favored her with a gaze colder than the Gulf of Sidra's treacherous currents.

"Trella, my love, you have confirmed my suspicions about my betrothed, and it grieves me." Hebeny's tone dripped with malice, belying her expression of regret. "But I cannot allow such perfidy to go unpunished, not even by a man as unblemished as Prince Rahotep."

Trella felt a moment's compassion for the poor man who was to wed her harridan of a mistress. She longed to look away as Hebeny's glance became pregnant with meaning.

"You know what to do," the girl said in a voice devoid of emotion.

Trella wished with all her heart that she possessed the courage to deny her lady's maleficent will. Faced with her own cowardice, she merely nodded and slunk off to obey her mistress's command.

Hebeny watched her go, waiting until the door shut completely behind her before moving toward it and sliding the lock into place. Confident she would remain undisturbed, Hebeny strode purposefully toward the darkest corner of her bedchamber. There, on an ornately carved round wooden table, sat a small altar formed of onyx. The black stone repelled the eye, swallowing all light so it seemed obscured from view. It was covered with a fine layer of dust, as none of the slaves would go near it even to clean it, fearing that it bore the evil eye and might curse them.

Closing her eyes, Hebeny raised her hands toward the altar, palms outward in perfunctory reverence. Head lifted proudly in reckless defiance, she whispered the forbidden words she had been taught in the secret underground temples of her homeland. The ancient language flowed effortlessly from her tongue, the incantation building in volume slowly as it gained in strength. The words of the caustic spell were sharp enough to pierce through living flesh. The room filled with dark power, weighing down the very air with malevolence until it seemed as though Hebeny would be unable to withstand the forces she had summoned.

The onyx began to glow, growing ever more luminescent as the incantation reached a fevered pitch. A gray pallor leached the color from Hebeny's tawny skin, and sweat gleamed upon her face, reflecting the stone's dark light. Her body began to sway back and forth, her black hair tumbling down her back as her head fell backward in a parody of ecstasy. Her shouts filled the room until the very stones resonated with the power of her words. The air grew hot, burning her throat and stifling her breath, but the young sorceress persevered through sheer force of will, her endurance bolstered by the depths of her rage and wounded pride. As her mortal flesh threatened to succumb to the spectral fires that singed her hair and blackened her skin, she abruptly ended her casting with a demanding cry.

"Come now before me, Lord Set, bringer of chaos! Hear your loyal servant's plea, oh vengeful one, and smite my enemies beneath your merciless heel." The prayer rolled easily from her lips, learned when she was but a child. Her father had long had plans for his only daughter and Psusennes II's son, but he would not see her go unprotected into a foreign land. Now a powerful priestess of Set, she called the fearsome god to her aid without hesitation or regret.

Hebeny stood unflinching as a strong wind whipped through her room, the air laden with scouring gusts of desert sand though her windows were tightly closed. All light fled as the wind extinguished every candle, leaving only the ghostly glow seeping from the small altar of stone. The wisp of illumination rose as smoke from the onyx, undisturbed by the gritty maelstrom. Suddenly, the shapeless fog curled in on itself, twisting into a tight coil until it coalesced into a bright sphere in the center of the room. Stretching and deforming with obscene undulations, the light morphed into human form.

An abrupt flash stole Hebeny's vision, but when her eyesight returned, she was met by the image of a viciously beautiful man. He stood where the light had been, his tall frame radiating the arrogance of unchecked power. Long hair tinged with the dark red of spilled blood fell down his back, and deep, ruby eyes promised an eternity of torment. His shoulders were broad, his carriage regal beyond that claimed by any earthly pharaoh. Chiseled muscles rippled beneath his blackened skin as he shifted and glanced toward the young girl staring up at him with a haughty gaze.

Hebeny's heart beat faster at the sight of him despite the hint of fear that shivered deliciously through her from head to toe. She bowed her head in insincere modesty as the god looked down at her. He chuckled briefly before the deep rumble of his voice caressed her ears.

"This posture of humility does not become you, little witch. Come now, lift your head and tell me what it is you would have of me. Your aura fair pulses with hatred, and the desire for revenge stains your very soul."

Hebeny glared up at the god, her dark gaze refusing to shy from his awesome presence. "My betrothed has betrayed me with a gods-spurned boy," she snarled, "flaunting his perversion in my face and naming me fool. I care not that he be a future pharaoh. I will not be mocked by one such as him!"

The god smiled as her voice rose to an enraged shout, amused by her puny ire. "But you do not love this prince, so what do you care with whom he slakes his lusts?" His tone dripped with mock confusion. "If this boy brings him happiness—"

"I will not be made to endure second place to some lowborn cur!" She spat upon the floor as though to cleanse the filth of Rahotep's perfidy from her mouth.

"And how am I to soothe your injured pride? Why have you summoned me?" the god taunted. He already knew what she wanted but nonetheless greatly anticipated hearing her request. Endlessly fascinating was the human capacity for petty spite, and the cruelty concentrated in this tiny girl captivated him more than most.

"Soon the boy will be dead, and I guarantee it will be done in such a way that the prince's depraved heart will be utterly destroyed. I ask only this of you, mighty Set: damn the slave's soul to eternal torment such that he will know the penalty for humiliating me. Once he is gone, I shall comfort what remains of my darling prince, showering him with every earthly pleasure until his will is enslaved to my own. And when he has at last reached the peak of happiness, I will tell him of his wretched lover's fate. Then I shall kill him myself so he might experience the endless delight of your tender mercies, my lord."

Hebeny fixed her haughty gaze unwaveringly on the god, never doubting that her wish would be granted. Her jaw fell agape, and she flinched in shock when her callous demand was met with mocking laughter.

"Compared to the scorpion's sting, you would not be embarrassed by the judgment." Set's mocking chuckle was like the rumble of quiet thunder. "But I am sorry, my pet. I cannot meet your request. Damn them though I might, their souls will simply meet again during the next cycle of their existence."

"Then tear their souls asunder!" she screamed, her slippered foot stamping on the stone floor in frustration. "If their love be true and not some base convenience, make them suffer the damnation of eternal loneliness. Let them be kept apart even throughout all the ages of the world."

Set laughed, the walls shaking with the force of his mirth. "This is no small task you set for me, girl. The prince and his lover are bound by Shai, the guardian of Fate, and none, not even I, may thwart him. Even if you were to kill them in this life, their spirits will be reborn to this world time and again, and in no life shall they be kept from each other. No, I am afraid this is an impossible request."

Hebeny glared at him, refusing to accept the summary refusal. "Then tell me, oh mighty Set," she grated, any hint of respect fleeing before her ire, "how might I see my desire fulfilled?"

The god favored her with a slow smile that was terrible and beautiful to behold. For the first time in her life, Hebeny felt the chill of true dread.

"If you would see your revenge done, then you, not chance, must be the author of their misery. It is within my power to set you at their heels throughout time immemorial. You will be able to follow them throughout the incarnations of their lives and thwart their love by your own cleverness."

An eternity to seek her revenge! The heady possibility of Set's proposal astounded her, and Hebeny's face brightened with malicious glee at his words. She opened her mouth to accept, when he continued.

"But know that as Rahotep and his sweet Tiye properly greet each life with innocent souls, you will retain all memory and knowledge of every life you might live." He watched her with a steady, knowing gaze as she paled. "The human mind was not meant to bear the terrible weight of the ages, but if you are committed to this path, this will be your test."

The sobering warning lay heavily on her. To never know the blessings of true reincarnation? It went against every tenet and precept she had ever been taught. How would it be to be a mere babe with years, even centuries worth of memories to endure? Could she truly withstand such a burden?

As doubt swirled darkly in her thoughts, sapping her will, a vision of her handsome prince and his accursed slave flashed before her eyes. She had once caught a glimpse of the boy as he trailed in his master's wake, and the devotion that had shone upon his face had shaken her to the core. The boy's feelings for his master were unmistakable, but she refused to call their degenerate affection love. Irrational hate filled her, searing away all foreboding. Hebeny raised her black eyes and met the amused regard of the god standing patiently before her, determination stamped upon her delicate features.

Set read the answer on her face and chuckled. She truly was a treasure, one he would be sure to cherish when the time came. "Then it shall be. You will be the agent of your own success, and it will be measured thus: Rahotep and Tiye will meet and love in the ages to come as they have in this life. If, however, you can turn their love to hate and set them against each other, even unto death, then you will carry on and may join them in their next life as the guardian of their destruction.

"But," he continued, his voice vibrant with perverse delight, "if you fail to defeat their love, which the very stars have proclaimed, and one of them ends your life while protecting the other, the cycle of your own existence will be forever sundered. You will not be reborn or take your final place in Anubis's kingdom. Rather, you must submit yourself to me and walk in the burning desert of madness for all eternity. Neither rest nor respite will you find, only the harsh embrace of chaos's sand and the scorpion's terrible sting. And worst of all, you will know that Rahotep and Tiye will be together forevermore, finding and loving each other throughout all the lives they may yet live.

"Now, my girl, do you agree to my terms?" Set gazed softly at Hebeny's ashen face, waiting for the inevitable moment when her fierce pride would overcome any notion of sense or self. Indeed, she did not long contemplate her latent ruin. With all the desperate recklessness and certainty of youth, Hebeny tossed her head, flinging back long black hair as she met his gaze with arrogant defiance.

"I accept. They will know only despair, I swear it, and I will honor you with their pain."

Set only smiled before disappearing without further discourse. Hebeny had but a moment to ponder the deal she had struck before her musings were broken by the sound of angry shouts.

CHAPTER 1

"WE ARE of one body and share one soul." His tone was steady, belying his pain as his sword buried itself deeply within his lover's belly. The beautiful boy collapsed against him, blood covering their white garments with a vivid, ghastly red. It was a long moment before he realized the pain spreading through him was not merely from grief.

Blood spread beneath their feet as the failing beats of their hearts added to the steaming pool. He looked into his lover's eyes and saw only sorrow and devastating regret.

Forgive me.

His heart heard the words the boy could not speak. He glanced down, but only the dagger's hilt could be seen, the length of it buried deep in his chest. He looked up at his lover once more, his strength failing as he graced the boy with a gentle smile.

"Mery," the boy gasped, his final breath cooling the blood that bubbled from his lips.

They both fell to the ground, their fall marked by a cry of horror. And somewhere out in the howling desert could be heard the malevolent laughter of a delighted god....

"GET YOUR shit together, Macon, or you'll be spending the rest of your career finding lost pets, *Detective*."

Mumbling an echo of the captain's warning, Brian stared down moodily at his glass. Not that he could bring himself to care that his career was spiraling down the toilet. He was only thirty-three, but he was already feeling burned-out. All the shiny idealism that had carried him through the police academy at the top of his class was long buried in the dirt and muck of too many bodies and not enough justice.

Ice tinkled against the sides of the glass as Brian gently swirled his drink. He took a sip, wincing at the harsh burn that identified the whiskey as less than top-shelf. Sounds of quiet conversation and the slick swish of waiters decked out in a server's semblance of black tie passed around him unnoticed.

As gay bars went, Blackjack's was more upscale than most. It was a bar in the truest sense, where guys could go and enjoy a drink and a leisurely chat without the pheromone-laden noise of dance clubs. An unseen sound system was piping in classical music, and the lighting was just low enough to create an intimate atmosphere while still allowing a man to see a potential evening companion clearly. Blackjack's was perfect for men who were fatigued by the club scene but still wanted to enjoy the openness of a sympathetic setting. Brian had occasionally gone there for more social reasons, but tonight he was there simply out of a desire to avoid anyone from work. He was pretty sure he was the only gay man working Homicide out of the 8th Precinct.

Feeling older than his years, Brian stared absently at nothing in particular. It wasn't a good idea to drink on a work night, but the whiskey was a necessary medicinal—a cure for his recent lack of sleep. His dreams had been disturbing of late, as much for the content as for their repetitiveness. Images of thin, dark-skinned arms wrapping around the neck of an olive-toned man dressed in the rich apparel of some impossibly ancient time drifted across his mind. He quickly took a deeper drink to distract himself before the picture could fully take form, but it wasn't easy to quell the feelings that lingered from the dream. Even now, hours after waking and after putting in a full shift at the station, the memory of the dream made him hard. The loving press of the taller man's strong, toned body again his smaller companion, the caress of the boy's seeking fingers against his lover's skin….

Brian squirmed on his bar stool, helpless to prevent his arousal even as he fought against it. He glared down at the amber liquid as the condensation from the glass coated his long fingers with chilly wetness. He could have simply chalked the visions up to his recent spate of abstinence if it weren't painfully clear there was far more between the dream couple than mere sex.

"Who gives a shit?"

He had no time for romance, imaginary or otherwise. Brian knocked back the rest of his drink and contemplated whether to get another. The bartender noticed his empty glass and looked over at him, but Brian didn't immediately meet the man's gaze. He was on duty tomorrow and couldn't afford the hangover or the derision he would face from overindulging.

Brian winced as he caught his reflection in the mirror lining the wall behind the row of liquor bottles. Lines of exhaustion etched the light brown skin of his face. The green hazel eyes that gazed back at him were slightly red, as much from the whiskey as the tiredness that had become his constant companion. Cursing his irritatingly low tolerance, Brian settled for tipping a cube of ice from the glass into his mouth and sucking on it. His tongue absently chased the taste of whiskey lingering on the cold surface as the bartender took the hint and turned his attention toward a waiting customer.

It had been a long day—hell, a long few weeks—and he was dog tired from his inability to get a decent night's sleep. Unfortunately, he couldn't blame everything on the high-budget porno that kept playing in his head every night. The dead body he and his partner, Angela Lovell, had investigated two days ago was the third in three weeks that hadn't fit the usual mold of street violence. The victim had been an unimportant, low-level member of the Cosmino crime family. What was odd was the precision of the bullet hole that had scooped out a sizeable portion of the man's brain. The coroner had been adamant that a run-of-the-mill handgun hadn't caused the wound.

Forensics had found the bullet in the wall of the victim's apartment, just as they had with the prior victim, another Cosmino flunky. And just like its predecessor, the bullet had been frustratingly clean of any markings or distinguishing characteristics. Their lack of progress in finding any useful clues about who was hunting mobsters had severely displeased his beautiful but bitchy captain. Not that anyone would miss the scum, but the longer the rash of hits continued, the worse the department looked. Captain Preston was a woman of ambition, and she refused to tolerate any black marks on her otherwise perfect record.

Too bad she sounded like a screeching crow when she was pissed. With her insults ringing in his ears like nails on a blackboard, the last of the ice dissolved on Brian's tongue. He glanced at the bartender's back, thinking that maybe just one more drink wasn't such a bad idea after all.

"Forgive me for bothering you, but please tell me exactly who has put such a disagreeable expression on your face so that I may kill them."

The unexpected words, spoken in a mild yet outrageously sexy accent, made Brian lift his head sharply. He blinked in astonishment at the man who had presumptuously taken the stool next to him. Resentment at having his solitude disturbed by some guy on the make bubbled up but died a swift death as he got a good look at his uninvited companion. The stranger's features were finely sculpted, his close-cropped hair a shade so blond as to be almost white. The man's ice-blue eyes were somehow warm as they gazed at him, instantly tempering Brian's glare into a helpless stare. He was undeniably gorgeous, but the unexpected shock of recognition that shot through Brian caused him to clutch desperately at the empty glass in his hand.

I know him.

The thought ran through him like a shiver. Somehow, he'd known this man his entire life. Shaking his head to rid it of the ridiculous notion, Brian scowled, more unnerved than annoyed. The man quirked an eyebrow at him curiously, but his unwavering gaze was expectant, as though he was confident he wouldn't be rejected. His expression was open and inviting, but behind his calm, glacier-hued regard, Brian could sense a hidden intensity, a keen focus that was determined to miss nothing. The man's focus suddenly sharpened, and Brian was nearly convinced the man sensed the slight change in his breathing and the quickening of his pulse. The stranger's gaze shifted downward almost before Brian realized the warmth in his cheeks was an aberrant flush.

Humiliated at the revealing streaks of color, Brian turned away and lifted his glass to his lips distractedly before remembering that he had already drained it dry. He blinked at the empty glass, his discomfiture rapidly turning to self-disgust before mellowing into amusement at a seduction well played. Lifting his glass in acknowledgement, Brian smirked and glanced at the man from the corner of his eye. "That's a creative line. Are you always so inventive?" His stomach fluttered when the stranger chuckled. Brian wondered when he'd suddenly become a randy teenager with his first crush.

"Well, not to dash your expectations, but let me follow with this: may I buy you another drink?"

Brian laughed in spite of himself as he turned to look at the newcomer full-on. That unsettling focus was gone, but he hadn't been imagining how handsome the man was. His gaze drifted surreptitiously over the stranger's fair, shapely brows, strong cheekbones, and thin yet sensuous lips. A prominent, slightly crooked nose kept his face from being too perfect, but even that flaw wasn't enough to relieve the noticeable tightness in Brian's pants.

"Sure, why not?" he answered, ignoring the voice in the back of his mind telling him this was a bad idea. Brian had a feeling this wouldn't end with just drinks, but after the day he'd had, he deserved a little selfishness. The man smiled at him, fueling the growing hardness between his legs and quieting the lingering guilt that niggled at his conscience. Brian stared at the man's finger as he lifted it to gain the bartender's attention. Wondering how he could possibly find an index finger sexy, Brian forcibly looked away as his stranger ordered a martini for himself and a refill of whatever Brian was having.

"This is a beautiful piece, *ja*?"

Brian blinked at the non sequitur. He glanced distractedly at the bartender as the man set a newly filled glass in front of him before looking back toward his companion. The soothing music was nice enough, but he didn't know a concerto from concrete. "Um, I can't say I've heard it before." For a moment, Brian was tempted to pretend he was more sophisticated than he really was, but he knew his cheap suit practically screamed "middle-class peon."

"Beethoven's *Appasionata*," the man elaborated. "The third movement. Do you hear how the strings strain through the arpeggios, almost as though they're fighting gravity?" His hand moved in graceful counterpoint as he spoke expressively about a clearly beloved topic.

Brian understood only one word in ten, but the man's deep voice, supremely suited for the gutturalness of his accent, only heightened his fascination. Brian quickly realized he would have been equally entranced if the stranger were reading from an actuarial table.

"I have occasionally heard this piece attempted with a full orchestra in this way, but the maestro intended it for the piano. No other instrument is truly capable of capturing the essence of his intent. The ebb and flow of emotions, like winds ripping through the trees of the Black Forest during a storm. Such powerful imagery created with the mere touch of hammers to strings."

After the second serving of alcohol, Brian was feeling pleasantly warm and decidedly less cautious than he had a minute ago. He stared as the man paused to sip his martini, mesmerized by the sight of his lips, which glistened with droplets of gin. The stranger picked up the speared olives from the glass and took one of them between his teeth to slide it free. Brian shifted uncomfortably on his stool. Sensing a lull in the conversation and eager for it to continue, he hazarded a guess as to his companion's nationality.

"You're European?"

The flash of straight white teeth made Brian realize he'd said something embarrassingly gauche. He wanted to be angry, but there was no hint of condescension in the man's demeanor, only amusement at Brian's obvious gambit.

"I am German. And you are American, *ja?*"

Because Europe isn't a country. Brian could almost hear the gentle correction. Fighting off yet another blush, he answered with a crooked smile that was more than a little sheepish. "Yeah, I was raised right here in the city. I've never been to Germany, or even out of the country for that matter." Brian felt a little better when the man's expression remained free of any hint of pity for Brian's lack of worldly experience.

"Um, the Black Forest, is that where you're from? Is it nice?" He would have winced at the banality of their exchange if he'd been a little more sober and the man gazing at him almost fondly had been a little less hot. As it was, he was willing to talk about the time he'd gotten sick on the teacup ride at Disney World when he was six if it would keep his companion talking. Thinking about why he was so unwilling to end this interlude made him uneasy, but the whiskey dulled the edge of his concern.

"Um, no. I grew up in Potsdam, when it was still part of East Germany. But when I was a child, I loved to read about the forest and its nearby mountains. I finally got a chance to visit when I was in college, and yes, it is very nice. Would you come to my hotel room with me?"

The question was so straightforward and without preliminaries that it took Brian a moment to process it. But when he did, his body was quick to answer before his mind could interfere. Swelling to full hardness, Brian resisted the urge to press his legs together to appease the sudden ache. The man watched him closely, his brilliant blue gaze taking note of the uncertainty Brian felt flit over his face.

This is ridiculous. Rolling his eyes, Brian shook his head as his shoulders moved in a silent, humorless chuckle. He was a grown man, far beyond the stage of trolling for pickups in bars, and all he could think about was following some stranger to his hotel? No way. He didn't have time for this, and he especially had no interest in hooking up with some guy from out-of-town who was just looking for some local color to enliven his evening. It was past time he did the responsible thing and went home to sleep off his impending hangover so he'd be ready for another day of the job he'd increasingly come to hate.

Bracing his hands against the edge of the counter, Brian lowered his feet to the floor so he could push his stool away from the bar. He turned to make some excuse he hoped wasn't overly lame when a warm hand fell atop his own.

"Please say yes. You don't have to be afraid of me."

Shit. Brian glared at the man and cursed him silently, wondering how in the hell he'd guessed the real reason Brian was planning to flee as fast as he could. A challenge darkened his gaze, daring the man to force the issue and give him an excuse to walk away. But the stranger merely stared at him with an emotion Brian did not dare try to identify but which caused his stomach to knot with something akin to anticipation. The man's gaze was direct and intense, filling him with need. The weight of the hand against his was disturbingly familiar, and a jolt of electric heat threatened to scorch him where they touched. Brian started to jerk his hand away and tell the bastard to go fuck himself, but the man squeezed his hand ever so slightly.

The invitation wasn't repeated, but the blue eyes examining his face for the tiniest reaction spoke loudly. As Brian returned the blond's steady gaze, a voice whispered an unknown word into his ear.

Mery.

"Yes."

Brian didn't even realize he'd spoken until he saw the pleased grin spread slowly across the stranger's face.

THE WALK from the bar to the man's hotel was short, and Brian barely remembered a second of it. He wanted to blame the whiskey for the shameful quickness with which he'd accepted the offer, but as a cop, he'd learned that lying to oneself was futile at best. This was lust, pure and simple. A beautiful, exotic stranger had invited him back to his room for a one-night stand. Hell, he was living every man's dream. Surely it was high time he allowed his libido to drown out his common sense.

Absorbed with trying to convince himself he wasn't being unforgivably stupid, Brian was grateful the man kept up an innocuous flow of conversation that required little response.

"I'm a freelance writer for a small music publication out of Frankfurt," the man said, responding to the question Brian guessed he'd asked.

"Music? Like what, bands?" Brian groaned silently as throaty laughter reached straight into his shorts.

"*Nein*, not exactly. The magazine focuses mostly on classical music. I travel around to attend various performances of different orchestras, chamber groups, and the like, and critique them for the magazine."

That explained how he was able to speak so fluently about the music playing in the bar. The *Appasionata*. Brian remembered how the word had rolled off his companion's tongue.

"I enjoy it because it gives me an excuse to see the world." The man chuckled again, and Brian feared he could easily become addicted to the sound. They stopped before the front entrance of a posh hotel. Brian reassessed his assumptions about how much a freelance writer must make as he followed the man through the hotel's sliding glass doors.

The lobby shouted elegance and money, neither of which Brian was used to. Compared to the long camelhair coat that hung so casually from the man's broad shoulders, he keenly felt the statement his own off-the-rack trench made as they crossed the well-appointed lobby. Several people glanced toward them, and the desk clerk peered curiously in their direction as they passed by reception. Self-consciousness made his shoulders tense, the obvious difference in his and his companion's financial status making Brian feel like he'd been bought for the evening.

Ignoring the looks, he stared at the back of the figure walking in front of him, distracting himself by applying his professional judgment to the man's physique. *Six two, 190 pounds*, he guessed. Four inches taller than him, ten pounds heavier, and if the man's supremely balanced gait was anything to go by, all of it muscle. So much for the image of some pudgy, effete desk jockey. The only thing that pegged the man as a writer was his pale skin, but that was as likely a product of genetics as anything. He certainly displayed no other hallmarks of someone who made their living sitting on his ass. *And what an ass it is,* Brian mused as his gaze drifted helplessly in that direction.

"Sir, may I help you?"

Brian turned to look at the man addressing him, his shiny, buffed name tag identifying him as Charles, the hotel manager. His weak chin was thrust forward, and lines of disapproval etched the skin around his prissy mouth. Brian realized he wasn't the only one who thought he didn't belong there.

Well, fuck me.

Brian surmised he was about to be politely ejected from this fine establishment and resisted the urge to flash his badge, punch the man in the face, or maybe both. *Let's see how he likes it next time he needs to call the police for something.* Not bothering to glance toward his companion's retreating back, Brian decided it was high time he put an end to this stupid scene. But just as he was about to say something that would surely prompt the manager to call for security, a hand fell heavily atop his shoulder.

"Is there a problem here?" His deep-voiced accent prominently on display, the man held the key card to his room discretely at his side, fingering it absently and telegraphing the fact that he was a patron of the hotel. The manager blanched beneath the hooded, icy blue gaze.

"Ah, no, sir. Well, I was just asking this gentleman what his business was."

"He is my guest. Do you require anything else?" The clipped tone brooked no further opposition.

Brian fumed silently as the manager made some stumbling excuse and assured his customer that there was no problem whatsoever. The urge to just make some excuse or other and head for the door was strong, but it died a humiliatingly quick death when the man gestured for him to go ahead of him, the killer smile aimed in his direction blinding Brian into obedience. Trying to ignore the way his heart skipped in response, Brian did as requested. They reached the elevator bank without further incident, but Brian felt his control over the situation was rapidly disappearing as the elevator came immediately at the man's call.

Although they were alone in the conveyance, the ride up was uneventful. Brian mentally shook his head, wondering what, exactly, he'd been expecting. To be thrown against the wall for a quick fuck? He'd obviously been watching too much porn. Brian glanced at his companion out of the corner of his eye, but the man was silent as he gazed up at the progression of lighted numbers on the display panel above the door.

The stranger was the epitome of that certain brand of European sophistication that American men, no matter how urbane, never quite managed to copy. It was more than the cut of his clothes or the glint of the gold chain at his throat. It wasn't simply the breadth of the shoulders that stretched the expensive material of his coat or the impressive chest that pressed against his fine woolen sweater. The neat cut of his fair hair and the precisely trimmed sideburns, the endless stretch of his legs in those tailored slacks—they merely added to the overall impression.

Brian drew himself up when he realized he was staring. It was then that he noted the tight set of the man's jaw and the way he held his hands clasped at his sides, clenched almost into fists. He was clearly annoyed at something, but Brian decided not to worry about what it might be. Instead, he joined in watching the floor numbers as he struggled to suppress the growing erection that was becoming more and more pronounced the longer they were together.

The elevator finally reached the indicated floor, and after a quick walk down the carpeted hallway, the man paused to swipe his key card in the electronic lock of room 1201. Brian knew he was paying close attention to meaningless details to avoid thinking about how ridiculously out of character he was acting. But that didn't stop him from indulging in the diversionary exercise.

The room was as elegant and understated as everything else in the hotel. A couch upholstered in dark chocolate leather sat in the middle of the room, flanked by a tall lamp on one side and a matching arm chair on the other. The couch faced a set of picture windows that stretched from wall to wall and showed the city in all of its nighttime glory. Brian walked over to the windows and looked out at the sea of pinpoint lights. If only he could fool himself that the beauty wasn't hiding so much dirt.

"Please allow me to apologize for the manager's rude behavior."

Brian started in surprise at the sound of his companion's voice, then shrugged. Why should he care that the hotel manager had been a pretentious jerk? "Don't worry about it. I've heard worse."

"That's a pity. I can't imagine that anyone would be intentionally rude to you."

Brian bit back a snort, thinking of all the crude things perps had said to him over the years. He didn't bother explaining that he was a cop. They hadn't even exchanged names, and that was a piece of information he didn't feel the need to share.

"Would you like a drink?"

When Brian turned, the man was standing next to a bar inset into the wall beside the door. A flick of a switch illuminated a bank of tastefully recessed lighting above the bar. Other than that, the room remained in shadow. The setting couldn't be described as anything other than romantic, and the undeniable ambiance sent Brian into panic mode.

"Look. You don't have to entertain me like we're on a date or something. If you want to fuck, let's fuck."

The man's self-assured smile faltered for the first time. "It's true that I want us to have sex, but there is no need to be uncivil. I did not ask you here merely for a *fuck*."

Brian felt ashamed even as he shivered at the way the man's accent turned the already provocative word into something downright sinful. He turned back toward the window to hide his discomfort.

"Sorry." He could barely hear his own mumbled apology, but his companion's ears must have been better than his own.

"Please, have a seat and let me pour you a drink. I have enjoyed our conversation. There is no reason to hurry."

Brian begged to differ, as his inexplicable case of nerves got worse. He wasn't some trembling virgin. He'd taken his share of cock in his day. But something about this man warned him that it would be dangerous to stick around any longer than it took to satisfy his libido. Brian ignored the little voice in his head that called him a coward.

"What if I want to hurry?"

The man watched Brian carefully as he slowly crossed the room, dropping his coat over the back of the couch as he passed it. Brian paused in front of him, swallowing his apprehension as he reached out and took a fistful of the man's soft sweater. He didn't react as Brian pulled him forward, but neither did he resist as their lips came together.

For a few seconds, the only contact between them was that light, innocent touch. Warmth, tenderness, and a disturbing sense of rightness flowed into Brian. *Why?* The question poked at the back of his mind. Why did this feel so perfect, so inevitable? But before he could come up with an answer, the innocent kiss abruptly changed, becoming all fire and heat, as gentleness turned into a blazing conflagration of mutual desire and all doubt was swept away.

Pa'sheri, come to me.

Brian was extremely grateful for the strong arms wrapped securely around his waist, uncertain whether it was the kiss or the mysterious voice in his head that suddenly turned his knees to water. All he knew was that he didn't want the kiss to end. Ever. The firm press of the man's lips was a revelation to his senses. He somehow knew just how hard to press, just when to bite, just when to thrust his tongue into Brian's mouth with deep, confident strokes. It was like this stranger had known him forever. Every caress, every hot point of contact—from the warmth of the hand kneading his ass through the fabric of his pants to the powerful thigh wedged between his legs, pressing tightly to his groin—reduced him to a quivering mass of need.

Brian was unaccustomed to being ruled by the base demands of his body. Over a year of celibacy was testament that he didn't just fall into bed with any handsome guy who glanced his way. Hell, all he knew about the man who was taking ownership of his mouth was that he was a writer and he liked Beethoven.

The ache between his legs didn't give a damn. The pulse fluttering in his throat didn't care about his reservations. Nothing mattered but the firm chest pressing against his own, the man's heavy heartbeat reverberating into his own body. The sensuous dance of the tongue claiming his mouth was all-consuming, finding and exploiting every sensitive corner as though they had been lovers for years rather than seconds. Brian moaned and wrapped his arms around the taller man's neck, holding on for sanity and dear life.

A throaty, unrestrained moan caught Brian off guard, and it took him a moment to recognize the voice as his. But he couldn't find the will to summon the embarrassment that would usually follow such a loss of control. Even in his younger days, he hadn't been promiscuous. In college, he'd been too focused on his career goals. Then in the academy, he'd just been too damned busy trying to survive the training to be overly indulgent in his sex life. Besides, after Dennis, he had become something of a loner, preferring the solitude of his dorm, or later his tiny academy apartment, to braving the dating scene. Now, years later, his social skills hadn't improved much.

But being here with this beautiful man… this wasn't hard. In fact, it was the easiest thing he'd ever done. A deep groan filled his mouth, prompting him to reciprocate in kind, the mutual sounds of pleasure resonating like a familiar song. Large hands swept down his back, and Brian felt the lingering warmth of soothing comfort in their wake. If he weren't so turned-on, he knew he'd be freaking out.

"You taste like cheap whiskey."

Brian barely had time to register the comment before the man dove in for another kiss.

"Umm, delicious."

Brian's laugh was lost as the man's tongue delved deeply into his mouth, as though seeking out the lingering flavor. Like everything else about his companion, he even tasted classy, like expensive vermouth, or what Brian imagined vermouth might taste like if he'd ever had any. When long nimble fingers abruptly went to work on the buttons of his shirt, it was almost a relief, but Brian couldn't help tensing as strong hands came into burning contact with his bare skin.

"W-wait." Wincing at the unsteadiness of his voice, Brian wrapped his hands around the man's biceps, holding him at bay as he raggedly dragged air into his lungs. He couldn't deny he wanted the man desperately, but things were moving too fast. His brain struggled to kick into gear against the drugging lust sapping his intelligence. He needed to give his cock a chance to calm down so he could think this through, so he could decide if he was honestly ready to allow some stranger to fuck him in a hotel room. A stranger who was doing very wicked things to his neck with his teeth and the tip of his tongue.

"Just—just wait a second." The breathiness of his tone was humiliating.

The man caressed his sides with slow, calming strokes, as if Brian were a skittish horse that needed reassuring. Brian was mesmerized by the contrast of the man's pale hands against his darker skin, the gentle touch steadying Brian even as his body thrummed like an instrument under the guidance of a master.

"Shhh, just relax. You don't need to be afraid."

In that instant, Brian became absolutely convinced that German accents should be illegal, or at least reserved for actors in adult movies. "Yeah, right."

The man chuckled. "If I am to give you cause for concern, I will ensure that you enjoy it very much." He flashed that killer smile again, causing something eager and greedy to clench in Brian's gut. "Come. We should take this elsewhere, *ja*? I'm too old to relish the thought of making out on the floor."

Brian laughed wryly, appreciating his companion's attempt to put him at ease. And damn him, it was working. "Yeah, my back would probably prefer a mattress."

Although the man relaxed at the display of humor, his grip was firm, refusing to let Brian escape. Warmth spread from their joined hands, radiating out to fill Brian's entire body, and he tried not to dwell on why the presumptuous gesture didn't piss him off.

The bedroom was probably as nice as the rest of the hotel suite, but Brian didn't see much of it. His entire world winnowed down to the press of the man's firm lips, the weight of his hands, and the wet heat of his tongue. Brian was amazed they didn't kill themselves as they maneuvered through the room in a complicated pas de deux. Clothing—Brian's tie and vest, the man's scarf and jacket—soon lay on the floor in an incriminating trail stretching from the sitting room to the bed.

His own hands were far from idle as he worshiped the rippling muscles of the man's firm, toned body. Brian had never been one of those gay men whose life centered around the gym and the guys who frequented them, but only a dead man wouldn't have appreciated the tantalizing swells and ridges. Brian pushed his hands under the soft fabric of the man's sweater, wanting it gone. Muscles smoothed and bunched intriguingly beneath his fingers, and when his companion moved back and obliged by lifting the sweater over his head, Brian had to forcibly close his mouth to stop from drooling.

A shaft of moonlight shone through the thin curtains pulled across the bedroom's floor-to-ceiling windows. The pale light made the man's skin glow in the darkness, highlighting the impressive yet understated swell of his pecs, the indentation of his defined abs, and the light dusting of blond hair across his chest. The hair thickened down the center of his stomach into a trail that led teasingly downward, disappearing beneath the waistband of his pants. Brian blinked, unsure if he should fall to his knees in reverence or simply jump him.

"Now it is your turn, I think," the man murmured, his hand lifting in Brian's direction.

Brian waited breathlessly for the man to touch him again, so he was more than a little startled when, instead of reaching for him, the hand reached past him toward the lamp sitting on a bedside table. Brian hastily grabbed the man's wrist. "What are you doing?" He felt stupid for asking such an obvious question, but he'd panicked.

The man looked at him curiously. "Well, I've not yet learned to see in the dark, so…."

Cocky bastard. Brian's lips twitched with the urge to return the man's gentle smile, but he still didn't let go of his wrist. Brian knew he didn't work out as much as he should, and he spent way too much time sitting at his desk eating whatever was at hand. Though he wasn't fat by any means, his body wasn't necessarily as tight and toned as it could be. In comparison to the godlike creature standing in front of him, he couldn't help but feel a little self-conscious of his less than fabulous physique. Plus, remaining in the dark would keep things more anonymous and impersonal. He had a feeling that injecting any more of himself into this encounter would be a very bad idea.

"Look, why don't we pretend like we're blind or something and that we have to use Braille to read each other. Sound like fun to you?"

The man gave him a crooked grin, but Brian could sense his reluctance to leave the lights off. Under other circumstances, he might have felt flattered, but the fewer sensory memories he carried away from this experience, the better. Brian breathed a sigh of relief when the man dropped his hand, abandoning his plans for the lamp in favor of wrapping his arms around Brian's waist. The next moment, Brian was cursing his brilliant idea when the man traced lightly up and down the knobs of his spine with his fingertips.

Hot air blew softly over the side of Brian's cheek as the man bent forward to murmur in his ear.

"I admit that I'm a little rusty, but I believe this says, 'I want your mouth on my cock.'"

Brian sputtered as the man dropped to his knees. He wanted to say he had been expecting no such thing, but when the man leaned forward to press his nose into his crotch, inhaling deeply to savor the musk of arousal, Brian's brain short-circuited.

"Fuuuuuuck."

Brian couldn't manage anything more coherent as a warm mouth closed around the ridge of his cock, the fabric growing wet as his companion sucked him through the maddening layers of his pants and boxers. The vibration of the amused hum against his swollen flesh was enough to drop him to the edge of the bed. Unfazed by his sudden change in posture, the man took advantage of Brian's seated position to unlace his shoes and slip them off, one after the other. As he did so, he traced up the middle of Brian's soles with his fingernail, the scraping sensation making Brian groan helplessly as his hips bucked against the man's mouth, hands scrabbling against the duvet for leverage.

Figures he'd find my second biggest erogenous zone in two seconds flat.

His pants were next, a practiced flick of the man's long fingers releasing the button holding his fly closed. Brian lifted his hips obligingly at the man's tug, and as the pants slid down his legs, he began to suspect he was in way over his head. He felt awkward and uncertain, as though his previous experiences with sex were nonexistent. *Wrong*, he admitted. He hadn't even been this nervous during his first time. Maybe it was the fact that Dennis had been just as naïve and eager. But the mouth sucking so expertly at his cock didn't belong to some awkward teenager.

The man followed the path of Brian's pants with his lips as he slipped them off. Warm kisses trailed down one leg from the edge of Brian's boxers to the top of his black dress sock. Letting the pants fall to the floor, the man ran his hands back up the underside of Brian's legs. Brian groaned at the featherlight touch, his hips shifting against the bed as a damp spot seeped through his boxers. He could hear his own breath rasping in his ears, competing with the pounding beat of his frantic pulse. He nearly whimpered when the man paused to toy with the sensitive area behind his knees, cataloguing yet another promising spot in his quest to drive Brian insane.

Brian tried not to get swept away, telling himself this was just like the dozen or so other make-out sessions he'd experienced over the years. But when the man's mouth reached his knee, pausing to lick at the rough skin and suck on the knobby curve, he admitted defeat. No one had ever made him feel like this before. He was afraid that he might actually come from someone sucking on his damned knee.

"You don't have to—"

Whatever objection he had been about to make was cut short, drowned out by his own moan as the man ignored him and returned to his previous task, now unhindered by anything but the flimsy material of Brian's shorts. Even that final barrier was soon breached as the slit that offered convenience to billions of men all over the world provided the perfect access to his throbbing cock.

"Arggggh, shit!"

Brian dug his fingers into the comforter as the tip of a warm, wet tongue traced slowly, lovingly, over the veins standing out in prominent relief along the swollen length. His toes curled, punching dents into the deep shag of the dark brown carpet. The muscles in his thighs tensed as shocks of sensation spread out from his cock, showering his body with white-hot sparks. Sweat broke out in beads over his skin, his body temperature spiking feverishly with every tantalizing caress.

The rasping swirl of the man's tongue circled the flared head of his cock, hesitating briefly to savor the fluid dripping from the weeping hole. Brian's lips fell slack as he struggled to draw in air. He mumbled incoherently, begging for the man to stop teasing. Yet the light touch never ceased, just the tip of the man's tongue making contact as it abandoned the leaking head to bathe his rigid shaft with slow, deliberate strokes. Brian reached down and threaded his fingers into the thick cap of close-cut blond hair. He tugged fretfully at the pale strands, desperate for the man to keep going but afraid he was on the verge of abandoning himself completely to this delicious torture.

As though he'd been waiting for just such a signal, the man's growl was a sexy threat as he abruptly took every inch of Brian's aching cock into the warm, wet cavern of his mouth. Brian cried out, heat racing through him like a bolt of lightning. The man's nose pressed against the tight curls at his groin as his thighs were pushed farther apart, a dexterous tongue laving the delicate skin at the base of his aching shaft. The man hummed appreciatively as he massaged Brian's thighs, gently kneading the tense muscles. He licked at Brian's cock, enjoying it like a rare treat, before sucking at it with a strong pull that drew the rod of flesh to the very back of his throat. Everything seemed to go white before Brian's eyes, his ability to think obliterated by the talented mouth flinging his will into oblivion. Only his voice seemed to be working properly. Every dip of the man's head and sweep of his tongue forced out an unbidden curse or helpless shout in appreciation of his skill.

Brian slumped forward, every ounce of concentration centered on his cock. A sudden tightness in his balls signaled his rapidly approaching downfall. "Ahh, please don't stop!" he panted, his hair dripping with sweat. "Please," he begged, knowing he'd die if the man left him now. He was so close he could taste it.

The man hummed reassuringly, and the vibrating purr signaled the end for Brian. His entire body convulsed as jets of viscous heat shot from his cock. The man swallowed the flood greedily, not stopping until the last drop had been coaxed from the softening flesh in his mouth.

Brian collapsed onto the bed, his limbs jerking with aftershocks as every ounce of strength bled from his body. He wanted to move, to touch the man's cheek with his hand, to offer a word of gratitude for the best blow job he'd ever had. But too many sleepless nights suddenly caught up with him, and all he could do was groan as the sweat cooled on his body.

He sensed movement and the resulting disturbance of air as his companion rose to his feet. Those same hands that had driven him so crazy tugged at his boxers, and at long last sent them the way of his pants. When the man lifted his legs and swung them over so he lay fully on the bed, Brian figured his ass was about to return the favor.

But the man simply raised him so he could pull the duvet from beneath him. Brian found the strength to open his eyes when the thick cover fell gently over him. The bed dipped from the heavy weight that settled beside him as the man lay next to him. Brian was acutely aware that other than the duvet, he was wearing nothing but his gaping shirt and his socks, but he simply yawned, too tired to care about his state of undress.

"What about you?" His voice was hoarse, presumably from his recent attempt to shout down the walls, and his cheeks grew warm at the humiliating memory. Although it was hard to tell in the dim room, he thought he could see the flash of the man's perfect teeth.

"Do not concern yourself. You look very tired." The man ran the backs of his long fingers softy down Brian's cheek. "Just sleep. I promise I won't molest you too much."

"Too bad." His snarky reply was the last thing Brian remembered as he slipped into sleep.

CHAPTER 2

"PA'SHERI, I love you."

Long arms wrapped securely against a smaller body, drawing the boy into a firm chest. Thin, dark fingers ran lovingly through a thick fall of black hair.

"And I you. Always."

BRIAN AWOKE with a gasp as the remnants of the dream faded, leaving him disoriented and horny.

Great, not again.

He groaned, wishing his dream buddies would give it a rest now and again—not that he didn't get a voyeuristic thrill from watching the handsome princely figure take his pleasure in his dark-skinned boy toy. Yet, sometimes, he felt a little jealous of their uncomplicated affection. Slowly, the images began to fade back into his subconscious, though they had seemed particularly vivid this time. His nose twitching as he caught a whiff of some unfamiliar, earthy scent, Brian tried to forget the smoke he'd seen rising from a stick of incense situated near the dream couple as they made love. He kept his eyes closed, enjoying the last few traces of the dream and realizing he had a serious case of morning wood.

Figuring he should probably think about getting up, Brian reached his arms out in a slow stretch. It was a beloved morning routine that popped and lengthened every muscle. He paused abruptly in the middle of the motion, however, when his right arm brushed against the pillow next to him. That should have been impossible, since he always slept on the right side of his bed. His arm shouldn't have hit anything but air.

Where in the hell am I? Images far more concrete than the mysterious dream instantly flooded his mind in swift response to the unspoken question. A wave of dread swooped in on their heels, and Brian groaned as he covered his face with his hands.

"What the fuck did I do?" he mumbled aloud.

Received the most amazing blow job of his life from the hottest damn guy he'd ever met, that's what. Brian cracked his eyes open into cautious slits, expecting them to feel gritty. Not only were they not sore and tired as sleepless nights usually left them, but they felt rather good. In fact, he felt good all over. No headache lay in wait to punish him for drinking too much the previous evening, and he didn't have so much as a sore muscle from sleeping on an unfamiliar mattress. He felt better than he had in nearly a month.

I should sleep here every night.

The quickness with which he put the brakes on that line of thought probably etched skid marks onto his brain. There had only been one man he'd ever slept comfortably with, and he was long dead. Having another body in bed with him made him feel vulnerable and usually guaranteed he'd spend the night tossing and turning. But last night, he'd slept like a log.

He wasn't really sure what to think, but the fact remained that he had slept—and slept well—with a total stranger. A fucking gorgeous stranger with an insanely sexy accent. Brian groaned as more of last night started coming back to him, embarrassed that his first sex in well over a year had ended with him leaving his partner high and dry while he fell asleep.

Well, that was easily remedied, and he could definitely use an outlet for the pent-up energy from his latest dream. Never let it be said he was a selfish lover. The sky visible through the window was the deep indigo of approaching dawn, though it was still a ways off yet. The room was pretty dark, but Brian didn't need to see for what he was planning. Rather, light would feed his insecurities and remind him how out of character he was acting. The ache in his cock spurring him on, he turned toward his new—what? Friend, partner, fuck buddy? Deciding that the latter moniker was the easiest to accept, he reached out to try out his extremely rusty powers of seduction.

Brian's eyes flew open fully when his searching hands found nothing but smooth linen. He sat up to confirm what his hands were telling him. Indeed, the other side of the bed was completely empty. He spread a hand over the sheets, feeling not even the barest hint of lingering warmth.

Well, fuck me.

So much for that. Anger and mortification warred for prominence in his mind. He wouldn't have pegged his erstwhile companion for an asshole, but it wouldn't be the first time he'd been dead wrong. A shadow at the foot of the bed resolved into a piece of luggage lying on a rack. So, he hadn't checked out, but he'd made himself scarce, obviously unwilling to engage in some awkward morning-after scene.

Taking the hint, Brian figured he might as well gather up his clothes and what remained of his pride and get the hell out before the man returned. He would surely appreciate Brian departing as efficiently as possible. And Brian bet that prick of a manager would enjoy watching him leave before first light, like some hustler who'd worn out his welcome.

Get your shit together, Macon.

For once, he agreed with his captain 100 percent.

Brian swung his legs over the side of the bed and his feet landed on his discarded pants. He grimaced at the thought of how wrinkled they'd be after lying on the floor all night. He might not be the snappiest of dressers, but he didn't have a ton of clothing suitable for work, so he was careful with what little he had. Groping for the lamp that had led to that whole stupid Braille game, Brian swore sharply as he knocked his hand against the edge of the night table. He hissed, the sharp pain that bloomed at the point of impact only adding to his irritation with himself and this entire situation.

"Just perfect," he muttered, annoyed with his own clumsiness. He shook his hand for a second until the sting began to fade and reached out a second time with more caution. Finding the base of the lamp, he followed the metal stem upward until his fingers touched the switch. Blinking rapidly as the sudden burst of light shriveled his irises, Brian looked down to begin the humiliating process of locating his clothes.

A note lay unassumingly on the night table next to a key card, the same key card the man had flashed at the manager so effectively.

Brian sat motionless for a long moment, staring at the two objects. Impatient with waiting for his mind to catch up, his body reacted violently to the seemingly innocuous sheet of paper and piece of plastic. His cock swelled to full mast, as though the man was right there driving him crazy all over again, and his hand reached for it instinctively.

One squeeze was nearly all it took, the mere memory of the man's touch ghosting over his skin almost enough to make him come. He seriously needed to get laid more often if all it took was one blow job to make him this needy.

One absolutely incredible blow job. No harm in giving credit where deserved. *And now this,* Brian mused as he stared down at the note and key card.

And just what in the hell was he supposed to think about those? He bit his lip uncertainly as he contemplated the possibilities. Maybe he'd been alone in considering last night some tawdry encounter he should forget as fast as he could. The key seemed to indicate, at the very least, that a repeat encounter wouldn't be unwelcome.

Helplessly, Brian fell back against the bed and shuffled his stockinged feet against the thick carpet as he slowly stroked his cock. Whatever the note and key signified, his top priority right then was to take care of the raging erection that was trying to poke a hole in his belly. He wanted to feel ashamed of what he was about to do, but he figured housekeeping had probably seen worse than sheets covered with dried come.

Indeed, it didn't take long. He was too far-gone for that. His shifting body bunched up the sheet, releasing a hint of the absent man's scent into the air. Breathing deeply, Brian indulged in the spicy tang of what was probably some expensive European cologne. Or maybe it was just the man's own unique scent. Whatever it was, it worked for him. His fingers became a teasing tongue, the palm of his hand an enveloping mouth as he worked up and down his shaft. His climax came on so suddenly, it caught him off guard. For one blinding instant, Brian deeply regretted that he didn't know the man's name, because that would have been the perfect moment to shout it out loud.

Brian collapsed onto the mattress, one hand still wrapped around his softening cock, the other resting heavily on his heaving chest. Slowly, his breathing and his heartbeat calmed into a more normal rhythm as sleep tugged at him again. But the sky visible through the window had already begun to lighten. His shift started at nine, and he'd be damned if he showed up at work in the same clothes he'd been wearing the previous day. He'd never hear the end of it.

Dragging himself reluctantly from the bed, Brian shuffled toward the bathroom for a much-needed shower. A flick of the wall switch turned on the bathroom light, and a quick glance down at his torso showed him just how huge a mess he had made.

"Ugh."

Shaking his head in disgust, he caught sight of a mark just above his right pelvic bone. It stood out starkly against his complexion, though his light brown skin hid most of the redness. The ghost sensation of warm lips sucking at his hip made him shiver. Brian suddenly recalled how the man had kissed him there right after swallowing every drop of his come and licking him clean. His cheeks flamed at the memory of the intimate guesture.

Stop acting like a freakin' girl. They were both men, and sex between men was messy. Big deal. Growling in disgust at his own embarrassment, he headed toward the stand-alone shower and turned on the hot water. The bathroom was decadently large, and there was a separate tub situated next to the shower. Brian wondered idly if anyone ever actually used the tubs in hotel rooms.

He studiously avoided any further self-examination in the mirror, telling himself he was simply in a hurry. Steam quickly began to fog over the cool surface, happily obliterating any unwanted reflection. Not that he was fooling anyone. He probably looked like he'd been royally fucked and had enjoyed every minute. The water was just short of scalding as he stepped into the stall, the glass door closing him off in a world of misty heat. Irritated with his procrastination, Brian snatched up the complimentary bar of soap from the holder bolted into the wall.

For whatever reason, Dennis chose that moment to unexpectedly come to mind. His best friend since they were both in diapers, Dennis had become his boyfriend in high school mostly because they were the only gay boys they knew, having come out to each other during their second year of middle school. They had kept each other sane through those long years of high school, offering much-needed sympathy when the lying and sneaking around became too much. They had been each other's refuge when a stupidly forgotten magazine in his backpack and an ill-hidden video in Dennis's bedroom resulted in nearly identical scenes of crying mothers and irate fathers. Only Dennis had been able to understand how hurt Brian had been at his parents' inability to accept his sexuality, particularly since, as an interracial couple, they had experienced their own share of intolerance. Almost inevitably, they had been each other's first, their pleasure coming from familiarity rather than any real passion.

Nothing he'd experienced with Dennis had remotely prepared Brian for what he'd experienced with the German stranger, with his easy manner and devastating smile that made Brian melt into his shoes. Brian clung desperately to the memory of his best friend as thoughts of the previous night threatened to sweep them away.

Whatever hadn't been washed was just going to have to wait. Brian pushed open the stall door and stumbled out after the outward rush of billowing steam. After grabbing a towel from the rack, he rushed out of the bathroom. He applied the towel haphazardly, then threw on his clothes, unable to feel the proper concern over the large wet spots he was transferring to the fabric of his shirt and pants.

Brian tried to convince himself he was simply eager to get home and change before going in to work. *Yeah, right.* He grumbled at his annoying inner voice to shut up. Sitting on the bed, he reached for his shoes, his fingers making a hash of tying the laces as he attempted to complete the task at record speed. He swore the next time he got picked up in a bar he'd wear loafers so he could make a faster escape. After lowering the final foot to the floor, he glanced at the nightstand to see if he'd forgotten anything. Of course, the first thing his gaze landed on was the note and the key card.

Laughing blue eyes that caressed him with a glance, a softly accented voice that dripped with confidence and innuendo, a touch that seemed to burn his skin…. A flood of remembered sensations threatened to set up permanent camp in his brain.

"I must be losing my mind," he moaned. Either that or the man had laid some goddamned Old World mojo on him. Berating himself for such an idiotic thought, Brian stood and started to walk away from the bed. A second later, he turned back and pocketed the note and the key card, calling himself a hundred kinds of fool.

The door of the suite closed behind him with a soft snick. Brian took a deep breath as he stood in the hallway, allowing the astringent odor of carpet cleaner to overpower the scent of sex that lingered in his nose. "That was really fucking stupid, Macon." Brian swore right then he'd never make use of the key card. Besides, the man would probably be checking out soon. Who could afford to stay in a place like this more than a few days? "Might as well take a souvenir in case I ever think of doing something this dumb again. Let tall, blond, and charming pay the lost key fee." After all, it was his fault for dropping such a tempting hint.

Brian refused to answer the inner voice that urged him to take the man up on it.

ANGELA LOOKED up at the squeak of a chair across the industrial tiled floor. Brian tried to ignore the silent weight of her gaze as he sat at his desk, which was situated facing hers, and turned on his computer. Fifteen years his senior, she'd been his partner during his entire six years in Homicide. She was tough as nails and as smart as a whip, a fact he wasn't entirely grateful for when a knowing smirk spread across her face.

"Did the toxicology screen on that kid come back yet?" he asked, keeping his tone neutral. "It was due yesterday."

The teenaged female had been found in a downtown back alley a couple of weeks ago, and they needed to know if the coroner had determined the cause of death. Brian always hated cases with young victims, their lifeless bodies a mockery of the natural order of things. Plus, the girl had been raped before she'd died, or maybe even after, so he was eager for any information that might lead them to her killer. Not that he was all that hopeful, given the frequency and anonymity of drug-related deaths in the city.

Unfortunately, Angela wasn't fooled by his dodge. The surprisingly firm skin around her dark green eyes crinkled as her smile got bigger and more annoying. "It was Ecstasy cut with something nasty, just as we thought. Meaning we'll probably never figure out where she got the stuff. 'E' dealers are a dime a dozen."

"Great."

She continued to grin at him, her gaze never leaving his face. Brian tried to ignore her while his ancient computer booted up, but her silent amusement soon got under his skin just like she meant it to. "Okay, what?"

"You sure seem perky this morning. What did you do, try a new brand of coffee?" Her eyes widened in mock surprise when he reddened right on cue. "No! Don't tell me you actually found a use for those condoms I gave you for your birthday last year?"

"Macon! Lovell! In my office now."

Saved by the yell, Brian thought.

Angela quirked an eyebrow at him when he pushed back his chair faster than was strictly necessary. "Don't think you've put me off, partner. I am a detective, after all."

Brian smiled despite himself when she tapped a finger to the side of her nose.

"I said now!"

"Ah, the dulcet tones of our lovely captain. Let's go see what's got her panties in a bunch today."

Angela made no secret of the fact that Captain Hayley Preston was not her favorite person, and Brian couldn't say that he disagreed. At thirty-seven, Preston was one of the youngest captains on the force and one of the even fewer women who had managed to attain that rank. From the day she'd arrived to take charge of Homicide, she'd made it clear Brian was on her permanent shit list for no apparent reason. He couldn't remember ever doing anything in particular to get on her bad side, but hell, you couldn't please everyone.

Brian and Angela both avoided looking in the direction of a certain desk situated nearest the captain's office, but they weren't any more successful at evading the notice of the man sitting there than they ever were.

"Pleasant morning, isn't it?"

Matt Roddy, Captain Preston's personal toady, smirked at them as they passed his desk. The captain was clearly in a foul mood, and he smelled blood. Roddy's beady gray eyes nearly glowed with malicious pleasure, anticipating what was sure to be a decidedly unpleasant experience for them.

"Good morning, Ratty," Angela replied. She blew him a kiss and slammed the door of the captain's office in his face, denying him the pleasure of witnessing their meeting.

"Don't bother sitting down. You won't be here long."

Brian turned from chuckling at his partner's antics just in time to see a file slide across the captain's desk, scattering a few neatly stacked papers in its wake. It was distressingly thick. He looked up reluctantly and winced as he met a fiery glare.

Hayley Preston was drop-dead gorgeous. Even though he was gay, Brian still appreciated her physical appeal. Flowing black hair and a honeyed tint to her skin hinted at exotic origins she'd never revealed. Her eyes were an arresting shade of liquid brown, her lips full and pouting, and on top of all of that, she had the body of a swimsuit model. Preston was the total package.

When he'd first met her, Brian had been catty enough to wonder if she'd slept her way into her lofty position, but he knew now it had been a grossly unfair assessment. The captain was smart and very good at her job. She'd been the one to crack the case of the serial killer who had terrorized the city for months several years ago. No one else had come close to putting together all the clues, not even the hotshot Feds the mayor called in to help the local police. Which was probably why she was so annoyed he and Angela had been less than successful at closing the book on the multiple mob murders that were giving the media daily boners.

"Yet another body for your collection, ladies and gents." Preston shot Angela a narrow-eyed glare when the older woman sighed and reached for the file.

"Who now?" Brian asked.

"Another member of Cosmino. But this time, it's not just one of the foot soldiers."

That the victim was from Cosmino wasn't a surprise. Everybody matching the murder profile had been from that organization. They all knew what that meant, and none of them were thrilled by the prospect.

"Goddamn mob warfare," Angela mumbled under her breath.

"Indeed." The captain sat back in her chair and folded her long legs as she rested her arms comfortably along the armrests. A heeled shoe swung from one elegant foot as she moved it back and forth. "Do I need to draw you a diagram?" She flicked long, slender fingers tipped with ruby red nails dismissively in their direction. "Off you go, children. And you'd better fucking bring me something useful this time."

Brian supposed that straight guys found it hot to hear obscenities fall from those perfect carmine lips. Personally, he just found it supremely irritating.

"How in the hell can she afford those clothes on what the city pays us? It's not like the brass does that much better than us grunts," Angela groused when the captain's door was closed safely behind them.

"She's clearly doing something right."

"Yeah, sleeping with the mayor probably."

Brian smothered a guffaw. And he thought he could be catty. His partner could give him lessons.

CHAPTER 3

"I WISH all of our crime scenes were this neat."

Brian nodded in silent agreement with Angela's assessment. The body was lying facedown in the middle of the living room floor, the head closer to the door, while the feet were pointed toward the single, dirty window. The window was one of those swing-out models, and it was wide open. Dried blood pooled beneath the head in a small circle, indicating the most likely area of fatal trauma and that the victim had died very quickly.

"You said it, doll. I hate it when deaders leave bits of themselves lying around. Next to godliness, as they say."

The medical examiner, Jeremy Vincent, had been in charge of the city's dead for nearly twenty-five years. Unrepentantly old-fashioned, Vincent was possibly the only man in the state Angela would let get away with calling her "doll." He was balding, growing a paunch, and needed bifocals to see, but he was the best at what he did, even though more than one detective thought his basset hound looks made grim crime scenes appear even more depressing. Several people wearing Forensics jackets were milling around, working on their evidentiary sweep. A couple of them were walking around taking pictures of every inch of the apartment.

"The victim was one James Talbot, according to the ID in his wallet." Jeremy pulled out a pair of latex gloves from the black case he lovingly called his "doctor's bag." As per procedure, he'd waited for the lead detectives to arrive before messing around too much with the body. He crouched down next to the victim's head, and Brian's knees ached in sympathy when he heard the resulting creaking from the older man's joints. His empathy quickly fled, however, when Jeremy took out a long metal probe from his bag and began poking through the victim's blood-soaked hair. Brian was suddenly very glad he'd only had time for a bagel and coffee that morning.

"The building superintendent found good old James after several residents began reporting a disgusting smell coming from his apartment," Jeremy explained. Brian was surprised it had taken them that long to complain. Even with the open window, the air was pretty rank. "I'm putting the time of death at, say, 2:00 a.m. the night before last? The super got a nasty surprise when he finally checked out the source of the stink." He glanced over to the corner of room, where a puddle of vomit added unpleasantly to the already noisome atmosphere.

"Single bullet to the head, huh?"

Jeremy glanced up at Angela and nodded. "Yep, just like the last three."

"Perfect." Brian felt the beginnings of a headache forming between his eyes and fervently wished he was back in the bed he'd left that morning. Quickly veering away from that unwise line of thought, he cleared his throat and glanced at his partner. "Why do I know this building?"

"Because it's a front for a Cosmino business. I probably mentioned it when I was regaling you with tales from my illustrious days in Vice. The Cosminos operate a brothel in several of the apartments. If I remember correctly, our boy James here was the head pimp." She barked out an amused chuckle. "I suspect he spent his last few hours of life availing himself of his girls." She glanced pointedly at the trashcan sitting in the corner of the room near the threadbare couch. Brian walked over to it and shook his head as he saw several used condoms lying on top of a smashed pizza box. He lifted up the lid of the box and saw the remains of missed toppings but no signs of rot or mold.

"You're good, partner." He returned her condescending smile with an indulgent smirk. "The party wasn't that long ago, maybe even only a little while before he was hit."

"Body's been photographed already, so here we go."

The medical examiner grabbed hold of the dead man's shoulders and flipped him over. Brian made a conscious effort to hold down the bile that rose into his throat as a clammy sweat broke out over his face. Angela ignored him when he turned away to compose himself. Every time he saw a newly dead body, man or woman, young or old, Dennis's face appeared superimposed over it like a death mask. He'd hoped after so many years he would have gotten over it, but it happened every damned time. If Angela noticed his rookie-like reaction, she never said anything. Still, she always gave him a moment to regain his composure when they reached a new crime scene. He loved her for it, even as he hated himself for needing her thoughtfulness.

"Clean exit wound. Bullet went straight through his head, just like with the others."

"Let's see if we can round anyone up." Angela's tone was brisk, her mind firmly on the investigation. "If James was having a party right before he was killed, his guests might have something useful to offer."

Angela headed toward the apartment door, but Brian paused and looked around. "Did any of the Forensics guys find the bullet?"

"Yes, sir." A freckled redhead walked over to him as though he'd been waiting for the summons. Brian repressed a wince and reminded himself that to a kid who was probably only in his early twenties, he was an old man. "We found the slug in the wall." He gingerly held out a baggie toward Brian.

Angela came to his side and looked at it over his shoulder. "Looks like the same large caliber as the others, a .45 at least. Is it clean?"

The Forensics tech preened under her gaze. "Yes, ma'am." Brian hid a smile when he felt Angela flinch. "Well, we'll have to take it back to the lab to know anything for certain, but I couldn't see a thing under my field scope."

"Okay, thanks." Brian nodded at the kid. "Let us know what you find out."

"Field scope." Angela snorted. "He probably means the magnifying glass he found in his Cracker Jack box."

"Now, now. Be nice." Brian patted his partner on the padded shoulder of her jacket. He'd never had the heart to tell her that style had gone out with the early '90s. "Let's split up and see if any of the girls know what happened to Jim Bob, here."

"I TOLD you, I didn't see nothin'."

Brian's jaw tightened as he listened to the woman blatantly lie to him. "The girl in 5A told me she saw you go into his room with two other girls around eleven the other night. Now, that's only a few hours before James was killed. You telling me he had a trio of free ass in his apartment and let it go after only a couple of hours? Tell me another one, sweetheart."

The woman was obviously strung out on something. Her twitchiness was due to more than nerves, and she looked like she hadn't had a decent meal in years. Brian had to question the dead man's taste, free or not.

"Okay, yeah, I was in his room the other night. But I swear I left before he got shot."

Brian cocked his head to the side as he often did when he heard something interesting. Angela said the habit made him look like an adorable puppy dog. "When did I say he'd been shot? I just said that he'd been killed, not how."

The woman paled as she realized her mistake. Her gaze darted up and down the empty hallway as though she was looking for help. Brian waited patiently for her to speak.

"Shit, man. I was pretty high that night. I don't really remember much."

Brian could believe that. "But you were there?"

The woman scratched the track marks marring the bend of her left elbow. "Yeah, I was there. Jimmy was workin' over one of the other girls—fuckin' her, I mean. He didn't do rough stuff." Brian nodded encouragingly. "Anyway, it happened real sudden like."

"What did?"

"The shot. It came outta nowhere. I didn't hear a bang or nothin'. It got Jimmy right in the head, just like that." She snapped her fingers to emphasize her point.

"Then what happened?"

"I ran like hell, that's what. Some sonofabitch was shootin', I sure as hell wasn't gonna wait around to be next."

Brian couldn't fault her logic. "Who were the other girls with James that night?"

"Don't know. I never saw them before. Just some girls from the street, I guess."

Brian reached into the pocket of his coat and pulled out a beat-up tin cardholder. He retrieved one of the embossed cards the commissioner had insisted all detectives carry and held it out toward the twitchy woman. "You remember anything else, you call me. Okay?"

"Yeah, okay." A moment later the door slammed closed in his face. He wondered how long it would take the woman to ditch his card.

He didn't want to jump to conclusions, but it smelled like a sniper hit. The living room window had been open—odd, since it was the dead of winter—so there was no telltale shower of glass on the floor to indicate that the shot had come from outside. That's why he'd thought at first that the shooter had been someone in the room. But a sniper? That changed things considerably. Either they had some crazy bastard on their hands who was a damned good shot, or someone had hired some serious muscle to wipe out the Cosminos. He didn't need too many guesses to figure that one out.

When he got back to the victim's apartment, Brian met Angela at the door. He told her what he'd learned from the prostitute in 2C.

"You think it was a sniper? Really?" She groaned. "Hell."

"One of the girls must have opened the window so the perp would have a clean shot. No other reason why it would be open when it's so cold outside."

"Meaning the hit was carefully planned. The captain's going to love that. Still, at least you got some information. I totally struck out. 'Nobody saw nothin'.' You know how it goes."

Brian nodded and popped his head into the apartment. "Jeremy, you got anything else for us?"

"Not right now. I'll let you know if I find anything once I have him on the table."

"All right," Brian replied. "Catch you later."

"More than likely."

Chuckling at the corner's gallows humor, Angela walked beside him as they made their way down the poorly lit stairwell. Once outside, they headed straight for their unmarked car. Angela paused beside the driver's side door and rested her hand on the roof, tapping out a mindless rhythm on the metal with the ignition key.

"The Milano family?"

Brian grunted. "Bingo."

"Goddamn mob warfare," she groused. "Don't they have anything better to do with their time? I know I sure as hell do."

Brian didn't bother replying as they got in the car.

"So, who's the guy who's got you all bright-eyed? Oh, don't think I've forgotten about the way you practically bounced into work this morning."

Brian thought about ignoring her but knew it wouldn't do any good. After all, Angela had two of the most important hallmarks of a good detective—good instincts and dogged determination. He gave the scenery passing by the car window one last wistful look.

"Just a guy I met at Blackjack's."

"Ah-ha. Didn't you promise to take me there sometime?"

Brian looked at her askance. "You'd probably be bored. Besides, I doubt Todd would approve."

"He wouldn't care," she replied breezily. "Not like any guys would try to pick me up, right?"

Brian smiled. "Probably not."

"Yeah, that's what we straight girls like about gay bars. All the fun with none of the creepiness. Anyway, you were telling me about having sex with an actual person?"

"You are so hilarious." He turned his gaze back to the window, as much to dismiss her silliness as to hide the warmth he could feel rising in his cheeks. "He was just some guy."

Angela scoffed and shot him a glare. "I know you far too well, partner, to believe that. You're hardly the type to hop into bed with 'just some guy.' So, what did he do to convince you to abandon the monastery?"

Brian sighed and decided he might as well be honest with her. It wasn't like he could just stall until they got back to the station. Knowing Angela, she'd just pull the car over somewhere until he spit it out.

"He wanted to know why I looked upset."

"Upset?"

"Yeah, about the captain getting up in my grill every day. About this damned case that we haven't managed to get a single break in." Brian ran a hand over his face to dispel the irritation that began to crop up at the mere thought of all the crap that was his life these days. "Anyway, I was sitting there, drowning my sorrows in some rotgut. He was kind enough to buy me a second glass."

"And?" Angela pressed after he remained silent for a few seconds.

"And he invited me back to his hotel room."

"And you went, right?"

"Yeah, I went."

Angela let out a loud "Ha!" that threatened to damage his hearing.

"I'm glad you're so thrilled."

"I am thrilled, and do you know why? Because you've been living in a cave of your own making for far too long, sweetie, that's why." She glanced over at him with an emotion close enough to affection rather than pity that he let it slide. "I remember what you told me about your friend from high school, and how you've been so reluctant to get involved with anyone since."

Brian shifted his body farther toward the window, his discomfort with the subject making him antsy.

"But, sweetie, Dennis died years ago. I know it must have been awful finding him like you did, beaten half to death by those lowlife juvenile delinquents. But from what you told me, Dennis really loved you. You can't tell me that he would have wanted you to live the rest of your life in an emotional shell."

An old pain started to knot and burn in Brian's stomach, one he'd lived with since Dennis's death. Angela was wrong. He hadn't merely found Dennis after he'd become another teenaged, gay-bashing statistic. His best friend for sixteen years had died in his arms, hemorrhaging from a busted spleen and a punctured lung pierced by his own broken rib. His last words had been gibbered nonsense, a product of the bleeding in his brain that had been named the official cause of death. Brian hadn't even been able to say good-bye because Dennis wouldn't have understood him anyway.

After surviving those last few months of high school alone, he had channeled his grief into determination and ambition. He wanted to become a police officer in order to protect those who couldn't protect themselves. Since the day of the funeral, he'd felt that, if only someone had been there for Dennis, they might even now be enjoying their lives together, as friends if nothing else.

Throughout his time in college, majoring in criminal justice, he had kept that goal in mind, but those long months in the academy had been beyond stressful. Fear that someone would find out he was gay and he would end up like Dennis had kept him celibate. But his desire to become a cop had been too strong to let him give up, and after graduating and being assigned to his first patrol, he'd felt he'd finally been given a chance to do something worthwhile in his friend's memory.

But all that bright idealism had long since been smothered beneath the reality of legal technicalities and expedient politics. There were no heroes in the world, and if there were, he certainly wasn't one of them. As the years went by, it became easier and safer just to remain detached in both his professional and personal life. If he stayed away from other people, then he wouldn't be crushed when he couldn't do anything to help them. He never wanted to feel like he had when he'd held his best friend in his arms as he bled to death on the inside, lying on a dirty sidewalk a mile from their neighboring houses.

Of course, Angela hadn't been fazed by his standoffishness. She'd forced herself into his heart with all of the blunt stubbornness that had made her excel in a traditionally male profession. Like a one-woman army, she'd carved deep holes in his self-protective armor and had pushed herself and her boisterous family into the chinks. Maybe that was why the man from last night had been able to affect him so deeply. It was all Angela's fault, damn her.

"So, what does he look like?" she asked when he remained silent. "Tall, dark, and cliché?"

"More like tall, blond, and gorgeous."

"Oooo, do tell!"

Brian smirked at her enthusiasm. "Blond, like I said, and blue-eyed. Maybe six-two, 190? All muscle, but not bulky. You know, more like a swimmer's build."

"I think I'm in love." Angela swooned.

Brian laughed. "Then you'll really like this part. He's from Germany."

Her jaw dropped, and she threw him a wide-eyed look before she turned back to watch the road. "Shut up! So, on top of everything else he has an incredible accent?"

"Yep."

"Sweetie, you must have done something right in a past life."

Angela laughed at her own joke, but Brian couldn't join her as an unexpected chill shot through him. Unbidden, the memory of the odd sense of familiarity he'd felt for the man came back to him. Shaking off the strange feeling, he looked out of the front window and saw that they were approaching the station.

"So, when are you seeing him again?" Angela turned into the station lot and looked around for an open space. "And what's his name?"

Ugh, Brian thought. He'd been dreading the latter question, knowing how she would react to the answer.

"I didn't ask."

Angela stopped the car dead in the middle of the lot. The sound of tires screeching assaulted Brian's ears as the car that had pulled into the lot behind them was forced to slam on the brakes. She ignored the angry honking as she stared at him.

"Oh, come the fuck on. You are not telling me you slept with a guy and didn't even get his name?" She rolled her eyes. "Boy, where did I go wrong with you?"

"Angela, you should probably move. And I didn't sleep with him exactly."

She shot him a glare but took his advice and headed for a parking spot. Brian glanced out of his window and shot a look of apology to the guy she had cut off.

"Don't sass me, Brian." He really did hate it when she treated him like one of her teenaged sons. "I'm not going to ask what you meant by that, but you are going to see him again, right? And find out his name this time?" Angela grabbed his shoulder when he opened the door and started to exit the car without replying. "Brian—"

"What would be the point, Angie? It was just a one-night stand." He tried not to squirm as she squeezed his shoulder tightly.

"Brian, I have honestly never seen you look, well, as content as you did when you walked into the station this morning. Not in six years of knowing you. And I know you didn't suddenly become Mr. Sunshine for no reason. This guy had something to do with it. So don't you sit there and tell me that it was just a one-night stand."

Brian could feel the key card burning a hole in his pocket. It had fallen out of his pocket when he'd changed pants at home that morning. As though the thing had called attention to itself just to taunt him, he'd stared down at it accusingly as it lay on his bedroom floor. He'd had every intention of tossing the damn thing into the garbage, but somehow it had ended up in the pocket of the pants he'd changed into. He didn't dare mention it to Angela, given the implication the man hadn't necessarily considered their moment together a one-off experience. Brian wasn't sure he was ready to let it be anything more.

"It was just a moment, that's all. And now I've got a really hot memory I can pull out when I need a good fantasy to jerk off to." Brian heard Angela sputter behind him indignantly at his crassness. He pulled away from her grip and got out of the car. "Come on," he called back as she did likewise. "I'll flip you for who gets to write up the report and deliver it to the captain."

BRIAN SQUINTED at the screen, his temple throbbing in time with the overhead fluorescents as he tried to finish proofreading his report. Angela's laugh rang out through the department as she chatted with her husband on her phone, her feet propped comfortably upon her desk. He shot her an evil glare, which she returned with a smile full of saccharine sweetness. He should have known better than to make a bet with her. She had the devil's own luck and was a less than graceful winner.

A shadow fell across his desk, and his mood didn't improve when he glanced up to find Matt "Ratty" looking down at him, his usual smirk in place. Brian stared in fascination at the strands of hair Matt had deluded himself into thinking were perfectly adequate to cover his rapidly thinning pate. A real shame, since he was only twenty-eight years old. Sympathy diminished his urge to smack the grin off the man's wormlike lips, but only the tiniest little bit.

"What's up, Matt?"

"Captain Preston is looking for you two. She's wondering why your report is late."

"Is she now?" Angela chimed in as Brian's knuckles peaked into white caps from his tightened fists. Matt didn't know how lucky he was she'd decided to run interference. "Well, why don't you run along and tell her we'll be right there. Brian was just making it all pretty for her."

Matt pouted at their apparent unconcern in the face of the captain's ire and favored them with a futile glare as he stomped away.

"A few days' suspension for hitting a fellow officer, right?" Brian sighed as he pushed back his chair after instructing his computer to print out a copy of his report. "It'd be like a vacation."

"I'll talk to you later, lover." Angela made kissy noises into the phone as she signed off with Todd. Brian was rather amazed at how hot and heavy they managed to be even after twenty-three years of marriage and two kids. Angela patted him on his arm understandingly as she walked past him to grab the report off the printer.

As Matt had warned, Captain Preston was extremely displeased they hadn't given her their report within an hour of their return and that its content was less than informative. "Yet another crime scene and you still don't have any new information about this damned assassin? Is that what you're telling me?"

She was in full bitch mode, pacing behind her desk in a long-legged strut. Brian's shoulders tensed defensively as her voice rose in pitch. "A witness confirmed our hunch that the hits are being done long-distance. We're waiting for the ME to complete his workup before we can say for sure, but it's very likely we're looking for a sniper."

Preston sneered. "Yes, that's very helpful. Maybe you can just flip through the fucking *Yellow Pages* and look under 'sniper' to find the killer!"

Angela folded her arms, hiding her hands in her armpits. Brian knew that she was restraining her fingers before they inadvertently flipped off their boss. He hated to say it, but the captain was right. Knowing how the hits were made did little to narrow down their list of possible suspects.

"Since only criminals have been getting killed, the mayor hasn't put too much pressure on the department to solve the case. But make no mistake," Preston said as she braced her balled fists on her desk and leaned toward them, "I take every new body as a personal affront." She glared at both of them in turn. "Now, I'm not trying to imply you're purposely screwing up this investigation, but I find it astonishing that after four bodies, you haven't brought me or the District Attorney anything useful." Her voice lowered into a disturbing mixture of consolation and menace. "I have found in my experience that it's not the crime scene that lacks evidence, but the detective who lacks the intelligence to find it."

Preston abandoned her standing pose and took her customary seated, cross-legged posture. Her chair rolled back slightly from her desk as she sat, revealing a scandalously short skirt that showcased her gold medal legs. Brian wondered if she thought she was some damn queen, sitting on her throne and hurling down judgment upon her minions.

"I don't need dead weight in my department, Detectives. I hope I am making myself perfectly clear."

Brian knew he hadn't imagined that she'd been staring directly at him when she'd spat out that last bit of snideness. If she wasn't careful, she'd ruin her hundred-dollar lipstick with her toxic attempts at pep talks. He wasn't sure why she'd always had such a hard-on for him, but ever since taking over Homicide, it was like she'd made it her personal mission to make his life miserable—criticizing his work, his reports, even his dedication to his job.

"Yes, ma'am, perfectly clear." He turned away before her icy glare could focus on him. As Angela preceded him back into the squad room, Brian struggled to retain the unaccountably good mood he'd been in when he'd walked in the door that morning. He was sorely tempted to punch Captain Preston in her perfectly lacquered mouth, gender and rank be damned. "A couple of weeks for assaulting the brass. Yeah, a wonderful vacation."

Angela snickered and shook her head in mock disapproval. He knew she'd be right behind him, waiting her turn.

"DAMN IT, Gio, I thought you said this guy was a pro?"

Giovanni Rivella—"Gio" to people who were afraid of him— glared at the older man. "If I said it, it must be true. So shut up, Mick. He'll be here."

"It's colder than a witch's tit in here." Mick growled as he jammed his hands beneath his armpits to keep them warm.

Gio ignored the complaint, resisting the urge to shiver and give away his own discomfort. He stood with his hips perched against a large metal desk, some circa-1950s office relic and the only piece of furniture in the room besides the folding chair, where Mick was huddling for warmth. They'd been there for nearly twenty minutes, and it was ten minutes past the time of their scheduled meeting.

"Why did you even bother hiring outside help? You're a pretty good shot yourself."

"Are you really that dense, or did your mama drop you on your head as a child?" Gio growled. "Like I'd want to have any direct tie to the shootings." He shrugged. "Besides, I might be able to hit more than the broadside of a barn, but I don't have anything on this guy. He's scary good."

"I gotta admit, those Cosmino bastards don't know whether they're comin' or goin' these days." Mick's phlegm-filled laugh rapidly devolved into a cough.

Gio looked away from him as his stomach turned. He took another pull from his cigarette, his attention fixed out the window on the entrance to the building a floor below. "By the time they figure it out, most of them will be dead, and the Milanos will have the run of this city like back in the old days."

"You wouldn't know 'the old days' if they dropped on you like a ton of concrete."

Mick probably thought he was whispering, but the old man was growing deaf. Gio's fingers twitched, but he reined in his temper and didn't reach for the handgun stashed beneath his stylish wool coat. He knew Mick couldn't stand him, considering him nothing but a young upstart who somehow thought he was capable of running the entire organization. But he was the big man's nephew, so even though he was only twenty-nine, Mick had to kiss his ass. In this business, blood mattered.

Back when Mick was coming up through the ranks, the Milanos had been the biggest game in town. Nowadays, they were playing second fiddle to the Cosminos, who had taken over the most lucrative underworld industries through sheer ruthlessness. But Gio had suggested a reckless plan for the Milanos to regain control of the city, and even Mick had eventually, though grudgingly, given him credit for coming up with it.

"Yeah, this guy you hired is slick as shit on ice," Mick said at a volume that made Gio wince. "But what's with his handle? Todd's Angle? What the fuck does that even mean, anyway?"

"It's *Todesengel*. It means Angel of Death."

The accented voice dripped with condescension. Gio jumped and spun toward the door to face the newcomer. Out of the corner of his eye he saw Mick do the same. Neither of them had heard the man come up the stairs, which was surprising considering how the old building creaked and rattled like an old whore at the slightest disturbance.

The lack of light in the hall seemed to emphasize the man's already imposing figure. He wasn't wearing anything that might hide his identity, merely a long, dark coat to block the wind. His hair was so fair he seemed to glow in the darkness. It had to be a liability in his line of work, but he'd just proven his ability to move with stealth. The man walked farther into the room, his icy blue gaze sizing them up with a single glance. It was clear he wasn't impressed.

Gio was the first to recover, hiding his discomfort behind his usual bravado. "We were just talking about you."

"So I heard. You were pleased with this last job?"

"Yeah." Gio rubbed his hands together. "Perfect as always. But this next one's really gonna knock their socks off. It needs to be done tomorrow tonight."

"As you wish." The hit man glanced down scathingly at the envelope Gio held out toward him. He'd expressed his dislike of the paper trail these dossiers created, but Gio's uncle was old-fashioned and preferred to do business in analog rather than use modern technology. He took the envelope without comment and placed it under his coat beneath his arm without looking at the documents inside. "Will that be all, gentlemen?"

Gio hopped off the desk and stepped closer to the tall blond. "What's your hurry? You've been doing such a good job, I thought maybe we could buy you a drink. You know, to show our appreciation." He chuckled, knowing the six-figure per hit fee they were paying him was more than appreciation enough. He reached out to put a friendly hand on the man's shoulder, but the frigid glint in the assassin's eyes stopped him cold.

Mick coughed reflexively, as though to break the sudden tension in the room. Gio saw him reach for the gun stashed in his waistband at the small of his back in case the hit man made a move, and then think twice about it. Something must have told the old man he wouldn't get far before he got shot for his trouble. Like Mick had said, this guy was slick as shit on ice.

"It would be most unwise for us to be seen together in public. My survival depends on our ability to act with discretion. I am sure you understand."

Gio swallowed as he backed away slowly. Any sudden moves and he feared he might pull back nothing but a bloody stump. Clearing his throat, he took refuge behind a mask of brashness.

"Yeah, yeah. Sure, man, I gotcha." With a few feet of space between them, his confidence began to return. "I should have your next assignment for you in a couple of days. Let's meet at, say, 10:00 p.m. day after tomorrow at that old warehouse over on Twelfth Street."

59

"Fine." The tall man turned to leave. "I will expect the remainder of my payment for my current assignment no later than noon tomorrow." He swept out as suddenly as he'd arrived.

"Holy fuck, that son of a bitch gives me the creeps." Mick gave an exaggerated shiver. "Come on, Gio. You can buy me that drink for draggin' my old ass out in the middle of the night."

"Whatever." Gio gave Mick his most charming smile. "Maybe you should find some sweet young thing to remind you how to use your dick, huh?"

The stairs creaked and groaned noisily as they started down them. Gio slapped Mick on the back, determined to take his own advice. Anything to forget about the "angel" who'd managed to scare the collective shit out of them.

CHAPTER 4

"WHAT am I doing here?"

Brian looked up at the hotel's marquee for a third time, but the name didn't change no matter how long he stared at it. He was indeed standing at the front entrance to the stranger's hotel when he should have been home in bed.

"I'm an idiot."

The realization didn't stop him from stepping closer to the sliding door until the electronic eye registered his presence. He paused, still trying to talk himself out of it, but when the door began to slide closed, he stepped though before it could.

After the unpleasant meeting with Captain Preston, his day hadn't gotten any better. Ignore her though he'd tried, he'd felt the laser focus of her glare every time she sauntered past his desk. Angela hadn't been any help, either, hounding him ceaselessly about whether he planned to see his mystery man again. By the end of their shift, he was about ready to strangle her. Adding insult to injury, his afternoon had been completely wasted when a rookie patrolman called them out to a suspected murder scene at an old woman's apartment. It took the medical examiner about five seconds to determine that she'd suffered from a massive coronary when her new neighbor's dog had barked too loudly. He felt sorry for the woman, sure, but it had taken time away from the actual murders he was trying to solve.

The second his shift had ended at five, he'd waved a perfunctory good-bye to his partner, leaving her in midsentence about her favorite new topic—his sex life—and headed to the gym.

After a half hour on the treadmill and a quick dinner at his favorite greasy spoon to ruin all of his efforts, he'd decided to cut his losses and head home. Lying in bed with a beer and some inane TV sounded like the perfect way to put the day behind him.

So how in the hell had he ended up downtown when he lived five miles away? Brian mumbled threateningly under his breath as he walked across the hotel lobby to the bank of elevators, but he didn't deviate from his path. He kept an eye out for the manager who'd harassed him the night before. The man was nowhere to be seen, and the young woman with the shiny nametag who stood behind the check-in desk merely sent him a pleasant smile and a nod. It was too bad. Some good old-fashioned hell-raising might have let him work out whatever had brought him there before he made a complete fool of himself by going any further. Brian sighed as the elevator arrived.

He hadn't really been paying attention too much the night before, except to the way the blond man's ass had looked in his slacks, but somehow he remembered the correct floor number. For the first time, he regretted the observational skills that made him a good homicide cop. A chime sounded with a chirpy ding when he reached his floor. Brian watched warily as the doors slid open, but nothing awaited him except an empty, softly lit hallway.

He wanted to blame Angela for keeping the stranger in his thoughts all day, but he knew it was his own fault he hadn't been able to get the man out of his head. Well, he was here now, and it couldn't hurt to relieve some tension. After all, what other reason could he possibly have for being there other than the promise of more mind-blowing sex?

Pants on fire. Shit. He'd always sucked at lying to himself. Sex wasn't the first thing that had come to mind as he'd realized where his subconscious had brought him. He had a ridiculous need to see the man's face, to watch it light up as he talked about long-dead Germans who wrote pretty music. If Brian were being completely honest with himself, he'd admit he just wanted to spend some more time with him.

"A complete idiot."

Sticking his hand in his pocket, Brian fiddled with the key card as he started down the hall. The room wasn't far from the elevators, and before he was ready, he was standing in front of a door bearing a familiar room number. Brian took a deep breath. *Last chance.* Though he wanted to think of this as no big deal, he recognized he was taking a profound step toward admitting it was time to let Dennis go, that he was ready to fill the gaping hole his friend's death had left inside him. He'd be admitting he was still capable of opening his heart up to someone.

Or maybe he was overthinking things, and he was just really horny.

Brian stood there for a long while, staring at the door. His hand closed and opened as though it couldn't decide whether or not to form the fist he would need to knock. Before he could chicken out, circumstances decided the matter for him. A chime sounded, and Brian panicked as he whipped his head toward the elevator bank. The man's room was directly down the corridor from the elevators, and whoever got off would see him standing there looking totally suspicious. That asshole manager had already mistaken him for an undesirable the previous night. Choosing not to press his luck, he reached for the key card that was burning a hole in his pocket and jammed it into the electronic lock.

The indicator light turned green, and Brian slipped inside just as one of the elevator's doors swished open. He braced himself to explain to the room's occupant why he had unexpectedly barged in without knocking, but the complete lack of light told him he was alone. Closing the door, Brian fell back against it and stared sightlessly into the room's dark interior.

"All of that for nothing, huh?" Brian wasn't sure whether he wanted to laugh or cry. Maybe the man's absence was a sign it just wasn't meant to be. It was somewhat comforting to know he could simply return to his solitary existence with no one the wiser, but at the same time, he experienced an unexpectedly intense swell of regret. Brian realized right then that, even without the prompt of the person coming off the elevator, he would have knocked on the door.

A wry smile curved his lips as he fingered the key card one last time. "That's that, I guess. Time to go home." His eyes had adjusted to the dark, and the light from the windows allowed him to see the low table sitting next to the couch. He walked over to it and was reaching out to set the key card down when the door suddenly opened behind him. Brian turned quickly, feeling like a burglar who'd been caught in the act. Light flooded the room, and he blinked against the brightness.

The tall blond saw him immediately, and the delighted smile that lit up his face made Brian's heart twist. He sensed he'd just gotten a much-desired second chance.

"You came back." The man dropped his coat carelessly across the back of the couch and prowled toward Brian. Brian heard the crinkle of something from the coat but spared it no mind as he feasted on the sight.

Damn, he's even more gorgeous than I remembered.

Brian thought it almost funny that his usual powers of retention should have failed him so critically. But looking at the man walking toward him, Brian realized his senses were simply inadequate to the task of appreciating him fully. The eyes fixed upon him were bluer than he'd remembered, the shoulders taking up his field of vision broader. Had he always been so tall, with those firm lips that simply begged to be kissed? The memory of what that mouth had done to him the night before was enough to make his face flame.

"I-I came to return your key," he stammered.

The man's smile grew as he gave the obvious lie all of the credit it deserved. "If that's really the only reason, why didn't you just leave it at the front desk?"

Gorgeous and smart. How was that fair? "I don't know" was all Brian could come up with.

The man's smile faded, and his blue eyes took on a serious cast as he invaded Brian's personal space. "Why lie to me? Why lie to yourself?"

Brian felt his eyelashes flutter when a long thumb whispered over his cheek. All the resolve he'd found while standing in the hallway abandoned him in the face of his companion's overwhelming physical presence. Getting away as fast as he could suddenly seemed like the most prudent course of action. He was finding it difficult to marshal his thoughts into something useful, however, as his blood abandoned his brain for parts south.

"Last night was a mistake. I don't do affairs."

A displeased frown transformed the man's expression, the kind amusement fleeing as something dark and focused took its place. "Is that what this is? A fleeting affair—tawdry and cheap—occurring once and never spoken or thought of again?" He moved even closer, obliterating the remaining distance between them. "I didn't think so. Did you?"

Brian's breath caught painfully in his throat, his pulse racing as the man spoke softly in his ear. Their only connection was the hand resting gently against his cheek, but he was fully hard, his arousal throbbing painfully in time with his heartbeat. The man was right. He hadn't wanted last night to mean anything, but it did. He was deathly afraid that it meant everything.

"No," Brian whispered.

The man smiled softly before taking the key card from Brian's hand and slipping it into his pocket. "Then I think you had better keep this, *ja*?"

As he leaned closer, his gaze fixed on Brian's lips, Brian figured it was high time to drop one more barrier. "What the hell is your name?" The question turned into a groan as firm lips brushed against his.

"Alrick Ritter. And yours?"

"Brian Macon."

And then all conversation between them ended.

The trip to Alrick's bedroom was far smoother this time. They already knew the steps of the intricate dance, moving and spinning in tandem, dropping clothing as they went.

"It was still dark when I woke up this morning, but you were already gone." Coming up briefly for air, Brian felt he had the right to ask, seeing how Alrick had practically given him permission to come and go as he pleased. "Did you leave in the middle of the night?"

Alrick grunted affirmatively before distracting Brian with yet another searing kiss. Brian nearly forgot what he'd been asking, but his detective's curiosity nagged at him to gather as much information as he could. "Why?"

"Didn't you read my note?"

"No." Brian didn't elaborate, deciding he'd rather eat nails than admit he'd been too afraid to read it.

Alrick tsked in disappointment, waiting to answer until he had removed Brian's shirt and tossed it to the floor somewhere behind them. "I received a call from the German office of the magazine I write for. I keep reminding them that America is many hours behind them, but with a deadline looming, they were unsympathetic that it was still nighttime here." Alrick moaned when Brian chuckled against his lips. "Believe me, I had no wish to leave you, but I didn't want to disturb you as I worked. So I found an all-night coffee shop with a Wi-Fi hot zone."

"Hotspot!" Brian gasped as Alrick ran his long-fingered hands up his sides, charting the lines of his ribs.

"*Was*?"

Alrick nibbled contentedly at Brian's neck as his hand wandered down Brian's stomach and found his belt buckle. Brian's breath stuttered as sharp teeth caught his skin, and a warm tongue soothed the small hurt a moment later.

"It's called a Wi-Fi hotspot."

Alrick smiled wickedly. "Hotspot." The word rolled obscenely from his tongue. "You mean like this?"

Firm lips tracked to a spot behind Brian's left ear that stole all remaining strength from his legs. How in the hell had he known about that? Brian's curiosity about Alrick's unerring ability to find his erogenous zones was forced to remain unsatisfied as Alrick explored said spot with single-minded thoroughness. The light from the sitting room didn't penetrate far into the bedroom, and it was as if they had crossed from day to sensuous night. Brian immediately felt bolder in the darkness. His cock ached as it grew impossibly hard, and all he could think about was how quickly he could get Alrick naked.

Alrick chuckled as Brian plucked fretfully at his sweater before remembering how clothing worked. Keeping his attention on the intriguingly sweet spot behind Brian's ear, Alrick helped him, lifting his head only at the last possible moment so the sweater could be removed completely.

Chest to chest, skin to skin—that first unobstructed touch was intoxicating. Brian thought he might combust at any second as they explored each other's mouths and bodies with searching tongues and demanding hands. He hadn't ever been this turned on just from kissing and a little heavy petting. Trying to toe off his shoes despite the tied laces, he was distracted as Alrick finally conquered his belt. The button and zipper holding his pants closed followed in quick succession, and he stumbled as his feet got caught in the sagging material.

"Careful." Alrick caught Brian to his chest, holding him easily as Brian grabbed him around his waist to keep from falling. Standing wrapped in each other's arms, they paused for a moment in their hasty undressing. Brian was amazed at how natural the position felt, but he didn't dare say anything about it. The sensation was too powerful and unexpected, the moment too fragile. Besides, there were far less emotionally treacherous ways to express himself.

"Let me get these off." Brian waddled the remaining distance to the edge of the bed and fell with an awkward bounce, more concerned with getting his shoes and pants off than with looking goofy. Before he could make much progress, Alrick kneeled in front of him.

"Allow me."

The position was eerily familiar, and Brian's cock twitched from remembered pleasure. But this time, Alrick merely gazed at him steadily as he carefully unlaced and removed both shoes and tugged Brian's pants past his feet. Not content to remain a spectator, Brian urged Alrick to stand and put his own hands to use, making short work of the button at Alrick's waistband. Since he was wearing loafers, Alrick was far more graceful than Brian had been as he bared his lower body. Brian made another mental note to add them to his wardrobe as he stared at the pale, muscular legs that slowly came into view.

Alrick stood motionless as Brian ran his hands up the sturdy length of his calves and corded thighs, his eyes narrowing to heated slits when seeking fingers slipped beneath the edge of his boxers. Brian watched the bulge at Alrick's crotch swell as he curved his fingers and dragged his nails close to the crease where thigh met groin. Hooking his hands behind Alrick's legs, he pulled him close and buried his face in Alrick's crotch. Inhaling deeply, he groaned at the heady scent that flooded his senses.

The sudden intrusion of light broke his concentration. Blinking rapidly, Brian couldn't help but take in everything the brightness revealed to him. He ogled the perfect form that bespoke hours of physical effort and the blessing of excellent genes, gazing in wonder at the particular shade of Alrick's hair, the perfect set of his jaw. An exquisitely detailed tattoo of an eagle with spread wings flying over a stylized ring of leaves was inked high on Alrick's left shoulder, and Brian stared at it in fascination.

He wasn't alone in his perusal. Alrick's searching gaze was like a physical caress as it traced over Brian's bared flesh. Brian's face grew warm beneath the careful scrutiny. Shooting a glare toward the offending lamp, his irritation quickly rose to cover his embarrassment. "I thought we'd settled this thing about the light."

"I want to see you. Tonight I don't wish to pretend that I am blind."

Brian turned his face away in a futile attempt to deflect Alrick's focus. Alrick ruined his attempt to hide, crouching down and boxing Brian in with a hand braced on either side of his hips.

"You don't need to look at me."

"What, so I should pretend that I am with someone else?"

Alrick's gaze was steady as Brian stared at him distrustfully. Brian asked himself how Alrick had known what he was thinking, and then simply accepted that his companion somehow had the ability to read his thoughts.

"I'm not as… fit as you." Brian was appalled with his own lack of confidence, but he couldn't ignore the difference in their physiques. Large hands suddenly grabbed him by the hips and drew him closer to the edge of the bed. Brian sputtered, both indignant and impossibly turned-on by the manhandling. Alrick paid him no mind, groaning appreciatively as he sank his fingers into the somewhat soft flesh of Brian's ass.

"Feels perfect to me."

Brian stared at him owlishly, taking a moment to bask under the brilliance of that gorgeous smile Alrick used so damn effectively. He startled himself by laughing. Shaking his head, he decided he'd finally met Angela's match in the stubbornness department. "Okay, okay. You win this time." His reward for his acquiescence was a deep kiss that continued long after he was lying flat on his back with Alrick's muscular body pressed hotly against his.

"I will hold you to that."

The growled response made Brian realize what he'd implied, but he was beyond caring right at that moment. He moaned as their arousals lined up, hot, swollen flesh seeking its mate through the maddening barrier of their boxers. Alrick shifted his hips slightly, his cock rubbing against Brian's in a small circle. A pleased smile curved his lips when Brian treated him to a delicious whimper. He repeated the motion, nipping at Brian's ear as he encouraged more of the sexy sounds.

Brian, on the other hand, was trying his damnedest to keep his wits about him long enough to remove the final layer separating them. He stroked his hands roughly down Alrick's sides, trailing his fingers though the thin slick of sweat that glistened on his pale skin. Alrick groaned appreciatively, shivering at the needy touch. Deeply involved in his exploration of Brian's skin, it took him a moment to react to Brian tugging at his hips. He lifted them obligingly when he realized what Brian was about.

Moving hastily in his impatience, Brian hooked his fingers through the waistbands of both of their boxers and pushed them down simultaneously. The elastic band of his own shorts slid maddeningly over his throbbing flesh, the excess stimulation making him hiss.

"Shit," he breathed as sensation arced through him.

An earthy laugh sounded in his ear. The heated swell of Alrick's cock flopped heavily against his own, and his curse rapidly degraded into a desperate moan. He'd only caught a tantalizing glimpse of Alrick's cock as it bulged beneath his boxers, but now, faced with the impressive reality, Brian's hole spasmed in greedy anticipation. Thicker and longer than his own quite respectable length, Alrick was a sight to behold. Brian was this close to begging to be fucked. Although it had been a long time since he'd last taken another man into his body, he felt no trepidation at Alrick's size. He just wanted him badly, and now!

"Mmmm, just like that." Alrick groaned as Brian took hold of his cock and began pumping him with long strokes. His hips thrust helplessly as Brian worked him, a steady dribble of slickness soon easing the passage of Brian's hand. He plundered Brian's mouth as a reward for his boldness, seeking out every sensitive surface and claiming ownership as though it were his right.

Brian drowned beneath the luscious assault. His hand lost its rhythm when long fingers flicked at his peaked nipples, worrying them until he writhed against the bed, feeling as though the sensitive nubs were tied straight to his leaking cock.

"Ung! If you don't fuck me right now," he growled, "I swear I'll kick your ass." A nip to Alrick's full lower lip reinforced the threat.

Alrick chuckled at the pathetic warning and abandoned Brian's lips to nibble at his throat in mock admonition. He growled in approval as a shudder rippled through Brian just before his thighs fell helplessly to either side. Cradled snugly in the newly formed valley, Alrick resumed the slow pump of his hips.

Brian gasped sharply as their cocks slid together. He felt Alrick smile against his skin at the sound but couldn't help repeating the breathy exclamation as Alrick licked at the long column of his throat. He hummed in appreciation as Brian grabbed hold of his ass with greedy hands, urging him to go faster. But Alrick seemed to be in no hurry, turning his attention to the tempting expanse of Brian's bare chest. As though he'd found a new playground to enjoy, Alrick took his time, kissing and licking his way down, relishing the salty taste of Brian's skin. The scent of their mutual arousal filled Brian's senses like the bouquet of a fine wine.

Brian was increasingly desperate to feel Alrick's cock in his ass. He was afraid he really might start begging if he didn't get it soon. Maybe that should have worried him, but right then he just didn't give a damn. The wicked tongue languidly playing with his swollen nipples definitely wasn't helping his mental state. Alrick sucked and licked at the brown nubs, and Brian arched helplessly beneath him as his cock was treated to the slow caress of Alrick's arousal. But the sharp nip of teeth against the throbbing peaks was the straw that finally broke Brian's sanity.

"Damn it, stop screwing with me!"

"Oh, I have not begun to screw you, *Liebling*."

When Alrick pushed himself up and shifted away, Brian sat up in a panic and grabbed at him. "Where are you going?"

Alrick's smile reassured him while exacerbating the maddening ache in his cock. "We must do this right, *ja*?"

Alrick crawled down to the foot of the bed, offering Brian a heart-skipping view of his naked ass. His cock hung heavily between his legs, swinging pendulously as he moved. Brian wiped away the drool from the corner of his mouth as Alrick rummaged briefly in his suitcase. Coming up with a box of condoms and a bottle of body oil, he smiled at Brian as he turned back toward him. Brian blinked, a little taken aback that he was so prepared when they had only met the day before. Of course, the supplies weren't necessarily meant for him. Noting his wary expression, Alrick watched him steadily as Brian felt his face warm.

"You must think me very presumptuous. Or rather, you must think that I always have sex when I am on business trips."

Don't be a schmuck. Brian wasn't so naïve as to think that a man as sexy as Alrick wouldn't be prepared at all times. It was unlikely he was ever short of offers wherever he went. Brian shook his head. "I don't care whether you always carry around rubbers and lube wherever you go if it means I don't have to wait for you to fuck me." After a moment of stunned silence, Alrick laughed out loud, his broad shoulders shaking with mirth. Brian decided he could learn to love that sound.

"Should I feel insulted?" Alrick said jokingly as he stalked back up the bed toward Brian. "I can assure you that I do not have 'a man in every port.'" He ran a thumb over Brian's lips, tugging lightly at the fuller bottom one. "I find that I am only interested in one man."

Brian felt relieved by the assurance even as that last bit made something tremble frenetically in his stomach. Focusing a little desperately on the matter at hand, he got to his knees and wrapped his arms around Alrick's neck. "Then why don't you just shut up and kiss me?"

Alrick didn't merely comply, his tongue pursued, captured, and wooed until Brian couldn't tell up from down. He felt lightheaded, marveling at the erotic sensation as Alrick sought out the unexplored surfaces of his mouth. Who would have guessed that just a kiss could bring him to the edge so quickly? It was as though

Brian hardly knew his own body and Alrick was the only one who could show him everything he was capable of feeling.

Brian moaned as Alrick's fascinatingly large hands clutched lovingly at his ass and squeezed. Alrick hooked his fingers, pulling Brian closer even as he pried the fleshy cheeks apart. Aware of little except the press of Alrick's lips and the caress of his tongue, Brian found himself moving forward until he straddled a pair of muscular thighs. They spread slowly beneath him, urging his own farther apart and adding yet another log to the inner fire that slicked his skin with sweat. His hips moved without conscious thought as the thick column of Alrick's arousal nestled heavily against his own.

Alrick circled Brian's pucker with a tapered finger, spreading a generous layer of oil over his entrance. "How does that feel?" he asked, applying his lips to that recently discovered area below Brian's left ear and earning another needy moan.

"F-fine."

Alrick pushed his finger in before pulling it back out slowly. He groaned as the muscular passage sucked at his finger. "Just fine?"

"Ahh!" Brian began to pant as another finger joined the first, stretching him gently but persistently. He could feel the strain as Alrick fucked him sweetly with his elegant fingers. But he sure as hell didn't want him to stop. Not ever. "It feels g-good."

"Mmm, that's better."

Brian could have sworn Alrick's accent suddenly grew thicker, as did the cock that was rubbing wetly against his. Brian slowly realized he was moving his hips in time with Alrick's thrusting fingers. He wasn't going to last much longer.

"That's it. Show me how you're going to ride my cock." Alrick drew his free hand up Brian's side and over his chest until his thumb found the tender peak of a taut nipple. Running his thumb over and around the brown nub, he worried it into a hard pebble as he continued stretching Brian's clenching hole. Brian moaned, feeling bombarded from all sides. Alrick swallowed the sound as he thrust his tongue in and out of Brian's mouth in a sensuous rhythm, keeping time with the pace of his fingers.

Brian broke away with a harsh gasp. "Holy fuck, I'm going to come!" The warning was almost a shout as the impending explosion drew ever nearer.

"Then come. Come for me, Brian."

The last thing he needed was to hear that gorgeous voice saying his name. As if that weren't enough, Alrick's probing fingers finally located his prostate and exploited the discovery mercilessly.

"No!" Brian jerked from the shock, shouting helplessly before burying his face in the crook of Alrick's neck to muffle his desperate cries.

"No?" Alrick questioned him unconcernedly. Denied Brian's mouth, he happily turned his attention to the swirling curve of Brian's ear.

Brian sank his teeth into Alrick's neck, trying to make him stop before he lost it completely. All he got for his trouble was a lusty groan and the slow roll of his nipple between a dexterous finger and thumb. Brian rushed to clarify, his sanity hanging by a rapidly fraying thread.

"Not until you're inside me," he whispered, feeling his face catch on fire.

Brian could hardly believe what he'd just blurted out. Always somewhat shy about the whole business, he had never been overly vocal during moments of intimacy, not even with Dennis. But Alrick had broken down his inhibitions to the point where he was willing to say whatever he had to in order to get what he wanted. And what he wanted was Alrick's thick cock buried so deep inside of him that he could taste it.

Alrick pulled back just far enough so they could look each other in the eye. Silently, he asked if Brian was sure, warning him that this was his last chance to change his mind. Brian let his lips answer for him, leaning down until he could press them against the firm, tempting line of Alrick's mouth. In a dizzying flash, he found himself on his back with his legs propped up on Alrick's shoulders. He watched eagerly, licking his lips as Alrick ripped open one of the foil packets he had retrieved from his suitcase and rolled a condom down his length, making a lusciously decadent show of it. Brian felt his cock pulse as if it were the one being squeezed. Molten blue eyes watched him in return, darkening as though Alrick could see the desire coiling in his stomach.

The broad head of Alrick's thick cock nudged against his well-oiled entrance. Brian instinctively grabbed hold of Alrick's forearms, relishing the powerful bunching of muscles as Alrick leaned over him, bracing himself on his hands. Brian turned his head and pressed his open mouth against one of those strong arms, sucking hungrily at the salty, pale skin. Somewhere above him, a voice growled in low, guttural German, and then Brian was shouting an epithet of his own as he was spitted like a willing sacrifice to some pagan god.

That first thrust of that beautiful cock went on and on, burning and stretching and filling him inch by glorious inch. Brian wondered if it would ever stop and prayed fervently that it never would. The friction was intense, the sense of fullness almost too much to bear. "*Mein Gott!*" Overwhelmed, Brian cried out in incoherent thanks to an entity he didn't even believe in. Barely realizing what he'd said, his passion only spiked higher when Alrick graced him with that killer smile.

"You know some German?"

Alrick's amused delight caressed Brian's ears as Alrick eased his cock out as deliberately as he'd entered. Brian shook his head both in answer and protest, flinging sweat over the duvet. "No, ngggh! I heard it in a movie." He was becoming far too enamored of Alrick's laugh. When had this thing between them moved so far beyond simple lust?

"That was very good. I shall have to teach you some more."

Brian hoped he saved the lesson for later. There wasn't room for anything in his head right then but how fucking amazing he felt. Alrick took advantage of his supine position and bent over, hitching Brian's legs higher over his shoulders so his next thrust went even deeper. Satisfaction gleamed from his focused gaze, and Brian closed his own in an attempt to shield himself from the intensity. He couldn't, however, stifle the moan that fell from his lips as he arched his back in acknowledgement of a direct hit to his prostate. Adding "flexible" to his list of talents, Alrick bent down, his back curving into a long, graceful arc beneath Brian's hands as he latched onto one of the puckered brown nubs rising from Brian's chest.

Powerful hips worked in a steady, unrelenting rhythm, pulling the hard, throbbing length of flesh from Brian's clenching hole before thrusting it back in deeply. The slap of heavy balls against his ass kept time like an X-rated metronome, and for some demented reason, the edgy arpeggios of Beethoven's *Appasionata* came into Brian's head. He groaned, knowing that if he ever heard that song again, he would instantly get hard. Even so, he instinctively wrapped his legs around Alrick's waist, trying to draw him even deeper.

Alrick applied his tongue first to one nipple, then the other, long fingers ensuring that the neglected twin did not feel abandoned. Brian had never thought of his nipples as being overly sensitive, but as in so many things, Alrick had proven that he could teach Brian a thing or two about himself. He swirled the broad flat of his tongue over the swollen nubs, twirling around and around before sucking hard at the tender peaks with firm lips. A sharp nip made Brian yelp, and then Alrick started the process all over again, switching back and forth, all the while keeping up the long, steady thrusts of his hips.

Brian clawed the pale expanse of Alrick's back with his short nails, uncaring that he left parallel lines of red marks in his wake. There was nothing for him but the slow torment of Alrick's tongue, the heady scent of arousal wafting up from the their heated skin, the fat head of the cock rubbing against his prostate as though there were no place else it would rather be. His own hardness was trapped between them, the joint planes of their stomachs massaging him as deftly and sweetly as a tight fist. A grunting, groaning moan cut through the panting and heavy breathing filling the room, and Brian had just enough remaining presence of mind to be mortified when he recognized the voice as his own.

"Don't cover your mouth," Alrick admonished when Brian slapped his hand over his face to muffle any more revealing noises. He took one of Brian's hands in each of his, and entwining their fingers, spread them wide to either side of Brian's head. "I want to hear you moan and cry out to me. I want to hear you call my name when you let go."

Brian realized after an experimental tug against the grip just how insanely strong Alrick was and that he'd never be able to free himself. Being restrained so securely made him feel helpless and exposed and protected and cherished, and… *fuck!* The confusion in his head, the throbbing in his cock, and the huge rod owning his ass flipped a switch somewhere deep inside. All the built-up tension exploded out in a pulsating torrent, and he shouted the only word that held any meaning.

"Alrick!"

Brian's throat strained with the force of his cry, the plea joined by a deep, animalistic growl as Alrick found his own release. He clenched frantically at the hands grasping his, holding on desperately as his climax swept over him in an endless series of pounding waves. And as he floated at the apex of his release, incomprehensible yet somehow familiar words whispered in his ear.

Mery, stay with me.

CHAPTER 5

RAHOTEP GRUNTED in irritation as he woke to muffled sounds. His eyes blinking open reluctantly, he glanced toward the window, but it revealed only the velvet darkness of night. A soft murmur and a warm body drew his attention, and his arms tightened fondly about the lightly snoring boy tucked against his chest. He began to drift back to sleep, but the discordant noise continued, peaking his concern. Rahotep eased Tiye away as gently as he could before standing and reaching for a robe. The racket seemed to grow louder as he unbarred the door and opened it onto a nightmare.

Palace soldiers fought viciously against a ragged group of slaves. Blood streaked the stone floor, making the flagstone dangerous and slick. The slaves, armed as they were with machetes used for cutting wheat and pitchforks grabbed hastily from hay troughs, were no match for the trained men they faced. Several lightly clothed bodies fell to the ground before the soldiers' coordinated defense. Shouting vicious curses, the remaining slaves took off down the hall with the soldiers in close pursuit.

Ice solidified into a ball in the prince's gut as he stared at the chaotic scene. Rahotep looked around sharply, his body tensing as an approaching figure caught his eye. He relaxed with effort as he recognized the pale but determined face of his personal guard. "By the gods, what has happened here?" he demanded.

"Sire, the slaves… they are rebelling!"

Rahotep bared his teeth in frustration at the obvious statement. "Yes, I can see that. I am asking you why? What has happened to enrage them so?" He glanced in the direction of the retreating sounds of battle. His gaze narrowed suspiciously as the most likely cause tightened the knot in his belly. "Is this my father's doing?"

"I do not know, my prince," the soldier replied. "But some of the slaves were shouting about an attack on their village, saying that many were murdered on the pharaoh's order! But I know of no such command!"

Rahotep shoved the man away and whirled back to his room only to be wrenched to a halt as he was confronted by Tiye's frightened stare. Awakened by the fearsome din, the boy had abandoned the bed and was standing as near to the door as he dared, naked save for the sheet hastily wrapped about his waist.

"Is what he says true?" Tiye cried.

Sparing not even a moment to answer, the prince hurried to where his sword hung mounted on the wall. If the soldier had not been misled, then his father was in mortal peril. No matter the virulence of the conflict between them, Rahotep had no wish to see the pharaoh dead.

"Please!" Tiye begged, dogging his heels, his brown eyes a frenzy of dismay. "Was there an attack on the slaves' village? My mother and brother are there!"

Tiye's desperation tore at him, and Rahotep forced himself to pause as he rushed toward the hall. He turned toward his small lover, taking a deep breath to calm himself before tracing a gentle finger over the boy's cheek. "I am not certain exactly what has happened, but I am going to my father now to see if I can make some sense of this insanity." He turned to go but stopped when Tiye came immediately after him. "No, I want you to stay here, safe and out of harm's way."

Rahotep leaned down and pressed a kiss to the boy's furrowed brow. "I will come back for you as soon as I can. Now," he ordered, "bar the door behind me!"

BRIAN AWOKE to find himself trapped beneath something large and warm that smelled really good. Alrick. After leading Brian to that first orgasm that had ripped him apart, Alrick had spent the long night coaxing out another, then another, until all Brian could do was collapse into a boneless, satisfied heap. Even half-asleep, Brian could feel his cheeks warm at the memory.

Now, consciousness was slow to return, but eventually Brian was lucid enough to realize he was still clinging to Alrick's long, muscularly lean form. Forcing his eyes open a crack, he glanced toward the window. The sky was noticeably lighter, so he knew he'd managed several hours of sleep. Still, he felt completely wrung out, sticky from the droplets of creamy heat that had cooled against his skin.

Brian tried to stretch his tired body, but the weight pressing him into the mattress hampered his attempt. As though alerted by his movements, searching fingers reached out to gently stroke his side, and something soft and wet caressed his neck, sending tingles from wherever it touched straight down to his toes. Exhausted though he was, Brian marveled as his body reacted with impossible swiftness to the firm thigh that slipped between his legs to rub maddeningly against his rapidly swelling arousal. He groaned heavily, his head pressing back into the pillow as his hips moved in an instinctive attempt to increase the sensation.

"Fuck me."

Brian didn't realize he had spoken out loud until he heard and felt Alrick's rumbling laugh vibrate against him. He kept his next bout of swearing to himself as his toes curled and his cock tried to react to Alrick's ridiculously sexy voice.

"If you care to stay for a few more hours, I will be more than happy to oblige."

Temptation. It wasn't called sweet for nothing. Brian actually spent nearly a full minute considering the offer before reality reared its pushy head.

"No, I have to go to work. After I go home and change clothes."

"Maybe you should just bring some here. Simply for your convenience, of course."

The hint was hardly subtle. A frisson of anxiety wiping out the last of his lethargy, Brian opened his eyes and looked up at Alrick. He narrowed his gaze suspiciously, not trusting that innocent smile one little bit. In lieu of giving an answer, Brian turned his attention to trying to struggle free from Alrick's embrace. What had he been sleeping with, a damned octopus? It took some doing, not at all helped by Alrick's deliberate attempts to change his mind. Swatting away the hand reaching unerringly for his spent cock, Brian finally managed to move out from under his living blanket.

Deciding to behave for a moment, Alrick propped up on one elbow and watched as Brian sat up and swung his legs over the side of the bed. Alrick never touched him, but Brian swore he could feel the slow caress of a heated gaze over his back. Seriously irritated at how easily Alrick could make him blush, Brian pushed off the bed defiantly, giving his appreciative audience an eyeful. His moment of brashness proved temporary as the nerves he'd so conveniently forgotten last night returned in full force. He studiously avoided the hooded gaze watching him so closely.

"Will you at least stay for breakfast?"

Haven't you already had it? Brian winced at the ungracious thought, wondering when he had turned into such a pissy little bitch. "No thanks. I appreciate it, but I think, no, I'm definitely running late."

A quick glance at the clock on the nightstand had him fumbling for his pants. Getting to work late was the last thing he wanted to do. No point in giving Preston any more excuses to ride him. Turning back toward the bed as he zipped and buttoned his pants, Brian's resolve slipped somewhat when Alrick treated him to a mighty stretch, the reach of his arms spanning the width of the king-size bed. The sheet covering his flat stomach slipped downward until Brian could see the hint of a blond thatch just a shade darker than the hair on his head.

Damn, he was actually drooling. Again. Brian turned away out of self-preservation and hunted up his socks.

"If I let you go now, do you promise to return?"

A biting comment about no one *letting* him do anything died a swift death. It wasn't like he wanted to go. But he couldn't just blow off work to lie in bed all day having mind-numbing sex. Brian shook his head sharply as he remembered just how incredible the previous night had been. No fantasy he'd ever had even came close to what

Alrick had made him feel. After throwing on his shirt, Brian bent to pull on his socks as he looked around for his shoes and tie.

"Yeah, I promise." He didn't look back around, not at all trusting the strength of his willpower. Shoes located, Brian stepped into them. He spied his tie on the floor near the door to the living room and headed toward it.

"Wait for a moment. Let me give you my mobile number."

Brian turned around cautiously, but Alrick pulled the sheet with him as he sat up. Brian sighed in relief and waited as Alrick scribbled down his number on the complementary hotel stationery.

"I will likely be very busy working on a new article tonight, but if all goes well, I should be available tomorrow evening." He tore off the top sheet of paper and held it out. Brian tried not to let his gaze linger on the smooth motion of muscles shifting beneath his fair skin. "Please call me before you come so I will be sure not to miss you."

"Sure." Brian looked up after pocketing the note, and his heart started to beat a little faster when Alrick smiled at him.

Fuck.

"*Auf Wiedersehen.*"

Yes, it was indeed difficult to walk with a hard-on. Brian shuffled as fast as he could toward the door, scooping up his abandoned tie along the way.

"Nice to know you finally got my message. You do know your shift started thirty minutes ago."

Angela's voice drifted to him before he reached the room housing their latest victim. She must have heard him coming up the stairs. Brian ignored the remark since she was absolutely right. He could have saved time by taking a shower in Alrick's room instead of waiting until he got home, but he wasn't stupid. Alrick probably would have joined him, which would have led to lots of other things, and he would soon find himself looking for a new job. He hadn't checked his voice mail until he was dressed, only then seeing that his partner had called to tell him about the new body.

"Our sniper friend has been busy again."

Angela spoke to him over her shoulder when he entered the room, giving him a minute to collect himself as he caught his first sight of the figure sprawled on the floor. Brian was surprised when he realized he was perfectly fine. For once, Dennis's face wasn't coming out to haunt him. Not taking the time to consider what that might mean, Brian stopped at his partner's side and watched with her as a man from Forensics took photos of the victim.

A uniformed patrolman had happened to see a freaked-out junkie running from the building early that morning. The officer was a rookie, which explained why he was in a neighborhood his fellows usually shunned. Otherwise, it might have been weeks before anyone stumbled across the victim. The junkie had found the body in a burned-out building that had long ago been scheduled for demolition and then forgotten. The building sat in the heart of the slums huddled in the dead center of town. Once, it had been a thriving neighborhood, but after years of rising crime and drug dealers deciding it was perfect for doing business, the area was nothing but a neglected shell of its former self. Adding to its woes, a few years ago a mysterious fire had wiped out all but a few of the habitable residences on this block.

The body lay faceup on the charred black floor, bloated and pale. A stain of blood that had bubbled up from the hole in the victim's forehead charted a grim course down the side of his temple, matting his hair.

"Who was he?" Brian asked.

"Pete Karabel." They waited as a woman wearing a Forensics jacket came over to them. She handed Angela a printout from the Violent Crimes database. "I ran a picture of his face through the computer and got an instant hit. Looks like someone lured him here with this." She held up a small bag of heroin in her other, latex-encased hand.

"He's Cosmino, all right," Brian mused, "but he's a total nobody, just a low-life enforcer. Can't imagine why anyone would bother to off this punk."

"Fear? Intimidation?" Angela scanned over the sheet of paper. "Someone's clearly trying to make the Cosminos shit themselves."

Brian read the victim's rap sheet over his partner's shoulder. "The same perp as the other hits, you think?"

"Yep. The 'scopes already pulled the bullet out of the wall." The Forensics tech twitched as Angela used the hated nickname. Brian thought that calling them "microscopes" was quite fitting. "Same caliber as the others, and I'll bet it will be just as clean."

"Great." Brian sighed deeply as he dragged a hand over his face. He didn't care if he had to cheat at their customary coin toss; he was not writing this one up. "Still nothing back from ballistics on the other bullets?"

"Not yet. You know they like to be thorough."

Which was a good thing, as ballistics was often their only evidence. But the waiting was damned frustrating. "So the only thing we know for sure is that the sniper uses a high-powered rifle and is an expert marksman." He moved over to the window, and Angela followed, stepping carefully around the body and the blood pooled beneath it. He hung back so she could stand in front of him as they looked up at the shattered glass. "Assuming the bullet came through here, the only direct line of sight is way over there."

The day was heavily overcast, and Angela squinted as she tried to make out the shadow of a building in the low light. The window was filthy, so she went over to the open doorway to get a better look. There was a clear line to a building sitting off in the distance.

"Shit, that has to be half a mile away."

"At least."

"So we're dealing with a real pro, not just some mook off the street. No way anyone in Milano has this kind of skill."

Brian shook his head. "Doubtful. And if the sniper is hired muscle, it'll be that much harder to find him."

"Heads."

Brian blinked down at his partner. "Huh?"

"I call heads." She slapped a quarter into his palm. "Happy flipping." Her chuckle floated back to him as she sauntered away.

THE CAPTAIN received Brian's report just as well as she had his last one, which was to say, not at all. The beginnings of a tension headache building behind his eyes, Brian glanced down wistfully at the crumpled piece of paper that had been hiding in his pocket all day next to the key card.

"So you got the digits, huh?"

Brian rolled his eyes as Angela snorted. Standing behind his shoulder in the most convenient spot for snooping, she read the neatly scrawled lettering written on the paper. Brian balled up the note in his hand and took the time to shut down his computer before answering. Let her suffer.

"You know you shouldn't repeat anything you hear Sam say." Angela's youngest son was a notorious user of slang, and his mother found it amusing to pretend to be young and hip by parroting him at every opportunity.

"Don't change the subject." She poked him in his arm. "Did you see your German dreamboat again or what?"

"Good grief, woman. Will you give it a rest for two seconds?" He picked up his coat and headed for the door of the open-plan room that housed Homicide. Angela grabbed her coat and purse and followed closely on his heels.

"I will not. I've been married for twenty-three years. Let me live vicariously."

Brian smirked, not believing for one minute that she and Todd didn't neck like teenagers every chance they got. He'd been an embarrassed witness more than once to their touching penchant for PDAs. No wonder her sons were so well-adjusted with such a loving home example to follow. Ignoring a small twinge of jealously, he made use of his longer legs to annoy her as he headed through the door leading to the emergency stairwell.

"Brian!" She was using her "ticked-off mom" tone, and he wisely paused at the top of the stairs until she caught up.

"I saw him again last night," he said after confirming that they were alone.

Angela's eyes damn near sparkled as she grinned up at him. She was clearly ecstatic and amazed he had actually had a repeat encounter with someone, as it had never happened since she'd known him. "Oh, sweetie, I'm so happy for you!"

"We're not picking out china patterns, Angie." Brian turned away from her slightly as his face flamed.

"No, but you look at peace for the first time in a long time. That makes me happy."

"Yeah, everybody's fucking happy."

"Don't be flip, Brian."

He had the nerve to feel sheepish at the chastisement. "Sorry."

She smiled up at him with benevolent forgiveness, making him feel all of twelve years old. "So, how do you feel about him?"

He'd been dreading the question even as he expected it. Brian shook his head. "I honestly don't know. I'm…." He stalled, looking down at his feet, unable to meet her concerned gaze. "All I know is I can't wait to see him again."

Angela placed a comforting hand on his arm. "I'm sure I don't have to tell you what that sounds like."

"Come on, Angie!"

"I won't say anything more," she said, interrupting his sputtered denial. A door opened somewhere above them, heralding noisy voices that suddenly echoed in the stairwell. She turned away and continued down the stairs toward the ground floor. "So I guess you aren't available for pizza night?"

Brian sent a silent thank-you to the pepperoni gods, though he knew the reprieve was only temporary. He wondered how long it would take her to invite her favorite new topic to dinner. No way she'd pass up an opportunity to size up his new boyfriend for herself. *Boyfriend?* Brian winced, amazed at how easily the term had popped into his head.

"Actually, he's busy with work tonight, so I'll be there."

"I'm guessing you finally asked him his name."

"Alrick Ritter."

Angela nodded approvingly. "Nice. You can tell a lot about a man from his name, you know. So, can we expect Mr. Ritter to join us for pizza night next week?"

Brian laughed, congratulating himself for his clairvoyance as they reached the door leading outside.

THE LOCK succumbed to the skillfully applied piece of wire with a quiet snick. The door was not so circumspect, but no one else was around to hear the rusty creak of its hinges. Alrick looked about cautiously, confirming he was alone as he stepped out onto the level surface of the roof.

Spring was only a few weeks away, but the air was still bitingly cold this time of night. He pulled the door closed behind him and blew onto his hands, working the left one to relieve the growing ache. He'd normally have worn gloves in weather like this, but he preferred to have them completely unencumbered for his work. He disliked any reduction in his tactile connection with his instrument when he was performing, and a skillful application of glue over his fingertips eliminated any risk he might leave unwanted prints.

His black clothing provided excellent camouflage in the darkness, a knit cap hiding the flag of his white-blond hair. The building was abandoned, and he gave a grudging compliment to his employer for providing good information. Walking as closely as he dared to the unprotected edge of the roof, he scouted the circumference of the building until he found his target.

He would so much rather be in bed with his new lover than out on this damn roof in the middle of the night. But this was the job, and it would pay very well. He couldn't afford to scoff at the money this assignment promised to bring. A gust of wind buffeted him from the side, and he hitched the strap of the gun case higher as he hunched his shoulders.

He hadn't completely lied to Brian that morning. He'd spent several hours writing for the magazine that provided him with such a convenient cover. Working freelance allowed him to travel to wherever his less public work took him, enabling him to stay however long he needed in a certain place without raising any questions or alarms. The article was a critique of a small-town orchestra and the halfway decent performance of *Carmina Burana* it had given the week before last. He wasn't a huge fan of Carl Orff, but he appreciated the composer's attempt to make a statement against the madness that had swept through his home country during the early twentieth century. He wished he had half the man's courage.

As they had so often during the past two days, his thoughts doggedly returned to Brian. The delicious scent of his honey-toned skin, the comfortable feel of his body, the beautiful sight of his easily aroused blushes. The man was a veritable symphony to his senses, stirring his emotions like one of Brahms's sweeping melodies. Alrick softly hummed the opening strains of the maestro's *Cello Sonata in E Minor* as he swung the case off his shoulder and laid it carefully on the ground.

A jaw-popping yawn interrupted the music, the bracing nighttime air doing little to alleviate his tiredness. He'd tried to take a nap after finishing the final draft of the article, but it had been less than restful. His sleep was disturbed not only by delicious memories of Brian, but also by the dream that had been plaguing him for some time. Only lately, rather than the usual flashes of images, the dream had become strangely intense and vivid. He knew enough to recognize the scenes that flitted across his mind as belonging to the Egypt of the ancient world, but he had no idea why his subconscious was determined to dwell on such a seemingly random subject.

Shaking his head to clear it, Alrick opened the gun case and looked down at the disassembled parts lying within. As he removed the various pieces of his weapon from the case, the chill of winter slowly replaced his emotions with ice. It was a ritual he endured every time he took up the mantle that was both his salvation and his curse.

Todesengel.

He'd fallen in love with the Arctic Warfare from the first moment he'd seen it in his marksman classes. The matte black surface seemed to absorb all light, diverting the eye with its simplicity and deadly beauty. It was not an elegant weapon. The Swedes had originated this particular version, the Psg 90, and they had chosen to emphasize function over form. The stock fit perfectly against the shoulder, the solid piece of metal broken only by the trigger and an opening where the thumb could grip to provide stability before flowing smoothly into the long straight barrel. There were few extraneous parts, the only piece not directly concerned with firing being the bracket designed to support the telescopic sight.

As each piece fit into its place, he became the gun. He might not enjoy killing, but he was damned good at it. He allowed his humanity to slip away as he assembled the weapon, avoiding the pain of thinking about the talents he'd neglected in lieu of this deadly skill.

Music had once been his best friend and his hardest taskmaster. His brilliance had revealed itself at an early age when a chance visit to Berlin with his mother when he was only four years old had opened up a whole new world to his young eyes. East Berlin's premiere orchestra, the Rundfunk-Sinfonieorchester, had been performing a free concert, and his mother and her sister had wanted to see them. He'd been less than enthusiastic at the prospect, squirming and fussing as he was dragged along through the ornate doors of the Konzerthaus Berlin. His impatient kicks at the upholstered chairs had earned him a painful cuff on the ears, but once the music had begun, he'd been transported.

Even now he could still remember the orchestra's matchless performance of *Tannhäuser*. The music had enraptured him, washing over him and filling his small body with emotions he didn't have the words to articulate.

He hadn't known what the large instrument was called at the time. All he knew was how affected he'd been by the sight of the old cellist sitting close to the edge of the stage as he'd hunched over the gracefully curving form. The man had been bent with age, his fingers gnarled and kinked with arthritis, but when he played, the years fell away. Alrick had watched him closely, staring with longing as the man danced across the strings with his bow. After the performance, his mother and aunt had praised him for sitting so quietly and listening so intently. They'd bought him some candy as a reward, but the only thing he'd wanted was a cello.

Fitting the Schmidt & Bender PM II telescopic sight into the bracket on top of the assembled rifle, Alrick banished the memory from his thoughts as he lowered onto his stomach. Music might have been his first love, but fate had intervened, obliging him to put down his cello and pick up a gun. He aimed at a building sitting off in the distance and looked through the scope as he focused on one particular window. Light shone through the window, and Alrick watched silently as a corpulent figure walked into view.

Indeed, Giovanni Rivella was occasionally good for something. Alrick smirked darkly as he remembered the information written in the dossier. Rivella thought he was so clever, using a hired gun to further his battle against the city's rival crime syndicate, but Alrick doubted the authorities would long be fooled by such a blatant ploy. He would have to be careful as long as he worked for the young mobster and not get caught up in Rivella's sloppiness.

As though he could talk when he'd failed so spectacularly to take his own advice. He'd been inexcusably careless since meeting Brian. Even as he'd applied his best efforts to charming Brian the previous night, he'd silently berated himself for being so foolish. And Brian was sharp. Alrick had been caught off guard at their first meeting when Brian had asked whether he'd grown up near the Black Forest, surprised he'd paid attention to such a minor, offhand comment. He hadn't lied when he told Brian that he'd longed to see the forest as a child, but he'd been with his German *Bundeswehr* Army unit, not in college, when he finally got the chance.

As he'd warned Rivella, his very survival depended on his ability to be discreet. He'd had no business picking up a man in a bar, but something about Brian had called to him, prompting him to abandon all of his carefully nurtured caution. It wasn't simply lust that had egged him on. He could have found countless ways to satisfy the needs of his body that were easier to persuade and less dangerous. Any number of men would have provided willing companionship for the night without names being exchanged or prompting any desire for a repeat performance. But within a minute of seeing Brian, Alrick had been completely smitten. It had to be him or no one.

So he would enjoy Brian while he could, until this job was completed and he had to move on or until caution finally won out.

Alrick was disgusted and amused as his thoughts lingered tenaciously on the beauty who'd practically run from his bed that morning while, at the same time, looking utterly reluctant to leave. He could only laugh at his pitiful lack of self-discipline, of that focus that had made him such an accomplished cello player and such a deadly marksman. Yet he couldn't stop himself. For once, his coldness threatened to abandon him as he prepared to take a life.

His target paused in front of the lit window. Alrick braced his rifle and quieted his breathing, though his mind refused to follow suit.

"Sorry, *mein Freund*." He spoke gently to the Arctic Warfare. "I fear you are no longer enough for me."

CHAPTER 6

BRIAN STEPPED carefully around the ugly stain covering a large part of the gaudy orange carpet. Drying blood definitely didn't go with that color. He watched as Jeremy examined the body while humming a jaunty tune.

"Matthias Riccoh." Snapping her notepad shut, Angela glared at the well-known face in disgust. "Well hell, there goes that theory."

The dead man was no stranger to the police, having his hand in many of the illegal dog fighting and underground boxing matches that constantly popped up despite their best efforts to stop them. But the most interesting thing about him was that he was the first victim who fell outside of the profile of the sniper's MO.

"Riccoh was Milano, not Cosmino," Angela groused. She held up the plastic evidence bag one of the 'scopes had handed her. "Same bullet. It was definitely our shooter, but this just doesn't fit."

Brian peered at the hole the large caliber slug had left toward the base of the victim's wall, indicating the shot had come from a high angle. "Not necessarily."

"What do you mean? It wasn't the sniper?"

"No, it was him. Or her," he said quickly before Angela could start in on him with her women's lib bullshit. "I mean our theory might not be dead just yet."

Angela scoffed. "How so? All of the victims up until now were Cosmino, meaning that, most likely, the hit man was hired by the Milanos. But now you're saying that they took a hit out on one of their own? What sense does that make?"

"It makes a lot of sense if you're trying to throw someone off your trail." He turned away from the wall and threw her a smirk over his shoulder. "Were you thrown off?"

She flipped him the bird, her nose turning up in the offended Victorian lady pose she affected so well. The incongruity never failed to tickle him.

"All right, bright boy. So now what? We still don't have any evidence that might give us a clue as to who we're dealing with."

Brian hummed thoughtfully. "I guess we could go shake down someone in Milano and see what falls out."

"Before you do that, you might want to go over to that building across the way."

The two detectives looked down at the medical examiner as he maneuvered his hefty bulk up off the floor.

"You got something, Jeremy?"

The ME nodded at Angela and nudged his toe at the edge of the stain surrounding Matthias's ruined head. "This is still fairly fresh. Plus, rigor mortis isn't nearly as advanced in this one as it was in the others when they were found."

"Meaning this happened, what, yesterday?"

"Sometime very early this morning, to be exact." He grinned at Brian. "And that's not the only thing. See how big of a mess his head is? The shooter was much closer than he usually works."

Brian was already walking over to the broken window. He looked out at the building that sat a few streets over and offered an unobstructed view to anyone who might have wanted to take a shot at old Matthias.

"That building right over there, huh?" Angela joined Brian at the window. "Think we might actually find something?"

"If it's only been a few hours, we should definitely take a look." He turned and headed for the door of the condo, trusting that his partner would be right behind him. "If you learn anything else, Jeremy—"

"Yeah, I know the drill."

"Shit, it's cold up here," Angela cursed as she stuck her hands into her coat pockets.

"It was probably colder last night." Brian reluctantly admired the sniper's fortitude as he pulled his trench coat closer around his body. He glanced over at the two forensics techs that had accompanied him and Angie over to the building. The 'scopes were already poking around, searching for any viable clues as to the sniper's identity.

They had started at the bottom of the abandoned building, checking every door to see whether their shooter had used any of the rooms as his base. Only when they reached the roof did they have any luck. The door was unlocked and undamaged, meaning the sniper was probably also a skilled lockpick. Brian was starting to like this guy less and less.

The four of them split up, each taking a quadrant of the roof. Stepping carefully, they looked closely over every inch of asphalt surface. A thick layer of dirt and debris covered the rooftop, making it difficult to search for anything that might indicate someone had recently been up there. Although he stared at the black-tarred surface until his eyes began to cross, Brian found nothing. He was about to go find his partner when one of the 'scopes called out. Angie beat him to where the tech was waiting at the edge of the roof facing the victim's building. The tech looked over at them, his eyes blinking behind an oversized pair of what looked like red ski goggles.

"Found the shooter's footprint, but not much else."

Brian cocked his head. "Footprint?" He saw nothing but some smudges where the sniper had tried to cover his tracks, but nothing more.

The tech smirked. "The shooter missed a spot." He aimed a device that resembled a spotlight at a clean portion of the asphalt next to the smeared dust. No visible light emanated from the device, and Brian glanced at the tech in confusion. "Oh, sorry." The tech removed his glasses and handed them to Brian.

Brian whistled when he looked at the lit area through the specs. "Not bad."

"Let me see." Angie took the glasses off his face and peered through them. "Guess our shooter isn't as clever as he thinks he is."

"He?" Brian teased. He chuckled when she stuck her tongue out at him.

"Kiss my girly curves. No woman has feet that big."

Brian nodded at the tech when the man wisely handed him his own pair of specs. He donned them and peered back down at the print. "The pattern of the tread is odd."

"It looks like a combat boot of some sort. Maybe government issue?"

Brian placed his own foot alongside the print. "Taller than me by the looks of it." His shoe was a couple inches smaller than the shooter's.

"No need to guess." The tech pulled a tablet and a cable from the backpack resting at his feet. He plugged one end of the cable into the tablet and the other into the light source. "Just give me one second… there. I ran a program that can provide some basic details about the shooter based on residual image of the print." He held up the tablet so Brian and Angela could see it.

"Six to six and a half feet tall. 185, 190 pounds?" Angela shook her head. "That's damn impressive, kid."

Brian snorted at the bright grin the tech sent his partner, as though she'd congratulated him for winning the science fair or something.

"As soon as I get back to the lab, I'll run the measurement through the domestic and foreign criminal databases to see if we get a match."

Brian sobered and waited until the tech and his partner wandered off to look for any more evidence the sniper might have inadvertently left behind.

"Foreign databases," he echoed. "Probably not a bad idea, but I really hope we don't have to call in the FBI on this one." He sighed and braced his hands against the raised rim of brick encircling the roof. "What do you think is really going on, Angie? Everything we can figure about the sniper pegs him as someone who can command top dollar for his services. So how in the hell did the Milanos find him? They may be big-time in the city, but in the grand scheme of things, they're small potatoes."

"You aren't wrong." Angela folded her arms, sheltering her hands beneath them as the wind blew stronger. "When I worked Vice, we partnered up with the Organized Crime taskforce a lot on cases. The Milanos have their hands in a lot of businesses and certainly aren't lacking in resources, but nothing ever pointed to them having any serious connections."

"Well, somehow they've managed to find themselves a major player." Brian looked over the edge of the roof toward Matthias's ruined window. It might not have been as far as the hit on Karabel, but he knew he sure as hell couldn't have made the shot. He didn't want to be impressed, but he was anyway.

"Come on, let's get out of here." Angela started back toward the roof access door. "Since my thirteen-year-old beat you so badly at checkers last night, I'll even write up today's report." Her laugh became muffled as she disappeared into the building. The 'scopes had already left, apparently satisfied they'd gathered as much evidence as they could.

Brian smiled and moved to join her. As he followed Angela down the stairs, he couldn't help but wonder what Alrick was doing right then.

When they returned to the station, Captain Preston was out at the department head meeting the commissioner held every month, so Angela took her time working on the report. "Ratty" came over to her soon after they returned, pretending he was harassing them on the captain's orders. Angela amused herself by ignoring him utterly, which of course drove him completely insane.

"Matt, why don't you go and do some actual work?" Brian looked down at the picture he was doodling, not bothering to acknowledge Matt when he turned toward him with his lips twisted in an unattractive sneer.

"I'm not the one with six dead mobsters on my plate and not a single inkling who the perpetrator is."

"It's five dead mobsters; and we don't need an 'inkling.' We've got evidence." Brian cocked his head as he darkened a line with his pencil. "You should try it sometime."

Angela smiled as she did a final save on her report and clicked Print. She watched Matt stomped away in high dudgeon. "I swear my teenagers are more mature than that man."

"He's got a crush on the boss. Can't blame him for trying to suck up to her."

"Oh, yes, I can." Angela pushed back from her desk and stood, then took a moment to stretch her back. She retrieved the printout and paused behind Brian on her way back. He'd drawn a geometrical shape that looked like a set of irregularly spaced steps and a stylized eye. Now, he was sketching a figure that looked like it was wearing a long goatee and a robe. Curious, she watched him work on the crudely rendered image for few minutes.

"Huh, looks Egyptian."

Brian glanced up at her. "What?"

"Those symbols. They look like some pictures Sam showed me the other day in his schoolbook. They're hieroglyphs. Sam's studying Egyptian mythology this month, and he's really gotten into it."

Startled, Brian stared down at what he'd drawn. He'd seen the symbols in his increasingly detailed dreams. This set had been on the wall right next to the bed where his horny dream boys had been engaged in their X-rated games. He wanted to feel stupid for not recognizing what he'd been seeing all this time, but he'd spent far more time sleeping through history class than paying attention. Egypt, of course. That explained a lot, specifically the strangeness of the men's clothing and the weird furniture and decorations in their room. But given how little he knew about the subject, Brian couldn't begin to explain how he'd suddenly become a freaking expert in Egyptology.

Disquieted, he balled up the scrap of paper and tossed it into the wastebasket beneath his desk. "Whatever. I guess I accidentally learned something while passing the museum on my way home from work."

Angela sniggered. "So it can be taught. Who knew?" She danced out of the way as he lobbed his pencil in her direction. "Forensics promises me that they'll have a report on the bullet from James the pimp's apartment early next week."

"Forensics promised you, or that cute redheaded 'scope promised you?" He laughed as his partner favored him with a sour expression. "Now who has an admirer?"

"Speaking of which, it's quittin' time. Don't you have plans?"

Brian shifted uncomfortably in his seat and glanced at his cell phone, which was lying in its usual spot on his desk. "I don't know. He told me to call first." He kept his voice low to prevent being overheard, unwilling to out himself at work.

"So call already." When Brian didn't move, Angela reached for his phone. "Fine, I'll do it. I've been dying to hear what he sounds like."

He snatched up the device before she could reach it and shot her a disgruntled glare. He looked around, checking if anyone had heard her slip of pronoun usage. No one was paying them any attention, but she gave him a sheepish grin, realizing her mistake. Standing, he grabbed his coat from their shared coat rack and headed for the door. Angela stared after him in consternation.

"Brian!"

"Night, Angie." He waved good-bye, phone in hand. By way of apology and to show that he forgave her, he opened it up and hunted for the number he'd programmed in only the day before while she could still see him.

MATT RODDY glanced toward Macon's retreating back as he left the department. A smirk teased at the edge of his mouth, but he tamped it down ruthlessly. Just thinking about the reason for his glee made him giddy. His gaze drifted toward the captain's door as he remembered the conversation he'd had with her earlier that day.

She'd called him into her office unexpectedly. As always when he saw her, he had to force his libido to behave. She was so unbelievably beautiful, she always left him tongue-tied. Swallowing, he tried unsuccessfully to control the unbidden reaction of his body when she looked up at him.

"Come in, Roddy, and shut the door."

He did as she asked even though he was surprised at the command. He'd never been in a closed room with her before, and the novel situation certainly wasn't helping with his growing problem.

"Captain?" He didn't trust himself to say anything more.

"I want you to follow up with Forensics regarding that ballistics report on the shooter Macon and Lovell are investigating. Have them run the tests again."

Matt blinked at her in confusion. "Um, okay. Why, what's wrong?"

She leaned back in her chair, one long leg crossed over the other. The posture hiked up her skirt and spread her jacket lapels apart so her cleavage was even more visible. Matt struggled to keep his gaze on her face.

"I'm afraid the evidence might have been tainted. I want them to double-check everything to ensure the results are accurate. The commissioner is breathing down my neck over this sniper case. We can't afford to be wrong about this."

"Sure, of course. But why don't you just let Macon and Lovell know your concerns?"

"They have enough on their plate following up with new leads. Besides, this is a team effort, right?"

He nodded hesitantly. Her request seemed reasonable, but something was odd. It didn't make sense for him to do something on a case without the lead detectives' knowledge. "I guess," he mumbled.

"Matt."

Her cajoling tone went straight to his groin. His palms started to sweat as she stood and flowed around her desk toward him. Her perfume filled his senses as she stopped mere inches in front of him. With her tall heels, she towered over him by a couple of inches. Her dark brown gaze was warm with sultry promise as she captured his.

"Please, just do this for me?"

He nodded, his voice trapped in his throat.

She smiled as she adjusted his tie. "Very good."

He stood frozen where he was when she turned and went back to her desk. She sat and pulled some paperwork toward her.

"That will be all." She didn't look up at him again.

Matt left her office determined not to let her down and trying to ignore the lingering knot of uncertainty lodged in his stomach.

CHAPTER 7

ALRICK SAT on the couch in his hotel room, toying with a glass of wine and pretending he wasn't listening carefully for a knock on the door. Brian had called earlier to say he wanted to come over, and Alrick was trying not to be impatient. So of course when the knock came, he was on his feet immediately. The couch was only a few steps from the door, but it seemed to take him forever to reach it. He'd guessed that, even though Brian had a key, he would be too shy to use it. Indeed, when he finally opened the door, Brian was standing there giving him that self-conscious, embarrassed look he loved so much. Tender warmth spread from his chest throughout his body.

"What's up?"

Smiling at the Americanism, Alrick stepped back so Brian could come in. "Not much. I was just having a drink. Would you like anything?"

"Sure. Whatever's easiest is fine."

"Whiskey on the rocks?"

"Yeah, that sounds good. Just as long as it's better than that stuff I was drinking at Blackjack's." Brian laughed wryly, making Alrick respond in kind.

"I assure you it will be. This hotel prides itself on providing only the best."

"Great, thanks." Brian took off his coat and looked around for somewhere to put it.

"Would you like to hang it in the closet?"

Brian glanced over toward the bar where Alrick stood fixing his drink. "Yeah. I guess I should act civilized once in a while, right?" He moved to follow the advice as Alrick chuckled at his self-deprecating humor.

Alrick didn't immediately think about what was in the closet besides hangers and his own jacket until he saw Brian pause and stare curiously into the small space.

"What's this?"

His stomach tightened instinctively before he forced himself to relax. "It is a cello." He walked over and stood behind Brian, looking over his shoulder at the large, black case. Habit and experience had prompted him to store his rifle in a far more secure location than his hotel room, but he liked to keep the stringed instrument close by. Even so, although he took it with him everywhere he went, he always made sure to lock it away whenever he arrived where he was going. The mere sight of it stirred up many emotions he would prefer remained buried, but perversely, he found he needed that reminder, painful though it was.

"Do you play?"

"A bit."

Brian hung up his coat and took the glass of whiskey from Alrick's hand. "Cheers." He took a sip, and the corner of his mouth turned up. "Way better than that other stuff."

"I am glad you like it." As Brian moved past him to head for the couch, Alrick started to close the closet door.

"Oh, um, would you play something? Our conversation at Blackjack's sort of piqued my interest."

Alrick froze for a brief moment, his stomach flopping queasily at the unexpected request. "It has been a long time. I'm rather out of practice."

Brian looked confused, his head cocking adorably to the side. "Then why is it here?"

Why, indeed? Alrick rolled his shoulders, a habit that manifested when he was uncomfortable. "I've had it since I was a boy. It was a gift from my mother." He looked back toward the large case. "I don't trust anyone else to take care of it. She died when I was fifteen," he continued after a slight pause. "I suppose it reminds me of her."

"Ah. I'm sorry," Brian said. He shrugged before taking another sip, clearly regretting bringing up such a personal topic.

Alrick couldn't help but stare as Brian licked a few lingering drops from his lips. He moved to close the closet door, but Brian's voice stopped him.

"I'm not really into classical music, but I kinda like the cello. There was that one song in that movie with Russell Crowe and Paul Bettany—*Master and Commander*. Do you know it?"

"The movie or the song?"

Brian shrugged. "Um, both, I guess."

Alrick nodded. "Yes, I've seen the movie." He pulled the case from the closet. "And I know which song you are referring to. It's 'Prelude' from Bach's Cello Suite No. 1."

Brian shrugged again. "If you say so. I didn't mean that you had to play it for me," he added when Alrick pulled the case from the closet.

Alrick looked over at Brian, noting the sincerity in his expression. He really hadn't been expecting anything but had merely been expressing his interest. Alrick began to relax as Brian's innocent curiosity chased away some of his old ghosts. Smiling ruefully, he carried the case over to the armchair sitting at a right angle to the couch and laid the case flat on the floor beside the chair before settling on the edge of the deep cushion. It wasn't the ideal for playing. A higher, harder chair would be much better. Still, it would do. He took the bow out of the case along with a small block of rosin.

"No, it's all right," he said as he rubbed the amber substance carefully back and forth over the taut strands. "Like I said, I'm just out of practice."

Brian sat back on the couch, making himself comfortable. Alrick was pleased to see he'd chosen the side closest to the chair rather than shying away to the other end. Setting the bow aside, he removed the cello from the velvet-lined case. Brian followed his movements intently as he began tuning the strings. He winced painfully at how bad they sounded, though, fortunately, none of the strings had gone completely slack.

"What are you doing?"

"Tuning." Alrick held his head close to the strings, plucking them before adjusting the tuning knob. "Each string has its own note, and if they aren't properly aligned, nothing will sound right." He plucked and adjusted again, humming quietly to himself, or so he thought.

"You're humming the note the strings should have? How do you know?"

Alrick lifted his head for a moment and smiled, pleased at Brian's curiosity, before returning to his work. "I have perfect pitch. That means I always know the correct pitch for any given note."

Brian's look of confusion at the unfamiliar term cleared, his eyebrows lifting as he whistled. "Wow, I'm impressed. I can't even sing in the shower without scaring away bugs and mice."

Alrick laughed out loud. "Singing may be difficult for you, but you can be tone deaf and still learn to play an instrument."

Brian shook his head and held up his hands in denial. "Nah, I'll leave that to the experts. I'd probably just break something if I tried. Coordination isn't my strong suit."

"Somehow I doubt that."

Maybe it was the way the pitch of Alrick's voice suddenly dropped, but Brian, who had seemed completely relaxed for the first time since they'd met, suddenly looked away from him, his light brown cheeks flushing with color. Sparing only half of his focus on tuning the high A string, Alrick let his gaze trace indulgently over Brian's handsome features.

"You know, I think this is the longest conversation we've had without getting physical."

Alrick watched gleefully as Brian realized what he had just said. The color in his face went from faint to flaming in an instant. "I would be more than happy to rectify that lapse."

Brian glared at him, embarrassment making him snippy. "No, you can just sit there and play like you promised."

Grinning, Alrick sat up at last and pulled the cello between his legs. He didn't miss the swallow that bobbed Brian's Adam's apple as he realized just how Alrick would have to sit as he played. He took a deep breath as he placed the bow on the strings. It truly had been a long time since he had played. He'd tried a few times after leaving the *Bundeswehr*, but those experiences had not been pleasant. For Brian, however, he would at least make the attempt once more.

"Bach's 'Prelude.' Let's see if I remember."

The bow vibrated the second, third, then fourth strings in rapid succession. The work was typical of Bach, a masterpiece of skillfully arranged yet deceptively simple arpeggios. Alrick had learned the solo piece when he was nine years old. An elderly woman who worked at the underfunded library where he'd spent so many hours listening to his favorite composers had given him his first introduction to the piece in the form of an old recording. Upon discovering that he'd taken up an instrument, she'd kindly provided him with the sheet music for free. He'd toiled for hours, practicing and practicing until he could play it perfectly from memory.

It came back to him easily now, his muscles remembering where his mind had forgotten. He closed his eyes as he played, the old, yellowed paper filled with those beautiful notes floating across his memory. His right arm was an extension of the bow, moving in a flowing rhythm that drew out the emotional strains effortlessly.

But his left hand soon betrayed him, as it had for the past eight years. A painful cramp twisted his fingers in a vise of agony. He grunted sharply as he abruptly removed his hand from the neck of the cello. Brian, who had been listening in rapt silence, blinked at him in confusion when he suddenly stopped playing and glared down at the offending appendage.

Brian inhaled deeply, as though he had gone some time without breathing. "That was beautiful. Why did you stop?"

Alrick tried to keep his expression neutral as he massaged his aching hand. "I was in a car accident several years ago and broke several fingers of my left hand." His tone was emotionless, although the tightness of his clenched jaw belied his indifference. "It has made playing rather… difficult."

Brian reached out and rested his hand on Alrick's shoulder. "Man, I'm sorry. You should have told me. I never would have asked you to play if I'd known."

Alrick shook his head. "No, it's fine. Actually, it hurts much less than it used to. I haven't been able to get that far into the piece since before the accident." He gave Brian a reassuring grin. "It felt good to play."

"Well you were amazing. I think you were having me on when you said you were out of practice. That was absolutely incredible."

Brian's eager expression brought a smile to Alrick's face. The throbbing in his hand lessened as though Brian's very presence were a soothing balm.

"How long have you been playing?" Brian asked. "I'm guessing you started when you were really young to be so good."

Alrick nodded, amazed at how little reluctance he felt to share his carefully guarded past with the man gazing at him so intently. "I was eight. My mother brought me my first cello—this one in fact—at a flea market. My father was a carpenter, and he restored it for me. It was far too large for me back then, but I've always loved it."

"Hmm," Brian murmured at the pleasant tale. "You must have had an excellent teacher."

"Actually," Alrick said with a grin, "I taught myself."

Brian stared at him. "Get out! Are you serious?"

Alrick laughed. "*Wirklich*," he replied, holding up his left hand and placing his right over his heart to emphasize his sincerity.

"Did you ever play professionally?"

Alrick glanced at Brian cautiously. He was beginning to feel as though he were being interrogated, but the open look on Brian's face quickly alleviated his suspicions. "No," he finally answered, though he didn't elaborate. Not out of caution, but because the truth hurt too much to remember.

When he was seventeen, he often earned pocket money by playing at a street market. A member of Dr. Hoch's, the premiere music conservatory in Frankfurt, heard him one afternoon and offered him a spot. He'd run home after talking with the man, eager to share his news with his father and younger sister.

It was 1992, the Wall had been torn down for several years, and all of Germany was caught up in the fervor of reunification. But the fall of the Eastern Block had not been kind to everyone. Access to the West and its capitalistic splendor had lessened demand for the local wares that had sustained the people of the former Democratic Republic for so long. Alrick's father had found his business foundering, his debts mounting day by day. Driven to desperation, he'd struck a deal with the remnants of the Russian mafia for some much-needed capital to keep his business and his family afloat.

Alrick's mother had died nearly two years before, after a long battle with cancer, and the resulting medical bills were crippling. Needing his son's help more than ever, Hans had refused Alrick's request to attend the music conservatory. Instead, he'd insisted that, after Alrick completed his compulsory military service in the *Bundeswehr*, he enlist, desperate for the steady paycheck his son would earn as a result. After learning that his father's business was in ruins, their home was mortgaged to the hilt, and everything they had, from the clothes on their back to the food on their table, had been bought with money from the Russians, Alrick had relented.

His dreams of music died as he put down his cello and picked up a gun, finding he had a rare talent for marksmanship that allowed him to rise quickly through the enlisted ranks. Within seven years, he became an *Oberfeldwebel*, a Sergeant First Class. Then it all went to hell.

"No," he repeated, his smile returning at the concern in Brian's gaze. Sad thoughts of the past had distracted him from his beautiful guest for long enough. He brought the cello upright again, seeking to recapture a lighter mood. "In fact, let me see if I can do better with something a little easier."

He placed the bow on the strings and set in on another piece that had a slower, steadier melody. The music invoked a dark, heavy, yet somehow sensual mood. It had always been one of his favorites, despite its fame.

"Okay, I definitely know that one."

"Yes, it's very popular."

"And it's called…?"

"'*Mondscheinsonate.*' 'Moonlight Sonata' in English, also by Beethoven."

"Ah! *Immortal Beloved.*"

"Eh?"

Brian gave him a sheepish, apologetic look. "Nothing. It was this movie about Beethoven that a friend of mine made me watch. Gary Oldman was in it, so it wasn't half-bad. Anyway, that's where I heard the song—" Brian broke off and stared at Alrick in shock when he suddenly stopped playing and threw his bow across the room.

"*Scheiße!*" Treating the cello with only a little more consideration, Alrick stopped just short of dropping it as he surged to his feet. His jaw clenched as pain radiated through his hand. Anger tore at him, and he came uncomfortably close to kicking the polished wooden frame.

"What the hell are you doing?" Showing no small amount of bravery, Brian stepped directly in front of Alrick, interrupting his agitated pacing.

Alrick stopped in midstride and glared down at him. The hesitancy Brian so often projected was nowhere to be found, as though witnessing Alrick's all too human show of frustration had broken through the last of his reserve. Seeing the concern in those incredible green hazel eyes, Alrick's fury bled away, only to be replaced by an intense sadness. The cramping in his hand served as a persistent reminder of how everything that had once been good in his life had been so cruelly wrenched away. He took a steadying breath, determined to calm himself before he lost even this new gift.

"Please forgive me for my outburst." Alrick winced as his hand throbbed in time with his heartbeat. "After my accident, it was some time before I received medical attention. My fingers were never set properly, and now even that simple piece is apparently too difficult for me." He sighed, feeling as if he'd failed Brian somehow. "I really did want to play for you." Alrick's breath stuttered to a halt when Brian reached out and cradled his aching fingers in his hands. They were a man's hands, large and capable and sure of themselves as they massaged away his pain.

"You can hum, can't you?"

Alrick's brow furrowed at the non sequitur. "Yes, of course." He hissed as Brian sucked his index finger into the warm cavern of his mouth. The soft caress of a tongue against the slightly crooked digit went straight to his cock, instantly leaving him impossibly hard. He shivered when Brian slowly withdrew the finger from the wet orifice.

Brian leaned close to him until their lips were a mere paper's width apart. "Then hum for me instead."

Alrick wasn't certain which of them closed that last distance. In the end, it simply didn't matter. The man who had been occupying his thoughts so incessantly was back in his arms. That was the only reality he cared about.

Brian slid his hands beneath Alrick's shirt and traced his fingers over the muscular plane of his chest. Before Alrick could react, Brian swept the shirt over his head and tossed it carelessly onto the floor behind them, then sent his own quickly after it. Alrick groaned as soft lips latched intently onto a pink nipple, his remaining ability to form a coherent thought draining swiftly into his cock. Shoes thudded to the carpet, followed urgently by pants and boxers. The air in the living room was cool against his bare skin, but Alrick barely noticed. Thrusting a naked thigh between Brian's legs, he grabbed the warm flesh of Brian's ass and drew Brian toward him, aligning their erections.

Brian threw his head back as their mutual hardness came into luscious contact. "Ah, yeah. Like that."

Alrick took eager advantage of the long column bared for his exploitation. He swept his tongue up Brian's neck with broad, slow swipes before taking a section of glistening skin between his lips and sucking hard. Brian grabbed at his shoulders as sharp heat bloomed beneath Alrick's mouth. After a long moment, Alrick lifted his head to admire his handiwork.

"Mine," he growled, the sight of the red mark arousing a fierce sense of possessiveness. Alrick laid claim to Brian's mouth, twisting as they fell onto the couch so Brian landed flush on top of him.

Brian parted his legs and straddled Alrick's muscular thighs. Moving his hips, he rubbed their arousals together, drawing a grateful moan from Alrick, who lay beneath him. The friction burned uncomfortably at first, but the fluid leaking from the tips of their mutual erections soon eased the way.

"That's it," Alrick murmured, kissing wherever he could reach. "Show me what you want." Reaching down, he clenched his hands around the soft mounds of Brian's ass and squeezed, loving the way his fingers sank into the slightly out of shape muscles. "Show me how you want to fuck me."

Brian inhaled sharply as his arousal throbbed in response to the suggestion. "Goddamn it, keep talking to me. I fucking love the way you talk."

Alrick chuckled deeply as Brian paid him back by attacking his neck and chest, leaving a multitude of red marks in his wake. He whispered endearments in German, his tone degrading to a growl as the tension built up with every thrust of their hips. Chest heaving, his flushed skin dripped with sweat. Brian's breath rasped over his heated skin in harsh puffs as if he were running a race. Brian reached behind him and peeled Alrick's left hand off his ass. Alrick started to protest, but his complaints ended swiftly when Brian drew his still-aching finger into his mouth. Again, the soft, wet pressure made him throb in reaction. He watched in fascination as Brian released his index finger, only to include his middle finger and then his ring finger.

"*Scheiße*—" This time, the epithet was a prayer rather than a curse. He recognized the tender gesture as a primitive attempt to soothe away his pain. An intense need for release came upon him suddenly, every slide of Brian's cock against his own flooding his nerve endings with sparks of electricity. Alrick tried to hold back, wanting to take Brian into his bedroom, where the king-size mattress and a box full of condoms awaited them.

But Brian chose that moment to exchange the three fingers he'd been sucking on so contentedly for his little finger, which was twisted awkwardly from the abuse it had received. Though he couldn't have been aware that the finger had nearly been crushed beyond use, Brian treated it with special care; the pressure of his mouth shaded away from the sexual and became almost familial, the soft sucking of his mouth designed to soothe away the pain in the mistreated appendage.

Alrick shouted as he succumbed to unspoken sentiment, his passion pouring out in shuddering waves and coating both of their stomachs with hot stickiness. Alrick's release triggering his own, Brian added to the spattered tableau, shouting nonsense as he exploded. He collapsed against Alrick, their breathing filling the room with a different kind of music.

"Crap, that's gonna sting in the morning. Next time, gotta use lube."

Alrick groaned in agreement, the skin covering his softening member already beginning to feel sore. "Indeed."

Brian wiggled on top of him, seeking to find a more comfortable position. "The light's on again. What is it with you and lights?"

Alrick smirked, knowing Brian was fully aware he had been the instigator this time. "I didn't hear you complaining before." He huffed as a finger poked him none too gently in his side. "Besides, I enjoy seeing the expressions you make when you are about to come for me."

"Bullshit. You just have some freaky lamp fetish."

Another wiggle, and amazingly, Alrick felt his cock stir with lazy interest.

"Why is it that curses sound so much cooler in German?"

"Because we invented it. Or at least that's what my father always insisted."

Brian stilled. "Is your dad still alive?"

Alrick's chest tightened, although the weight of Brian pressing down on him somehow lessened the familiar pang. "No, he died many years ago." A pair of arms held him a little closer.

"Sorry."

Alrick knew he shouldn't encourage such personal questions, but he merely shook his head, knowing Brian would be able to feel the movement. "It is hardly your fault."

"Do you have any other family?" Brian's words began to slur, and Alrick bid a reluctant farewell to his plans of continuing things in the other room.

He was being interrogated again, but he was too relaxed and contented to care. "A younger sister," he replied

"What's her name?"

"Rosamunde."

Alrick began to drift off as exhaustion slowly overtook him. He'd been up very late the night before taking care of business and had not rested much today, too eager at the prospect of seeing Brian again. It was a dangerous game trying to live in two such wildly incompatible worlds. Could a cold-blooded killer really fall in love? He grunted sleepily as something stroked his shoulder.

"Nice tattoo. What does it mean?"

Alrick hoped that Brian was far enough gone that he didn't notice the sudden tension in his body. "Nothing in particular. It's just a souvenir from a misspent youth."

There was no answer save for a soft snore.

CHAPTER 8

TIYE WATCHED helplessly as his prince rushed from the room. He wanted badly to follow, but he did as bidden. His heart pounding loudly in his chest, he wrestled with the solid plank of wood that served to secure the door. Tiye hastily pulled on his discarded skirt and sat on the bed, only to leap to his feet again a second later, unable to contain his nervous energy. The bone-rattling clang of metal and the chilling shrieks of pain and death swelled in the hall as the fighting neared once again. A loud thud banged against the door, and Tiye wondered grimly whether it was the falling of a body that had caused the terrible sound.

But the pounding soon resolved itself into the sound of a determined knock. Tiye hesitated only a moment before rushing to unbar the door. His prince's name was on his lips as he flung open the heavy wooden slab only to have his hopes dashed. A regal beauty stood in the doorway, seemingly impervious to the violence that raged behind her. An older woman cowered behind her, trying to make herself as small and inconspicuous as possible. The young woman swept into the chamber as though it was her rightful place, and Tiye instantly perceived her identity.

"Lady Hebeny," he said with surprise, bowing nervously in greeting. Tiye looked behind her into the hall, but amazingly, the hall was empty of all but dead bodies. Shivering at the morbid scene, he closed and locked the door behind them. "Why are you here?" he asked his unexpected visitor. "It is dangerous to be out during this madness."

"It is this very tragedy, my dear boy, that has brought me to you," she said hastily, waving away his words. She met his gaze fully for the first time, and her eyes were not nearly so cold as he had imagined. "I have just heard it from my woman, Trella. Whispers of an impending rebellion amongst the slaves reached the pharaoh, and he had his personal guard raid their village. Several of the ringleaders were put directly to death, including—"

She closed her eyes, her voice choking with the tears that spilled down her cheeks. Made bold by the dread coiling in his gut, Tiye stepped toward her impatiently and grabbed her hands. He stared into her eyes beseechingly, anxiety sharpening his gaze.

"Who? Who was killed?"

"Your mother and your brother were accused," she whispered.

Tiye could only stare at Hebeny, her words screaming in his mind like the raging of a storm. "My mother and brother?" he echoed, his tone weak and distant as his voice faltered.

"Trella says that your brother, at least, escaped, though he was wounded. He roused the rest of the village, and they came to attack the pharaoh. Even now, your brother has gone to kill Rahotep's father!"

Tiye turned without a word and raced toward the door, flinging away the heavy bar in his panic as if it weighed nothing. He fled from the room, tears blurring his vision as a single, horrible thought chased itself through his mind. His brother, Nakhti, had gone to kill the pharaoh, and his lover had gone to see to his father's safety. Even though they were often at odds, the prince would never allow his sire to be killed. And if Rahotep and Nakhti should meet....

THE APARTMENT building was gaudy and pretentious, fitting the nouveau riche attitude of the neighborhood's residents. The penthouse taking up the entire top floor was by far the worst. Access was possible only by way of a private elevator, which required a key to operate. The long hallway between the elevator and the front door of the penthouse featured an oriental rug worth enough to feed a family of six for a decade. A heavy gilt-framed mirror, surrounded by a dozen tacky paintings of dogs as circus performers, interrupted the bare expanse of wall. A tall, hulking giant of a man in dire need of a neck stood guarding the door, his massive torso straining the seams of his shirt and a pair of sunglasses making his blank expression even blanker. Giovanni Rivella might not have needed the protection of a full-time bodyguard, but having one constantly at his beck and call apparently did his inflated ego a world of good.

Hayley had always considered the place unbearably tacky.

From her vantage point in the bathroom, she could see Gio lying in his oversized bed, propped up against thickly stuffed pillows. Both the bed and the pillows were covered in varying shades of black and purple satin. Gio had told her once he liked living like a pimp. She'd been singularly unimpressed.

Naked but for the gold chain lying across his respectably pumped chest—courtesy of a regular course of steroids—he bent his right arm at the elbow, smiling in approval at the resulting mound of his bicep. She rolled her eyes in disgust. Gio never failed to be awed by the sight of himself, but she didn't share his infatuation.

"Yo, babe! What's the holdup? Get your sexy ass out here." He reached down to rub eagerly at his uninspiring cock, randy from a long night of clubbing, booze, and amphetamines. "Gio junior needs some attention."

Hayley continued massaging cold cream onto her face, calmly ignoring his crude outburst. He would wait for her like he always did because he found her irresistible. She'd made certain of that.

She turned the tap and waited as warm water filled the sink. A few quick splashes removed the majority of the cream, and an efficient swipe with a towel took care of the rest. Glancing up into the mirror, she studied her reflection with cold detachment.

She was beautiful, but then, she was always beautiful. No matter the ethnicity into which she was born, glorious black hair, stunning brown eyes, and olive-kissed skin always defined her. In every life she'd lived for nearly three thousand years, her features were the only constant. Perhaps the North African heritage of her first life had been imprinted on her very soul, following her from incarnation to incarnation. Or perhaps that bastard god, Set, simply delighted in tormenting her with the constant reminder of her past.

Not that her appearance made any difference. Beauty meant nothing when you were doomed to spend eternity living out an ever-repeating hell.

She hated this time more than all the others through which she'd lived. The fast-paced soullessness technology had brought to the world made her long for the elegance of days past. Once she'd worn silks and exquisite jewels. She'd danced the complicated steps taught by masters and watched as men fought over her in deadly games played with swords and, later, pistols. She'd ridden in golden chariots and on magnificent steeds and had enjoyed all the wonders of the ages as civilizations rose and fell around her.

But this world was lacking in both beauty and taste. For all of the conveniences of "modern life," it bored her. The shabbiness of the clothing, the tastelessness of the food, the horrid banality these people called music. She sometimes wondered how the human race had survived instead of dying out beneath its own hideous inconsequence.

More than anything, however, she hated the men of this time. They were weak, vulgar louts who barely knew how to scratch their own balls, let alone how to truly satisfy a woman. When she thought of the magnificent specimens of masculinity she had known across the years, it was enough to make her weep. How could the pitiful creatures that dared lay claim to the male gender compete with the likes of Hannibal and Julius Caesar, Salah ad Din and Peter the Great? Emperors, kings, and knights of untold beauty and power had once hung upon her every word, fighting for her favors and submitting to her slightest whim. But now she was reduced to this.

She cast a derisive eye over the tawdry décor reflected behind her in the mirror. Thinking of what awaited her in the next room, her mouth twisted in revulsion. How poetically tragic the twist of fate that doomed her to follow two particular men through time, sacrificing everything she might make of her endless lives in order to spend her existence attempting to thwart their base relationship.

But she couldn't stop. She could never stop. The threat of what awaited her should she fail pressed her ever onward down her unending path.

Through the vagaries of her curse, she was destined to stumble across at least one of the men whom she'd hated enough to sacrifice eternity. If she discovered one, she never had to worry about seeking out the other, for they would find each other without fail. Her desire for vengeance had carried her strongly through those first incarnations, and she'd taken great delight in destroying her perceived enemies. But after her first few lives, she had grown weary of the evils she was obliged to commit as she facilitated the lovers' betrayal and ultimate destruction. She'd tried to outsmart Set, who had eventually fallen out of consequence to the people of the world. Ignoring her oath, she'd lived as she pleased without giving the slightest thought to her curse. But as she had quickly realized, avoidance was impossible. As in every lifetime, one of the men crossed her path, and as though Set had thrown a black stain on her soul, her ire had compelled her to fulfill her promise. Although the dark god might have become nothing more than a myth, there was no escape for her as long as his frightful power continued to hold true.

And so it was in this incarnation as it had been in all the others. She'd enjoyed a brief respite for the first twenty-one years of her current life, but when she suddenly found one of the men she was doomed to hunt, the innocent normalcy of her life came to an abrupt end.

She'd stumbled across her target while visiting a boyfriend at his college campus. A senior herself, she'd barely given the skinny freshman a second glance when he nearly bowled her over while rushing off to some activity or other. But even with only that brief look, she'd seen past the fleshy trappings of his body to the true form of his soul. Rather than a medium-toned, brown-haired young man of average height, his pretty green-hazel eyes wide with embarrassment as he apologized to her profusely, she'd seen an image from a far distant past. Hatred and hopelessness had churned in her gut in sickening turns as she accepted the time had come, once more, for her to play her part in her never-ending tragedy.

She'd followed the young man that day, learning that his name was Brian Macon and he was studying criminal justice. Working on a hunch, she applied to the police academy the very next day. She'd shown a surprising aptitude for police work, and by the time Macon made detective, she was already rising quickly through the ranks, her natural intelligence and a three-year head start giving her an edge. When an opening for captain came in the homicide unit at his precinct, she was poised to exploit the opportunity. Her quarry was now firmly under her thumb, where she could set the stage for his downfall when the time came. All she had to do was to wait for him to find the soul to whom fate had bound him, and when he did, she would be ready to destroy them both.

But before she could discharge her duty to the bloodthirsty god, she was forced to this disgusting expedience.

The bathroom light flicked out, and Gio watched hungrily, licking his lips as she emerged wearing a lacy black number. He'd given it to her as a gift, and seeing her in it got him going every time. "About damn time, babe. You know you can't keep a stud like me waiting."

Hayley walked over to the bed and paused as she looked down at the man who was her sometime lover. She schooled her features with long practice, hiding her disgust. "You know I'm worth it, darling."

Gio loved it when she talked to him like some tawdry movie starlet from the early years of cinema. It was an easy persona for her to portray. Those sultry vamps of the silver screen had been the last women she'd truly admired. She slipped into bed, gritting her teeth as he immediately grabbed her ass and pulled her close to his sweaty body. At least he wasn't completely hideous. He was over twelve years her junior, and sometimes she wondered if he realized how old she was. She took great pains to hide the passage of years, that being the one thing that continued to rankle no matter how many lives she lived.

Hayley feigned interest as he planted sloppy kisses over her neck and chest. Digging her fingers into his thick hair, she held him in place as he nudged the neckline of her negligee below her breasts and went to work. Her stomach turned as he licked and sucked over the full mounds. "So tell me, have you decided on your friend's next target?"

"Aww, babe, you wanna talk shop now?"

Her lips tightened with impatience. Gio generally didn't mind when she wanted to talk about his business. He thought it extremely amusing that he was fucking a police captain. She'd met him shortly after taking over Homicide. He'd been walking out of Central Booking, brash and cocky from beating some petty rap using his uncle's influence. When she'd learned who he was, she'd decided to introduce herself by accosting him in the back room of a nightclub and giving him an extremely skilled blowjob. Long experience had taught her to never let a possible pawn go unused, and Gio had proven to be a particularly valuable stooge. She sometimes wondered if he ever stopped to think how little sense their relationship made. Probably not. He rarely thought with anything except his fists and his dick. Gio's favorite topic, besides himself, was his latest project: wiping out the Cosminos. He was thrilled with the man he'd found to do his dirty work and thought he'd been turned on to the German assassin by an associate of his uncle's.

Hayley smirked as Gio indulged himself with the ripe, brown peaks that puckered beneath his tongue. She ran her long, sharp fingernails over his scalp as he sucked at her nipples, noting his shiver with nothing more than clinical interest. Never in a million years would Gio have guessed that his hired killer had, in fact, been deliberately dangled in front of his nose by his new girlfriend.

Abandoning her breast for more tempting prospects below, Gio slid down her stomach, his wet cock leaving a disgusting trail of slime along her leg. She found it within herself to forgive him, however, when he pushed up her negligee and buried his head between her legs. A throaty sigh slipped from her lips as he quickly hit his stride, licking and sucking the tender folds of her sex, his tongue fucking her with eager jabs. She relaxed as her body reacted despite her intellectual repugnance.

If he had to be good for something, it might as well be this. Even though she selfishly enjoyed Gio's eagerness to go down on her, it rarely made her come. Still, she would make him service her until she was satisfied. It was the least he could do to thank her for the privilege of letting him touch her at all. Tightening her grip on his hair, Hayley smiled as he grunted in pain. Disgusting lout. She moaned when he hit a particularly good spot.

As her body hummed, she allowed her mind to drift pleasantly with thoughts of the day when Macon or the German, or preferably both, were dead. Those times when she managed to make them kill each other were always her favorite. If she finished them off soon, she'd have years left to enjoy the benefits offered by the power and prestige of her job. Hell, she might even find a man she could tolerate long enough to get married and have a kid or two.

But she was getting ahead of herself. First, Macon and the German had to be dealt with, and when it was all over, she'd take immense pleasure in slitting Gio's throat and watching him bleed out like the squealing little pig he was. He groaned as she dug her nails deeper into his scalp, the vibration making her shiver.

"That's right, pig," she whispered. "Squeal."

CHAPTER 9

"WHERE ARE the pictures from the scene?"

"Forensics hasn't sent them up yet."

"What the hell are they waiting for? I'm not a damned psychic."

"Psychics see the future, dumbass."

"Shove it. My point is that I can't visualize the crime scene just by closing my eyes and saying 'Abracadabra,' can I?"

The entire station was in an uproar, and it wasn't just their precinct. A city council member's daughter had turned up dead in an alley the night before, a drunk couple who'd been looking for a semiprivate place to screw having stumbled across her in the wee hours of the morning. Preliminary reports indicated she'd been robbed and then raped before being stabbed to death. It was nasty and high-profile. The media was all over it like wolves on a kill, and the distraught councilwoman was harassing the mayor, demanding to know how something like this could happen to her precious baby in her very own city. The mayor hadn't been slow in shifting the blame.

Harried detectives rushed back and forth, shouting at each other as they tried to piece together the few scant clues they had. The dank alley where the girl had been found hadn't yielded much, and they were down to grasping at straws.

Brian stayed out of the fray as much as possible, but since every available body had been pulled into the case, he wasn't having much luck. The victim had been a freshman at the local college, so he was currently looking through the girl's high school yearbook, trying to determine if any of her schoolmates looked like they might turn into a rapist within a year. The brains over at the FBI's criminal behavior unit had recently put out a book of guidelines for profiling suspects, and the commissioner was a big proponent of using them. Rule number one for rapists: it was usually someone the victim knew.

"This is pointless." Brian slammed the book closed. "She was probably just out clubbing and ended up at the wrong place at the wrong time. Doesn't the captain know that we're up to our ears in that other small, insignificant matter she's so interested in?"

"As if she cares," Angela replied. She was engaged in her own pointless task, going through the victim's half-dozen social networking profiles. "The commissioner is leaning on all the brass to find somebody to hang for the girl's murder."

"So the captain's just sharing her pain, huh? Great." Brian looked up to see his partner staring at him with a raised eyebrow. "What?"

Angela remained silent as she continued to smile at him serenely.

"Angie, why are you staring at me?"

"Because once again, my dear boy, you're positively glowing. Get too much sun? Or maybe just enough of something else?"

"Do you kiss your sons with that mouth?"

She laughed. "Don't play the prude with me, mister. How do you think my boys got here? Storks?" Her expression grew thoughtful. "So, it's really going well, then?"

Brian glanced down at the cover of the yearbook. He thought of his own, which was hidden in the back of his closet, and the picture of a certain person that had never been included. "You were right, Angie, as usual. It's time I put the past behind me and moved on with my life. Dennis wouldn't have wanted me to live like I have been, closing myself off to anyone who might cause me to feel something." He rubbed a palm over the embossed logo of the dead girl's high school. "Life's too damn short. If anyone should understand that, it's me, right?"

Angela nodded at him. "What you're doing now, what you've dedicated your life to, he couldn't have asked any more than that. Every time you help bring a killer to justice, every time you help give a family some closure, you're honoring Dennis's memory. He'd be proud of you, sweetie."

Brian felt something warm expand in his chest. Maybe, just maybe, he did still give a damn about this job.

"It's been nearly two weeks now," Angela said, interrupting his thoughts. "So, what's he like?" she whispered.

Brian frowned. "What's what like?" he asked in kind.

Angela rolled her eyes. "What's he like in bed?"

Brian stared at her in disbelief at her nosiness, his face flaming as he wondered whether to be offended or whether he should brag. But before his blush could grow any brighter, the door separating the homicide department from the rest of the precinct burst open with a loud bang. Captain Preston swept in, her long legs rapidly eating up the distance between the door and her office. She looked royally pissed and ready to take it out on anyone who crossed her path. As no one was feeling suicidal, the hum of conversation in the room fell to nothing.

"Guess the meeting with the mayor didn't go so well."

Brian pretended he hadn't heard Angela's low-voiced mumble, deciding he lacked her courage. He turned his face toward the wall beside his desk as the captain passed by, unwilling to risk catching her gaze. Studying a brown spot where one of his predecessors had used the wall to hastily extinguish a cigarette, Brian waited until he heard the click of her high-heels recede to a safe distance. He was just releasing the breath he'd been holding when the captain's voice rang out into the silence.

"No one had better even think about going home until this case has been solved. Consider yourselves on lockdown."

"Shit," Angela cursed as she reached for her cell phone. "Better tell Todd and the boys not to expect me home at a reasonable hour. Good thing Jonathan has recently discovered that not only girls like to cook. I swear, Todd and Sam would starve if it weren't for him."

Brian chuckled. "Because it's not like you can boil water." He nimbly dodged a hastily wadded-up piece of notepad paper as the man who had groused about the lack of photos passed by his desk. Sympathizing with his impatience, Brian stared after him absently as he left the department, presumably to go and harass Forensics in person. There really wasn't much they could do until the 'scopes processed the evidence they'd collected at the scene. The mayor and councilwoman's expectations aside, solving cases didn't happen by magic and wishful thinking.

The thought naturally brought to mind his own pending case. Of course he felt awful for the poor girl who'd had her life cut short so tragically, but there was another killer out there he still needed to find. His thoughts fully occupied by two very different mysteries, Brian jumped when his cell phone buzzed, the vibrations making it skip across the surface of his desk. He snatched it up before it could bounce off and hit the floor.

"Macon."

"I hope I'm not catching you at a bad time."

Everything going on around him seemed to fade away as the deep voice purred in his ear. Brian spread his legs unconsciously to accommodate the growing bulge between his thighs. "Not really. What's up?" Brian realized this was only the second time he'd spoken with Alrick over the phone. That would have to change. Alrick was wasted as a journalist or whatever the hell he did. He was born to be a phone sex operator.

"Well, I would tell you, but I believe you have phone decency laws or some such thing, *ja*?"

Brian laughed as much at the recognition that he was flirting over the phone like some love-struck adolescent as at the suggestive joke. "Yeah, you're right. So keep it clean. I'm at work."

"Ah, then I hope you will be leaving from there before eight o'clock tonight."

"Why, what's going on at eight?"

"I have to critique a performance of Mozart's *The Magic Flute* at the city college tonight. I'd love you to join me, if you're interested."

Brian hesitated, his heart speeding up at the question's implication. "Sounds like you're asking me on a date." He laughed nervously, unsure whether he should just pass it off as a gag.

"Yes, that's exactly what I'm doing. Do you not wish to go?"

Crap, he's serious. Brian bit his lip, ignoring the curious glance Angela shot him as she talked to her husband. *Come on,* he scolded himself. *What's the worst that could happen other than falling asleep during the middle of the show?*

"I didn't say I didn't want to go. But I'm not entirely sure I can get away tonight from work. There's a lot going on," he added vaguely.

Brian wasn't sure why he hadn't told Alrick he was a cop. It wasn't as if he was ashamed of what he did for a living, but something made him leery of revealing his occupation. Maybe he was just afraid that someone as cultured as Alrick would think his job was a little too blue collar, never mind that he had a college degree.

"Ah, I see. Well, I suppose our first date will have to wait until another time."

Brian's stomach fluttered as he heard the disappointment in Alrick's voice, hating that he'd put it there. Suddenly, he wanted nothing more than to make Alrick smile again. "Don't worry about it. I'll figure something out. Just tell me where I should meet you?" Brian imagined the grin that lit up Alrick's face.

"*Wunderbar.* Meet me in front of the performance hall at about a quarter to eight. That will give us plenty of time to get to our seats. Oh, and by the way—"

"Yeah?"

"Be sure to wear something pretty."

Brian ended the call, smiling despite himself. "Asshole."

"Was that the dreamboat?"

Brian nodded as he looked over at his partner. "Yeah. I've got a hot date with Mozart."

Angela's nose crinkled. "Mozart?"

"Yep. I'm going to see, um, *The Magic Flute*, I think it was. Over at the college." He gave Angela a suspicious glance when she laughed out loud.

"You're going to an opera?"

"I don't know. Am I?"

She laughed again and shook her head. "You sure as hell are. Oh, sweetie, it must be love."

For once, Brian didn't feel the need to contradict her. He looked down at the yearbook lying on his desk, which brought his thoughts back to how he should be spending his evening. He sat back in his chair and groaned.

"But how am I going to get out of here? If I just bail, the captain will have my balls for beignets."

"Hmmm." Angela pursed her lips as she pondered his dilemma.

Brian felt a niggling hint of worry when she suddenly perked up and threw him a bright-eyed grin. "I don't like that look."

"Oh hush and listen up. You said the show was at the college, right?"

"Yeah. And?" Brian waited while Angela riffled through the stack of papers on her desk.

"Here it is. This is the list of the victim's friends her mother provided when she was interviewed this morning. They all attended school with her. So—"

"So, I have a perfectly legitimate reason for needing to go there today."

"Bingo." She passed the list over to him. "Ain't police work grand?"

Brian smirked as he looked over the list and wondered how he could get his hands on a decent suit on such short notice.

BRIAN FELT a little silly as he stood in the hallway of the victim's dorm, wearing the suit he'd hastily borrowed from Angela's oldest son. It was tight across the chest and a bit too short for him, but he hoped his black socks, which matched the color of the suit's pants, would make that fact a little less noticeable. He was just lucky that Jonathan was a good-sized kid.

Angela's suggestion had been right on the money. The first few names on the list she'd given him hadn't proved very helpful, but he struck gold with the third. The young man, Frank Harper, had been with the victim the night before at a club. He'd been nervous at first because it was obvious that, just like the councilwoman's daughter, he was several years too young to be in a place that served alcohol. But Brian had assured him he was just after information that might help solve the girl's murder.

The kid explained that he'd gone out with his girlfriend, the victim, and the victim's best friend. Frank had left the club early to take advantage of the hints his girlfriend had been dropping all night, but he assured Brian that the victim's friend had stayed with her at the club after he and his girlfriend had left. Armed with the friend's name and room number, Brian headed that way.

It was after seven o'clock at night, but the girl answered her door right away when he knocked. If her hysterical crying was anything to go by, she had indeed been very close to the victim.

"Polly Jones? I'm Detective Macon." Holding up his badge, Brian waited patiently as the girl blew her nose. It took a few minutes, but she was eventually able to quiet her sobs long enough to speak.

"Have you found out what happened to Tara?" She was a pretty young lady, although her prolonged bout of crying had played havoc with her complexion. Her nose was as red as her eyes, and splotches had popped up all over her face.

Brian gave her his most sympathetic look. "Not yet. That's why I'm here. I just came from speaking with Frank. He told me that you all were out at Sweeney's last night. Is that right?"

"Uh, well, you know—"

"Don't worry. I'm not here to bust you for underaged drinking."

Polly looked relieved. "O-okay. Then, yeah, we were there last night."

"What time did you leave?"

"Um, I'm not sure. I was pretty wasted." She shot him an uncertain glance, but he merely nodded reassuringly. "Wait, I think the bar was giving last call, so it had to be around 2:00 a.m. or so."

"And did you leave the club with Tara?"

She nodded. "Yeah, we left together, but we weren't alone."

Brian's ears perked up at the new information. "Who else was with you?"

"This guy who'd been trying to pick Tara up. I don't know him, but I've seen him before. I think he's in her psych class. I mean, he was—" Polly broke into a fresh round of sobs. Brian waited in the hall while she retreated into her room to retrieve a fresh handful of tissues. "I'm sorry," she apologized when she returned.

He shook his head. "It's okay. So, you said this kid was in her class? What's the exact name of the course?"

"Beginning Psych 101."

"And can you describe him for me?"

Polly began to calm as she sensed that she was being helpful. "Yeah. He's our age, seventeen or eighteen, brown hair, gray eyes. Maybe your height or a little shorter?"

Brian had pulled out his notepad from his trench coat pocket and was taking notes as she spoke. "And how about his weight? Fat? Thin?"

"Um, average, I guess. A little heavier than you, I think, but not really fat?"

Brian wasn't sure whether he had just been insulted, but he simply nodded. "Anything else? Some other distinguishing characteristic that would help us identify him?"

"Yeah, he has braces."

Brian cocked his eyebrow. "Braces at his age?" He felt a bit proud of himself when she giggled.

"Yeah, he's kind of a dork. That's why Tara wouldn't give him the time of day for a long while. He's been trying to get her to go out with him since, like, the third week of school. But we were both really trashed last night, and I guess she was feeling generous."

"They do say that alcohol is the best beauty treatment in the world." Smiling at her, he flipped his notepad closed. Replacing it in his pocket, he exchanged it for his card holder. "Here, if you think of anything else, don't hesitate to give me a call."

She took the card he held out toward her. "Okay, I will. Oh, and Detective?" Brian paused in the act of turning away from her door and looked questioningly at her over his shoulder. "When you catch the bastard, I hope you cut his balls off."

Brian felt his lips crook up at the corner as he nodded. "I'll see what I can do."

ONCE HE was back outside, he considered himself officially off the clock. He had the best lead he could have asked for, but it would take a bit of time to locate this braces-wearing psych student. And in the meantime, he had a date he needed to find.

Not having a map of the campus handy, Brian asked a passing student where he could find the performing arts center. It was, of course, on the quad. Marveling at the groupthink that apparently had infected the designers of American colleges, he headed in the indicated direction. After a short walk, he came across a wide-open grassy area that stretched several blocks in each direction and spotted a particularly large building. It was butt-ugly, in his opinion. Rather than being fashioned using traditional right angles, it seemed to explode out like a possessed flower. But it was clearly the right place. Groups of well-dressed adults and passably attired college students thronged toward the main entrance. A large banner stretched between the columns framing the multiple sets of steps leading inside.

"*The Magic Flute*," Brian mumbled as he read the name of the opera he'd been invited to see. Opera? He shook his head, wondering what in the hell he was doing there. He had never seen an opera in his life. Heck, musical theater in general remained an unknown quantity. Yet here he was, ready to sacrifice a few hours of his life just because he was a sucker for a certain blond, blue-eyed German cello player. Well, if he did fall asleep in the middle of the thing, he at least hoped he wouldn't snore.

Brian looked around at the crowds, wondering just where his date was. He didn't have to search for long, since Alrick wasn't exactly difficult to spot. Standing a head taller than most of the people around him, he radiated a distinguishing air of elegant maturity. The lights from the performing center caught the white-blond of his hair in a halo effect as he turned his head this way and that, clearly looking for Brian in return. Brian stared for a long moment, wondering what cosmic favors he would owe in his next life for the opportunity of knowing this incredible man.

The fanciful thought was cut short when Alrick looked in his direction. Brian forced himself to breathe normally as Alrick came toward him, a broad grin stretching his sensual lips as he weaved through the crowd with all the grace of a dancer. Swallowing hard, Brian willed his body to behave, with limited success.

"You made it. I was worried for a moment that you might lose your nerve."

Brian laughed, refusing to admit that he'd never once considered not showing up. "Here I am, though I have no idea what I'm in for. Don't blame me if I pass out on you."

Alrick smiled down at him. "I am not concerned. The performing arts program at this school is supposed to be very good."

Having no opinion on the matter, Brian merely smiled. "I'm just glad at least one of us will know what's going on."

"I'll try and explain the acts as they happen. It will be in German—" Alrick grinned as Brian stared at him in horror. "But the plot is easily understood."

"Yeah, okay, if you say so. What's it about, anyway?"

"Oh, the usual. A boy who falls in love with a girl and has to fight through many obstacles to win her with the help of his *Zauberflöte*, his magic flute."

"Sounds simple enough."

Alrick nodded. "Indeed." The crowd had thinned noticeably, and people were streaming steadily up the stairs and into the building. "Looks like they'll be starting soon. Shall we go in?"

Brian was somewhat relieved when Alrick didn't offer him his arm. He still wasn't entirely comfortable being out in the open like this. Glancing up at the improbable roof of the center as they neared the entrance, Brian shook his head. "What's up with this building? Some crazy architecture project gone awry?"

Alrick chuckled. "No, it's so the music will reflect properly."

Brian frowned in confusion. "What do you mean?"

"Here, look." Alrick pointed upward. They had made it inside, and Brian saw the same insane pattern on the ceiling of the theater. "Right angles swallow sound and don't allow the audience to hear properly. By slanting each section of the room like so, the acoustics are better."

Brian shrugged. "I'll have to take your word for that." He noticed they weren't the only two guys there as a couple and felt his self-consciousness abate somewhat. It was very unlikely that he'd run into anyone he knew, but after witnessing the shit heaped upon a guy in the academy who'd been less than circumspect about his sexuality, Brian had been careful to the point of paranoia. There was no sense inviting trouble. Still, it was nice to be able to sit so close to Alrick, their arms pressed together from the tightness of the seating.

"I truly hope you enjoy the performance."

Brian glanced over and felt a warm tingle as Alrick smiled at him gently. "I'm sure I will."

CHAPTER 10

ALRICK SHIFTED in his seat more from a desire to feel Brian's arm bump against his rather than from any discomfort. Even if the performance turned out to be horrible, this was still shaping up to be one of the best nights of his life. Even now, his body hummed with electricity at the discrete touch. His spent cock stirred ever so slightly, the memory of being buried deeply in Brian's delicious heat urging it to life. If he could, he'd gladly spend the rest of his life discovering just how far he and Brian could crawl into each other's bodies before they could no longer be separated.

He'd felt compelled the moment he had seen Brian sitting so forlornly at the bar. The sense of connection with an utter stranger had shocked him, but the instantaneous attraction had gone far beyond the mere physical. It was like he'd been looking for something but hadn't known that it was lost until he'd found it. And now that he had, he couldn't let go.

As a young man, he'd dreamed of enjoying a performance of beautiful music with the man he loved, and he did love Brian; there was no denying it. He just had no idea what to do about it. It wasn't as though he could stay in the city forever. The demands of both of his jobs and the risk of discovery simply wouldn't allow for such foolish self-indulgence. The looming prospect of his upcoming assignment for Giovanni grew all the more distasteful. Every murder he committed took him further and further away from Brian, every lie he told compounding his guilt.

For a moment, he tortured himself by imagining how much simpler things would have been had he met Brian before his life had imploded. But things weren't different. His reality could not be changed, no matter how much he might wish it.

The warmth of Brian's arm seeped into him, chasing away the chill of the late winter's night. A problem for another time, he decided, determined to just enjoy himself and to relish every moment he got to spend with Brian. The lights dimmed, and a spotlight came up as a young man wearing a tuxedo walked across the stage, a baton held motionless in his hand. Bowing, he paused to bask in the adulation from the audience before taking his place behind a large stand covered with a thick ream of paper. Brian leaned back, surprise reflected on his face, when the section of the stage where the man stood began to lower into the floor.

"Huh? What's going on?" he whispered.

"The orchestra is below the stage," Alrick explained softly. "The platform will descend only partially. See? The conductor's position will enable him to see both his musicians and the performers."

"Clever."

Alrick smiled as the conductor raised his hands. He brought them down sharply, and the lyrical strains of the overture filled the hall. Although he made certain to watch the performance with a critical eye, Alrick allowed himself to become immersed in the music. In his opinion, this was by far Mozart's best work, compelling and playful in turns as it transported the listener to the magical realm of fairy queens and desperate lovers.

He leaned toward Brian occasionally, offering translations and commentary where he thought they'd be most effective. He whispered closely in Brian's ear, enjoying the way Brian shivered from the heated brush of his breath. The story of the handsome prince and his foolish servant unfolded before them, the soaring arias and comical refrains giving brilliant life to the tale of a young man willing to overcome any trial to win the hand of the girl he'd been promised.

As Alrick explained the meaning of the lyrics to Brian, he suddenly realized just how relevant the story had become to his own life. He knew what it meant to want someone dreadfully but to fear that the difficulties separating them might prove insurmountable. After all, what right did a man who killed for money have to live happily ever after?

This likeness is enchantingly lovely
I feel it, as this heavenly picture
My heart with new emotion fills.
Can the feeling be love?

"Yes, it is love alone." Alrick hummed the words quietly to himself in German. He hooked his fingers through Brian's, his heart twinging with a bittersweet pang when Brian returned the gesture with a gentle tightening of his grasp.

"SEE? YOU didn't fall asleep."

Brian laughed as they walked down a path leading away from the quad. His hand still tingled from where Alrick had been holding it for the past two hours. He stuck it in his coat pocket, telling himself it was to block out the wind and not so he could preserve the sensation. "It wasn't half bad at that. I didn't expect to laugh out loud, but that Papa-whatever guy was pretty funny."

"Papageno. Yes, every good opera needs a court jester, and he is more effective than most."

Brian didn't know if Alrick knew the campus any better than he did, but he followed Alrick's lead without comment as they drifted farther away from the crowds leaving the theater. They were soon in a darker section just off the quad, and he realized the dimly lit area was a small park. The shadows of trees loomed over them as they wandered aimlessly along the path, the waxing moon providing the only light.

Isn't this romantic? Smiling wryly, Brian decided he wasn't complaining.

"So who was your favorite character beside Papageno?" Alrick asked.

Brian didn't hesitate. "The Queen of the Night."

"Really? Why?"

"She reminds me of someone I work with."

Alrick chuckled. "That sounds ominous."

"Yeah, she's definitely queen of all she surveys. We're just the peons slaving away, subject to her every whim."

Alrick made a sympathetic noise. "The queen is a very intriguing character. Her arias are particularly difficult. It's said that she has some of the highest notes that any singer has ever had to produce."

Barely listening, Brian kicked at a pile of leaves as he walked at Alrick's side.

"Mozart's own sister-in-law premiered the role."

"Um-hmm."

"There's a spider on your head."

Brian stopped and looked up at him with a raised eyebrow. "Really?"

Alrick laughed. "I just wanted to see if you were paying attention. You seemed lost in thought."

Brian glanced from side to side, noticing they were completely alone on the dark path. "I was."

"What were you thinking about?"

"Whether I had to give you an engraved invitation before you kissed me."

Alrick went completely still for a moment, clearly shocked at Brian's boldness. Then his lips turned up into a sly smirk, and Brian quickly found himself wrapped in a pair of strong arms. Even through the barrier of their coats and clothing, he could feel Alrick's body heat flowing into him, making a mockery of the biting chill.

"Your wish—"

Words gave way to the soft press of lips. The gentle slide of Alrick's against his sent a tingle all the way down to his toes. Brian tried to urge Alrick's lips apart with his tongue, but Alrick stood firm, allowing nothing but the soft, intimate caress.

Groaning with frustration as his cock began to swell, Brian reached up and tugged on the lapels of Alrick's long coat, trying to convey his dissatisfaction with the teasing pressure. Alrick answered his urgency with a murmured sound of amusement, indicating his delight at Brian's desperation. Brian resorted to calling him names in his head because he had no desire to move away from those lips.

The soft kiss went on, broken only by the playful nips Alrick bestowed on him as he took the plumpness of Brian's lower lip between his teeth. Brian groaned, his body reacting both to the gentle bites and the sound of softly teasing laughter. But he found Alrick's weakness when, in a fit of pique, he wedged his leg between Alrick's and pressed against his own growing hardness. Brian had only a moment to congratulate himself before his mouth was invaded by a searching tongue and he lost the ability to think at all.

"You are a minx." Alrick's growl filled Brian's mouth and resonated straight to the growing ache between his legs.

Brian's moan was half-protest, half-encouragement. He grabbed Alrick's shoulders, kneading the solid curves as long fingers buried themselves in his hair to hold him in place. Alrick's tongue deftly sought out all of those secret places only he had discovered.

Not fair. The silent complaint burned away as lust swept over Brian like a flame. Yet again, he thought he might actually come just from being kissed. Alrick moved his hand slowly down his back to settle on his hips. Brian gasped into Alrick's mouth as the hand pressed Brian flush against him, the hardness beneath Alrick's coat coming into demanding contact with his own.

"I want you." Alrick's accent deepened as his excitement increased.

Brian reacted with humiliating predictability to the sound of the guttural vowels. "Nnnn," he whimpered, responding the only way he was capable of right then. Letting his hands speak for him, he reached beneath Alrick's coat and groped for the hem of his sweater. His greedy fingers had just found a strip of warm flesh when Alrick groaned and pulled away from the kiss.

"Wait," Alrick breathed, holding Brian in place when he growled in protest and attempted to draw him back in. "I have no wish to be arrested for public indecency on a college campus. After all, we can't even use the excuse of being irresponsible students."

Brian blinked up at him as his brain tried to return to working order. The moment he was capable of a coherent thought, he groaned in mortification and buried his reddening face against the soft material of Alrick's coat.

"Shit."

"No, don't go yet." Alrick pulled Brian back when he tried to push away. "Give me a moment, if you would."

Brian laughed wryly. "Yeah, I'm pretty sure I could poke a small child's eye out with this thing right about now."

"What a lovely thought."

"Pervert."

"You said it."

They stood quietly for a moment, hugging each other close as they attempted to restore themselves to decency. Brian wondered whether he would ever manage it as long as Alrick kept holding him. Finally, he felt collected enough to move away and stifled a sigh of disappointment when Alrick let him go.

"When will I see you again?" Alrick brushed a thumb over Brian's kiss-bruised lips. Brian bit at it playfully, shooting him a mock glare.

"You're not helping, you know. Anyway, I've got something really pressing going on at work, so it might be a few days before I'm free again. Can I call you?"

Alrick frowned down at him, obviously displeased at the lack of certainty. The fierce expression made him look even sexier. Brian buried his hands in his pockets to keep from trying to touch.

"It shouldn't be too long. I made some good progress with the project today." Brian wondered again at his vagueness. Before he could decide whether he should just be honest, Alrick nodded.

"All right. But don't blame me if I hound your phone if I haven't heard from you in a few days like you promised."

Brian grinned and shook his head. "It's 'blow up your phone,' and don't worry. I don't think my libido would forgive me if I stayed away too long." He expected Alrick to return his amusement, but Alrick's frown deepened.

"Is that all this is to you? Just sex?"

When did this get so heavy? Brian wanted to protest the seriousness, but as Alrick continued to watch him silently, Brian's desire to play it off faded away. Alrick was right. This thing between them—whatever it was—had gone far beyond sex. Hell, hadn't he just sat through two hours of people singing in a foreign language for this man? If that wasn't love, what was?

"No, it's not." He stretched up and pressed a kiss against Alrick's warm lips. "I'll call you soon."

Alrick nodded, the harshness of his features gentling as he returned the kiss. They walked back toward the quad in silence, their hands clasped firmly together.

"NICE DOIN' business with you, Tony." Giovanni Rivella laughed as he pocketed a large envelope and walked out into the darkness, leaving the bodies of Tony Conti, the third-highest ranking man in Cosmino, and his two body guards to bleed out on the floor of the dirty warehouse.

Alrick watched through his riflescope in annoyance. He didn't appreciate having to take out multiple targets at once, but Rivella had offered more than triple pay for the job. It would have been foolish to turn him down.

He methodically went through his usual checklist as he packed away his rifle. He was running low on ammunition. The specially made bullets he used, fashioned to minimize the ballistics markings the barrel would leave behind, weren't cheap. Thinking about how many shells he would need to order, his mind drifted back to earlier that evening. Had it only been several hours since he'd parted reluctantly from Brian after the concert? He found it hard to believe the grisly sight of dead bodies could exist in the same world as the joyous delight that had graced Brian's handsome face as he watched his first opera.

Alrick suspected Brian wasn't even aware of all of the emotions he'd revealed. Surprise, amusement, tension, joy. Those impossible eyes had followed everything going on without missing a moment. Alrick thought about what other musical performances Brian might enjoy. Maybe a jazz session, or there was that orchestra he needed to review the week after next.

"Making plans? Not a smart move, Ritter." Alrick sighed when he realized how far into the future he was thinking, as though he had that prerogative. Tony Conti hadn't been some nobody. He was one of the richest men in the city. From his position, Alick had been able to hear much of Rivella's taunting conversation with his victim. Apparently the young mobster had just managed to con Conti out of several lucrative deeds to Cosmino business. Whatever Rivella was up to, he was clearly ramping up his timetable as well as the profile of his victims, and if that was the case, it was unlikely this job would last much longer.

In all honesty, that was perfectly fine with him. He was rapidly growing sick and tired of Rivella's games. Rivella was a punk, and an unpredictable one at that, which made him dangerous. He might have thought he had everything under control, that he held both the city and his rivals in the grip of fear, but Alrick was all too aware of the dangers of hubris. There was always something beyond your ability to control waiting to trip you up. Rivella wouldn't be on top forever, and when he finally fell, Alrick wanted to be long gone.

But that meant leaving the city and leaving Brian.

Alrick's jaw clenched, his body rejecting the very thought. He snapped the gun case closed and ran his foot over the spot where his body had lain in order to foul any evidence of his presence. He glowered as he remembered the Riccoh hit. Rivella had wanted it to happen just before dawn. Alrick had been forced to leave his location quickly as the sun began to lighten the sky, unable to perform his usual cleanup ritual of ensuring he hadn't left any other incriminating evidence behind. Damn Rivella and his unreasonable requests.

It was past time he ended his association with the Milanos. Rivella was getting bolder and equally more careless. He couldn't afford to be around when the younger man imploded. As for Brian....

Alrick squinted against the cold wind that blew across his face, trying to ignore the answering ice that gripped his heart.

CHAPTER 11

BRIAN NODDED at Angela as they took up flanking positions to either side of the door. Several uniformed officers were spread out behind them as backup, filling the small second-floor hallway of the rundown apartment building. Since he and Angela had cracked the case, they got the position of honor, such as it was. The bulletproof vest he wore was heavy and uncomfortable, but he wouldn't have dreamed of going into a situation like this without one. Weapon at the ready, Angela took a deep breath, making her own vest expand slightly over her ample chest as she waited for Brian to knock.

A warrant had gained Brian access to the college's enrollment records. It hadn't taken him long to find the guy who'd almost gotten lucky with the councilwoman's daughter. At first, Angela had thought they'd found their killer, that Tara had spurned him after leading him on all night and that he'd attacked her in a frenzy of frustrated desire. But after they'd tracked him down, a far different story had come to light.

They'd found the kid, one Lloyd Taylor, in an area hospital. It had only taken one look at him to realize his injuries hadn't been caused by a slight girl like Tara. Someone had used his freckled face for a punching bag. He was disfigured by a mass of ugly bruises, and his braces had torn his lips to shreds. Lloyd had suffered a concussion and only regained consciousness earlier that morning. As soon as he saw their badges, he had started talking, desperate to tell someone about what had happed to Tara.

"I was with her when we left the club that night, but I didn't know we were being followed."

"Followed?" Sitting in a chair next to his bed, Angela kept her voice gentle so as not to exacerbate the kid's trauma-induced headache.

"Yeah, it was her ex-boyfriend, Bobby Gibson. He caught up with us a few blocks from the club and started screaming and shouting at Tara, calling her a 'slut' and a 'fucking cunt.' Uh, sorry, ma'am."

Angela smiled reassuringly. "Do you know this Bobby guy?"

"No, not personally. He and Tara were still together at the beginning of the school year. I saw him pick her up from class a couple of times. I must have overheard his name at some point."

Brian hid a smile behind his hand. More like Lloyd had made it his business to find out who his competition was.

Angela nodded at the kid and urged him to continue. "Then what happened?"

"Tara yelled at him to leave her alone, that they were through. She told me to come on and grabbed hold of my arm to pull me away. That's when he jumped me."

Brian, who was standing back from the bed as Lloyd talked, frowned as a full body shiver racked the young man's body. He glanced away out of consideration for the kid's dignity when tears began to course down his puffy face.

"I've never even been in a fight before, you know. I didn't know what to do."

"It's all right, hon." Angela gave his hand a motherly pat, careful not to jar the IV taped to his skin.

"What happened to Tara?"

Lloyd looked up at Brian in response to his question, wiping the tears away from his face. He winced when he hit a particularly sore spot. "I'm not really sure. The last thing I saw, he was dragging her away. She was crying my name. I guess she was worried about me." Lloyd smiled at the thought that the girl of his dreams had cared about him after all, before breaking down into sobs as he remembered that he would never see her again.

"All right, Lloyd." Angela stood and put away her notepad. "You get some rest now, and please give me a call if you think of anything else."

Lloyd took her card without comment, his sad gaze directed down toward the white sheet covering his lap.

It had only taken a phone call to find good ol' Bobby. Tara's friend, Polly, had known exactly where he lived and didn't hesitate to give up the information when Brian shared what Lloyd had revealed. They waited only until forensics analyzed the DNA sample Lloyd had provided—a rush job courtesy of pressure from the mayor's office—and it proved not to be a match for the seminal fluid found on the victim. Once he had been exonerated, Lloyd's story had been enough to convince a judge to give them a warrant for Gibson's arrest.

Brian pounded on the door with the side of his fist. "Bobby Gibson? This is the police. We want to talk to you, Bobby. Open up."

Silence met his request. Deciding that was good enough to announce their presence, Brian silently counted to three, his mouth forming the words so the others could follow. He was interrupted by the sound of scrambling footsteps and grunting and then the crash of breaking glass. Sensing their quarry was making a run for it, Brian stepped back and let the uniformed officer standing directly behind use the battering ram he was carrying to break in the door.

"Police!" Brian looked around as he shouted and caught sight of a burly figure trying to squeeze through a broken window opposite the door. "Freeze, asshole!"

Ignoring him, the man scrambled past the broken glass, his upper body already through the window. Brian launched himself across the room and landed on the man's back as he grabbed him around the waist, grunting as he hit a solid wall of muscle. *Great, the guy would be a fucking football player.* A couple of officers rushed to his aid and helped him manhandle the guy back into the room and down onto the floor.

Sitting on the perp's back, Brian fumbled for the handcuffs in his pocket. "You Bobby Gibson?"

"What the fuck do you want? Get offa me!" The harsh voice was muffled by the threadbare carpet covering the floor. The man moaned as Brian pulled his arms sharply behind his back. One of them was slick with blood, the skin slashed by the broken windowpane.

"Answer my question, dickwad. Are you Bobby Gibson?"

"Yeah!"

"Then you're under arrest for the murder of Tara Parsons. You have the right to remain silent."

Reading Gibson his Miranda rights, Brian snapped the cuffs into place around his meaty wrists before hauling him to his feet with the assistance of the two officers who'd helped him subdue the oversized jerk. Gibson was a good-looking kid, probably closer to twenty-five than eighteen. Hadn't Tara's mom told her that it wasn't a good idea to get involved with older men? Although, given the look of this guy and his apartment, it was obvious she'd been slumming when she hooked up with him. It was highly unlikely her mom had known anything about Bobby.

"You ain't got nothin' on me!"

"After you jerk off into a little cup for us, I'm sure we'll have plenty. Didn't your daddy teach you to use a rubber when you rape and murder a little girl?"

"Man, you're talkin' shit. I want a lawyer."

"We'll get around to finding you one after you cool your heels in central lockup for a few hours, how does that sound?"

Protesting loudly, Gibson struggled as several uniforms led him from his apartment. Angela came to stand next to Brian as they watched Gibson's noisy departure. She glanced over at him when he rubbed at his shoulder.

"You all right, sweetie? That was some tackle."

Brian chuckled, his lips pulling into a wry smile. "Yeah, well, I'm not a teenager anymore, that's for sure."

Angela grinned. "You sure looked impressive, flying across the room. My hero!" She batted her eyelashes at him.

He narrowed his eyes as he looked down at her. "If you want to thank me, how about you write up the report?"

She waved away his suggestion. "We'll flip for it like we always do. Let's see if that superhero vibe helps you in the luck department."

"Heartless wench."

She blew him a kiss as they followed the exodus of people out of Bobby's former apartment.

"Why can't our other case fall into place as neatly as this one did?" Brian sighed. "I don't know, Angie. Do you think we're doing something wrong?"

She shook her head. "I think we're doing all we can do. We just have to wait for the evidence to come in."

"What the hell is taking Forensics so long with that ballistics report, anyway?"

Angela shrugged. "I heard they were rerunning the tests for whatever reason. They're just being thorough, I guess, but like I told you before, they promised me it would be back soon."

"I hope so. That reminds me, now that this circus is over, I need to follow up with that tech who was with us at the Riccoh scene. Hopefully he hit on someone in the crime databases fitting our sniper's profile." Brian worked his shoulder again. "I don't know about you, but once this report is filed, I'm knocking off."

Angela threw him a sly smile. "Got a hot date?"

"If I have anything to say about it."

She laughed out loud. "What, no more being coy and evasive?"

Brian shook his head. "It's been nearly three days since I last saw him." They were well back from the rest of the officers, but he kept his voice low. "I'm too horny to be coy."

Angela patted him on his arm. "Good for you. But I'm still making you flip me for the report."

DELICIOUS SMELLS filled the car from the bags sitting in the passenger's seat. Brian steered expertly with one hand as he held his cell phone to his ear with the other. Chewing absently on his bottom lip, he waited for the call to go through.

"*Ja?*"

"Alrick? It's Brian." He was a bit surprised Alrick didn't know it was him, since his name should have come up on caller ID.

"Ah, Brian. Please forgive me. I am working on the *Magic Flute* article. I didn't look at my phone before answering."

Brian's stomach knotted as he sensed his plans falling to pieces. "Oh, I gotcha. Well, I'll let you get back to it, then."

"Wait," Alrick interrupted before Brian could disconnect. "Did you want to come over?"

"Yeah, but if you're working—"

"I have only about another hour to go. Why don't you keep me company?"

Brian squirmed in his seat as Alrick's low, suggestive tone massaged his ears. "If you're sure I won't be disturbing you."

Alrick chuckled warmly. "Oh, I'm sure you will be, but I certainly don't mind."

Brian's mouth quirked up at the corner. "All right. I got take-out. Is Chinese okay?"

"Sounds wonderful. I will see you soon, *ja*?"

"Yeah, in about ten minutes."

Ending the call, Brian felt a silly grin spread across his face. He never would have thought a few weeks ago that the prospect of sharing Chinese take-out with a guy as he typed away on a laptop would be his idea of the perfect evening.

Traffic was fairly light for a weeknight, so he made even better time than he'd predicted. He nodded politely at a few of the hotel staff he recognized as he walked across the lobby. The asshole manager who had caused him such grief during his first visit merely noted his presence before glancing back toward the computer at his station without comment. Brian wondered how many of them had guessed why he was there so often. Deciding he didn't really give a damn what they thought, he whistled off-key as he hit the elevator call button. It came quickly, and soon he was arriving at Alrick's floor. Swinging the aromatic bag from his fingers, he strode down the hall to the now-familiar room number and knocked. He still had the key card but was uncomfortable at the thought of just barging in unannounced.

A welcoming smile was already on Alrick's face as he opened the door. He leaned against the doorframe, arms crossed over his broad chest. "I didn't give you that key just for show, you know."

Brian shrugged. "What can I say? My momma raised me to have some manners." He slipped past Alrick, taking care to make as much contact as possible.

Alrick's hooded gaze promised his unsubtle suggestion would definitely be acted upon. "Something to drink?" he offered as Brian hung his coat in the closet.

"Sure. Do you have any beer?"

Alrick's glance was full of mock indignation. "I *am* German."

Guessing that meant he did indeed have beer, Brian grinned and made himself at home on the couch. He took the food out of the bag and spread the containers across the coffee table. "Let's see, I've got General Tso's chicken and Hunan beef, one with vegetable fried rice and one with white rice. Which do you want, or do you want to try some of each?"

"I'll try a little of each. I haven't had much American Chinese food."

"American Chinese food?"

Alrick chuckled. "Trust me, this isn't what Chinese people consider real Chinese food." He placed a bottle of beer on the table beside the food and dropped a kiss into the curve of Brian's neck. Startled at the unexpected gesture, Brian jumped a little before deciding that he enjoyed Alrick's easy shows of affection. He picked up the bottle, noting that it was a brand he'd never heard of. Curious, he popped the top open using the edge of the table.

Alrick quirked an eyebrow at him. "Impressive trick."

"I didn't spend all my time in college studying."

Alrick laughed at his dry delivery. Brian didn't bother sharing that he'd spent much of his time in college drunk, trying to erase the image of Dennis's blood-covered face from his memory.

"So you've spent some time in China, then?" he asked as he grabbed one of the paper plates and a set of the plasticware the restaurant had provided.

"Some."

Alrick loaded a plate and took it back to the armchair without elaborating further. Greedy for information about Alrick, Brian was tempted to press for more. But when Alrick retrieved his laptop from the floor next to the armchair and opened up the top to bring it out of hibernation, Brian decided against it. Kicking off his shoes, he stretched out on the couch with his feet up as he settled back with his own full plate.

Pausing now and again to take a fork full of food, Alrick worked steadily for the next hour. Brian didn't see him using any notes. Either he kept them on his laptop or he made up what he wanted to say about the performance as he typed. Thinking about the article made Brian curious as to the man's work. "Do you have any copies of other stuff you've written? Sorry, I didn't mean to interrupt you," he said hastily when Alrick glanced up.

"No, it's fine." Alrick nodded toward the bar. "I think I put a copy of the latest issue over there. It has an article I wrote about a small chamber group out of Portland, Oregon."

Brian carried his plate with him as he went in search of the magazine, which he found where Alrick had indicated. *Musikgeschmack* was written in large block letters across the title page. Brian struggled with the word for a moment before giving up. "How do you say the name of the magazine?"

Alrick pronounced it for him slowly. Brian wanted to be ashamed when the sound of the foreign word on Alrick's lips made his cock swell. But sexy was sexy, and Alrick had that quality in spades.

"It means 'musical taste.' Not the cleverest title, but it's a decent enough publication."

Flopping back down on the couch, Brian skimmed the table of contents. It was all in German, of course, but he recognized the name Alrick Ritter. Flipping to the indicated page, he amused himself for a few moments trying to pretend that he could read what Alrick had written. After a while, he tossed the magazine onto the couch, stopping before the crazy language could give him a headache.

Besides, it was much more fun staring at his companion. Alrick was typing away, concentration etching a furrow down the center of his brow. Brian wanted to lick the indentation. He sighed, feeling only slightly disgusted with himself. He marveled at how quickly Alrick's features could shift from playful to serious. Chewing absently on his plastic fork, Brian let his gaze rove over Alrick's body, from his neck, across his shoulders, down his arms to his hands as they danced over the keyboard. Brian bit his lip as his body reacted to the delicious picture Alrick presented. Damn, he looked as good sitting at a laptop as he had when he had been playing his cello.

You've got it bad, son.

"*Fertig.* That should do it for now." Alrick abruptly closed his laptop and set it back on the floor, distracting Brian from his X-rated thoughts.

Alrick rolled his shoulders, and Brian's hands twitched with the urge to relieve his stiffness. If he felt anything like Brian did after typing up a report, he would surely appreciate a massage. Before the intention was fully formed, Brian was on his feet. Alrick had closed his eyes as he stretched, so he flinched when he felt hands on his shoulders. He looked up at Brian questioningly, but he was soon groaning thankfully as strong fingers dug into the tight muscles.

"Mmm," he mumbled, "that feels good."

Brian smiled. "We aim to please."

He spent the next few minutes working out the kinks he could feel beneath his fingers. Fortunately, Alrick was wearing a thin, short-sleeved shirt, so he didn't have to work too hard to apply pressure where it was needed. As he started in on Alrick's upper back, his gaze drifted downward on its own accord. Having never seen Alrick from this vantage point, Brian practically drooled as he admired the slabs of muscle that filled out the upper parts of his shirt. Brian looked down the length of Alrick's arms, ogling the swell of his biceps and the cords defining his forearms. But when his gaze landed on the man's hands, the regulator governing his mouth decided to flip off.

"You were really hot playing the cello the other day." Brian bent over, running his hands down Alrick's arms as he took his earlobe playfully between his lips. "It looked like fun. Do you think you could teach me?" His brain instantly caught up with his mouth as he felt Alrick stiffen slightly beneath his hands. The memory of Alrick's frustrated anger and the pain he had experienced while indulging Brian's last thoughtless request came rushing back. Standing quickly, he backed away awkwardly, cursing his insensitivity. "No, never mind. I didn't mean it. Just forget I asked."

"No, it's all right." Alrick stood and turned to look at Brian. His smile held only the faintest traces of bitterness. "I would be glad to share my love of the instrument with you, even if I can no longer play so well. Besides, I have no objections to seeing my two favorite things in this world sitting together."

Brian was torn between basking in the sentiment and feeling like an ass, but Alrick seemed sincere in his offer. "Okay, then."

"Why don't you take it out of the closet while I clear away our leftovers."

Brian went over to the closet and opened the door. His coat was partially hiding the black case, so he held it out of the way with one hand while retrieving the case with the other. The weight of it caught him off guard. "Man, this is a lot heavier than I expected."

Alrick chuckled. "Indeed. Violins and violas are for boys. Only real men play the cello." His expression turned mischievous as his smile grew. "Of course, bass players say the same thing about cello players."

Brian smiled uncertainly, having to take Alrick's word for it. Musician humor was a bit beyond him. He handed over the case and watched as Alrick unlatched it and took the instrument out.

"Sit here." Alrick patted the back of the armchair before studying Brian critically. "I think you should take off your sweater. It will make it more difficult for you to feel connected to the instrument."

Brian looked at him skeptically. "Uh-huh. You just want me to strip." Angels would have wept for the innocence shining from Alrick's blue eyes. Brian had to laugh as he drew his sweater off over his head. He wondered just how many people had fallen for that look.

Alrick waited until Brian had settled in the chair before handing him the cello. "Hold it between your legs. You'll have to spread them wide. Wider," he instructed when Brian continued to sit too modestly.

Brian glanced up at him doubtfully, but Alrick kept his expression completely bland. Having no way of knowing if Alrick was being genuine or just messing with him, Brian complied without comment. When Alrick knelt in front of him and picked up his hand, Brian's thoughts quickly wandered to a place that had nothing to do with learning how to play the cello. He tried to pay attention when

Alrick carefully positioned the long stick strung with what looked like hair in his hand.

"This is the bow. It's what makes the strings produce sound. You specify the notes that you want using your left hand, but that's secondary. How to use the bow properly is the most important thing you should learn. Without it, you will sound like this."

Holding Brian's hand around the bow, Alrick placed it on the strings and moved Brian's hand back and forth. Brian cringed at the squeaky, eerie noise that erupted. "Ouch."

"Yes, ouch. So, bowing technique first. Then I will teach you about the different strings."

Brian waited patiently for Alrick to show him how to use the bow, but Alrick hesitated. He looked at Brian's hand consideringly for a moment before nodding to himself. Brian blinked when a firm grip on his arm drew him to his feet. "It will be better if I show you like this."

Alrick settled onto the chair and pulled Brian down in front of him. Long legs pressed firmly on either side of his own, and Brian groaned as he fought against the instant reaction of his body. *This isn't going to end well*, he thought. Strong arms wrapped around him as Alrick covered his hand with his own. Or rather, maybe it would.

"Hold the bow like this. Yes, that's perfect. Now, just relax and feel the way the bow moves over the strings."

Brian exerted no effort of his own, simply allowing his right arm to be moved however Alrick wished. With the bow seated properly against the strings, he was amazed at the rich sounds that rang out into the room. His cock began to harden as the cello vibrated against his inner thighs. He tried to ignore it, but the press of Alrick's chest and ripped stomach against his back only added to his growing problem. Not that he was alone. That definitely wasn't a flashlight digging into his ass. Brian scrambled for a topic to distract himself.

"You're really good at this, at teaching." Brian heard the slight breathiness of his voice. He swallowed a groan as Alrick's muscular arm bunched against his as Alrick directed the movement of the bow. "How come you don't do it for a living?" The sudden tension in

Alrick's body passed so quickly that Brian convinced himself it was his imagination.

"My sister asked me the same question after I recovered from the accident. But like I told her, I wasn't strong enough to watch others playing day in and day out, to see their joy from doing what I no longer could. I know that's awful."

"Not at all," Brian said, shaking his head. He couldn't imagine what it would be like to have such an incredible gift ripped away so tragically. He certainly couldn't fault Alrick's feelings, not when it was that very humanity that he found so appealing.

"Besides, my father's business left behind some debts that a teacher's salary wouldn't cover. Working for the magazine was a more lucrative proposition. And it allows me to help my sister. She's married with a small child, and her husband is self-employed. Sometimes it's a struggle for them to manage, since she stays home with the baby."

Alrick had stopped playing as he spoke. Brian took the bow from him and laid it and the cello carefully on the carpet. He turned and knelt in front of the chair as he met Alrick's questioning gaze. His chest ached with a suspicious tightness as he fell into an ocean of deep blue. "You're a good man."

Alrick parted his lips to speak, but Brian captured them before he could make a sound.

CHAPTER 12

EVERY NERVE in Alrick's body sparked as his senses focused on the warm press of lips. Brian's spicy, masculine scent filled his head, making him dizzy. Brian moved to kneel in the chair, fitting his knees into the narrow space on either side of Alrick's hips. He lowered himself so they fitted together from lips to groin. Alrick wrapped his arms around Brian, holding him tightly as their swollen arousals moved against each other. He met Brian's excited groan with a deep growl and pulled Brian closer. Heat rose between them, bringing a flush of sweat to his skin even as an icy hand of fear gripped his heart.

Alrick was afraid that if he relaxed his hold even a little, Brian would be taken from him. Or worse, he might run away of his own volition. He walked an extremely fine line with untold happiness on one side and unendurable anguish on the other. The slightest slipup on his part would bring all of his newfound bliss to a crashing end, for although Alrick had shared more with Brian than he had with anyone besides his sister, those truths were tainted by lies. If even one of them came to light, Brian would surely leave him in a heartbeat.

Brian had called him a good man, but Brian was the one who was perfect. How could such a wonderful man ever love a killer?

Brian seemed oblivious to the desperation in his embrace. He thrust his tongue deep into Alrick's mouth, all the while sliding his arousal maddeningly against the hard ridge beneath Alrick's own zipper. Alrick groaned helplessly when Brian reached beneath his T-shirt and traced eager fingers over the heated skin covering his abs and chest as he lifted the shirt upward. He protested when Brian released his lips to whisk his shirt off over his head, but Brian didn't leave him wanting for long. Alrick tilted his head back, taking a deep breath as nimble thumbs caressed back and forth over his peaked nipples.

"*Ja*, keep doing that."

Brian chuckled deeply as he ran his tongue up the long column of Alrick's throat. "Oh, I intend to," he warned.

Not content to remain a passive participant, Alrick made short work of the button at Brian's waist. He slid the zipper down carefully, making sure his knuckles *accidentally* brushed against Brian's arousal. Brian whimpered obligingly and sank his teeth into Alrick's neck.

"*Gott!*" Alrick panted for breath when soft, wet sucking replaced the sharp pain. He instantly went from comfortably aroused to painfully hard. Brian's surprised exclamation barely registered as Alrick thrust his hands down the back of his pants, got a solid grip, and lifted them both out of the chair.

"Holy shit!" Brian wrapped his legs around Alrick's waist, holding on for dear life. "Don't you dare drop me," he threatened, then countermanned his own order by trying to bury his tongue down Alrick's throat.

That was the least of Alrick's worries. All he cared about was getting them both to the bed before he came in his pants.

They let out loud huffs as they fell on top of the mattress, bouncing a few inches from the force of the impact. The lamp was already on, but for once, Brian was too distracted to complain about it. They toed off their shoes blindly, mouths melded together as their footwear hit the carpet with muted thuds.

Alrick moved down so his mouth was level with the gaping waistband of Brian's pants. Taking the hem of Brian's shirt in his teeth, he lifted it, tugging when the shirt got caught beneath Brian's back. Breathlessly, Brian took the hint and arched his lower back, allowing the shirt to be pulled up over his stomach. Alrick smiled when Brian tried to suck in his gut before Alrick could notice his lack of a six-pack. He attacked the warm brown flesh with his lips, kissing up the center line of coarse, dark hair before licking his way back down.

"Ah, fuck me!" Brian groaned as his cock rose and tried to escape from the confinement of his boxers. He bit his lip in a vain attempt to stifle an unmanly cry when Alrick nuzzled at the rod of flesh poking him in the chin.

"In time, *Liebling*. Be patient."

Brian reacted to the teasing with characteristic directness. Grabbing Alrick's shoulders, he pulled him up and pushed him over onto his back. "You be patient. I'm about to go crazy."

Alrick fully appreciated the sentiment. Brian kissed him savagely, and he shivered as a threatening growl resonated into his mouth. He offered no resistance as Brian laid siege, proclaiming with every sweep of his tongue his right to be exactly where he was. Laying his hands across Brian's back, he stretched his fingers wide to cover as much skin as he could.

Restless and demanding, Brian feasted on Alrick as if he were a banquet. He nibbled and licked his way down Alrick's torso, lingering over the nubs that broke the broad expanse of his chest. "Anyone ever tell you how cute these are? Like little pink cherries."

Alrick's laugh turned into a needy moan as Brian worshiped the tender buds. He toyed with each one in turn, the encircling ring of colored flesh pebbling, as if trying to discern whether they tasted like the delicate pink fruit they apparently resembled. Alrick's cock throbbed against Brian's stomach, weeping with excitement as Brian worked over the heavy slabs of muscle covering his chest with biting kisses.

"Fuck, and you smell so good I want a taste."

"Brian—" Alrick hissed, his stomach muscles jerking as sharp teeth worried the taut skin covering them. He murmured something and realized he was speaking in German, begging Brian to stop tormenting him. Knowing Brian wouldn't understand, he rested his hand atop Brian's head, hinting at what he wanted. He could feel Brian's smile against his skin, but he graciously moved down to where Alrick so desperately wanted him to go.

Reciting a poem he'd learned as a child, Alrick hoped the innocent verses would help him stem the rising pressure coiling between his legs. He wanted to wait, to enjoy this for as long as he could, but *verdammt*! Brian was taking his sweet time, meandering aimlessly as he pulled down Alrick's boxers just past his hip bones and applied hot, wet kisses everywhere except where Alrick needed them.

"Brian, *bitte*. Please!"

His voice cracked, but he didn't care that he sounded like an untried adolescent. Brian uttered an absent, questioning noise but didn't stop running his tongue back and forth across the mark left by the elastic band of his boxers. When Brian opened his mouth and sucked at a circle of pale flesh, Alrick bucked up with a loud groan, wetness leaking from his cock in a steady stream. Finally, Brian pulled his boxers completely off, and Alrick cried out when the waistband scraped over the sensitive flesh of his hard cock. Soothing the hurt with a long swipe of his tongue, Brian grinned as the flushed rod bounced upward once it was free, leaving a wet trail as it landed against Alrick's taut stomach.

"*Scheiße*! Brian, you are making me die!" His accent thickened as his command of English began to slip.

Brian laughed with a decided lack of sympathy. "Not so cocky now, are you?"

Alrick kicked his pants and boxers out of the way, paying little heed to the smug tone in Brian's voice. Clearly Brian was holding some sort of grudge for what Alrick had done to him their first night together, but Alrick was beyond caring. "Whatever you say. Just, please, your mouth—"

"Hmmm? You mean like this?" Brian pressed a gentle kiss to the weeping tip, smearing the wetness over his lips.

Spreading his legs wide, Alrick moaned desperately as, at long last, Brian took pity on him. With devastating skill, he took Alrick all the way down his throat in one smooth motion. Unable to breathe, Alrick bowed his body upward as his hips pushed into the wet, engulfing heat. Sweat stung his eyes, and he shook his head to fling the beads of moisture from his hair. His hands gripped at the sheets, the distant sound of ripping fabric not even making an impression. All he heard was a cacophony of music playing in his head and a loud, shouting voice that he belatedly recognized as his own.

Brian worked him with a single-minded dedication that proved he really enjoyed sucking cock. Alrick would have been jealous of whoever else Brian might have done this with if he'd been able to think. As it was, he could only feel. Brian's hot tongue caressed up and down the underside of his shaft, the soft press of his lips surrounding him like a velvet glove. The thrilling scrape of his teeth was a delicious threat as Brian's throat massaged the head of his cock with every descent. Caressing hands rubbed up his flanks and over his chest, blunt nails dragging tauntingly over his peaked nipples and down his stomach.

Alrick was certain he could never feel more incredible than he did at that moment until Brian slipped his lips from around his cock and took a tight, swollen ball into his mouth.

"Ungg, Brian, *ja*!"

Chest heaving with hard, rasping gasps, he buried his fingers into Brian's hair, trying not to pull at the thick curls as his body jerked uncontrollably. Brian subjected first one side of the round sac, then the other, to his thorough attention, and then that beautiful mouth was back on his cock and a long, slick finger probed with gentle determination at his entrance. Alrick's vision went white. His body loosened reluctantly as Brian eased his finger inside his passage. It had been a long time since someone had touched him like this, and the fact that it was the man he loved was almost too much to bear. The finger pulled out slowly, and he heard the squish of lube being squeezed from the bottle he'd started keeping conveniently in the nightstand drawer. This time, two fingers slid past the muscular ring, plunging deep inside. He felt a slight twinge of discomfort as the fingers eased apart, stretching him....

And then he was there, shouting fit to wake the dead as his body clenched and shuddered. The glorious feel of Brian's mouth as his cock pumped out jets of white fire kept the sparks flying long after he was completely drained. He moaned plaintively, his throat raw from the force of his gasping breaths, and it was a few moments before he was able to form a coherent thought. When he finally opened his eyes, he saw Brian propped up on his arms, leaning over him with a satisfied grin. Alrick huffed in exhausted amusement when Brian licked his lips.

"Remember how to speak English now?"

Alrick smiled, reaching up to caress his cheek with a shaky hand. "Maybe. But I could be convinced to forget again."

Brian's gaze darkened as his lips curved with a smirk. "I'm kinda rusty, but I'll do my best."

He reached over to the already-open drawer in the nightstand, and Alrick closed his eyes, taking a deep breath as he heard the sound of tearing foil. He tensed nervously for a moment when Brian lifted one of his legs and draped it over his shoulder. Over ten years had passed since he'd granted anyone this privilege, and he tried to force himself to relax. Before he could get too lost in his thoughts, however, a thumb brushing across his cheek prompted him to open his eyes, and the gentle expression on Brian's face suddenly made all of his tension bleed away. He took a deep breath as the thick head of Brian's cock pressed into him. Sweat beaded on his brow, his body protesting the burning stretch. Brian's hardness penetrated deeply with a long, slow slide, its passage eased by a lube-slick condom and Brian's careful preparation. Alrick sighed at the incredible feeling of fullness when Brian's balls finally came to rest against his ass. Warm lips pressed softly against his in an unspoken question, and after a moment, he smiled.

"Okay," he breathed.

It was many hours before he was able to say much of anything else. When he finally regained consciousness, he rolled over and buried his face in the hollow below Brian's chin.

Brian chuckled as Alrick's tired groan rumbled against his neck.

"You're not the only one who's exhausted. My poor body isn't used to the marathon session I just put it through." Brian stretched, his bones popping audibly in protest. But when he settled down, Alrick could see he was smiling.

"You are in a good mood."

Brian turned to bury his face in his pillow, but Alrick stalled him with a kiss. When he pulled back, he gazed down at Brian for a long moment, still not quite able to believe how fortunate he was. He watched in fascination as color bloomed subtly in Brian's cheeks.

"I am, and it's because of you, really."

Alrick smirked. "Well, I should hope so."

Brian batted him away halfheartedly when Alrick sucked on his neck. "No, not like that. Well okay, not only like that." He tunneled his fingers into Alrick's hair. "I had a good day at work, and it's thanks to you. If you hadn't asked me to go to the opera, I wouldn't have thought to question people at the college, which gave me a break in the case I was working on. Well, it was really Angie's idea, but I did the legwork."

Alrick lifted his head and looked at him, his brow furrowed in confusion. "Case? What do you mean?"

"I'm a cop." Brian bit his lip. "A homicide detective, to be more exact."

Alrick blinked, grasping for something to say even as his mind went blank. "Ah, I see. That sounds like a dangerous but very important job. I'm sure you're very good at it." He brushed his thumb over Brian's lower lip. "Do you enjoy it?"

"Usually, although my captain can be a real bitch sometimes."

"The Queen of the Night?"

Brian grinned ruefully. "Exactly. Anyway, I was working a case of a dead girl, the councilwoman's daughter who was killed?"

Alrick nodded, indicating he'd heard the news.

"She went to school at the college where we saw the performance, and when Angie knew I was looking for an excuse to leave work and meet you there, she suggested I question some of the victim's friends. It turned out to be just the break we needed."

"Who is Angie?"

"Angela Lovell. My partner of six years and my sometimes work mother."

Alrick frowned. "Don't you mean work wife?" He thought his voice sounded normal, or at least he hoped so.

Brian rolled his eyes. "No, trust me. It's like the two sons she gave birth to aren't enough for her. My folks and I aren't all that close, so she thinks I'm deprived. She enjoys sharing her family with me, and truth be told, I love her for it."

"She sounds like a special person."

Brian laughed. "Let's see if you say that after she's convinced you to come to pizza night. She's dying to meet you, you know."

"Is she now?" Alrick feared his face might crack from tension as he smiled.

"Yeah. Anyway, I wish all my cases could go so smoothly." Brian stretched again before flopping back down to the bed and closing his eyes. He moved closer to Alrick until they were touching. "This one I've been working on for a while now has me stumped. A bunch of mobsters have been getting killed by a hired gun. The guy's a pro. Hasn't made a single false step. But I'll get him—"

Alrick watched Brian closely as he fell asleep, a bone-deep cold invading his body in spite of the duvet and the warm body lying against him. He didn't know whether it was consideration or shock that kept him immobile. A police officer? A detective? This had to be some cruel cosmic joke. He couldn't believe the universe hated him this much, no matter how much he deserved it.

He should get out now, just slip away and disappear. Although he hadn't made as much from Rivella as he'd planned, it would have to be enough. There would be other opportunities, other ways for him to make enough to clear his father's debts. The situation had suddenly become far too dangerous. It was madness to remain in the city when the very man hunting him was the one lying right next to him. Was the one he wanted more than anything.

Alrick remained still as he gazed into Brian's face, marveling at how beautiful he was. He pressed his lips against Brian's forehead and closed his eyes, his lover's heat pressed against his side eventually allowing him to drift off to sleep despite the crushing weight of inevitability bearing down on him.

CHAPTER 13

"MERY! PLEASE do not leave me!"

"All will be well, Pa'sheri."

Sounds of battle clashed outside the door of their sanctuary. The boy pressed his thin body against it, trying to bar his lover from going out into the madness.

"No, I am afraid for you."

"Do not fear. I will never leave you."

THE DREAM was slow to recede back into his subconscious, leaving Brian dazed. He glanced at the clock one more time, hoping he might have just misread it the last ten times. But no, he was nearly an hour late for work, and he still had to go home and change.

"This is the last time I run out of here in the same clothes I had on the night before."

"So, you will bring a change of clothing here, then?"

Brian glanced over at Alrick standing at the foot of the bed wearing nothing but a towel after his second shower of the day. Brian had actually woken up in plenty of time to get to work that morning, but the rather disgusting state they'd been in had made him agreeable to Alrick's suggestion of a shower. And it wasn't as if he'd complained when Alrick joined him, although sharing a small space while wet and naked had, of course, led to other things. An hour later, they'd finally passed out in a satisfied stupor, which was the cause of Brian's current predicament.

Brian groaned as he gave the clock another glance. "Yeah, I guess I should, huh? No use in trying to preserve my maidenly honor at this point."

Alrick smiled. "No, probably not."

"Damn, if the captain doesn't kill me, Angie will. 'Responsibility is the hallmark of a good cop, my boy.'" Brian finished tying his shoes and pulled on his undershirt. Noticing that Alrick hadn't commented on his falsetto impression of his partner, he turned to look at him. Alrick was staring at the carpet, looking a million miles away. "Something wrong?"

Alrick glanced up at the question. The easy smile that curved his lips made Brian wonder if he'd just imagined the absent expression. "What would you say to going away with me for the weekend?"

Brian blinked at him for a moment, waiting for the punch line. When none was forthcoming, his face flamed. "What? You're serious?"

"Quite. I want to spend more time with you without having to worry about you running away at first light."

Brian sputtered. "I haven't been running away. I have to go to work. And as for first light…." He looked at the clock again, but it wasn't counting backward. But this was a conversation they needed to have. "Alrick, where do you see this thing between us going? It's not like you live here. This is your hotel room, not your condo. I know you travel around a lot for your job. Hell, I'm guessing you're here on a work visa. How long can you stay in the country?" He shook his head. "I don't know, maybe it would be better if we just keep this casual. You know, seeing each other when we can. That way when you leave it won't be—"

"Won't be what? Sad? Painful? Because I assure you, it would be both for me." Alrick had waited patiently as Brian whipped himself into a frenzy of doubt. But now, for reasons Brian couldn't begin to fathom, he looked almost angry. A muscle jumped in his clenched jaw, and Brian was annoyed he found the tic sexy. "Yes, I travel for my job. Yes, I will have to leave the country at some point. But I will come back, as often as I possibly can."

Brian shivered as a deep blue gaze pinned him where he stood.

"It will be… difficult for us to be together, this is true. But I am willing to make the effort, because the one thing I do not want is to lose you."

His heart pounded so loudly in his ears Brian could hardly hear himself think. Such a huge confession was the last thing he'd been expecting, and he didn't know how he should feel. It was frightening and exhilarating all at the same time. Butterflies danced manically in his stomach, and he felt lightheaded. He wanted to flee from the sudden awkwardness that had sprung up between them almost as much as he wanted to stay. But the one thing he didn't want to do was lie.

"I don't want to never see you again."

It took a moment for Alrick to work out his convoluted grammar, but once he did his entire body relaxed, the tension bleeding away from his tall frame. Brian felt a far more pleasant flutter in his gut when he was treated to a gentle smile.

"Then you will go away with me, *ja*?"

Brian told himself that this was nuts. How could Alrick really expect such a crazy long-distance relationship to work? He didn't even know where Alrick spent the majority of his time or if he ever spent more than a few weeks in one place. But Alrick was right that it was worth the effort to at least try. Brian watched greedily as Alrick walked toward him. It was so worth it. However, spending an entire weekend together was a big step to take with a man he had known for such a short time, no matter how right it felt.

"Let me think about it, okay?"

Alrick pulled him against his tall, muscular form. Brian's eyes closed helplessly as a clever tongue slipped past his lips. He was on the verge of just saying to hell with work for the day. If he got suspended for dereliction of duty, he'd have that much more time to spend in bed with his new lover.

Lover. He kinda liked the sound of that. The warm appendage that had invaded his mouth spent several long minutes relearning all of the secret places that made him squirm. Brian moaned in protest when Alrick eased away from him.

"You'd better get to work."

Brian looked up, wondering if he had hurt Alrick's feelings. That was the last thing he wanted to do, but things had been moving so fast, he just needed to slow it down, if only for a little while.

"I'll let you know soon, I promise."

ALRICK FOLLOWED Brian into the living room, stealing another kiss before Brian disappeared, the door swinging shut behind him. He stood there for a long moment, staring at the door and wondering if he'd gone insane.

If his intentions had been less than sincere, it would have been a decent plan. Getting Brian—Detective Macon—out of town meant he wouldn't be able to continue his investigation. He still hadn't heard about anyone finding Conti, and taking Brian away would allow the trail to grow cold. A weekend full of hot sex and attractive scenery would be the perfect distraction.

In truth, though, those were nothing more than convenient excuses. He just wanted to spend some time together with Brian away from all the obligations and lies that lay between them like landmines, just waiting to be tripped. Alrick was well aware that the risky game he was playing had become far more dangerous now that he knew Brian was a policeman. But walking away from Brian was something he was simply not prepared to do. It had been so long since he'd just allowed himself to enjoy being alive. From the moment he'd first taken a human life, he'd shut away all emotion, his heart lost for years in icy darkness.

Then he'd met Brian, and suddenly, he wanted to live again.

He glanced over at his cello, which was still lying on the floor where they'd abandoned it the night before. Sighing, he returned it and the bow to its case. Although he'd taken immense pleasure in the interruption, the diversion of Brian's visit had left him with a looming deadline and an article that needed revising. The pleasant memories the sight of the instrument aroused weren't at all conducive to work. He smiled darkly, wishing this really was his most urgent concern. After putting the case back in the closet, he fell into the armchair and opened up his laptop. His cell phone was in the bedroom, charging, and he tried without success not to listen in case it rang.

An icon on the lower part of his screen indicated he had a new e-mail message. It was from his sister. His smile became genuine as he opened it up to read.

Guten Morgen, Alrick. I hope this finds you well. It is still very cold here. I don't know if it is so cold in America, but I made you some gloves to keep your hands warm. I will send them to you as soon as I have finished them.

Alrick knew from long experience how slowly she knit and that it would likely be next winter before he ever saw those gloves. Still, he always appreciated her attempts to mother him. He clicked the Reply button and stared at the blinking cursor for a long moment, thinking of what he wanted to say.

Rosa, I've met someone....

BRIAN WAS just sitting down at his desk when Angela tossed a sealed envelope onto the scarred wood surface. He picked it up, noticing that the envelope was unmarked.

"What's this?"

"The ballistics report."

Brian's head snapped up, and his gaze flew to meet hers. "Well it's about damn time. Did your boy toy tell you why they reran it?"

"Ha-ha, very funny."

"I'm telling you, that redhead has the hots for you."

"Leave off, Mr. Comedian. He's young enough to be my son. In fact, he did tell me that Roddy made the request, but he guessed the order came directly from the captain."

"What, she ordered them to redo the tests?" Brian frowned up at her. "Why?"

She shrugged. "Don't know for sure, but the kid said there was some concern about the evidence being contaminated or some bullshit. Plus, she apparently instructed Forensics to show her the reports first before they were given to us."

Brian's expression darkened further. What in the hell did the captain want with the report? Unless she didn't trust that he and Angie could interpret it correctly for themselves. He wouldn't put such a dick move past her. But then, why not rub it in their faces when she made whatever brilliant deduction she thought them incapable of? Why hadn't she called them into her office when she first got the report?

"Well, go on. Open it up."

His partner's voice cut into his circling thoughts. Deciding the mystery of the captain's odd behavior could wait until later, he stuck his thumb under the sealed edge of the envelope. It opened without giving him a paper cut for once, and he pulled out a thin, spiral-bound volume. Angela braced a hand on his desk and leaned over his shoulder as he flipped through the pages.

"Which bullets did they test?" she asked.

"Looks like the ones from the first three scenes: the drug runner, the loan shark, and the pimp. Let's see, rifling impressions, tool marks…."

A lot of it was technical gobbledygook he couldn't care less about. Finally he found a page written in plain English. Angela bent closer to read it. Brian bit his tongue, remembering the beatdown she'd given him last time he mentioned that she might need glasses.

"There, gun identification. What's that part say?"

"Hmmm." Brian scanned briefly down the page. "The analyst says that the evidence was faint, but there was enough of a trace left on the bullets to identify them all as having been fired from the same gun."

"We already knew that we're dealing with a single shooter. What else did they find?"

"How about this? They identified the make: an Arctic Warfare rifle."

Angela wrinkled her nose at the information. "Arctic Warfare? Sounds like something out of a comic book."

Brian snorted. "I'll do some research to see what I can find out about the weapon."

"No, I'll take care of it." Angela patted him on the shoulder. "You're off this weekend."

"Oh, right. Thanks, I almost forgot."

When Brian had been in middle school and he'd tried to get out of trouble by lying, his mother had told him to give it up because he was horrible at it. He'd hoped the years had improved his ability to prevaricate, but when his partner raised a skeptical eyebrow at his mumbled statement, he realized they hadn't.

"So, do you have plans for the weekend?"

Brian shrugged and focused his attention on neatly returning the report to its envelope.

"Brian…."

God, he hated that tone. But he had to give Angela credit; she'd mastered the art of using nothing but a name to convey ultimate disapproval. It was no wonder she was able to keep the three men in her life under her complete control with so little effort. Or rather, make that four men.

"—for the weekend."

Angela gave him an annoyed look. "What was that?"

"I said, Alrick asked me to go away with him for the weekend." Brian got a sinking feeling in his stomach when she beamed at him.

"Really? Oh, sweetie, that's wonderful!"

"Is it?"

"What do you mean, 'is it'? Of course it is!" Even though she took care to keep her voice low, her enthusiasm was irrepressible. "A man that you clearly care for a whole lot has asked you to spend several days away together. Hon, that's huge! Back when Todd and I were dating, there was a point I wasn't sure how he really felt about me. I would have been a whole lot less nervous about our relationship if he'd made me such an offer." She leaned closer, dropping her volume even more. "Sweetie, there's no reason for him to go through all of the trouble and expense of arranging a getaway for the two of you when you're already giving it to him for free. Not unless he's really serious about you." She straightened up a bit, looking thoughtful. "He is paying, right?"

Brian figured he said something like "I guess so," but it was hard to hear over the roaring rush of blood setting fire to his face.

But whatever his response, it apparently satisfied his partner. She clapped her hands together, her grin returning full force.

"Then there you have it. So where are you going?"

"I don't know."

"What, he didn't tell you, or is he letting you choose? That's awfully sweet of him."

He squirmed. "I mean, I don't know if I'm going."

Compared to the constant background hum of the busy squad room, Angela's silence was deafening. Never in six years had he experienced her being so quiet. He glanced up at her out of sheer curiosity and in the next instant wished he hadn't. She fairly radiated disappointment.

"Why in the hell wouldn't you?"

"Angie—"

"A blind person could see how much you care about him. Your entire demeanor lately practically shouts it. I know I've said it before, but honestly, I have never seen you so interested in something. In someone."

She propped her hip on his desk. Brian tossed the envelope onto his desk and slouched back in his chair. She was obviously settling in for a long lecture. He picked up his pen to give his hands something to do and followed it carefully as he twirled it between his fingers.

"You remember the day we met? I'd been in Vice for nearly ten years, and although I enjoyed my time there, I was ready to take it a little slower. Not too many fireworks when your clients are dead, right?"

It was an old Homicide joke. Brian forced a smile, but he never raised his gaze from his twirling pen.

"I was excited to get a new desk in a new office and to meet my new partner. But do you know what I thought the first time I saw you?"

Her serious tone made him look up at her. "What?"

"I told myself not to get too attached, because this guy's going to eat his gun within a few years."

Brian stared at her in shock. She had never told him that before. "Why in the hell did you think that?"

"Oh, it wasn't anything in your psych profile or anything like that," she said, reading the thought in his owlish expression. "It was simply a hunch I got because I'd never met anyone as detached as you, someone so completely disconnected from life. I could tell that something awful had happened to you in the past, and whatever it was, it seemed like you had just given up."

Angela shook her head. "You looked like such a sweet kid. I didn't want to wake up one day to the news that I had to look for a new partner after I'd finally broken you in. That's why I practically forced my family onto you. I thought that if I made you feel a part of something, maybe you'd want to stick around for a while. I know I was pushy about it, but in all seriousness, I was afraid for you. And even though you eventually let us in, you still kept something of yourself locked away, like you were afraid to let yourself be happy. Like you felt you didn't deserve to be.

"But ever since you met Alrick, it's as if you've finally stepped into the sun after years of living under a cloud. Whatever it is that you feel for him, sweetie, I think he's given you a reason to really live again." She cupped his cheek in her hand. "It would be a shame if you gave that up just because you're scared."

Brian shook as she spoke. She had dug up his deepest uncertainties and brought them out into the open, forcing him to confront them. Her hand was soft against his face, and it smelled like the cheap, flowery hand lotion her sons gave her every birthday. He knew why they liked it. The scent was like a warm hug wrapping around his senses. It was a mother's hug.

He had tried hard to forget everything about the day he'd found Dennis lying near death on the street. As his friend had slowly bled to death internally, Brian had yelled his head off, calling for help. Someone walking down the street heard his cries and called for an ambulance, but by the time it arrived, it had been too late. The EMTs didn't even bother trying to resuscitate him. Brian had been distraught, screaming bloody murder when the paramedics had tried to take Dennis's body and leave him behind. He'd thrown himself across the gurney, refusing to let them carry him away. In the interests of expediency, they'd bent the rules and let him ride along to the hospital.

Brian's parents had found him there, sitting listlessly in the emergency waiting room. Dennis's folks had already arrived and were in with the doctor who had pronounced their son dead.

Only been a few weeks prior, Brian's mother had found the gay magazines he'd foolishly hidden beneath his mattress. His father had railed at him, threatening him with the promise of military school if he didn't abandon his deviant behavior. Brian had run to his mother, begging her to try and reason with her husband, but when he went to hug her, she'd recoiled from him. And then, in the hospital, when he turned to her for comfort, distraught over the death of his best friend, his parents had barely been able to look him in the eye.

Not for the first time, Brian felt jealous of Angela's boys. "But what if it doesn't work out, Angie? I mean, sex is one thing, but what if I actually let myself fall in love with him and he leaves me?"

"But you already do love him, don't you?"

Brian blinked up at her. His chest tightened, and for a moment, he couldn't breathe. She watched him steadily, her open face inviting his trust and demanding only that he be honest with himself.

"I don't know, Angie," he finally replied after a long, comtemplative silence, "but I'm going to figure it out." In an instant, the tightness faded away. Brian inhaled deeply, feeling like it was the first time he had been able to do so in years.

Angela smiled at him, and with a final pat to his cheek, she eased off his desk. "Good. So, be sure to let me know where you'll be this weekend when you find out. In case any emergencies come up."

Her nonchalant reaction to such an earth-shattering revelation on his part made him laugh. Sometimes Brian thought that if he were straight, he'd seriously try to steal her from her husband, the fifteen-year gap in their ages be damned. Now was definitely one of those times.

"Ten-four."

She nodded matter-of-factly when he saluted. Sitting down across from him at her desk, she started typing something on her keyboard.

"Brian?"

"Yeah?"

"If you don't call him in the next five minutes and tell him that you're going, I'm going to fill every drawer in your desk with rotten fish."

Brian rolled his eyes and glared at her. She never stopped typing, but her lips curved upward in a tiny smirk. Taking the hint, he reached for his cell phone.

CHAPTER 14

ALRICK SAT in his rented car, tapping his finger against the steering wheel in time with Wagner's driving rhythms. He'd hoped the sweeping melody would keep his mind off where he was and why he was there, but the neatly sown fields stretching as far as he could see kept the distraction from being successful. It had taken him less than an hour to drive here from the city, and he was amazed at how quickly the dense urban center he'd been staying in had fallen away.

In some ways, the rural areas of America weren't all that different from similar locales in Germany. But somehow they seemed so much more remote than the farmland that sprawled across portions of his homeland. Perhaps it was the sheer size of this country that made everything seem so distant from everything else.

Or maybe it was the anxious tension in his stomach that made him feel so alone.

It had been a long time since Viktor Privalov contacted him. Alrick had hoped it would be a longer time still, but it seemed Privalov's patience was wearing thin. A long-time member of the Russian mafia, it was Privalov's organization that had rescued Alrick's father when he'd been drowning in debt. Hans Ritter had known he was making a deal with the devil, but visions of his children starving because of his inability to provide for them had forced him to swallow his pride.

And his common sense, Alrick thought uncharitably. Sometimes he found it difficult to muster any sympathy for his father. His current situation was entirely due to Hans Ritter's recklessness. Doling out death and violence should not have been his life, and he cursed his father for forcing him into it.

His father was similarly to blame for his long stint in the *Bundeswehr*. He'd hated it at first. At eighteen, having known nothing but the doting love of his parents and sister, he'd found it difficult to acclimate to the strict regimen and stricter discipline. Although, with his naturally gregarious personality, he'd quickly gotten to know his fellow trainees very well. The fact that he'd found not a few of his new compatriots quite attractive went a long ways toward helping him acclimate to his new life.

From the first blush of adolescence, he'd known he was attracted to men, but he also had enough sense to keep that knowledge to himself. Until he left home, he had indulged in only a few clandestine meetings that never went further than sloppy, inexpert kisses and enthusiastic groping. But now he was a man surrounded by men, and he'd soon realized that other people considered him extremely attractive. While homosexuals were allowed to serve openly in the *Bundeswehr*, everyone knew of the unspoken rule that some things were better kept to oneself. But having the will, he'd cautiously found a way.

During the course of basic training, he had discovered he was surprisingly proficient at marksmanship. The rifle training and long-distance shooting that many of his peers found so difficult came to him as naturally as breathing. He didn't know why he'd excelled at sharpshooting. When a friend in his unit had asked him in the midst of trying to stick his hands down Alrick's regulation pants, all he'd been able to say was that he saw the bullet as a melody speeding along the background symphony of wind velocity. The barrel of his rifle was the first note, and the target was the last. All he had to do was play through the deadly music from beginning to end and the target would be struck.

After entering his infantry unit, his skill had only increased, and it wasn't long before he was recognized by his unit commander. As he continued to excel, he was often given the most important assignments, meeting and exceeding all expectations with ease. He'd received one commendation for marksmanship after another, and one day his commanding officer had come to him with a stunning offer, to be a sniper in the *Bundeswehr's* antiterrorism division. The honor was considerable, but he'd hesitated in accepting. The life he had desired for so long was slipping further and further away. After finishing his service and earning enough to put a significant dent in his father's debts, he had planned to finish his interrupted pursuit of a musical education. At the age of twenty-seven, he knew it would be nearly impossible to achieve his dream of becoming a professional. Most musicians started when they were very young, as he had before his life had been derailed by circumstances. But he figured if he could not perform professionally, he could at least teach.

Two years later, however, he'd found himself dishonorably discharged with an injury that put the final nail in the coffin of his hopes. He'd never figured out how his sergeant major had discovered his sexual proclivities. He hadn't lived as a monk, but neither had he advertised his homosexuality. Maybe his superior had seen him in some incautious, unguarded moment and had discovered the truth. Or maybe he had just been a sadistic ass.

The sergeant major of his unit had caught him alone in their barracks one night, his fellows having gone to a local tavern to celebrate a job well done after saving a small village when the Danube had overrun its banks. The bastard had tried to rape him, and when he'd resisted, had used Alrick's own gun to smash his left hand into a mass of crushed bones and broken dreams.

Alrick looked down at his left hand, which had curled into a protective fist at the memory. Even all these years later, he could still feel the blinding agony of the bones being crushed. It was almost ironic that his unit mates had chosen just that moment to return from their bar hopping. Caught literally with his pants down, the sergeant major had been forced to scramble for an excuse. Fortunately, a convenient one had been lying beneath him, passed out from the pain of a broken hand.

The official records said Alrick had initiated the advance on his superior, and when the man had refused, that he'd pursued his deviant passions with violence. Who was to argue otherwise? There were no witnesses, and the sergeant major had been a highly decorated soldier who had served with distinction for two and a half decades.

His friends had tried to take him to the infirmary right away, but the sergeant major had insisted on making a show out of charging him with insubordination and having him arrested and thrown into the brig. In the end, he'd ended up spending nearly two days locked up before his military lawyer came to visit him and saw the swollen mess at the end of his left wrist. He'd received the best medical treatment the Army could provide, but he had gone too long without care.

Any hope he'd had of ever playing the cello again was forever ruined. It had been just one more flake of misery in the avalanche that had buried him.

The sound of an engine made Alrick look up from his clenched hand. Although it had healed enough to be functional, he'd never recovered the full use of it, and even the smallest exertions of dexterity caused severe agony. But he didn't need his hand to be perfect to hold a rifle or to get through this meeting.

The car pulling up behind him was unfamiliar, but the man sitting behind the wheel was not. Viktor Privalov's blocky, unattractive features were instantly recognizable. Alrick didn't know how old the Russian was, but he had to be well into his sixties. He wasn't overly tall, but he made up for it in sheer bulk, which had probably once been pure muscle but had long ago run to fat. He looked like some Cold War-era Soviet caricature.

But Alrick wasn't foolish enough to underestimate him. He'd made that mistake once when Privalov had first approached him about clearing his father's debt. It was the first and last time he'd done so. The man hadn't risen to the upper hierarchy of the Russian mafia by being a nice guy. Privalov always put forward an air of joviality, but his toothy smile was sharklike and just as dangerous.

The driver's side door of the nondescript car opened, and the older man eased his bulk from behind the wheel. Alrick waited until Privalov was standing beside his obviously rented vehicle before pausing the CD player in his own car. Silence replaced Wagner as he opened his door. The shoulder holster beneath his coat tucking the reassuring weight of his Glock against his ribs, he unfolded from his seat and stood to meet the Russian.

"Ah, Alrick. Wonderful to see you, as always. You are looking very well." Privalov spoke English, as he said it was always polite to use the language of the soil you were standing on. Listening to the man's thickly accented voice, Alrick wondered if he sounded so foreign to Americans. He nodded with polite reserve.

"Mr. Privalov."

"How many times have I told you to call me Viktor, eh? We are old friends by this time."

Alrick didn't bother returning his friendly laugh. He knew Privalov thought of him as uptight and overly serious, and he saw no reason to dissuade him of that opinion. The only relation he wanted to have with the Russian was of the purely business variety. "You left word that you wanted to meet with me."

Privalov sighed in mock sadness at Alrick's disinclination for false civility. "Fine, have it your way. Yes, I did want to speak with you. My comrades and I have become concerned with the amount of time your family is taking to retire your debts. We think maybe you need to be reminded that we are not running a charity."

Alrick feared his teeth might break beneath the force of his clenching jaw. "Mr. Privalov, I have managed to pay you back nearly a half-million Euros since my father died, and before that he gave you over fifty thousand. That is seventy percent of what I owe you. I promise you, I am making every effort to honor our agreement."

Privalov shook his head, his jowly face making him look like a basset hound as he frowned sadly. "My boy, there is interest to consider. I am afraid your debt has increased significantly since your father first came to us for a loan. Even with the big name you have made for yourself, you still have not paid it off." He clasped his hands on top of his large belly. "And after all I did to help you."

The muscles in Alrick's neck and back tightened as he tensed with anger. Oh yes, the Russian had certainly offered him a way to repay his father's debt, but at the cost of himself.

Two months after he'd left the *Bundeswehr* in disgrace, Privalov had found him sitting in a bar a few miles from his father's shop. His father had offered to let him take up the permanent job that had always been meant for him, but his injury made using the necessary tools very difficult. Alrick had seen his father grow old before his eyes, the stress of no longer having Alrick's military income to depend on wearing away at him and aging him before his time. He would be dead less than a year later, right after Alrick had earned his largest payment up to that time for a job.

Alrick had taken to drinking heavily, though the alcohol had only increased the black depression that threatened to bury him. He'd felt like a failure, a worthless man and an utter disappointment as a son. He'd been indulging in his preferred medicinal when Privalov had offered him his first job as a hit man. He'd heard of Alrick's reputation in the *Bundeswehr*, and had presented the opportunity as a win-win for both Alrick's family and Privalov's organization.

Privalov's offer had seemed too good to be true, promising Alrick a hefty fee of 10,000 Euros. The job had been a hit on a Polish police chief who had been making trouble for the Russians. A dedicated public servant, the chief had made it his mission to root out the organized crime syndicates that held Warsaw in their grip. Although he would be ashamed of it later, at the time, Alrick hadn't asked too many questions. He hadn't even known who the target was. All he'd known was that Privalov was paying him more money than he'd ever seen at one time. Privalov had even given him an Arctic Warfare rifle fitted with a Schmidt & Bender PM II telescopic sight for the job, the same model he had used in the *Bundeswehr*.

The weapon had felt like an old, dearly missed friend in his hands, the grips fitting his hold as though it had been made for him. Thinking of nothing but how much the money would help his father, Alrick had taken out his target with all the deadly efficiency that had earned him countless medals and commendations. He'd felt no trepidation, it not being the first time he had killed on command. It was only later that he'd learned whose life he had taken, but by then he had already earned the first dark stains on his soul. Using the threat of harm to his father and sister, Privalov kept him on a tight leash. That first job was soon followed by others, and eventually, his clientele expanded beyond the Russian mafia. His reputation had grown quickly, and within a few years, he'd become one of the most sought-after assassins in Europe and the Americas.

His only peace came from the knowledge that his father had died before learning that his son had become a monster.

"Believe me, Mr. Privalov, I have taken many jobs that I probably should have avoided in my efforts to make good on my promise. I even entered a legitimate occupation so all of the blood money goes toward my obligation to you. But I can't earn everything that I still owe from a single hit. Please, I ask you to give me just a little while longer. My current job is very lucrative and will make a sizable dent in the remaining amount."

Privalov looked at him skeptically. "Yes, I know about this arrangement you have with the idiot Italian, Rivella." He turned his head to the side and spat into the dirt. "The man and his organization are a joke."

"But his money is good. I swear, it won't take much longer to pay everything off in full."

"You have said this to me before, Alrick. I trusted you, but my patience can only be stretched so far. You might say otherwise, but I know you are extremely selective in the assignments you accept. That may be good for you, but it is not so good for us, eh? I think maybe you do not work hard enough. Maybe you need some incentive."

The threat was hardly subtle. A ball of ice solidified in Alrick's stomach. "What sort of incentive?" Sharp spikes of dread speared into his gut when the Russian smiled pleasantly.

"Rosamunde, your sister? She is a very lovely girl. What a beautiful child she and her devoted husband have brought into this world. It would be such a shame if her husband and son were to lose her."

An animalistic growl tore from Alrick's throat as fear for his beloved sister filled his heart. "You will not hurt her!"

"Hurt her? Oh, you mistake me, my boy. If she were hurt, she would not be able to work, *da*?" Privalov's eyes were cold, belying the shark's grin that spread across his face. "Such a lovely girl. She is a little old, perhaps, but I'm sure many men would pay good money to enjoy her charms." He watched with clinical detachment as Alrick turned red with fury, almost as though he was more curious than pleased at Alrick's frustration.

Alrick held on to his temper by a thread. Killing the man would do him no good. Privalov wasn't the only one in his organization who knew of his debt. There would be others to take Privalov's place, and they would surely be less than pleased if their boss was murdered. Unbidden, a soothing melody began playing in Alrick's head as he forced himself to calm down.

"That will be unnecessary, Mr. Privalov. The Milano job isn't over yet, and I've already had inquiries for several others when this one has ended. You will have your money in the allotted time."

Privalov spread his arms as he approached Alrick. Steeling himself, Alrick tamped down the desire to snap the man's neck when he was grabbed in a friendly embrace. Alrick always wondered if Privalov's lack of caution around him was because he trusted him or because he knew that Alrick would be insane to try anything. Alrick's expression remained impassive when the three traditional kisses were pressed to his cheeks.

"Then we understand each other. This is very good!"

Alrick tried not to stumble as a heavy clap landed on his arm. The years had not robbed Viktor Privalov of his power in any sense of the word. He would do well to remember that.

"Until next time, my boy."

The rental car sank low on its tires when the large man sat behind the wheel. Alrick remained standing beside his car as he watched the Russian drive away in a shower of gravel. He hadn't been exaggerating the amount of money Rivella was paying him, and he did indeed have more opportunities waiting in the wings. But the very thought of them made his heart sink. The melody running through his mind suddenly resolved itself into Bach's "Prelude."

Brian's song. That was how he'd come to think of it. He'd never forget the night Brian had first asked him to play. That was when Brian had seemed to break free of whatever had been holding him back, the night he had opened himself fully, prompting Alrick to respond in kind as they'd enjoyed each other's bodies. Of course, that facade of openness could be nothing more than a farce as long as he and Brian remained on completely opposite sides of the law. Alrick had experienced many moments of regret since first accepting Privalov's offer, but never before had he been so desperate to walk away from the inescapable mess his life had become. All he wanted was to be free to love Brian the way he wanted to, the way he needed to.

The Russian was long gone when he finally gathered himself enough to return to his car. He'd just shut the door when his cell phone rang, the name that flashed across the display making his heart race.

"Brian? Is everything all right?"

"Yeah, why wouldn't it be?"

Alrick smiled, finding Brian's touchiness adorable as always. "It's just that you rarely call me in the middle of the day. What's up?"

Brian snorted at the colloquialism. "You've been hanging around me too long." The line was silent for a moment when he paused. "Um, I just wanted to tell you 'okay.'"

"Okay about what?" Alrick frowned in confusion.

"Okay, I'll go with you this weekend. Just let me know where we're going so I know how to pack."

Elation and trepidation fought for equal space in Alrick's chest. His continued pursuit of Brian was an exercise in utter futility. His meeting with Privalov had only reinforced that painful fact. Alrick knew the smart thing would be to rescind his invitation and cut off all future contact with the detective. He ruthlessly silenced the inner voice that preached caution.

"I'll e-mail you the web address for the inn. It's on a lake, so bring something you wouldn't mind getting wet in. Also, there will be opportunities for hiking."

"Sounds like fun."

Alrick could hear the smile in Brian's voice. He realized he would gladly be damned as a fool rather than give up even one precious moment with Brian. "Then I will pick you up this evening, say around ten?"

"That's fine. And, Alrick? I'm sorry for waiting until the last minute. I should have accepted when you asked." Brian sighed. "I was just being an idiot, but don't worry. Angie set me straight, so to speak."

Alrick thought his grin might split his face in two. "I'm just glad you agreed to go. I will see you tonight."

"Yeah, okay. Um, *auf Wiedersehen.*"

Brian's pronunciation was terrible, but it was like beautiful music to Alrick's ears.

CHAPTER 15

BRIAN LOITERED on the stoop of his apartment building, trying not to pace as he glanced at the cars coming down the street. A light above the front door illuminated the space around him, but he kept out of the direct glare, attempting to remain less conspicuous out of habit. The approaching cars kept going past him, their headlights nearly blinding him. Pulling up the collar of his coat to block out the cold, Brian sighed as he bumped his toe against his small suitcase. He should have asked Alrick what type of car he'd be driving.

Angela had helped him tidy up the paperwork lingering on his desk, so he'd been able to leave the station that evening without worrying about something hanging over his head, waiting for his return. She'd been positively giddy when he told her he'd accepted Alrick's invitation. Several people had glanced curiously in their direction when she let out a happy whoop, grabbed his head, and planted a kiss on his cheek. He'd taken it with humiliated good humor, telling her that she was more excited than he was.

Yeah, right. He tensed as another car turned onto his street and cursed at the disappointment that filled him went it continued on like the others. This was ridiculous. He was a grown man. It made no sense that he was fairly bouncing in anticipation of spending a romantic weekend away with his boyfriend. He caught himself before he could kick his bag again and tried to stop fidgeting like he was five years old.

So of course when the next car that turned onto his block slowed as it approached him, the butterflies in his stomach immediately resumed their complex mating dance. It was dark despite the streetlights, and he couldn't see through the car's windows. *It might not be him.* Brian took a deep breath and told himself to calm the hell down. *The driver might be waiting for someone else.* But the butterflies won when a light came on inside the car and he caught sight of bright blond hair and a deadly smile.

Brian couldn't help the answering grin that spread across his face. Maybe he'd been a junior high school girl in a previous life. Resigned to making a fool of himself, he picked up his suitcase and headed down the stairs. The trunk popped open, and Brian stored his bag next to the one already sitting there. That smile was still waiting for him when he opened the passenger side door and slid into the empty seat.

"Hey," he said, hoping he didn't sound as nervous as he thought he did.

"Hi, yourself."

That voice got him every damn time. Brian felt his heartbeat quicken, and he was grateful for the distraction of fastening his safety belt as he tried not to squirm in his seat. "I don't mean to be rude, but thanks for being discreet and not getting out of the car."

Alrick nodded as he shifted into drive. "It's fine. I know you're a police officer, so I wasn't sure how openly you live."

"Not very." Brian appreciated Alrick's intuitive understanding of his situation. He watched Alrick drive for a moment and noticed something about his body language that made him smile. "You usually drive a stick, huh?"

Alrick glanced over at him in surprise. "How did you know?"

"You've kept your right hand on the gear shift ever since you put it in Drive, and your left leg keeps twitching like you want to use it on the clutch." Brian laughed when Alrick blinked at him. "Oh, come on. What sort of detective would I be if I couldn't figure out that much?"

"I'll remember not to underestimate you in the future." Alrick gave him a lopsided grin as he turned his attention back to the road. He looked over again briefly when Brian's jaw cracked with a mighty yawn. "Tired?"

"Yeah. It's been a bear of a week."

"Well, we have a bit of a drive to reach the inn. Why don't you get some rest? Do you mind if I put on some music?"

Something soft and instrumental filled the car. Brian relaxed into the seat. "Sounds like a plan." He closed his eyes for a moment before opening them as a thought interrupted his attempt to nap. "You never told me what this inn is like or even where it is."

Alrick smirked. "You didn't look at the website I sent you?"

"I didn't get a chance. I had some last-minute stuff to wrap up at work and ran out of time, and I don't have a computer at home." Brian rolled his eyes when Alrick sent him an amused glance. "Yeah, I know. I'm a dinosaur."

"Hardly. There is nothing scaly about you."

Brian's breath hitched when a large hand came to rest on his thigh. Alrick's warmth seeped through the thick denim of his jeans. "That's so not helping with the whole sleep thing." A soft chuckle rose over the music as the hand gave him a final squeeze and a fond pat before returning to the gearshift. Brian tried not to feel disappointed. "So, about the inn?"

"Oh no." Alrick shook his head. "Since you did not do your homework, I prefer to remain mysterious. We'll be there soon enough, and then you can see for yourself."

Brian was already dozing, the classical music and drone of the car's engine quickly lulling him to sleep. He thought he might have mumbled something in response, but he was gone before he could be sure.

"Time to wake up, sleeping beauty."

Something soft pressed against his forehead, and Brian struggled to open his eyes, blinking as the overhead light hit him. When his vision cleared, he focused on Alrick, who hovered mere inches from his face, gazing down at him with vibrant blue eyes. That color, which should have been as cold as glacial ice, never failed to fill him with heat. Brian's eyes drifted shut as Alrick kissed him gently.

The kiss wasn't urgent. It was slow and comfortable, like they had all the time in the world just to be close to each other. Brian raised his arms and wrapped them around Alrick's neck as a tongue licked at his lips, seeking entrance. Parting his lips in response, Brian leaned forward, trying to close the distance between them.

"Ow." Brian glanced down ruefully as a hard stick dug into his side, and not in a good way.

Alrick chuckled, disappointment obvious on his face. "Perhaps this isn't the best place for this." As though he couldn't resist, he ducked his head and gave Brian one last kiss.

This one was far more passionate than the last, and Brian groaned in protest when Alrick pulled away. He let out a loud, gusty breath as he flopped back against his seat. *Making out in a car in the dark. Check.* "All I need is a school ID and braces."

"What was that?"

Alrick had opened his door and swung his long legs out of the car. Brian glanced over to see Alrick looking back over his shoulder at him. His laugh was self-mocking as he shook his head and followed suit.

"Never mind."

It was eerily dark, the full moon hanging directly over their heads providing the only light. Not that there was much to see. They were clearly miles outside of the city. If he looked hard, Brian could discern the skeletal remains of winter-bare trees interspersed with a few spiky pines.

"Damn, it's cold out here." His breath rose into the air in a smoky plume.

"It's always cooler away from the city. The asphalt and concrete hold heat. Not so with grass and dirt."

"Hmmm." Brian heard something rustle in the darkness and peered into it, trying to see what it was. A sound from over his head was more familiar but no less unexpected. "Was that an owl?" A chuckle was his only answer. He shot Alrick a dirty look. "Hey, I'm a city boy. I'm not used to all of this nature stuff."

"Then this will be a good experience for you. Come, grab your bag and we'll go."

Brian looked around as he complied. His eyes had begun to adjust to the dark, and he could tell they were in some sort of parking area. There were two other cars, but no signs of anything else. "So where's this inn of yours?"

"Patience." Alrick smiled at him as he retrieved his suitcase and shut the trunk. "We have to take a short walk through the woods. Do you think you can handle it, city boy?" The smile grew into a teasing grin.

Brian stuck out his tongue and struck out on the path he could see leading from the lot. Laughter rang out behind him, and he shook his head as a surge of warmth chased away the cold. Alrick drew even with him, his long legs easily erasing Brian's head start. Dead leaves crunched under their feet as they walked. Brian winced, wishing he'd brought a hat as his ears began to ache from the chill.

"It's almost spring, but looks like winter isn't giving up just yet. Are you sure we'll be able to spend any time outdoors while we're here?"

"Would you mind if we didn't?"

Brian felt a tingle in his lower belly at the suggestive tone. "No," he answered honestly. Alrick grinned at his directness. "But since we're here, wherever here is, it'd be nice if we could take full advantage of our stay."

"Then you're in luck. I checked the weather report before I came to pick you up. It's supposed to be lovely this weekend."

"Are you sure? It is March."

Alrick smiled at him. "Trust me, *Liebling*. We will have a wonderful time."

"What does that mean?"

"What, *Liebling*?"

Brian nodded. The tingling in his belly grew worse when Alrick merely quirked his lips in a sexy grin in lieu of answering.

As Alrick had promised, they'd been walking for less than five minutes when the trees suddenly fell away as they came into a clearing. The area was almost bright due to the lights blazing from the building in the center of a dark ring of trees.

"Whoa."

"It's nice, *ja*?"

Even in the darkness, Brian could see the inn exuded a sort of quaintness that placed it a cut above some plain old motel. The first floor was skirted by a wraparound porch, and several long benches and chairs provided places for guests to sit and enjoy the fresh air. Curved balustrades formed the porch railing, breaking only where a set of steps led up to the porch from the cobblestone walkway. Bay windows bordered by white shutters fronted the first level of the converted house, shaded by the porch roof that swept up to the second level. Three stories above the ground, more bay windows indicated there were at least six rooms available for rent. The three rooms on the upper floor had dormer extensions that continued the bay window theme all the way to the top of the inn.

Brian followed Alrick as he headed up the steps and across the porch. A bundle of dried herbs wrapped around a bell hung on the front door, and they bounced with a soft tinkle as Alrick pushed it open. The entry hall was crammed full of china cabinets filled with curios and dishes, a theme that carried through into the sitting room they traversed as they walked farther into the converted home. Knickknacks covered every available surface, and pictures and portraits from a bygone era created a wallpaper effect. The sitting room was furnished with sofas and overstuffed chairs, while another room held a piano and more upholstered armchairs.

Through an opening toward the back of the house, they could see a dining room featuring a beautiful fireplace and a long table of gleaming, well-polished cherry wood. Delicious smells wafted from the dining room, and as they moved through it, they could see that the door to the homey kitchen, which was set conveniently off the dining room, was open. Several platters of food were set out on a sideboard and lightly draped with linen cloths to allow guests access to late night snacking.

The reception area was situated toward the back of the house. The woman at the front desk looked like somebody's grandmother, her blue eyes faded yet twinkling, her full cheeks rosy, and her silver hair tightly curled to within an inch of its life.

"Welcome to O'Malley's Folly. I'm Mrs. O'Malley. How can I help you boys?"

"Why do you call it a folly?" Brian asked. "It's a lovely place."

The woman's hearty laugh was slightly raspy, as though her throat suffered from a lifetime of producing the boisterous sound.

"Oh, aren't you a dear? It was my husband who came up with the idea for this inn, and in the beginning, it was a complete disaster. So it seemed fitting."

"The name's Ritter. I have a reservation."

Brian watched the innkeeper uneasily as Alrick gave her his information. He wondered what she would think about two obviously unrelated men checking in together. But the smiling woman didn't bat an eye.

"You boys are in luck! One of the top floor rooms is available. Those have much higher ceilings, perfect for tall lads such as yourselves."

With that, she handed Alrick a double set of keys and waved them on their way. Brian glanced at her over his shoulder as he followed Alrick to the wooden staircase, but all he received in return was a friendly wink. Blushing, he smiled at her in return before joining Alrick, who had already disappeared up the stairs.

Their room reflected the antique store vibe of the rest of the house, but there was plenty of space for them to set out their own personal items. The bathroom, located down the hall, was communal for everyone on that floor. But the best part of their room, in his opinion, was the single queen-size bed that ensured they would have to get as cozy as possible to both fit on it.

"So what do you think?"

Brian could hear the slight wariness in Alrick's voice as he waited for Brian's approval. He didn't hesitate to reassure him. "It's fantastic. I'm glad I didn't see what it was like beforehand. It was a really nice surprise." Brian stepped closer to Alrick and gave him a peck on his lips. "Thanks for bringing me here." He felt his stomach flip when that smile he loved so much beamed down at him.

"I know that it's a bit cold out, but do you want to look around the grounds some before we turn in? If we stay close to the inn, we should be able to see well enough."

Although Brian relished the thought of walking arm-in-arm with Alrick under the moonlight, he could see the tiredness in Alrick's face. "Nah, you drove while I slept. Why don't we just call it a night? We have almost two days to freeze our asses off."

Alrick chucked. "Ye of little faith. I tell you, it will be very pleasant this weekend."

"Uh-huh. I'll believe it when I'm not cold."

Working around each other like they'd been doing so for years, they arranged their luggage and took turns using the shower situated in the claw-foot bathtub. Of course, when Alrick returned to their room wearing nothing but a towel low around his hips, sleep became the last thing on Brian's mind. Alrick was running another towel over his hair to remove excess water, and some of it had fallen onto his bare skin to cling in tempting droplets. Brian touched his tongue to his lips with the urge to lick them away.

He tried to hide his sudden arousal, but as always, Alrick read him like an open book. The corner of Alrick's mouth quirked up as his eyes darkened several shades. Brian was wearing only pajama bottoms, and when his nipples began to harden beneath the man's caressing gaze, Alrick honed in on them, his smile turning mischievous.

"Hmmm, maybe I'm not so sleepy after all."

Brian glanced from one side of the room to the other, wondering just how thin the walls were and whether there was anyone else staying on their floor. Alrick closed the space between them until they were pressed chest-to-chest, leaning in until their lips were almost touching. "Don't worry. I'll make sure you don't scream the place down."

The tongue that swept into Brian's mouth silenced his indignant protest. Eyes fluttering closed, Brian forgot about anything that didn't have to do with the man taking ownership of his mouth. He hadn't slept with that many guys, but he could say with unequivocal certainty that Alrick was the best kisser he'd ever known. All of those trite clichés about the earth moving, stars sparkling, knees turning to jelly—damn if they weren't all true.

Brian moaned deeply as his cock went from zero to aching in an instant. Alrick groaned his approval when Brian pushed his hips forward so his arousal met the intriguing bulge beneath the white towel wrapped around Alrick's hips. Alrick's long arms encircled Brian's waist, and he palmed Brian's ass greedily, pulling his hips even farther forward. They rubbed against each other instinctively, and the towel quickly succumbed to the shifting friction, falling into a forgotten pile on the floor.

The heat between them rose as the thin fabric of Brian's pajamas became the only barrier between them. Brian slid his hands around Alrick's sides, enjoying the bunching and smoothing as firm muscles shifted beneath shower-warmed skin. He traced up Alrick's broad back, his fingers curling unconsciously as damp heat teased his sensitive palms. Alrick sighed into Brian's mouth as Brian raked his nails gently over the pale surface. Brian came up for air for a brief moment to make his wishes known.

"My pants… off!"

He pushed his tongue deep into Alrick's mouth in gratitude as the hands cupping his ass shifted to delve beneath the soft fabric of his pajamas. It was amazing how quickly he'd become so thoroughly addicted to Alrick's taste. Their tongues wrestled, seeking mutual satisfaction rather than dominance, but the contact was broken when Brian's head dropped back as Alrick squeezed the warm, soft globes in his hands.

Alrick took Brian's bottom lip between his teeth, nibbling and sucking on the plump flesh as the front of Brian's pajama bottoms grew damp with the evidence of his growing excitement. Brian barely registered the hazy sensation of moving backward, his sense of balance a mess due to the lack of blood in his brain. The backs of his legs hit something, and the room suddenly tilted. Letting out a startled oomph, Brian found himself lying faceup on the mattress, staring up at the ceiling.

He threw Alrick a narrow-eyed glare as Alrick stood by his legs, gloriously naked save for the pleased smirk on his lips. "That was smooth, you bastard."

"I thought so."

Alrick reached down and hooked his fingers in the waistband of Brian's pajamas. He tugged them down slowly, baring his lower body inch by inch, the slightly cool air raising gooseflesh on Brian's skin as it was revealed. Brian felt as if he were being peeled like a banana, especially since Alrick looked like he dearly wanted to eat him up. The chill in the room succumbed readily to the scorching heat of Alrick's gaze as it inched downward, following the path of the pajamas. Dark blue eyes caressed the length of his cock, and when it was finally clear of the sliding fabric, it sprang upward to flop eagerly against his belly.

Brian groaned, mortified as the swollen brown tip leaked against his stomach. He turned his face into the covers, managing to hide only one burning cheek from Alrick's scrutiny.

"Do you know how much it turns me on when you act shy like this?"

Brian opened his mouth to express his skepticism at the silly comment, but whatever snarky response he'd been preparing was forgotten when Alrick applied his tongue to the moisture on Brian's belly, lapping up the little pool that had spilled from his throbbing cock. The sight nearly short-circuited his brain.

"Fuck—"

"Mmm, yes. Very soon."

Brian wasn't sure whether Alrick's growl was a promise or a threat, but either way it went straight to where he hurt the most. Heedless of his plaintive moans, Alrick ignored Brian's weeping arousal and shifted upward along his stomach, running his tongue along the lightly furred area around Brian's navel. He dipped his tongue into the indentation, taking a moment to swirl it around as he lingered.

Brian's hips jerked off the bed as the sensation ran through him like an electrical shock. "Ahh, Alrick, come on, man!"

"You Americans are so impatient. You want everything now." Warm puffs blew against Brian's skin as Alrick continued to lick his way upward as he spoke. "Wouldn't you rather I took my time and gave you all the pleasure you could ever want? Hmmm?"

Brian grunted as Alrick bit at the flesh covering his ribs. Firm lips fastened around the spot a moment later and sucked at the small hurt. "I might be dead later." A low chuckle stroked his ears as Alrick ran his hands slowly up along his heaving sides. He swore he could hear Alrick's accent in his laugh. It was sexy as hell.

"Is that so? Then perhaps I should do this before you expire."

"No, not there! Unghh!" Brian had never thought that his nipples were particularly sensitive, but apparently he just hadn't met the right guy. Alrick took his time, circling the brown nub with the tip of his tongue until the areola puckered and Brian was squirming against the bed.

Alrick raised his head for a moment to study his handiwork. "Yes, that's very nice."

Brian expected him to give his other nipple the same treatment, but clearly Alrick wasn't finished torturing him just yet. The broad surface of Alrick's tongue massaged the sensitive peak with wet, obscene circles. Around and around it went until Brian could feel a trail of saliva running down his side. And still the maddening caress continued, the rough surface stimulating him until he could feel it in his toenails. His cock was leaking like crazy, bouncing against his stomach as he panted. His legs moved helplessly against the bed, making a wreck of the sheets as he spread them apart in a wordless demand. Alrick fitted himself between them, the hard plane of his stomach rubbing against the tight balls and aching hardness nestled there.

"Nnnngg! For the love of… shit!" Brian grabbed at Alrick's head, not sure whether it was to hold him in place or to push him away. *Holy fuck, I can't believe I'm going to come from this!*

Light began to flash behind his eyes, heralding his climax, when Alrick finally took pity on him. His hooded blue gaze was so dark his eyes appeared black. His lower lip glistened with wetness, his chest moving rapidly as though he too were fighting for control.

"Did you like that?"

Brian tried to give him a dirty look, but it was all he could do to keep himself together. He let his head flop back onto the bed. "Fuck."

Alrick's smile was downright wicked. He rubbed the tender nub with his thumb until Brian moaned. When he was satisfied, he lowered his head and started in on its twin. Brian tried, he really did, but Alrick was too damn talented. As though he had all the time in the world, Alrick licked and sucked at Brian's chest, bringing him to the brink several times as he shifted from one throbbing nipple to the other. Brian was rapidly approaching the point of no return, and when he felt the shock of sharp teeth closing carefully around his flesh, he lost it.

Shouting out phrases that would have made a sailor blush, Brian came hard and didn't give a damn how loud he was being.

Every sensation gathered low in his belly and then rushed out through his cock in pulsating waves. It moved like it had a mind of its own, jerking as streams of white shot from the tip. And just when he thought he'd been turned completely inside out, a large hand wrapped around him and stroked, coaxing out a few last drops.

Brian collapsed on the bed, lying in a boneless heap, his stomach coated with the sticky remains of his release. He felt lightheaded, as though his brains had spurted out along with everything else. His heart thundered in his chest, its decibel level rivaled only by his rasping breaths. It was only when his body started to return to normal that he noticed the firm lips sucking gently at his spent member. And damn if it wasn't showing signs of life.

"Alrick, I can't," he whimpered.

The sucking continued, joined by a few tentative licks, as though Alrick was testing to see if he was too sensitive. Brian swore he could feel the bumps of Alrick's taste buds, but he never made more than that one token protest. It felt too good. The soft caresses continued, joined occasionally by the exhilarating scrape of teeth. Brian moaned as his thighs were nudged farther apart. Alrick made himself comfortable, settling in to wait for Brian to catch back up.

It took less than twenty minutes before Alrick's patience paid off. Brian couldn't help feeling like a bit of a stud. When was the last time he'd gotten hard again so quickly after coming? Clearly the rules didn't apply when a blond German god was taking your cock down his throat. Brian decided to just go with the flow, burying his hands into thick, close-cut hair as Alrick bobbed tirelessly on his rapidly stiffening rod. His hips began to pump, keeping pace with the lips surrounding him in a tight ring. Brian cried out when a slick finger probed at his twitching entrance. Alrick hummed as precome dribbled from the tip of Brian's cock, coating his tongue. The vibration made Brian's balls pull up against his body.

"You'd better fuck me in the next five seconds or I'm gonna shoot in your mouth." Brian groaned as Alrick drew off his cock with one last, long suck. The bulbous tip slipped from between Alrick's lips with a loud pop.

"As tempting as that sounds, I'll have to enjoy that another time." Alrick opened the drawer of the small nightstand next to the bed. He reached inside and pulled out a foil packet. Brian guessed the other man had put them there along with the lube while he was in the shower.

God bless German efficiency.

Alrick held the foil in one hand and ripped it open with his teeth, his other hand busily keeping Brian rock hard. A growl rumbled in Alrick's throat as he rolled the latex over the purple head of his cock and down its impressive length. Brian reached up to grab Alrick's shoulders and pulled him down until they were face-to-face. His lips curved as he reached down with the other hand and took hold of Alrick's thick hardness. Alrick gasped as much from Brian's impishly naughty expression as from the feel of the firm strokes working his pulsing, latex-covered hardness.

"I'll bet you could hammer nails with this thing."

Alrick moaned into his neck. "I'd rather hammer you."

Brian laughed huskily. "That was so cheesy." He licked at Alrick's lips before staring into his eyes. "So go ahead, then. Do it."

Brian grabbed hold of the comforter as his legs were lifted and pressed against his chest. Alrick stared down at the exposed place begging for his attention, and with a look of regret, he dipped his head and ran the flat of his tongue over the brown pucker.

"Nnngg!" Brian cried out. "Alrick, please!"

"Another time, I swear, but not now. I'm at my limit."

Alrick slid his lubed cock into Brian's body, the thickness stretching the clenching flesh with a sweet burn. The muscular ring sucked him in, as though unable to wait even for the first thrust. Alrick slipped into his native tongue as he forced his hips forward and buried his length in Brian's heat. Brian lost the ability for coherent speech in any language as his ass was plowed and his ears were treated to a rumbling Teutonic caress.

They were both too close for it to last long. The bed began to creak, the frame put to the test by the male bodies moving frantically against each other. They were dripping with sweat, and the scent of arousal filled the air around Brian, flooding his senses and raising his lust to a feverish pitch. Mindlessly releasing the bedcover, he grabbed Alrick's shoulders, holding on for dear life. His legs wrapped around lean hips as he pulled Alrick as close as the laws of physics allowed.

"Ah, yeah. Faster!" Brian raised his hips in time with Alrick's downward thrusts. "Shit, fuck me," he urged, modesty failing in the face of uncontrollable need. "Unng, I said harder!"

Answering Brian's demands, Alrick let out a dark sound of pleasure as, after a few more powerful thrusts, he released his pent-up desire. Brian followed swiftly, his passion uncontained as it poured between them, coating their stomachs for a second time. A shared groan filled the room, and then there was silence as they collapsed against each other.

The first thing Brian felt after the tremors subsided was the deliciously warm weight pressing him into the bed. The second was the sweat soaked blanket against his back and the stickiness gluing them together. "Eww. What in the hell are we going to tell the cleaning lady?"

A tired chuckle vibrated against his chest. "That we are enjoying our vacation very much."

Brian let out a sharp sound of amusement. "Come on, blondie. I don't fancy spending the night with my legs hanging off the edge of the bed."

After a few minutes of exhausted effort, they righted themselves. Alrick pulled Brian close to him as he settled into his preferred position for sleeping.

"Shouldn't we take a shower?" Brian asked.

"Umm, later." Alrick's words were slightly slurred, and a second later he was gone, his long, pale lashes resting motionlessly against his cheeks.

What am I, a teddy bear? Brian barely had the chance to wonder why the thought made him want to smile before he joined Alrick in sleep.

CHAPTER 16

ALRICK WOKE reluctantly as a shaft of sunlight penetrated the uncovered transom above the window, hitting him in the face. He groaned, turning his head away so the beam landed on his pillow instead. His chin brushed against a textured softness, and he looked down at a mass of curly, dark brown hair. Brian was still asleep, his cheek pillowed against Alrick's shoulder.

Smiling wistfully at the sound of his gentle snores, Alrick brushed his thumb lightly over Brian's slack lower lip. *I could get used to this.* His smile faded as he reached up slowly, careful not to disturb his companion, and ran his fingers lightly through the messy brown mop. Brian's hair was remarkable, the curls looser than other men of African descent he'd known, but still not completely overcome by whatever other blood he carried. Everything about Brian was beautiful, from his gorgeous eyes to the importance of his chosen career.

Alrick stifled a sigh as the thought of Brian's job threatened to darken the brilliance of the morning. Possible solutions to this irreconcilable situation spun around in his head, each one less viable than the last. Brian was a man who upheld the law, and Alrick had spent nearly a decade breaking it. What future could they possibly have together? Nevertheless, he wanted one desperately. He had never met anyone like Brian, had never felt so strongly for another person, and it had happened almost effortlessly, despite his innate caution. Meeting Brian had been the first good thing to happen in his life in a very long time.

Repeating the movement of his thumb, he gazed fondly at the glistening surface. Even Brian's tendency to drool was fascinating. He shook his head, both amused and frightened by just how far-gone he was. Alrick suddenly wished he were someone else.

"Ummnnn." Brian turned his face into Alrick's shoulder, rubbing his face against the firm swell of muscles and leaving a trail of drool in his wake.

Alrick chuckled as his skin was coated with saliva. "Are you finally awake, or do you plan to stay in bed all day?"

A single hazel-green eye opened and peered up at him. "Would that be a bad thing?"

Alrick sucked in a sharp breath when the hand that had been resting on his midriff started venturing down toward more promising territory. Brian had just taken him into a teasingly loose grip when a loud gurgling growl ruined the mood.

"Perhaps I should feed you first?" Alrick bit his lip to keep back the laughter that was trying to escape.

Clearly embarrassed by the noisy demands of his stomach, Brian rolled his eyes in an unconvincing show of nonchalance. His feigned brashness did nothing to lessen the redness in his face. "Hey, I haven't eaten since lunch yesterday."

Brian sat up and stretched with a pleasurable moan. As he watched the display of golden brown skin shifting over sinew and muscle, Alrick began to rethink his idea about leaving the bed to get food. They could always see if room service was available. But Brian had already thrown back the covers and was getting to his feet. The new view sought to destroy any willingness Alrick might have had to leave their bed let alone the room. Alrick knew he was unabashedly ogling, and when Brian glanced back at him, his blush deepened as their gazes met.

Alrick's cock hardened beneath the sheets as Brian's bashful smile hit him right in the gut.

"Race you to the shower!" Brian shouted as he turned and headed for the door.

Alrick laughed and allowed him only a few seconds head start.

BREAKFAST was a leisurely affair. Mrs. O'Malley served food buffet-style for several hours to accommodate the guests' differing schedules. Only three other couples were staying at the small inn. One was a young married couple still caught up in the newness of marital bliss. They seemed incapable of keeping their hands to themselves for more than a minute at a time. The other two were pairs of women. The two college-aged girls were friends enjoying an early spring break, but the other couple had Brian trying not to stare and failing miserably.

He'd never seen a lesbian couple before outside of the club scene, but they were perfectly nice and perfectly normal. They also recognized that he and Alrick were more than just two friends enjoying the great outdoors. The brunette of the pair noticed his surreptitious glances as he filled his plate and shot him a knowing smile before turning back to her girlfriend. The redheaded one brushed a lock of hair away from the brunette's face, the gesture one of familiar affection.

Brian wasn't sure if he felt more reassured or just more self-conscious.

Full of Mrs. O'Malley's hearty country spread, he and Alrick decided to see what lurked beyond the walls of their room. Brian had brought a warm jacket, but he hardly needed it. It was shaping up to be a fine morning, just as Alrick had promised. Settling for a flannel shirt over his undershirt instead, he ignored the I-told-you-so smirk that curved Alrick's lips.

The inn was even more impressive in the daylight, resembling something out of a Brothers Grimm story, only without the hungry witches or talking animals. Just past the immediate clearing of trees around the building, the woods spread out as far as he could see. The city, with all of its grime and seediness, seemed a world away. Brian decided he could really come to love this place and wondered if Alrick would come here with him when the seasons changed.

It was the first time he'd dared think of the two of them in a future sense. Brian marveled at the changes being with Alrick had caused within him. Somehow, without even realizing it, he had become hopeful.

They chose a hiking path at random and headed out, meandering without a sense of destination or urgency. Many of the smaller mammals were still hibernating for the winter, but several species of birds kept them company while they walked.

Brian kicked his booted foot through a pile of dead leaves, enjoying the resulting crackle as he gazed up at the leafless canopy. "Do you know what all these trees are called? You seem to be quite the nature buff," he said when Alrick glanced at him questioningly.

Alrick chuckled, his blue eyes shining as he took in the stunning winter scenery. "Well, I wouldn't go that far, but I've spent my fair share of time outdoors."

Brian would never have thought that the woods could be so lovely with nothing around but bare branches and pine trees. But the towering trunks flaring outward into their bony protrusions held an undeniably harsh beauty. Not as beautiful as the man walking beside him, of course. It was as if the sunlight was making love to Alrick's hair, striking sparks off the white blond strands. Not for the first time, Brian thought he looked like some Italian master's version of an angel.

"So what's that one?" Brian pointed to a tree off to his left.

"A pine tree."

Brian cast an incredulous glare at his hiking partner. "Oh, ha-ha. Yes, I know it's a pine tree. What type of pine tree is it?"

Alrick's smile was regretful. "I must confess, I am far less familiar with the flora here than I am with Germany's. I didn't come to America until I was an adult, and when I have done so, I'm generally far too busy to indulge in nature walks. In fact, this is the first time I've managed it."

"So, we're both babes in these woods, huh?" Brian laughed at his own joke, and Alrick grinned before casting a curious gaze toward him.

"What about you? We're only a few hours from the city, and you said that you grew up there. You can't tell me you spent all of your childhood in the city limits. Your father never took you camping when you were a boy?"

The abrupt shift from companionable chatter to tense silence must have alerted Alrick something was wrong. Brian kept his face downcast so Alrick was unable to read his expression. Alrick reached out and took his hand, and after a few moments, he squeezed it in return.

"I wasn't really close to my parents when I was growing up." Brian kept his attention on the path just in front of his feet. He was silent for a long while after making the revealing statement. Alrick didn't try to break the quiet, but eventually Brian felt compelled to continue.

"I was a teenager when I realized I was gay, but there must have been some hint even I wasn't aware of. My father was always, I don't know, sort of uncomfortable whenever he was around me, like there was something about me that bothered him." Out of the corner of his eye, Brian saw Alrick frown, but he didn't interrupt. "It wasn't like I was some little nancy boy who hated sports. I still play a mean game of b-ball when I have the time." He shook his head. "Maybe he just noticed that it wasn't girls I checked out whenever we went someplace. I guess my dad had better gaydar than I did."

"Did he confront you about it?"

Brian sighed. "Only when he couldn't deny it anymore. My mom found my stash of porn mags beneath my mattress one day. Stupid place to hide them, right? She usually made me clean my room, but that one morning, I guess she'd gotten fed up with my laziness."

"They didn't take it well." The remark wasn't a question. Alrick tightened his grip on Brian's hand sympathetically.

Brian figured Alrick probably knew how it felt to be a young man coming to grips with the realization that he was different. "You might say that. They didn't disown me or anything like that, but that was the day my father stopped pretending he gave a damn about me."

"I'm sure that's not true."

"It was bad enough that my mother would flinch whenever I tried to hug her after that. Like she was afraid I was infected with something that she might catch if I touched her."

"Brian," Alrick murmured.

"But my father pretended like I wasn't there, like I was a ghost in my own home. I still find it hard to believe my parents could be such bigots when they knew what it was like to feel discriminated against. It wasn't like my grandparents were thrilled when my folks decided to get married. To this day, I've only met them a handful of times." Brian gritted his teeth as the memory of his parents' unreasonableness stung him anew. "If Dennis hadn't been there for me back then, I honestly don't know what I would have done."

Alrick's brow furrowed as his frown deepened. "And who is Dennis?"

Brian froze, realizing what he had let slip. He had never told anyone about Dennis except for Angela, and it had taken him years to share that pain with her. Every time he spoke of his friend, it was like giving him away one piece at a time. And when that last piece was gone, he would have nothing left.

They had stopped in the middle of the path. Alrick was watching him closely, blue eyes filled with that incongruous warmth that never failed to amaze Brian. He had shared more of himself with this man than he had with anyone else in his life. There were sides to him even his partner didn't know about, but Brian felt like he could tell Alrick anything and he would understand. Alrick had shown him that he could open his heart without fear of having it torn out and crushed. He looked up at Alrick in wonder as his anxiety began to fade.

He makes me feel safe.

"Dennis was my best friend when I was a kid. We grew up together, practically since we were in preschool. We went all the way through to high school together, always in the same class, on the same sports teams. Not a day went by that Dennis wasn't there."

"You were lovers?"

Brian nodded, smiling sadly at the slight hint of jealousy in Alrick's tone. "Yeah. We came out to each other in middle school. There was only the two of us, so we got together mostly by default. But I did love him, even though it was more as a brother than anything else. We were happy in our insulated little world, hiding from everyone else."

Alrick took hold of his other hand, holding both of them securely as he caressed the backs with his thumbs. Brian felt a comfortable tingle radiate out from the light touch.

"Where is he now?"

It was inevitable Alrick would ask the one question Brian didn't want to answer. But if he was going to trust Alrick, he couldn't be half-assed about it.

"He's dead."

Alrick hissed in surprise, rocking back slightly on his heels at the unexpected answer. "What happened to him? No, forget I asked," he said immediately after. Brian guessed his complexion somehow reflected his sudden queasiness.

"It's okay." Brian took a deep breath. "Some thugs from the neighborhood followed him home one afternoon after school. We'd been there late because of basketball practice. I was the junior captain of the team, so I stayed to help plan the roster for that weekend's game. It was almost Thanksgiving break, and it was already getting dark out, so Dennis went on home without me." Brian paused, his throat tightening at the terrible memory of that day. "He was half-dead by the time I found him not even an hour later."

"What do you mean, you found him?" Alrick's pale complexion was ghostly, his eyes narrowed in horror.

"We lived only a few houses from each other, so of course we took the same route home. He was lying on the ground not too far from his house, moaning, his face covered with blood. There was so much blood, it was even coming out of his mouth. I found out later that it was because of his internal injuries. The guys who'd jumped him had broken a couple of his ribs, and his right arm was fractured in several places, probably from when he'd fallen to the ground."

"*Mein Gott*," Alrick whispered, squeezing his hand tighter. The sensation barely registered, Brian's ability to feel consumed by the ache in his chest.

"You know the first thing I thought when I found him? I was pissed that he wasn't going to make Saturday's game." Brian laughed harshly. "How's that for being selfish, huh?" The wind felt cool on his face, but Brian realized he was crying only when

Alrick took his face in his hands and gently wiped away his tears with his thumbs.

He spoke faster, the words tumbling from his mouth as though they needed to be heard. "Someone called for an ambulance, but by the time it came, he was already dead. The police found the kids who were responsible. They were seniors at our school. They confessed to beating Dennis because they'd seen him kissing some guy behind the school gym and 'wanted to teach the little faggot a lesson.' They swore they hadn't meant to kill him." Brian's laugh was utterly devoid of humor. "Isn't that crazy? My best friend died because he was cheating on me."

He tried to hold back his sobs, but when the first one escaped, the next one followed swiftly, then the next, until he couldn't stop them. Alrick pulled Brian against his chest, holding him so tightly he could barely breathe.

"That is why you became a policeman, *ja*? Because of your friend?"

Brian nodded against Alrick's shoulder, unable to answer with words.

"What you have done with your life, helping others, is very noble. Such a wonderful way to honor him."

The feel of Alrick's arms around him seemed to absorb his hurt, and Brian clung to him, desperately wanting Alrick to take it away. Alrick tilted Brian's head back gently, and his tender gaze replaced Brian's chill with a warmth that reached down to his toes.

"I wish my own life had such purpose."

The soft breeze blew quietly, swirling the fallen leaves around their feet as they kissed on the brightly lit path.

CHAPTER 17

Hebeny did not even bother to watch the boy go as he fled from the room. She calmly seated herself at the prince's dressing table, smoothing her hands along the polished wood and mentally planning the placement of her things. If Set held to his promise, the boy would be killed in his attempt to save his brother. She smiled at the delicious thought of Rahotep's grief at his lover's death. The prince would be hers to torment as she saw fit, and no one would ever know that it was she who had set things in motion.

Unable to bear the sight of the girl she had helped raise, Trella slunk away and slipped from the room. The corridor was littered with the bodies of slaves and soldiers alike: some torn by sword and knife, others lying with their flesh ruined by Hebeny's foul craft. This was all on her head. She was the one who had planted the false report that the slaves were planning a rebellion. Trella's heart ached with guilt, but it was what had become of the woman who sat celebrating her vanity even while this travesty of betrayal swirled about her that the aging slave truly regretted.

Trella had raised Hebeny from the time she was an infant, and she blamed herself for the girl's wickedness. She'd wanted to speak against the general's plans to have his daughter trained in the black arts, fearing what harm such knowledge might do to her charge. But Sheshonq I was not a pleasant man, and she'd held her peace for fear of her life. It had been so hard watching the girl's descent into darkness, witnessing her malicious pride grow year after year. Trella had prayed every day that her mistress might be saved, that the general's wicked plans might be thwarted. But such hopes had been in vain. Now, Hebeny's iniquities put even the general's plots to shame, and Trella cursed herself for her despicable cravenness.

Trella froze as she spotted two figures stealing quietly down the hall toward the prince's chamber. The slaves were armed with large blades covered in the blood of those they had slain. Their intent was apparent in their hard gazes: they sought the prince's death. A desperate, horrible plan formed in Trella's mind. The slaves would find their prey, only not the exact prey they had been seeking. The time had come for her to repent, and perhaps she could also save her lady's soul, in the girl's next life, if not in this one. Maybe when Hebeny was reborn she would at last find peace.

Trella slipped back into the prince's chamber before the men spotted her but left the door ajar just a sliver. Glancing around for somewhere to hide, to one side of the room she spied a door that led to a small storage area. She glanced toward Hebeny, but the young woman ignored her, seemingly content to gaze at herself in the reflective plate of beaten metal sitting atop the table as she pondered whatever new treacheries she was plotting. The old woman's eyes stung with tears as she firmed her resolve and abandoned the girl to Shai's will.

Secreting herself in the closet, Trella barely had time to close the door behind her before the men burst into the room, their murderous gazes instantly falling on the startled girl dressed in the finery of royalty. Caught off guard, Hebeny was powerless to save herself. Spitting epithets of hatred, they fell upon her.

IT WASN'T the smoothest surveillance she'd ever done, but so far, her quarry hadn't realized they were being followed. Standing within the meager shelter the bare trees provided, Hayley watched as the two men continued their walk. They weren't holding hands, but they walked close to each other, arms and shoulders brushing together.

Gods, these two never changed. They still made her sick to her stomach. The recent exchange between them had been charged with emotion, but they were still acting like a couple of newlyweds, which was a good sign. Hayley swore she spent as much time playing matchmaker as anything else.

She'd learned of Macon's plans for the weekend through a series of cleverly placed listening devices. After taking over his Homicide unit, she'd put bugs anywhere and everywhere that might prove advantageous. His cell phone, in particular, hadn't been difficult to get her hands on. He had a bad habit of putting it on his desk in the morning when he arrived at the station and leaving it there as long as he was in the building.

Sensing a choice opportunity to see where the men stood with each other, Hayley followed Macon and his blond lover out of the city. She'd made sure the German didn't spot her, following them at a safe distance all the way out to this godforsaken wilderness. When they finally exited off the highway, she'd gone one exit farther before doubling back. She'd spotted their car in the parking lot, realizing they had already headed toward the inn. Rather than risk being spotted, she stayed where she was. Not that she hadn't spent many nights in far less comfortable situations, but she hated sleeping in her car. It was just one more tick mark in the long list of grudges she held against them.

At first light, Hayley had scoped out the inn, hoping to catch sight of them. When they'd headed off down one of the hiking trails, she'd moved into the woods, a powerful pair of binoculars allowing her to keep them in sight. A rueful smile quirked her uncharacteristically bare lips as she saw them give in to temptation and lace their fingers together.

Once again, Shai had spoken. The wheel of destiny turned for all souls, and for hers most of all. That treacherous bitch, Trella, may have hastened her demise all those centuries ago, thus thwarting all of her delicious plans for Rahotep, but she would have died eventually anyway. In the end, she'd chosen this endless, accursed existence for herself, and now she had to live with the consequences. The alternative, to suffer the burning madness of the desert goddess Sekhmet's cruel judgment for all eternity, was simply unthinkable. It didn't matter the depths to which she had to sink; she would do everything in her power to avoid that fate. Now, the time had come once more to fulfill her bargain with Set, to turn the prince and his upstart slave against each other and ruin them in this life.

Fortunately, they had made things laughably easy for her. She couldn't have planned this better if she'd tried. Hayley moved to a better vantage point to keep the men in sight as they walked around a bend in the path. They looked so blissful on their merry little woodland tour, but their happiness wouldn't last. Not once they discovered the truth about each other.

A cop and a hit man? It was like the punch line to some gloriously bad joke. Fate had practically done her work for her. Even without her self-serving interference, she didn't see how they could possibly overcome such a tragic situation. She was thoroughly tempted just to let things take their inevitable course, but with her own eternal soul at stake, she couldn't afford to leave anything to chance. As always, it was up to her to sow the seeds of their destruction, thus ensuring her own survival.

It galled her no end that she was so often the instrument of what little joy they experienced together, and this incarnation was no different. She'd worked hard to bring Macon and the German together, wanting to get her onerous task over with so she could get on with the rest of her life. Once, long ago, she'd been content to let them find each other before playing her part, and her negligence had nearly ended in disaster.

Born to the barbaric peoples of Britannia, she'd spent much of her life living in fear of the mighty Roman Army. Never before had she so hated an incarnation, but she did her best to survive it. As always, she'd found the bastard prince and his slave in due time. The prince had been reborn as a centurion and his slave as a druid priest. She hadn't believed that even Shai could bring them together, but somehow they ended up in the same small town. The Britons had kept their priests safely hidden from the invading Army in an attempt to preserve their endangered religion, and it was only after the soldier's brigade had been scheduled to sail back to Rome that she realized they hadn't even seen each other. While she would have been more than content to let them remain apart, her curse wasn't so forgiving.

The youngest daughter of a minor clan chieftain, she'd been powerless to intervene. For once, she feared she might be unable to fulfill her ancient debt. Gripped with terror at the prospect of failure, she'd fretted mightily about what to do. Fortunately, the night before he was scheduled to sail, the centurion had fallen ill, and she'd begged her father to call on the priest to tend to him. Hoping to ingratiate himself with the invaders, her father had acted eagerly on her suggestion. Once they'd been put into such close quarters, the result had been inevitable. They fell madly in love, and with a few well-placed whispers, she'd sealed their doom.

The Romans attacked a nearby village to quell a rumored uprising, killing everyone down to the smallest babe and razing it to the ground. In a fury of grief, the priest turned on the centurion, attacking him with a dagger that was intended to be used only for religious ceremonies. When the centurion was found dead by the druid's hand, the Romans were quick to put the priest to death. It had all worked out as it should, but she'd sworn from that moment on to always take an active role in her own destiny.

Taking that lesson to heart, after she'd found Macon, Hayley had been impatient to locate his accursed soul mate. The sooner they met and fell in love, the sooner she could go about turning them against each other. While waiting for the promotion to captain that would allow her to infiltrate Macon's life, she'd taken a vacation to the south of France. She'd been lying on the beach, enjoying the plentiful sunshine, when a stunning blond man had walked past her reclining chair. Her first instinct had been to let him know that she was available. Her second was to stare in shock as she'd recognized him for who he truly was.

It took months of careful searching using every resource at her disposal, but eventually she'd found out everything about him, including his less than savory profession. Filing the information away for future use, Hayley had returned to the States to accept her promotion and her new assignment to Homicide. After several years spent patiently waiting for the perfect opportunity, the developing mob conflict in the city provided the opening she'd been looking for. The nephew of the Milanos' boss had been an easy target, and it hadn't taken her long to ingratiate herself with the muscle-headed idiot. She'd quickly realized that putting out for Gio was the easiest way to pump him for information. After a few disgusting weeks, he'd told her about his plans to take over the criminal underworld, and it had been almost laughably simple to put the German hit man on his radar.

Having gotten them in the same city, she'd turned to figuring out how to get them to meet under innocuous circumstances, but they'd been ahead of her. She didn't know how but found each other they had, and now Macon and the German were clearly in love. All that was left to do was bring them crashing painfully—and fatally—back down to earth.

The two men disappeared from sight around the curving path. Hayley watched until she couldn't see them any longer, but she didn't follow. Her loathing toward them was just as strong as ever, even after the passage of so many centuries. Such was the curse Set had placed on her heart. Apparently he had been unwilling to leave her continued hatred of them to chance, so her ire was never allowed to cool. To see them was to wish for their destruction. Even so, this was the part she dreaded. It would be far less complicated if all she had to do was kill one of them, but Set's commandment was much more insidious, for she had to find a way to turn their love to deadly hatred.

Hayley went back toward her car and forced herself to think about what was to come.

CHAPTER 18

THE ROOM was dark when Brian opened his eyes. He squinted at the clock sitting on the nightstand, staring at it until the glowing numbers resolved themselves into something readable. It was after seven.

By the time they returned to the inn, he had been exhausted. Opening his past to Alrick had been cathartic but emotionally draining. Alrick had suggested they spend the rest of the day relaxing in their room. Brian felt guilty about wasting any of their weekend, but Alrick had insisted, melting Brian's cares away with soft kisses and heated touches. They'd whiled away the entire afternoon in bed making love before finally falling into a restful sleep.

Brian rubbed his face against the firm warmth lying beneath him, Alrick's impressive chest once again acting as his pillow. It was becoming quite the habit. He smiled wryly and snuggled farther into the unyielding muscle, amazed at how unconcerned he was that they had crossed so irrevocably into couple territory. A loud gurgle rumbled against the hand he'd rested on Alrick's stomach. Brian snickered, his hand moving up and down as Alrick laughed with him. He looked upward to see soft blue eyes gazing down at him.

"Now who's hungry?" he teased. "It sounds like we'd better find some food before you decide to eat me."

Alrick grinned wolfishly, and Brian's cheeks colored as he realized what he had said. Quiet laughter followed him as he crawled over Alrick and slipped out of the bed.

"Perv." Brian rolled his eyes, a smile playing about his lips as Alrick smirked at him unrepentantly.

It took them a while to make their way downstairs to the dining room, the act of dressing proving nearly as stimulating as its reverse. After Brian had smacked Alrick's hands away from his ass for the umpteenth time, they reached the ground floor and followed the smell of food eagerly. Entering the dining room, they found that the group from breakfast had grown in their absence.

Another married couple had checked in while they'd been messing around in bed. The wife was a tiny, gregarious woman with honey blonde hair and bright green eyes. Her husband, who was just as blond but with unexpectedly dark brown eyes, was not nearly as outgoing as his wife. He glanced around at the other diners indifferently as he worked on a large helping of Mrs. O'Malley's pot pie.

Brian felt some sympathy for the man. Although he often had to speak to strangers during the course of investigations, it always proved an uncomfortable experience for him. Shyness wasn't the best quality for a detective, but it wasn't something he could really help. He always did better when there was someone around to deflect attention away from him. Dennis, who'd been by far the more outgoing of the two of them, had served that function when he was young, and later, Angela was always the first to step up when there were introductions to be made.

Now, Alrick slipped naturally into the role, keeping up their end of the conversation for both of them. Brian tried to be discreet as he watched Alrick engage the other diners, but the man was endlessly fascinating. Everything about him was graceful, each movement flowing into the next with a minimum of wasted effort. His own lack of coordination was conspicuous by comparison as he accidentally bumped the back of Alrick's hand while reaching for a pepper shaker that resembled a fat garden gnome. Alrick glanced at him and smiled, all the while debating enthusiastically with the perky wife and the college girls about who deserved the title of the greatest baroque composer, Bach or Händel.

Brian felt a warmth in his chest as Alrick laughed heartily at something the wife said. He knew what name the emotion deserved and felt he was finally ready to acknowledge it, at least to himself.

"Killer dinner, Mrs. O!"

The other guests nodded, smiled, and otherwise indicated their agreement with the young woman who had so artlessly complimented the chef.

"Why, thank you, dear." Mrs. O'Malley favored her with a pleased smile. "Everyone be sure to get seconds, and don't forget to try the pineapple upside-down cake. I just took it out of the oven." She laughed when everyone groaned at the thought of eating yet more food, but that didn't stop the wave of people heading to the buffet table for another helping.

Brian was very much enjoying his perfectly cooked steak and potatoes au gratin. Even the broccoli had tempted him enough to try some, the dark green florets tender, deliciously seasoned, and loaded with butter. Mrs. O'Malley didn't serve alcohol, saying that she preferred a peaceful, happy establishment, but the wide variety of freshly squeezed juices she did offer was plenty satisfying. Filled with good food and surrounded by pleasant company, it took a minute for Brian to realize that the chill he suddenly felt wasn't due to a crack in the well-caulked windows.

He didn't know what made him look toward the silent man sitting across from him. The man hadn't said a word, seeming content to let his wife speak for him, but when Brian caught his eye, the piece of buttered roll he'd just swallowed turned to cement in his throat. Reaching for his glass of apple cider, Brian coughed, trying to clear his throat. Alrick glanced at him questioningly, but he just shook his head, dismissing his concern. Using the cover of drinking, he looked back over at the man on the other side of the table.

He hadn't imagined it after all. The blond man was glaring at him, his expression brimming with disgust. A knot twisted in Brian's gut, replacing all of the contentment that had filled him moments before. He wanted to ask the man what in the hell his problem was, though he already had a pretty good idea. Lulled by the comfortable atmosphere, Alrick had dropped the reserve he usually employed for Brian's sake. His touches were a little too

familiar, his chair pushed just a bit too close to Brian's, his smiles more gentle than a man would usually bestow on a male friend. Not that it was any of that jerk's business. His anger increasing along with his anxiety, Brian opened his mouth to confront the man when Alrick laid a hand against his back.

"Are you all right?"

Brian turned toward him with an overly bright smile, cursing Alrick's perceptiveness as he tried to play it off. "Yeah, something just went down the wrong way." Hoping that he'd managed to deflect Alrick's attention, he forcibly calmed himself, refusing to let the ass sitting across from him ruin their dinner.

Determined to ignore the homophobic bastard, Brian cut off another piece of his steak and pretended that it didn't suddenly taste like cardboard. Ironically, the man's wife was engaged in happy conversation with the lesbian couple. She laughed at something the redhead said, the near guffaw drawing his attention. Since she was sitting next to her husband, Brian couldn't help but catch another glimpse of him out of the corner of his eye. The next instant, he found himself staring in shock at the drastic change in the man's demeanor.

Gone was the glower. Instead, his belligerent gaze was glued to his plate, and he had gone deathly pale. The angle of his downcast head seemed exaggerated, as though he wasn't so much interested in what he was staring at as he was afraid to look up. Brian had no clue what could have happened to prompt such a reaction. He frowned at the man, puzzled, but decided the freak wasn't worth his concern. Shrugging, he glanced over at Alrick.

"Think you have room for dessert…?"

Brian's voice trailed off, shock robbing him of his ability to speak. Alrick's fork was still in his hand, but he wasn't eating. Instead, he was looking fixedly at the other blond man. His blue eyes were like chips of ice, the glacial cold that had never been there for Brian filling the air between them with frost. Brian's heart skipped a beat, astonishment freezing him in his seat. If someone had asked him earlier that day, he would have sworn on his badge that Alrick didn't have an intimidating bone in his body. Apparently he would have been dead wrong. Brian shivered despite himself, feeling as though he was suddenly sitting next to a total stranger. He'd gotten similar impressions from people before, but only from the worst of the perps he'd arrested, and the comparison nearly stole his breath.

Those were the eyes of a killer.

"Yes. I'm very eager to try some of that dutch apple pie I saw sitting next to the cake."

Brian blinked when Alrick spoke to him. As though the last few moments had been nothing but a figment of his imagination, Alrick was smiling at him, his gaze as warm as ever. The abrupt shift was disconcerting, and Brian immediately began to doubt what he thought he'd seen. His uneasiness vanished, no match for that smile he loved so much.

Alrick, a killer? It was such complete and total nonsense he vowed he would never mention his moment of stupidity to another living soul.

"I call dibs on some of that. You can help me with a piece of that pineapple monstrosity sitting over there in the corner."

Alrick chuckled. "Deal."

"BRIAN, PLEASE relax. I promise we won't capsize."

Brian didn't bother responding, too busy gripping the sides of the rowboat with white-knuckled tension. He glared at the water lapping at the wooden hull of the small boat, as though daring it to come over the edge. A light breeze blew over the lake, creating small swells, one of which sent the boat into a gentle rocking motion.

Alrick chuckled as the wood creaked beneath the force of Brian's grasp. "Would I have brought the brand-new MP3 player I got just for the trip out here if I thought there was the slightest chance it would get damaged? There's hardly any wind at all. We'll be fine."

Moving cautiously so as not to sway the boat, Alrick reached over and pried Brian's hands away from the gunwales. Brian glared at him nervously but gave in to the gentle urging, probably figuring that resisting would only increase their chances of capsizing. He slipped off his seat and slowly crawled across the bottom of the

shallow craft until he reached Alrick's knees. Smiling in encouragement, Alrick helped him turn around and settled him on the seat between his legs so Brian's back was pressed against his chest. A dragonfly buzzed around their feet, and only the beautiful strains of Mahler's Fifth Symphony disturbed the quiet of the lake.

Perfect.

When Alrick had suggested spending the morning enjoying the lake located a mile from the inn, Brian had scoffed, assuming he was joking. It was only after he'd rented a rowboat from a shop on the lakeshore that Brian had realized he was serious. Noting Alrick's enthusiasm for the outing, Brian had kept his reluctance to himself, though he'd looked decidedly less than thrilled. Now Alrick understood why. Still, the springlike weather had already prompted the stirrings of new life, and every so often, green buds peeked out among the dry branches. Insects, fresh from their winter hiding places, danced across the surface of the water only to get plucked off by the hungry fish lurking below the surface. While spending another day in bed with Brian was a delightful notion, it really would have been a shame to waste such a gorgeous day.

As Brian leaned back against him, Alrick wrapped his arms around his waist and squeezed lightly, hoping Brian would relax and enjoy the excursion. Soon enough, the tension melted from Brian's body as his fear of the water gave way to the tranquil splendor of nature.

"I can't swim," Brian mumbled. "How did I let you talk me into this?"

Alrick pressed a kiss to the soft flesh behind his ear. "I have you. Besides, it's beautiful out here, *ja*?"

"Yeah, it is pretty. And it'll be even nicer if you make sure I stay in this boat."

Alrick chuckled and hugged him closer. He could feel Brian's heart beating against his folded arms, the warmth of the sun filling him with pleasant warmth after months of biting cold. "Like I told you, I will not endanger either you or my MP3 player. You're both far too precious to me."

Brian snorted in wry amusement. "Now I feel really special." He glanced idly at the electronic gadget lying next to Alrick's thigh. "This is a nice song."

"Mmmm," Alrick hummed in agreement. "It's one of my favorites."

Brian chuckled softly. "You really know your stuff about classical music, don't you? Your folks must have been really proud of you. I guess they were been pretty upset when you had your accident and couldn't play anymore."

Unwittingly, Brian had strayed into painful territory. Brian must have noticed his sudden tenseness because he turned around with a questioning gaze. Alrick didn't know what sort of expression he might be wearing, so he picked up the oars again and began to row, taking them farther from shore. Brian stared at him for a moment, obviously curious about Alrick's sudden change in mood, but he didn't comment. After a moment, he turned to look back toward the retreating beach, giving Alrick the opportunity to marshal his emotions.

"My father was older when I was born," Alrick explained after a few moments of continued silence. "His ideas were old-fashioned, and he didn't appreciate my desire to play music. As I got older, he was more concerned that I learn a trade than in indulging my wish to pursue what he saw as a wasteful hobby."

Brian glanced back toward him, his eyes a little sad, as though he understood everything that Alrick wasn't saying. "But I'll bet your little sister loved to listen to you play, didn't she? I know I would have." Brian smiled ruefully when Alrick blinked at him, amazed at his perception. "What about your mom? You said she bought you your first cello. Did she want you to play professionally?"

The man was relentless. Alrick supposed that it was a required personality trait for a detective, but talking about his past would eventually bring them into territory that was best left unexplored. So he cut off whatever else Brian was about to ask in the most pleasant, direct way he could.

Brian stiffened at the unexpected kiss, but it was only a moment before he parted his lips, letting Alrick delve deep inside. He moaned as Alrick thrust his tongue into his mouth, exploring all of those familiar places he had spent so much time charting. Alrick reached beneath Brian's shirt, spreading his hands across intoxicating expanses of warm skin. Thoroughly distracted, Brian

moved onto his knees, deepening the kiss as he turned farther around on the narrow bench....

"Shit!"

Brian froze, his eyes going wide with terror as the boat rocked from side to side, water sloshing over the edges. Once he was satisfied that he wasn't about to drown, he glared at Alrick, daring him to laugh, but Alrick was far too interested in what he'd started to do anything but try to pull Brian back toward him. A needy growl rumbled low in his throat as he wrapped a hand around the back of Brian's neck and urged him closer.

"Alrick, I swear to God, if we end up in the water, I will kill you." Brian's eyelashes fluttered as Alrick leaned forward and spoke against his lips.

"Then I will just have to fuck you very slowly so as not to rock the boat."

"No freaking way!" Brian growled. "I have no clue how deep this lake is, and I'll be damned if I find out firsthand."

Before Brian could work himself up into full blown complaint mode, Alrick had him lying flat on his back at the bottom of the boat. With their body mass located in the dead center of the craft, the rocking slowed until the boat moved only with the gentle swell of the lapping waves. Alrick could see Brian's fear fading as something else rose urgently in its place.

"You're crazy." Brian breathed heavily as the tip of Alrick's tongue ran over the ridge of his chin and licked slowly down his throat.

"Crazy for you."

Brian laughed, the sound changing to a moan as the fingers that had been roaming beneath his shirt found his peaked nipples. "I have got to teach you less cheesy English."

Growling with amusement and lust, Alrick lowered his head and nipped at Brian's throat. He was gratified when Brian's snark faded into a hitched sigh. He licked over the long brown column of skin before looking down at his handiwork. The reddened spot glistened as the sunlight hit it. Brian's head was tilted up and to the side, baring his throat. His full lips were parted, as though he wanted to taste everything that was happening.

Schön.

That was the only word that came to mind to describe the image of the man lying beneath him. Beautiful. An intriguing mix of shy innocence and wanton boldness. What could he do to keep from losing him? What could he possibly do when they seemed destined to be enemies? Feeling the sudden need to mark what he so desperately wanted to be his, Alrick placed his lips against Brian's throat again, this time sucking hard until Brian let out a grunt just on the edge of pain. Brian's eyes blinked open, confusion swimming in the green-hazel depths. He placed his fingers against the stinging spot.

"What was that for?"

Alrick had the good grace to look shamefaced. "I wanted to give you something to remember me by."

Brian quirked an eyebrow as he smirked. "Why, are you going somewhere?"

An ache squeezed Alrick's heart at the question, but he managed to hide his anxiety, showing Brian nothing but a suggestive smile. "Not yet. But I'm sure I will be coming."

Brian groaned at the bad pun, but the sound was swallowed as Alrick fell on his lips. Blindly, Alrick groped for his jeans pocket without relinquishing his enjoyment of Brian's mouth. After retrieving the condom and lube he'd wisely stashed inside, he pulled Brian's jeans and boxers free and set about preparing his lover's body. Brian scrabbled blindly for the bottom of Alrick's shirt. A growl rumbled in Alrick's chest as Brian pulled his shirt off and flattened greedy hands against his skin. Raking his fingernails over Alrick's nipples, Brian threw his head back against the wooden planks of the hull as he was fondled, visibly losing himself in the gentle motion of Alrick's fingers inside of him.

Alrick hissed as Brian's blunt nails played thoughtlessly over the sensitive nubs on his chest, but he never slacked in his task. When Brian's rapturous moans began to sing out over the stillness of the lake, Alrick finally abandoned his remaining composure. Replacing his fingers with his latex-covered hardness, he rose onto his knees and hooked Brian's legs over his shoulders. After taking firm hold of Brian's hips, he thrust home into his lover's heat. He wasn't gentle, needing more to imprint himself on Brian's body—if not his heart—than to be considerate. Not that Brian seemed at all to mind his forcefulness. Alrick hissed, wincing as insistent fingers dug into the muscles of his back. Incredibly, the pain just made the pleasure all that more exquisite. He whispered guttural approval into Brian's ear as he buried himself over and over again into his body.

"YEAH! AHH, fuck!"

Brian shouted encouragement in time with Alrick's strong thrusts. The cock filling him felt huge, splitting him open as Alrick forced him to take every inch. He couldn't remember Alrick ever being quite so rough, usually preferring hearts and flowers to raunchy sex. But now, he seemed to have lost the veneer of civilized behavior. This was base and animalistic, and Brian was loving every minute.

"Unngg, just like that." He wrapped his legs around Alrick's hips, riding along with the heaving momentum. "Ahh, harder!" Brian knew he was acting like some slutty bitch in heat, but he couldn't have cared less. He just hoped he could convince Alrick to do this again sometime. The boat moved in the water as their bodies heaved, but he hardly noticed the motion. He trusted Alrick would protect him if they should overturn, but he would be extremely pissed if it happened before Alrick finished pounding him through the hull.

Brian's dazed eyes caught sight of the intriguing tattoo that marred the pale skin of Alrick's shoulder. *As if he needs something to make him sexier*. Deciding to punish Alrick for overkill, he licked and sucked at the mark, biting the hard swell of muscle beneath it when he got a growl and a particularly vigorous series of thrusts for his trouble.

Each one scored directly on his prostate, and Brian damn near screamed. He hung on to Alrick for dear life as his body shattered, coming apart as he cried out Alrick's name. Alrick was right behind him, the hard rod of flesh inside him pulsing as it let loose with a torrent of heat Brian could feel despite the condom. A surge of resentment filled him, and he realized that he wanted the thin layer of latex to disappear so he could feel everything. The thought didn't scare him, and he didn't have the wherewithal to wonder if he should feel worried about that.

"Oomph." The wind was knocked out of him as Alrick slumped on top of him. He heard a barely coherent mumble that he interpreted to be an apology and ran his hands over Alrick's broad back in silent dismissal.

"*Autsch!*"

Brian blinked at the unexpected exclamation. "What was that?"

"Sorry. I said, 'ouch.'"

"What, did you hurt yourself? Maybe you should warm up and stretch next time you want to screw on a moving surface." Grinning, Brian shied away as Alrick sat up and smacked him playfully on his hip.

"*Nein*. I think I've gotten a sunburn."

Brian frowned. "But it's still winter. The sun isn't that strong."

"I am much paler than you, *ja*? Your American sun is maybe too much for me."

Brian glanced at him skeptically before taking a look. "Hmmm. Let me see. Oh wow."

He whistled in sympathy as he saw the red patch covering Alrick's back. It was only colored, not blistered, so he didn't think it was too bad, but he was sure it hurt. He remembered the summer before last when he'd gone to the park with Angie and her boys. Sam had insisted on running around with no shirt and had gotten a nasty burn complete with blisters. Brian winced in sympathy.

"Sorry I doubted you. Here, let's get dressed and get back to shore. Maybe Mrs. O'Malley has something you can put on that."

He helped Alrick with his shirt before worrying about his own clothes. Alrick maneuvered carefully so as not to stretch the reddened skin of his back, and Brian couldn't help thinking he was rather cute when he was helpless. Brian had put on his boxers and was reaching for his jeans when he noticed the stains on the wood. He groaned as he pushed his legs into the denim. Alrick looked over at him curiously.

"What is it?"

"We've made a freakin' mess of that old guy's boat."

Alrick chuckled as his gaze followed Brian's accusatory finger. The dark splotches were evident and unexplainable unless they wanted to reveal way too much information to the boat's owner. "In that case, I guess there is only one thing we can do."

Brian threw Alrick a wary glance when his expression grew thoughtful. "And that is?"

"Wash the boat."

Brian didn't have a chance to protest or prepare himself as Alrick pushed hard against one side of the hull, neatly flipping the craft over. They both went flying before landing in the water with a loud splash. Cursing the German bastard to a thousand burning hells, Brian panicked as he went under. The water closed over his head, his saturated clothing dragging him down. It was eerily quiet, the sky making the water above him shimmer. He tried to reach for it, but his frantic kicks got him nowhere. Damn his cheap ass parents for never springing for swimming lessons. But before he could even feel his chest tighten from a lack of air, strong arms wrapped around his waist and drew him upward. Brian gasped as his head broke the surface of the lake.

"You son of a bitch! What the fuck?" He coughed, trying to clear water from his nose. Out of the corner of his eye, he could see the overturned boat floating serenely a little ways off.

Alrick was grinning at him like a madman. Brian found himself pressed tightly against his chest, their heads nearly even as the other man treaded water to keep them afloat. A soft, wet kiss touched his lips, and he responded before remembering he was pissed.

"Don't think I'm going to forgive you just like that," he groused, pulling his head back as far as he could. "Why the hell did you do that? I told you I couldn't swim."

"Because the water feels good on my back." Tightening his hold, Alrick pulled Brian closer so their hips were pressed together. "But mostly so I could hold you like this. It's nice having you completely dependent upon me for once."

Brian stared at him in confusion. *What the heck was that all about?* "Couldn't you have waited until we were on dry land before going all macho on me?" Brian tried to pout but failed miserably as Alrick nipped at his bottom lip. "And your MP3 player's at the bottom of the lake now. I thought you said it meant more to you than anything?"

"No, you do."

Brian's heart flipped in his chest as that beautiful smile hit him at point blank range.

"Besides, now we will have to spend the afternoon naked as we wait for our clothes to dry, *ja*?"

Brian rolled his eyes, holding on to Alrick like he was a life buoy as he was kissed again. He could have mentioned that they both had a change of dry clothes in their room, but he suddenly had no desire to argue with Alrick's self-serving logic.

After they returned to the inn, they sought out the proprietress for help with Alrick's sunburn. When they showed her the damage, Mrs. O'Malley cast a critical eye over Alrick's back, her lips pursed in disapproval. Brian hid a smile when he caught the appreciative sparkle in her faded gray eyes at the muscle that shifted smoothly beneath Alrick's reddened skin.

"Son, didn't your mother ever tell you about the importance of sunscreen?"

"The sun isn't as strong where I'm from, ma'am. But you're absolutely right. I will be more careful in the future."

Brian coughed to cover the laugh that tried to escape as the elderly innkeeper's round cheeks turned pink beneath the charm of Alrick's conciliatory smile. Lady killer, gay killer, either label would work. Brian watched with amusement as she handed over a bottle of aloe vera ointment.

"Put a good dollop of this on the burn for the next day or so, and you'll be right as rain. I'm sure your friend will help you with the hard to reach spots." Mrs. O'Malley glanced at Brian, raising an eyebrow in satisfaction as his face heated. "You boys still planning to check out today?"

"Yes, ma'am, but we've enjoyed our stay very much." Alrick beamed at her, and Brian would have sworn he saw her fan herself. She waved them off cheerfully, pretending not to stare in the vicinity of Alrick's butt as they walked up the stairs.

"Seducing little old ladies. Have you no shame?" He closed the door of their room behind them as Alrick gingerly removed his shirt.

"I did no such thing. I was just thanking her for her kindness."

"Uh-huh. I see that I'm going to have to keep an eye on you."

Brian turned his back toward Alrick, the blinking message light on his cell phone catching his attention. It was a good thing he'd left it in the room for safe-keeping. He smiled when he suddenly found himself surrounded by powerful arms. There was a restless stirring below the waistband of his jeans as his back was pressed flush against a warm, firm surface. Damp heat from Alrick's chest seeped through his wet undershirt as playful lips nibbled teasingly at the side of his neck.

"I assure you," Alrick murmured solemnly, "you have nothing to worry about."

Brian shivered, not sure if it was from the butterfly kisses or the weight of Alrick's promise. The light on his phone was still blinking, and he grabbed at the excuse it offered before his racing heartbeat could give him away. "Why don't you hop in the shower before I put the gel on your back?" After retrieving his phone, he looked through his missed call log. "I have a message from Angie I need to check."

With a final kiss, Alrick grabbed his toiletry bag and left the room, shutting the door behind him to give Brian privacy. Brian stared at the door for a long moment. *Gone for two seconds and I miss him already.* Shaking his head, he dialed into his voice mail, wondering how he'd fallen so far so fast.

Brian, it's Angela. I forgot to mention before you left that the boys are off from school tomorrow. Some sort of administrative school holiday. Anyway, since I have some leave time, I'm going to take the day off with them. Give me a call if you get a chance. Otherwise, I'll see you on Tuesday.

After deleting the message, he called her back.

"Hello?"

"Angie, it's me."

"Oh, hey. I wasn't expecting to hear from you. Everything going okay?"

"You don't waste any time, do you?" Brian smirked when she laughed with no sign of shame. "Yeah, everything's fine. Just letting you know that I got your message, so enjoy your day off."

The line remained silent for a long time.

"Angie? You still there?"

"Sweetie, you're not telling me what I want to hear. I want to know how your weekend was, and by that I mean have you finally figured out how you feel about Alrick?"

Brian paused before giving the deflecting, knee-jerk response that was on the tip of his tongue. He realized her question didn't scare him nearly as much as it would have even two days ago. "Yeah, I have." He had grown tired of denying it, especially to himself. Angela knew him so well, he was sure she could hear his answer in his voice.

"Oh, sweetie, that's terrific. It's about damn time!"

Brian laughed. He could almost hear her grin through the speaker. His amusement only increased when the next words out of her mouth were exactly what he'd been expecting.

"I want to meet him the moment you get back. In fact, since I'm off tomorrow and I know you're not due in until the afternoon, why don't the two of you come over for pizza tonight?"

"We're a few hours outside of the city, but we're all packed and ready to check out. Besides, Alrick got a sunburn, so he probably won't mind if we cut out a little early. I'll ask him when he gets back."

"Gets back? Where is he?"

"Taking a shower."

"And you're talking to me? Boy, where are your priorities?"

Brian could hear her clucking her tongue in mock disappointment as he disconnected the call without answering. He glanced back at the closed door and headed toward it a second later, telling himself that he was just following his partner's orders.

CHAPTER 19

"YOU SURE you don't mind? We don't have to go. I can call Angie and tell her that you're not up to it. I told her about your sunburn."

"Brian, it's fine. You've mentioned how much your partner means to you. I would love to meet her."

In truth, Alrick was less than certain this was such a good idea. It was bad enough exposing himself to one police officer without meeting yet another, especially when they were both working to catch him. But he couldn't pass up the opportunity to become further entrenched in Brian's life. He knew he was all but untraceable, his anonymity and caution ensuring that neither Brian nor his partner would find out anything about him except for what he chose to reveal. And that, of course, was half the problem. He wanted to tell Brian everything, to confess the truth and share everything with him. Even if it meant losing his freedom for the numerous crimes he'd committed, he wanted to be relieved of the burden of secrecy.

Brian was driving so Alrick could sit at an angle in his seat and keep from pressing against his sore back. He felt extremely foolish for getting hurt in such a childish way, but he wouldn't have traded the experience of having Brian's gel-covered hands all over him for anything. In order to preserve their only set of dry clothes, Brian had decided that both should strip completely while he applied the palliative. Alrick had barely been able to remain still when Brian straddled his ass, his cock lying temptingly in the exposed furrow. Not content to concentrate on Alrick's back, Brian had covered him from head to toe with the cooling gel before taking advantage of their mutual nakedness. As a result, they left the inn a bit later than originally planned. It was a good thing that Brian was an officer in this state. If they got pulled over for speeding, he would probably be able to get out of it with nothing more than a tip of a state trooper's interestingly shaped hat.

Alrick tried not to fidget as the miles sped by. Some of it was due to his discomfort, but mostly it was nerves. He felt like a prospective groom who was about to be presented to his intended's family. The thought made him smile, as did imagining how mortified and pissed off Brian would be if he knew what he was thinking.

The sun was long gone by the time they pulled up in front of a modest single-family home located in a quiet neighborhood just inside the city limits. Brian glanced at the glowing clock on the radio with satisfaction. Given the time of year, it wasn't all that late, even though the moon was shining high in the sky.

"For some reason I thought we'd gone farther out of town, since it took longer for us to get there."

"That's because I don't drive like a maniac."

Brian stuck his tongue out at him only to have it chased back into his mouth. Several interesting minutes passed before Brian pushed Alrick back just far enough so he could breathe. "Come on. I'm sure Angie knows we're out here. She's probably figured out why we haven't gotten out yet and is just being polite."

"A woman after my own heart."

Alrick grinned as Brian threw him a mock glare. He joined Brian outside the car and looked over the split-level as they walked to the front door. What he could see of the small yard looked well-tended, and the white siding was completely free of smudges. They had parked on the street, and as they went up the driveway, he noticed a basketball hoop hanging over the garage door. A couple of bikes were leaning carelessly against the side of the house. Clearly, crime wasn't a problem when Mom was a cop. The home looked well-cared for and quite inviting.

Alrick swallowed, trying to force down the lump that had risen in his throat. He rubbed his moist palms against the legs of his jeans and admonished himself to grow up.

Brian's prediction proved correct, for the front door opened before they reached it. The silhouetted figure was short and slightly stocky, as befitted a mother of two grown boys. As they got closer, the porch light revealed an attractive, smiling face. Her hair was light brown without a hint of gray to be found. Dark green eyes twinkled up at him, fairly shining with approval. He smiled back at her, hoping he would be able to earn it.

"Hey, Angie," Brian said, sending his partner an exasperated smirk. "Been waiting long?"

"Oh, you hush up." Angela seemed to grow a bit taller for an instant, and Alrick realized she had sucked in her stomach and straightened her back as she looked up at him. His smile grew, and he reached out to take her hand. "And you must be this Alrick I've been hearing so much about."

"It's a pleasure, *Fräulein*," he murmured, pressing his lips against the soft skin covering the back of her small hand. Brian laughed when his take-no-prisoners, ex-Vice partner with nearly twenty years on the force turned as red as a beet.

"Oh, um, well…." Angela was completely flustered. She blinked up at Alrick as though in a trance for nearly a minute before the sound of Brian's snickering brought her back to herself. She glared at him, using the opportunity to get her act together. "Why don't you two come on in? We ordered four large pizzas, but with Sam and Jon in the house, if we don't hurry, everything will be gone."

Brian stepped back to allow Alrick to go ahead of him as Angela disappeared into the house. He pulled on Alrick's arm to hold him back for a second. "You're good, but you'd better watch out for her husband if you're going to keep on with the flirting. He played defensive tackle in college."

Alrick threw a smile over his shoulder. "I told you, I have eyes for no one but you." He chuckled when Brian poked him in the lower back below the worst of his burn, the prodding finger quickly replaced by a gently urging hand.

After inviting them to drop their jackets onto the coat rack sitting just beside the door, Angela led them down a short hallway. The hardwood floor was polished to a high shine, and Alrick felt bad about walking on it with his shoes. Pictures lined the hallway, some in sepia and black and white, bespeaking their antiquity, and some in color showing varying combinations of Angela, a man, and two boys. When they entered a room off the hallway, Alrick found himself in a homey den looking at the faces he'd seen in the pictures. The two boys, around twelve and fifteen he guessed, were tall and handsome, their faces a pleasant mish-mash of the woman who had given birth to them and the huge man who was coming toward him with a meaty paw extended in greeting.

"Brian! Good to see you, son."

"Todd, what's up, man?" Brian visibly braced himself, clearly from long practice, to keep from stumbling at the enthusiastic pat the bearlike man landed on his back.

Angela's husband had to be six-and-a-half feet tall if he was an inch, and all of it thick muscle that had only slightly run to fat. His eyes were a nondescript gray, but they radiated welcome, as did the broad grin he turned on Alrick. "And it's Alrick, right?"

"Yes. It's a pleasure to meet you." Alrick resisted the urge to wince as his hand was squeezed in a friendly vise.

"Whoa, your accent is sick! Where are you from?"

"Sam, don't be rude." Angela smacked her younger son on the back of his shaggy brown head.

Alrick laughed. "You have a good ear, Sam, though I guess it's not hard to hear. I'm from Germany."

"You mean like with the Nazis and stuff?"

"Sam!"

"Yes, that's the place. But that was a long time ago. It is not like that anymore."

"We've been learning about World War II in school. I had to do a report on it a few weeks ago. Wanna see it?"

And just like that, Alrick found himself accepted into Brian's family. He didn't doubt that was what these people were. The man who was usually so reserved in public and had taken so long to open up to him was relaxed and smiling as Alrick had only recently seen him. It was clear that they loved Brian and he loved them just as much in return. After learning what he had about how Brian grew up, Alrick was extremely grateful to them for showing Brian what a family should be.

"Sam, don't monopolize the poor man. He's Brian's guest, not one of your friends from school." Angela shook her head, her hands poised on her hips in classic disapproval. Sam hung his head, a disappointed expression darkening his young features. She went over to him and pressed a noisy kiss to his ear, smirking when he batted her away like a fly. The boy blushed violently from the unbearable embarrassment of it all. "Here, why don't you help your father and brother arrange the pizzas on the table while your uncle and I get the plates." By "uncle" she meant Brian, who threw Alrick an unapologetic, you-asked-for-it grin as he and Angela disappeared into the hallway.

Alrick stood back as the men opened up the pizza boxes, folding the tops under so grease wouldn't get on the table. The operation was completed with military efficiency, obviously the product of long practice. He took the opportunity to watch Angela's and Todd's oldest son. The boy was very handsome but seemed much more reserved than his younger brother. He hadn't once met Alrick's gaze, and Alrick had yet to hear a sound from him. For lack of anything else to do at the moment, Alrick decided to introduce himself.

"I didn't catch your name." He held out his hand politely. The boy blinked at it for a moment before raising his startlingly bright green eyes to meet Alrick's. A becoming flush of pink colored the teen's cheeks, and Alrick smiled as he hazarded what was probably not too wild a guess. He squeezed lightly when the boy's hand slid into his for a brief moment.

"Jonathan."

"It's nice to meet you, Jonathan. Is that your basketball hoop out by the garage?"

The boy shook his head, his hands now safely tucked in the pockets of his raggedy jeans. His T-shirt-covered shoulders were narrow, but Alrick could see the potential for fast growth, particularly considering his father's stature. His head, covered by a thick mop of light brown hair, was only a bit lower than his, and Alrick figured that the boy was already close to Brian's height.

"No, it's Sam's. He's on the team at his school."

"So are you, Jon."

Alrick glanced over at Sam, who was watching them with nosy interest, before he looked back at the shy teen. The boy's head had dropped even farther, and what Alrick could see of his face had gone pinker. "What sport do you play?

"Soccer."

"Oh really? I'm sure you know that soccer is very popular overseas. Germans love it. I used to play soccer when I was a boy with the other kids in my neighborhood."

All hints of bashfulness fell away from the teen at Alrick's words. Jonathan looked up with a broad grin that made him look a lot like his mother, his green eyes lit with enthusiasm for his beloved sport. By the time Brian and Angela returned from the kitchen with plates, napkins, cups, and a couple of two-liter bottles of pop, Alrick was deep in conversation with the Lovell men about the finer points of *Fußball*.

"If I can dare to interrupt this moment of male bonding, could one of you give your poor mother a hand?" Sam and Jon leapt to answer her call. Alrick smiled and stood from the couch to take a plate and a napkin from Brian.

"Making new friends?" Brian asked while the others were busy with the final setup.

"*Ja*," Alrick answered with a laugh. "I like your partner and her family very much." He basked in the look of pleasure that crossed Brian's face. Making Brian happy made him happy, and if there hadn't been impressionable youngsters around, he would have answered that lovely smile with a very inappropriate kiss. He settled for reaching for a thick slice of pepperoni pizza before sitting back on the couch. Brian flopped next to him and attacked the pie that was covered with every topping under the sun.

"Were you in the military?"

Alrick stared at Angela, the pizza slice midway to his mouth. "I'm sorry?"

"Oh, nothing really. Just something about the way you carry yourself reminds me of some of the guys I served with. I was in the reserves for about five years," she explained when Alrick continued to look at her blankly. "The Army helped me pay for college."

"Ah, I see." Alrick rested the slice on his napkin to keep the toppings from falling to the carpet. "All young men in Germany are required to serve for a short while, but I left when my obligation was completed."

"You never told me that."

Alrick felt Brian's gaze on his face. He bit into his pizza casually, trying to ignore the knot in his stomach. "It wasn't the most pleasant of experiences, so I don't often think about it." The cheese-covered bread tasted like cardboard as he swallowed. "Service is only required for nine months. It was just a small thing."

"Oh! Hey, Mom. Mr. Peterson said he's gonna flunk me in algebra if I don't do better on my next test. I told him I studied, but I just don't get how to solve equations...."

Alrick blessed the self-centeredness of children as Sam yammered on. Horrified at the prospect of their son doing badly in a school subject, Angela and Todd were thoroughly distracted from Alrick's awkward explanation. Jon grinned evilly at his brother, teasing even as he promised to tutor him if he wanted help. Alrick took it as a positive sign that they felt comfortable discussing such private family matters in front of him.

Brian leaned close to his ear, speaking softly so he wouldn't be overheard. "I probably should have told you about Jon in case he acts weird around you. He's—"

"Gay? Yes, I guessed." Alrick eyed the speck of cheese that clung to Brian's bottom lip with jealousy. "Is that why his mother seems so comfortable with our relationship? Because she wants to give her son a positive model to follow?"

Brian smiled as he looked over at the handsome teen. "Partially. But it's mostly because she thinks of me as one of her kids, or maybe more like a younger brother. She just wants me to find Mr. Right."

"And have you?" Alrick watched him carefully as Brian's gaze met his.

"Maybe."

Alrick grinned as Brian took refuge in another piece of pizza. "I'm sorry that I didn't mention that I had been in the service. It was a long time ago and didn't seem important."

Brian shrugged. "Don't sweat it. They say a few secrets make for better sex, right?"

Alrick stared at him for a long moment until his brain was able to accept that such a provocative statement had come out of his bashful lover's mouth.

"Mmmph!" Brian tried unsuccessfully to talk around a mouthful of pizza and Alrick's tongue.

"Eww, gross!"

The cozy den filled with laughter as Sam voiced his opinion about such icky adult shenanigans.

Three boxes of pizza and two dozen rounds of Pictionary later, Brian and Alrick said their goodnights to a chorus of loud "boos" from Sam and lingering, disappointed glances from Jonathan. Todd waved as he washed down yet another slice with a swig of pop.

"Alrick, I hope you know you're welcome back at any time." Angela smiled up at him as she walked them to the door.

"In other words, you had better be here for the next pizza night. Right, Angie?"

Angela tiptoed up to press a kiss to Brian's cheek. "Such a smart boy," she said indulgently, giving his face a gentle pat. Both men laughed. Alrick bent his head to return the gesture on Brian's behalf. He just smiled when the flustered woman pressed her hand to her cheek. "Oh, you are a troublemaker, aren't you? Go on, then, get out of here." Brian sent her a mock glare when she smacked Alrick on his ass. She just blinked at him innocently. "What? It was staring me in the face. What was I supposed to do?"

They were still laughing over Angela's outrageousness when they pulled up in front of Brian's apartment building. "I really do like your partner. I think she would get along well with my sister. They both seem to have no problem exercising absolute authority over the men in their lives and making them love every minute of it."

Brian chuckled. "Yeah, that sounds about right." He put his hand on the door handle but just sat there looking out of the window and chewing on his lower lip. His head was tilted up, and Alrick figured he was looking toward his own window. He was about to ask if something was wrong when Brian spoke.

"Do you want to come up?"

Did he even need to ask? Brian's apartment remained the one place he hadn't shared with Alrick, and Alrick wanted desperately to breach that final threshold of Brian's existence. If he really was contemplating the insane things that were scrambling around in his brain, then he wanted to know everything about the man for whom he was willing to risk his freedom and possibly his very life.

"Yes, I would," he answered simply.

Brian turned slightly, allowing Alrick to only catch a glimpse of his face in profile. "Then come on."

BRIAN LOOKED around his apartment as he closed the door behind them, trying to see it with fresh eyes. Not that it helped the view. It was small, dingy, and decidedly lacking in the elegant appointments of Alrick's hotel room. In other words, it was perfect for a single man living on a cop's salary.

"Brian, I'm not a bat."

"I swear, what is it with you and lights?" Brian's grumble was barely audible, yet somehow Alrick heard him. He made his way carefully to the lamp at the far side of his living room as Alrick chuckled. "Bats have good hearing, so you definitely qualify."

"It's just that I pay close attention to everything that you say."

A second after the lamp came on, Brian was pulled backward into a warm embrace. Clearly Alrick could see perfectly well in the dark if he'd navigated the disaster area that was Brian's living room without mishap. Books and old magazines, a couple of sets of neglected dumbbells, and every other manner of odds and ends were strewn about. Angela complained loudly every time she came over, threatening to break in and clean when he wasn't around. He'd managed to hold her off thus far by telling her that everything was carefully organized in a manner known only to him, so she had better not touch a thing.

"I like your apartment. It's cozy."

"Bullshit. It's a dump."

Alrick spun him around. "But it's your dump. Now, where's your bedroom?" he asked in between kissing Brian senseless. Pointing generally in the right direction, Brian had to depend on his memory of the layout of his apartment as they made their way without coming up for air.

"Oomph."

Brian fell hard on the mattress. He barely had time to recover his breath from Alrick landing on top of him before his mouth was more intriguingly occupied with other things besides breathing. Alrick tugged busily at his clothing, the offending pieces flying through the air, draping haphazardly on whatever surface was nearby. Blindly, Brian returned the favor, greedily seeking out the tactile enticement of Alrick's warm skin. He tried to push Alrick away for a moment, the attempt faltering as firm lips attacked his throat.

"Wait a sec."

"And why would I want to do that?"

Brian shivered as the flat of a hot, wet tongue ran over the mark on his throat that Alrick had made earlier during their gymnastics in the boat. It was still sensitive, and he felt the lick all the way down to his toes. "'Cause I'd rather stop now and grab lube than have to worry about it later."

"Hmmm, good point." Alrick rolled away and watched Brian scoot off the bed and head toward the bathroom. Brian felt his gaze on his ass like a physical touch. "It's too bad the other bottle got lost in the lake."

"Dumped in the lake, you mean. And whose fault was that?" Brian returned holding a bottle of body oil. The bedside lamp had been turned on, and he glared at the man who was lying propped up on one hand, smiling at him.

"And you call me prepared?"

Brian tossed the bottle onto the bed, missing Alrick's grinning face by inches. He flopped down after it and lowered his head to take Alrick's bottom lip between his teeth. "Don't think I make a habit of bringing guys into my room. See these sheets? I haven't changed 'em for a month. Anyway, Angie gave me the oil for my birthday as a gag."

He watched as Alrick turned his head to sniff at the bed. "Smells like you. I like it."

"You're such a perv."

Brian's grousing was cut short by the tongue that seemed intent on reaching the back of his throat. It was cool in the apartment because he'd left the heat off while he was gone, but he instantly broke out in a sweat. Alrick was like the sun, burning him with a touch. Brian had always found him unbearably sexy, but somehow this felt different, like he could explode just from the large hands caressing his sides and the lips devouring his own. Everything felt more intense having Alrick there in his own space.

"Alrick," he whimpered, panting into his mouth as he clung to his broad shoulders.

"Shhh, I've got you."

Brian tried to calm down, to regain some control before he embarrassed himself. With a low growl, he pushed Alrick over on his back. Bracing on his elbows, he tried out a wicked grin just to see if he could pull it off. "You do, do you?"

Alrick just smiled and casually folded his hands behind his head.

Apparently not. Brian rolled his eyes, annoyed with Alrick for seeing through his attempt to play the vamp and at himself for being so utterly vanilla. Deciding just to go with the direct approach, he leaned down and took Alrick's nipple between his teeth. *Better*, he thought as he was rewarded with a soft hiss. Brian looked up, capturing the darkened blue eyes that were intently following his every move. He held Alrick's gaze as he licked his way down Alrick's incredible stomach. "You have got to tell me how to get abs like this."

Alrick's chuckle turned into a groan when Brian's tongue delved into his navel. The pillow beneath his head dented as his fingers dug into it. "Hmmm, I don't know. I rather like you a bit soft. *Ow!*" Alrick laughed when Brian bit at his hip bone in retaliation for his teasing. The small pain was quickly forgotten in the next moment when his hard cock disappeared deep into unbelievably wet heat.

Tears stung Brian's eyes as he took Alrick in as far as he could, but Alrick's taste was just too amazing to worry about a little thing like breathing. The broad head tickled against the back of his throat, and Brian moaned as he felt his own cock leak in reaction.

"*Ja, sauge mich!* Suck me!"

Long fingers tangled in Brian's curls, tugging at them fretfully as he slid slowly up the impressive length, carefully scraping his teeth along the pulsing flesh. He looked up the span of Alrick's body, his heart skipping a beat at the incredible sight. Alrick's head was flung back, exposing cords of sinew and muscle that stood out from his neck in sharp relief. His massive chest heaved as he panted, struggling not to give in to Brian's seduction.

Brian licked at the weeping tip of Alrick's thick cock, the steady dribble matching the fluid dripping from his own aching length. The flavor was as intoxicating as the musk that rose from Alrick's body in an unmistakable signal of his excitement. But as much as he wanted to swallow everything Alrick was willing to give him, there was another part of him that was even hungrier. One hand scrambling for the bottle of oil, Brian licked up Alrick's torso in one long swipe, not stopping until his tongue reached the curve of Alrick's strong chin.

Alrick watched him closely, his blue eyes shadowed with lust. Brian stared down at Alrick in wonder as he slathered the fragrant oil into the palm of his hand. His body clenched in reaction when Alrick's gaze darkened even further as he worked the thick shaft pressing against his stomach with long, firm strokes.

Alrick lifted his head from the pillow and nipped at Brian's chin. "Tell me what you want," he growled.

The thickly accented purr poured over Brian's ears like hot, sweet chocolate. "Fuck," he hissed as his cock throbbed impatiently.

"Hmmm?"

Brian moaned as Alrick swirled his tongue inside the shell of his ear. And to think he'd always hated that before. He didn't bother trying to answer, realizing there was no way he'd be able to form a coherent sentence. Instead, he let his body speak for him. Sitting up, he positioned himself over the column of flesh rising up from the nest of hair covering Alrick's groin. Locking his gaze with piercing blue, he slowly eased downward, impaling himself inch by glorious, excruciating inch.

"*Scheiße*! Condom?"

"Unghh! Don't want it." Brian shook his head, sweat flinging from his soaked hair. He knew he was being unforgivably careless, but hell, if he was willing to trust Alrick enough to let him into his bed, then he figured he was willing to risk a disease or two. Besides, if Alrick wasn't the healthiest specimen of manhood he'd ever laid eyes on, he didn't know what was!

"I swear to you. I'm safe."

"Sure, whatever. Just keep talking." Brian lifted up slowly, the friction against his tender entrance burning like delicious fire. "Ahhh, yeah!" His head fell back helplessly as he lowered back down. Alrick's fingers dug bruisingly into his hips, not trying to direct his movements but betraying Alrick's need to maintain another point of connection between them. Brian spread his hands wide against Alrick's chest, feeling the heavy thud of the heart beating beneath his palms.

"You like my voice?"

Brian's head jerked as he nodded. "Hell yeah." He could feel Alrick's groaning laugh beneath his hands, between his thighs, and in the thick, hot flesh he was riding. He sped up, needing more of that perfect friction.

"*Warum*, hmmm?" Alrick growled as he squeezed the soft flesh of Brian's ass. "Why do you like it?"

"Shit, I don't know!" Brian whimpered. "I just do." He curled his fingers, kneading fretfully at Alrick's smooth, toned pecs. Alrick's hips surged upward to meet his downward momentum, and Brian pressed hard into the tempting firmness to keep his balance. Large hands traced up the front of his torso, making him moan as clever fingers plucked at his nipples like they were the strings of an instrument.

"Then shall I tell you how beautiful you are?"

Brian couldn't believe how embarrassed the question made him. If he hadn't already been flushed from being fucked so brilliantly, he knew he would have done so then. Still, he found himself nodding in response.

"And shall I tell you how wonderful I think you are?"

"Idiot." Unable to withstand Alrick's scrutiny another second, Brian slumped forward, pressing his chest against Alrick's as he buried his burning face in the crook of his neck. Alrick bent his knees, bracing his feet against the bed to better maintain the intimate connection. The change in angle caused his next thrust to hit a spot that made Brian's eyes cross. "Nnng, close," he breathed.

The fingers that slid through his hair to massage his scalp didn't help one damn bit. Trapped between their stomachs, his cock twitched eagerly as the resulting friction milked even more fluid from the swollen tip. He bit into the bold design of Alrick's tattoo as he started to lose it.

"And shall I tell you how much I love you?"

The whisper was so soft as to be barely audible, but the words seemed to echo endlessly in his head, tipping him over the edge into a maelstrom of blinding white. Brian shouted Alrick's name as he released his passion, an answering surge of delicious heat filling him as Alrick groaned deeply beneath him. Long minutes passed before the light faded away, leaving only the weak glow of the shaded lamp next to the bed and the harsh rasp of their breathing.

Brian felt like he'd been put through the spin cycle, but his heart was impossibly light. The cooling sweat on his skin tickled, and he was stuck to the man below him by perspiration and the tackiness of his drying come. The softening flesh filling his ass slipped out along with an unpleasant seep of wetness. Yet, he was thoroughly convinced that, if he never moved from that spot, he would die a happy man. Eyes closed, he enjoyed the lingering tingles that flitted over his skin even as his brain slowly succumbed to exhaustion. He smiled as strong arms wrapped around him and tried to pull him even closer.

"You could be the prince," Brian mumbled. Warm lips pressed gently against his forehead.

"Hmmm?"

"Just this weird dream I keep having. Two guys who like to screw like bunnies in my head almost every night."

Alrick's chest vibrated with a low chuckle. "Sounds kinky."

Brian smiled. "You'd think, but that's just it. After they finish, they always end up cuddling. Kinda pathetic for a wet dream, huh?"

"You said one of them is a prince?"

Forcing his eyes open, Brian looked up at Alrick's thoughtful tone. "Yeah, at least I get points for creativity." He licked and kissed the red mark his teeth had left in Alrick's shoulder. "What about it?"

"I've had a similar dream."

Brian stared at him in surprise. "What, about a prince? No shit. So, tell me about it."

"It is set a long time ago. In ancient—"

"Egypt?"

They stared at each other in silence, the only sound coming from the cars passing down the street outside of the bedroom window. Brian shivered like someone had just walked over his grave. Then, a second later, he felt really stupid. The corner of his mouth lifted in a wry grin.

"Right. Like we've been having the same dream." He pressed his lips hard against Alrick's. "I think too much sex has addled our brains. Maybe we should try celibacy for a while? What do you think?" Brian yelped as he found himself on his back with six-foot-two of incredulous German looming over him.

"I think that is a terrible idea. The worst idea I have ever heard."

They kissed with tired enthusiasm for a few minutes before giving up the ghost. Brian snickered as Alrick's blond head dropped heavily against his chest.

"Sleep now. Sex later."

"*Ja*. Now that is a good idea."

Brian toyed absently with Alrick's damp hair. "So are you going to tell me what *Liebling* means?"

Alrick's lips curved against his skin. Brian looked up as Alrick lifted his head so he could gaze into Brian's eyes. He shivered as vibrant blue answered wordlessly. Even if it didn't precisely mean "love," the sentiment was crystal clear.

"You're such a sap."

Alrick grinned. "So it would seem."

"I love you too," Brian whispered, filling the silence that had come over them as they gazed into each other's eyes. He was surprised how easy it had been after all his worrying. Large hands gently framed his face, and a surge of warmth spread out from his chest as firm lips pressed a light kiss against his forehead.

"PA'SHERI, DO not be afraid."

"But, Mery, she will take you from me."

The man pulled the smaller form to his chest, wrapping him in an unbreakable embrace. "It matters not what trials the gods give us. We will always be together."

"Until the ending of the world."

CHAPTER 20

BRIAN HELD up a manila file, waving it at his partner as she made her way to her desk. "Morning. I hope you enjoyed your day off. This came in shortly before I clocked out last night."

"What is it?" Angela hung up her coat and stored her purse in the bottom drawer of her desk.

"Three bodies were found at an old abandoned warehouse in the industrial district."

"Since we're involved, I'm guessing it wasn't some crack party gone horribly wrong."

"Tony Conti and two of his associates."

Angela's jaw dropped as she blinked at him in shock. "Holy shit. The Cosmino money man?"

"One and the same."

"So it was another hit?"

"Yep. They found our sniper's signature at the scene. Three bullets, one for each victim. Cause of death was a single head wound. Ballistics is checking the bullets to see if they can match them to the other hits, but it's a safe bet that they were all fired from that Arctic Warfare rifle."

"Speaking of which," Angela said, "I had some luck with my research while you were gone. I thought it could wait until today. No reason to ruin your date."

"Many thanks," Brian chuckled.

Angela unlocked her file drawer and took out a folder. She pulled out a couple of sheets of paper and held them out to Brian. "The Arctic Warfare is pretty popular with both military and militia outfits, legit and otherwise, and it's the particular favorite of sharpshooters in the German Army."

Brian looked up from the Internet printouts she had given him. "The German Army? If what Alrick said about military service being compulsory is true, then, what? We also have to start with the entire adult male population of Germany? Christ."

"At least the ones who are really good shots, and that's if it wasn't someone from one of those other groups that use it. Really, it could be anyone."

Brian sighed heavily. "So, then, this doesn't help us a whole heck of a lot, does it?"

Angela got up from her desk and patted him on the shoulder as she walked past him. "I'm going to grab a bagel and some coffee. Want anything?"

He held up his half-empty mug. "I'm good." After taking a sip, he wished he'd taken her up on her offer. Puckering at the bitter, lukewarm liquid, Brian skimmed over the printouts.

It was fortunate for his computer keyboard that he'd been holding his mug only a few inches above his desk, because when it slipped from his suddenly nerveless hand, only a little coffee splashed out. The shallowness of his breath was amplified in his head even over the sudden ringing in his ears as everything seemed to go out of focus except for one thing.

The printout featured a colored image of a silver, braided lanyard with a medal hanging from one end, the type of decoration that might be worn on the blazer of a full dress military uniform. He'd never seen it on a medallion like that, but the symbol cast onto the bronzed surface was hauntingly familiar. Brian stared at it until the image seemed to burn itself into his brain. He grew dizzy, as though all the blood had drained away from his body. Running a hand over his face, he could feel the beads of sweat that had formed on his suddenly clammy skin.

He was afraid to look at the description that was written next to the picture in neat, featureless typeface, but he knew he had to. It was his job to catch the bad guys. To find out everything he could until the case was solved. It wasn't as if he could just hide from the truth, no matter how much his stomach roiled in protest.

Schützenschnur: decoration for weapons proficiency for enlisted soldiers.

"Oh my God."

"Brian? What the heck is wrong with you, sweetie? You look like you've seen a ghost." Angela's expression was full of concern as she took in his sweaty appearance.

"I think I ate something I shouldn't have this morning." His chair clattered back as he surged to his feet.

"Brian!"

He ignored her and everyone else as he rushed to the men's room. The door was opening as he reached it, and he slammed into the smaller figure that was coming out.

"Hey, watch it, Macon!" Matt Roddy's cross face screwed up unpleasantly as Brian almost knocked him to the ground. "Asshole," he mumbled when Brian didn't even pause to mumble an apology.

Brian made it to an empty stall just seconds before his breakfast forced its way out. He heaved uncontrollably, the stench making his eyes water and triggering his gag reflex in a vicious cycle. Even after nothing was left, he dry-heaved until he thought his stomach would turn inside out. When it finally stopped, he hit the flush button and sank weakly to the tiled floor as his legs gave out. A knock rattled the stall door, and he shoved a hand against it to keep it closed.

"Hey, man, you okay?"

"Yeah. Thanks, Brad," he said to the other detective. "I just ate something that didn't agree with me."

Brad chuckled. "Gotta watch those food carts, man. Convenient don't necessarily mean smart."

Once he was safely alone, Brian held his head in his hands, rocking back and forth slowly on the floor as he tried to reason away what he had seen. Surely there were other German sharpshooters who'd served in the Army, and it was entirely possible that one of them had been hired to come to the city and kill mobsters.

Brian groaned, shaking his head at his pathetic attempt at denial. It fit too damn well, how he'd just seemed to appear soon after the murders began, how he was always out of touch at times that matched the ETDs of the bodies. It couldn't just be some crazy coincidence.

But how could it be true? It didn't make any sense! The memory of his touch still lingered—the tender affection in his gaze, the soft press of his full lips. It clung to Brian's skin, comforting only a few minutes ago, but now mocking him like some cruel joke. Only he wasn't laughing. He wanted to tear his skin off if doing so would destroy the millions of fleeting recollections that were whirling around in his head like some demented carnival ride.

The printout lying innocently on his desk screamed at him from several rooms away. The image of the symbol on the medal blazed clearly behind his closed lids even through the tears that seeped out from beneath his lashes. The proud profile of the eagle, wings outstretched as it hovered over a wreath of leaves.

It was a perfect match for Alrick's tattoo.

"TIYE, GIVE me the dagger." Rahotep flinched as Tiye's vacant eyes stared past him. "Tiye, please—"

"He was my only brother, and he was no traitor."

"FEELING ANY better?"

"Yeah. Whatever it was, I think I got it out of my system."

If only that were true. After dragging his body off the bathroom floor, Brian had forcibly pulled himself together. Water splashed onto his face washed away the sweat, although one look in the mirror told him it hadn't done a thing for his pallor. Trying to put on a brave face, he'd returned to his desk to reassure Angela. Of course, she hadn't been fooled one little bit.

"I don't know, Brian. You look like shit."

"Thanks a lot. I thought you were supposed to humor the sick." He grabbed a glass of water on his way back to his desk and took a deep swig, both the rinse out his mouth and to deflect her attention.

"Are you really sick? You seemed fine until you were looking at that stuff I found on the Internet. I didn't have a chance to look at it too closely. What the heck did it say?"

"Macon! Lovell! In my office."

Brian didn't think Captain Preston's harridan tone had ever sounded so welcome. Angela continued to eye him with skepticism as they answered her summons.

"I know you got that ballistics report before you both decided your beauty sleep was more important than work. So you'd better have something earth-shatteringly informative to tell me."

Neither detective bothered to mention that their vacations had been their first days off in over six months. The captain was in fine form, sitting in her chair in her characteristic "queen" pose. She was wearing some Dolce Prada whatsit ensemble that probably cost more than either of them made in a year. Her dark hair was artfully tousled to look like she'd just gotten out of bed, a style that had probably taken hours to achieve, but her brown eyes were sharp and looked utterly unwilling to accept any bullshit.

"Ballistics IDed the weapon as an Arctic Warfare sniper rifle," Angela explained.

"And what does that tell us?"

"Nothing much, I'm afraid. We know our shooter might be ex-German Army, but then again, he could be with any number of paramilitary groups. Apparently, the Arctic Warfare is very popular with marksmen all over the world."

The captain eyed Angela's practical pantsuit with distaste. Brian was concentrating on keeping his stomach in line when her gaze skewered him where he stood. "What about you, Macon? Have anything to add to your partner's lackluster report?"

Brian opened his mouth to answer when something in her eyes made the words stick in his throat. He suddenly got the sense that she could see through him, right down to his bones. It was as if she knew he'd possibly discovered who the sniper was, as if she knew it was the man he'd been sleeping with for the past few weeks. God, the very thought nearly made him sick all over again.

Get a grip, he scolded himself. The captain might be a very perceptive woman, but she wasn't a freaking mind reader. He took a deep breath. "No, ma'am. I don't have anything else at this time. We're hoping the Conti hit will provide more information."

You're lying. You know who it is, but you can't bring yourself to admit it.

Brian shivered as a chill ran down his spine. If he didn't know any better, he could have sworn he'd heard her voice in his head, but when he looked at the captain, she was glaring at Angela in annoyance. Squeezing his hands into fists, Brian tried to convince himself he wasn't going crazy, he was just having a really bad day.

"That's just fucking perfect." The captain's lips pursed into an attractive "O" as she let out a gusty breath. "I'm sure the commissioner will be thrilled at how unconcerned you are with not being any closer to solving this case than you were a month ago." She gritted her teeth before leaning back in her chair and gazing at them from beneath her lashes. "So, what's your next move, since forensics seemed to be a bust?"

"Brian and I talked earlier about leaning on Giovanni Rivella and seeing what dripped out of his oily hide. It's pretty clear that whatever's going on, the Milanos are behind it, so he's probably our best bet at this point."

"Fine. Go. And if he gives you any lip, threaten to haul him in on unpaid traffic tickets." Preston laughed shrilly. "I'm sure that sleazy bastard has a few floating around in the database."

"For once, I actually agree with her," Angela murmured as she led the way out of the captain's office. "See any flying pigs around?" Brian saw her glance at him out of the corner of his eye when he didn't respond to her joke, and he forced a smile trying to ward off any suspicion on her part. He figured he'd done a crap job of it when she frowned at him, but fortunately, she didn't say anything about his mood as they gathered their coats and headed to the parking lot. He was grateful when she took the wheel of their unmarked car without his asking.

"You sure you're up for this, sweetie?" Angela asked once they were sitting in their unmarked car outside of Rivella's apartment. "Gio will keep 'til tomorrow if you want to go home."

Brian looked up to the top story of the building, annoyed that the little twerp was living the high life in an expensive penthouse while he had to content himself with his tiny apartment.

His brain instinctively shied away from thoughts of his place. The shock was still too fresh. Gripping the car door handle, Brian fought to suppress the perverse stirrings of his body the mere thought of Alrick caused even as his stomach flipped in denial. The more he pondered his recent discovery, the more difficult it became to wrap his mind around the concept that the hands he'd seen create such beautiful music, the hands that had touched him so gently, were the same hands that had murdered half a dozen people.

Maybe he'd remembered Alrick's tattoo wrongly and what he thought was a perfect match was nothing more than a passing resemblance. But even as he tried to convince himself of his mistake, he knew that he had an incredible eye for detail. He had to with this job. If the tattoo was identical to badges given to enlisted sharpshooters, it was highly unlikely that someone who had only served the compulsory time period would be eligible for one. And if Alrick had lied about that, what else had he lied about?

Brian's mind spun from one conclusion to another until he wanted to rip his head apart. Ignorance had to be preferable to this horrible uncertainty.

"Brian? Okay, that's it. I'm taking you home."

"No, Angie. I'm sorry. Just thinking about what we should say to Gio."

Angela stared at him closely for a long moment, but just as he began to sweat beneath her scrutiny, she looked away, turning her gaze upward to the penthouse. "No idea. I guess we can't just knock on his door and tell him that we know he's connected to the murders, can we?"

"WE KNOW you're connected to these Cosmino murders, Rivella. It would be real convenient for you and your little gaggle of pals if the Milanos were to become the only mob in town."

"We're this close to getting a warrant for your arrest, and if you want to be in a position to cut a deal with us, this is your chance to start talking."

A feral grin spread across Gio's face as he looked at the two flat-foots standing in his foyer. The woman was a bit long in the tooth, but it was obvious she'd been a looker in her day. The man, however, looked like he had a not inconsiderable stick jammed somewhere that didn't see a lot of sunlight. Gio leaned against the door jamb, crossing one foot over the other as he got comfortable, ready to appreciate the show that had landed on his doorstep.

"Are you serious? I mean, come on, Detectives, I'm not some jag-off just off the boat. If you really had something to threaten me with, you wouldn't be appealing to my better nature. So why don't you just toddle on back to your little precinct instead of bothering helpless civilians, huh?"

"Helpless, my ass, you little shit. No one else has anything to gain from knocking off the Cosminos." The man's jaw was clenched so tightly Gio wondered if it would shatter.

"Well, except for every other law abiding citizen of our fair city who would be more than happy to be rid of them."

The woman glared at him with exasperation. "We know your uncle or one of his lieutenants hired the shooter."

"And right now," the man interrupted, "we're far more interested in the gunman than we are in your small-time ass. Just give us a name, something that we can use, and we'll be on our way."

Gio sighed heavily, trying to radiate as much false sympathy as he could muster while stifling a laugh. "I really am sorry, Detectives, but I've got nothing for you." He stepped forward and slapped a hand on the male cop's shoulder. Gio was a little irritated that the guy was a good three inches taller than him, but the frustration on the man's face helped to soothe his battered ego. "But I'll tell you what, next time I feel like dabbling in police work, I'll be sure to call you first." He winked at the female cop and slammed the door in their faces.

Gio laughed as he heard the detectives make their way back to the elevator, and his amusement at the pathetic encounter lasted well into the evening. Thinking of the reason the cops had come to visit, however, tempered his enjoyment of the memory somewhat. It was time for the Death Angel to make his next hit. Gio was a little pissed, because although it had been almost a week since Tony Conti had his mind expanded all over that warehouse floor, the creepy German was nowhere to be found. Gio had left messages for him in all the places he'd been instructed to use when he wanted to make contact. So far he hadn't heard anything back. Maybe he'd been working the guy too hard, and hell, everyone needed a vacation. Or maybe he was holed up with some little honey getting his rocks off.

Titillating thoughts about who the German might be screwing were interrupted by the sound of the doorbell. Heading toward his front door, Gio glanced at his watch and wondered who was coming to see him at ten thirty at night. The disgruntled putdown he'd prepared died when he opened the door. It was another cop, but a sexier piece of ass he'd never laid eyes on.

"Captain Preston." He grinned at the woman standing in his doorway. "To what do I owe the pleasure?"

Hayley swept past him without a word, her long legs easily eating up the distance from the front door to his bedroom. Gio closed the front door and turned to watch her walk. She was wearing a thigh-length fur jacket and a pair of red stilettos. When the jacket suddenly hit the floor, his jaw tried to follow. She was wearing only a scrap of black lace that hid nothing, matching garters, and fishnet stockings. Her dark eyes burned right through his clothes, instantly setting his crotch on fire. Hair flaring in a wide arc, she turned and disappeared into the room.

GIO WAS halfway undressed by the time he joined her. Hayley was waiting for him on his bed, and he fell on her with all the enthusiasm and grace of a rutting dog. She forced herself to moan when he latched onto her neck with a sloppy kiss. The sex was just as uninspired. After he finally rolled off her, she turned on her side to look at him as he lay on his back, basking in self-congratulations for his imagined prowess.

"I understand you had a couple of visitors earlier today." She drew her nails over his chest, watching idly as red marks rose in their wake. Gio groaned, shivering at the slight hint of pain.

"Yeah, two of your murder police by the looks of 'em. Heh. What a great name."

"I'm glad you approve. What did they want?"

Gio hissed when she scored a nail over his nipple. "Evil bitch."

"Best to remember that, lover. Now answer my question."

"They were just sniffing around for information about my project. Stupid bastards. Like I'd tell them anything."

Hayley smiled. "Oh, believe me, one of them already knows everything."

Gio sat straight up, the bedsheet falling back to reveal the dark patch of hair that began a couple of inches below his navel. He stared down at her in horror. "What the fuck do you mean by that?"

"Shhh, relax." Hayley knelt up and pushed him back down to the bed none too gently. She tossed the sheet away and straddled his naked hips. His cock stiffened immediately, but she didn't let him penetrate her. "It's not you he's after."

"Who, that depressed looking son of a bitch? He said the cops are mainly looking for the hit man. Is that true?"

"For him it is. Trust me, lover, he couldn't care less about you. There's only one man he wants."

"I don't get it. Why would he be more interested in the shooter than in the one who hired him? I thought you guys were always going for the big score, not trying to net the guppies."

Hayley merely smiled at his confused expression, letting his atrocious metaphor go without comment. She lowered her head and kissed him, her hair falling around them like a curtain as she explored his mouth with her tongue. She would rather miss this when he was dead. He might be an obnoxious twerp, but he was a decent kisser.

Gio squinted up at her when she let him up for air. "I don't get you, babe. Why betray your own people by fucking around with me?"

Surprised at the insight his question showed, Hayley considered how to answer. "Because there's something more important to me than my career."

"And what would that be?"

On a whim, she made a decision. "Shall I tell you a bedtime story?"

"What the fuck are you talking about? Ouch!" Gio pressed his fingers to his lips after she bit him, growling in annoyance even after he realized that she hadn't broken the skin.

"Hush. Pay attention and there might be a reward at the end." Hayley smiled wryly as he shut up. "Once upon a time there was a foolish girl who met a handsome prince."

"And they fell in love and lived happily ever after? I've heard it before." Gio's grin lasted only for a second when she scowled down at him at the interruption.

"No. The girl wanted power, and the prince was the way to get it. She gave up her home and even her name in pursuit of her dream. But on the night of her wedding, she discovered that her prince loved another. Her heart burning with rage and thwarted ambition, the girl struck a foolish bargain with an evil god. She demanded that he curse the lovers and destroy them. The god warned her that fate herself had joined them, but the arrogant girl vowed she would take it upon herself to keep them apart. And so the god set her on the lovers' heels throughout eternity like a hound on the scent of blood. Time after time, destiny brings their souls together, and the girl is doomed to follow them, never living her own life as she seeks to destroy theirs.

"Do you feel sorry for this poor girl, Gio?"

"Hell no. She sounds like a dumb bitch."

Anger flashed through Hayley, but it was gone in an instant. Unable to deny the truth of his crude assessment, she chuckled before pressing a far gentler kiss to Gio's lips. "Perhaps. But since she's stuck with the deal she made, she'll just have to make the best of it, right?"

Gio didn't bother asking her what she was talking about, most likely because she'd wrapped her hand around his dick and was working it with long, firm strokes. Raising herself back up, she sank down on him and let him fill her.

"If I asked you to do something for me, Gio, would you do it?"

"Yeah, baby. Ughh, whatever you want."

"Even if it's dangerous?" She squeezed her inner muscles, staring down at him as his eyes rolled back into his head.

"Fuck! Yeah, anything."

"Good boy, Gio."

His response was lost in the deep groan that rumbled from his throat. For a little while, Hayley allowed herself to pretend that it really was just a stupid story about a stupid girl. She knew it would become real soon enough.

SHE'S NOT coming out.

Matt sat outside Giovanni Rivella's apartment, looking up at the softly lit window of his penthouse. It wasn't the first time he'd followed Hayley. When he'd tailed her home one night after they'd both pulled a late shift at the station, he told himself he did it out of curiosity. The second time, he'd been forced to admit he was obsessed with the beautiful, untouchable woman who held so much power over him. Suspension was the least he'd get if anyone ever found out that he was stalking his superior officer. He'd ignored the risk, having convinced himself that he was in love with her, but now, he didn't know what to think.

"What's going on, Captain? What in the hell are you doing here?"

He waited for another hour, but there was still no sign of her. Matt finally started his car and pulled away from the curb, uncertainty a hard lump in his gut.

CHAPTER 21

"*HALLO?*"

"Rosa? *Ich bin's.* It's me."

"*Bruder*? I can barely hear you. This connection is awful."

Alrick smothered a laugh. "Are you in the cellar?"

"*Ja.* How did you know?"

"Maybe if you go upstairs, the connection will clear up." He heard the dull clop of feet on old wooden stairs. The faint static that had been on the line disappeared.

"Okay, how about now?"

"Much better. How are Heinz and little Gerry?" The line remained silent for a long moment. He sighed. "Rosa—"

"Another deposit arrived in our bank account, Alrick. It was very large."

"I'm glad it reached you safely. Little Gerry begins school soon, *ja*? I'm sure he'll need new clothes and supplies."

"*Verdammt*, Alrick! Enough of this. To be able to send this much money, *Bruder*, what are you doing? And don't tell me that you're just working for that magazine. No writer makes so much!"

Alrick clenched his jaw. He'd been floating ever since leaving Brian's apartment the other morning. His shy beauty had finally admitted that he loved him, and all he'd wanted was to share his good fortune with the other person he loved most in this world. But his sister was no fool. "Rosa, please. I'm just trying to help you so you don't have to work so hard. I don't want you to worry about father's debt. Just leave that to me, *Schwesterlein.*" He heard a muffled sniff as though she was trying to hide the fact that she was crying.

"You haven't called me 'little sister' in years. Oh, Alrick, every time you send me money like this I'm afraid to death that it is covered in sin."

Alrick's blood ran cold. "What do you mean, Rosa?"

"A man came to see me. A Russian named Viktor Privalov."

The phone creaked from the force of his grip as he leapt to his feet. "Are you all right, Rosa? He didn't hurt you or Heinz?" That *Scheisskerl* had actually had the nerve to speak to Rosa in person? The mere thought of his sister being in the same room with that bastard made him want to break something, preferably Privalov's head. "Or… *mein Gott*, is Gerry okay?"

"We're fine, Alrick, but what that man said about you, about what people pay you to do…."

The bombshell stopped Alrick in the midst of his furious pacing. He sank back down onto the sofa with a heavy thud.

"He told you?"

Rosa voice was thick with tears. "He said maybe I should consider helping you clear father's debt by—"

The lunch he'd recently eaten threatened to abandon him as bile rose into his throat. "No, Rosa! I can deal with this. Promise me you'll stay away from him. You don't need to get involved."

"I would never do as he suggested, Alrick. But you—"

"Rosa, please listen to me."

"*Nein*, just tell me that it isn't true." Her sobs were so heavy he could barely understand her. "Please, tell me that he was lying to me!"

His silence was damning. Only moments ago, his heart had been light as air. Now it sank like a stone.

"Alrick, you are an artist! You were meant to spend your life filling the world with beautiful music. But you have thrown it all away to, what, become a killer?" Her pained whisper cut through him like a knife. "What have you done?"

"Brian told me he loves me, Rosa." He wasn't sure why he felt compelled to tell her that when he had just broken her heart.

Not even sharing such wonderful news could repair the damaged he'd done.

Rosamunde didn't speak for a long time. Alrick thought she might ridicule him for thinking of something so trivial when their family was in danger of being torn apart. He didn't know how things would ever be the same between them. The closeness that had sustained them since childhood suddenly seemed unbearably fragile. How could she ever forgive him for becoming a monster?

"You love him too, *ja*?"

Her tone was calm, and a painful laugh burst from him at the question. He should have known better than to underestimate her. She was fiercely protective of those she cared about, and nothing he could do, no matter how terrible, would ever change that. Tears stung his eyes and burned his throat as he nodded. Realizing she couldn't see him, he cleared his throat so he could speak.

"I do."

"Then, Alrick, if you have truly given your heart to this man, you must turn yourself in, for his sake if not your own." Her voice cracked, catching in a little sob as she inhaled. "You must find yourself again, *Bruder*, find who you truly are. I know this isn't you. I love you, Alrick, but this cannot go on."

"I know, Rosa." A tear ran down his cheek unchecked. "Heaven help me, I know."

ANGELA SAT at her desk the next morning, tapping a pencil against her lips as she glanced over the information she'd pulled about the Arctic Warfare. She still couldn't figure out what had set Brian off so badly. That lame story he'd given her about eating something bad? No way was she buying that. She'd seen her partner go plate for plate with her husband and the bottomless pits that were her sons. No, there was something she was missing.

After they'd returned from their useless visit to Gio's, she'd sent Brian home to recover from whatever it was that had him looking like death warmed over. He'd promised to come in today, though. Angela glanced at the clock on her computer. It was only eight thirty, but Brian was already late. She stared at her phone for five minutes before giving in to the urge to call him. Her phone rang as she was reaching for it.

"Detective Lovell."

"Angie, it's me."

"You'd better be walking up the stairs, buddy. It's not polite to keep a lady waiting." She expected him to come back with some suitably dry response, but the seriousness of his tone surprised her.

"Sorry, Angie. Um, whatever was wrong with me yesterday got worse after I went home. I spent the entire night staring at the bottom of my toilet, if you know what I mean."

"Uh-huh. Okay, I'll cover with Preston for you. But Brian, you'd better be in here tomorrow with a note from your doctor explaining how you were near death, or she's going to have my ass for dessert after she finishes with you."

The line was silent for a long moment before she heard a heavy sigh. "I'll try. Thanks, Angie."

She shook her head as she replaced the receiver. *What in the hell is wrong with that boy?* Maybe he really wasn't feeling well. If that was the case, she hoped he called Alrick over to take care of him. One look at that face was guaranteed to cure any ills. Remembering how cute the two of them had been at pizza night brought a smile to her face.

"Where's your partner, Lovell?"

Angela rolled her eyes. "What's it to you, Roddy?" She almost laughed when he blinked at her in surprise for using his real name.

"I heard you got that report from ballistics the other day."

"Yeah, and?" she prompted when he didn't follow up on his comment.

"Get anything useful from it?"

"Not really. The 'scopes were able to identify the weapon, but as for the shooter, he or she remains, as yet, a complete mystery.

"Oh. Too bad, then."

Angela thought he looked almost disappointed at the news. She couldn't imagine why he would be. It wasn't his case. If anything, she would have thought he'd enjoy crowing over their continued failure. "Was there something else you wanted, Matt?"

"Huh? Oh, no. Better luck next time, I guess."

She shook her head as he wandered away. She hated thinking uncharitably about anyone who wasn't a perp, but she couldn't help herself. "What a weirdo."

IGNORING THE insistent flash of the message light, Brian tossed his cell phone away as he stared at nothing. He was huddled on his sofa, where he'd spent the night to avoid going into his bedroom. All of the lights were off, and the drapes were pulled tight. If he'd been in a reflective frame of mind, he might have realized he was using the darkness to distance himself from Alrick any way he could. Alrick had always wanted to see him in the light, had wanted him completely exposed. Now, all he wanted was to hide away.

Hurt and anger. He felt them both keenly, though he wasn't sure which one featured the most prominently in his muddled emotions. Alrick had looked him straight in the eye and lied to him. With every touch and caress, with every sweet word, he'd lied. Had it all been some elaborate setup? Alrick must have known Brian was a cop even before he'd told him. This whole interlude was probably just a game to him, a thrilling episode of hide-and-seek. Brian didn't want to believe it, but what other explanation was there? Why else would such a fascinating man show interest in someone as unremarkable as him? Doubt piled up on top of humiliation. Brian wanted to hate Alrick for turning his entire life upside down for nothing but his own sick, twisted amusement.

Not that Alrick was the only one to blame. Brian was just as angry at himself. How could he have been such a fool? Hadn't he kept his heart locked away all of these years for this very reason? He of all people knew how dangerous it was to love someone. Everyone he'd ever cared about had either shunned or abandoned him. It figured he'd be betrayed just when he finally allowed himself to feel again.

And the worst part was that this betrayal hurt far worse than his parents' careless neglect or the stupid perfidy that had led to Dennis's death. He'd never loved anyone as much as he loved Alrick. Even now, all he had to do was close his eyes to see those incredible blue eyes and that smile that had so captivated him from the moment they met.

Fury burned but was unable to overcome an even more powerful yearning. Brian was bone tired, but he dared not try to sleep in his bed. Alrick's scent was still there, and Brian didn't trust his body, not when the memory of Alrick's presence was still so fresh. Brian dropped onto the sofa and closed his eyes. Sleep tugged at him, though his racing thoughts refused to let him succumb. He desperately wanted to just ignore everything, to hide from the world in his dark apartment even though brooding was an indulgence he couldn't afford. He still had a job to do.

Opening his eyes suddenly, Brian stared at the tiny shaft of daylight peeking through a pinhole tear in his drapes. That's right. He had a job to do. So what if he'd been having an affair with a killer? Boohoo. Shit happened. But if he wanted to catch him, he would need to learn everything he possibly could about the man who had been fucking his ass and lying to his face.

And just maybe, he would discover that it had all been a terrible mistake. God, he would give anything for that to be true. Even with everything that he suspected, his heart still wasn't ready to give up and let go. That was why he hadn't been forthcoming with Angela. He was still hoping that, by some miracle, he'd jumped to conclusions in thinking that Alrick was the hit man. Brian groaned as his stomach churned against itself, the mere possibility opening up a burning hole in his gut. He hadn't eaten since yesterday, afraid he would just throw it up again.

Fuck, Macon, you won't figure anything out lying here like some pathetic little bitch.

Brian pushed off his couch, pausing a moment to take a deep breath in order to overcome the resulting nausea. After a quick shower to take care of the sweat his nightmares had left behind, he would throw on some clothes and head to the library. He didn't relish the thought of going out in public, but he needed to do some research without the eyes of the department or his partner's caring gaze looking over his shoulder. For the first time, Brian really regretted not owning a computer. It didn't matter; he could find everything he needed at the library.

Brian headed for his bathroom, feeling better now that he had some sort of plan. He pointedly ignored the fact that he never once turned on the lights.

ALRICK STOOD motionless in the cold, dirty vestibule as he waited for the man he was there to meet. The old apartment building was long abandoned and had probably already been condemned. The hallway leading from the front door was shadowed, only a few bulbs still functional among their broken companions. A tiny squeak near the dusty stairwell told him the dwelling wasn't completely free of residents.

Normally, he'd be annoyed at being forced to cool his heels, but today he was grateful for the change of scenery. He couldn't bear spending one more minute in his hotel room with no one but himself for company. After his revealing conversation with his sister the day before, he'd wanted desperately to see Brian. He'd tried Brian's cell phone most of yesterday afternoon and all last night, but he'd been unable to reach him. He would have gone over to Brian's apartment, but he didn't want to seem intrusive. Although their relationship had grown into something special, it was still new and fragile. He didn't want to risk it by being presumptuous, and it wasn't as if he could just walk into the police station and ask his lover out for lunch.

Missing Brian just added another layer to his restless anxiety. The precarious uncertainty of his life had left him feeling off balance. The memory of his sister's tears haunted him still. Rosamunde was right; he couldn't go on like this. Being a killer for hire was destroying him, every pull of the trigger eating away at his soul. The money he made, as necessary as it was, was black with the taint of its source.

As images of his sister's and Brian's beloved faces filled his head, a rush of certainty abruptly settled over him, quieting his mind even as his body tensed at the prospect of what had to be done. It was time to end it, to bury the killer before the man he'd been was gone forever. He would do as Rosa had asked. He would turn himself in and pay for his crimes. Maybe then he could make her smile again. Maybe then he could finally be worthy of Brian's love.

But not right away. Coward that he was, he wanted to enjoy his freedom for just a little while longer, to spend as much time as he possibly could with the man he loved. He wasn't naïve. When Brian found out who he really was, it would be over between them. His lover would haul him away in irons and leave him to rot, which was no more than he deserved. He wasn't ready to give up this dream, not just yet. So for now, he would remain selfish and hold on to Brian for as long as fate allowed.

And that meant doing this one last job for Rivella. Wrapping the identity of *Todesengel* around himself like a blanket of emotionless ice, Alrick prepared to sell his soul one final time. After this was over, he would never again take a life with the skills in which he'd once taken such pride. Every cent he'd earned from Rivella would go to Privalov. It wouldn't cure his debt completely, but it would go a long way toward easing the burden. As for the remainder… somehow, he would find a way.

His first task would be to make the *Todesengel* disappear as though he'd never existed. He wasn't overly concerned about the people who'd hired him in the past. Some of his employers had been criminals like Rivella, but many had been far more respectable and politically connected. They wouldn't want to have any association with him. He didn't usually meet clients face-to-face, Rivella being a rare exception. The mobster had made their meeting in person a prerequisite to forming a contract, and the money had been too good to pass up. Most of the people who hired him could have passed him on the street and either wouldn't know him or would be very motivated to pretend they didn't.

He didn't trust Rivella nearly as much. The mobster would have to be silenced, especially since Alrick planned to spend much of his time in this city in the future. After this last job was completed, he would take out Rivella and the old man who had sometimes accompanied the young mobster to their meetings. What were two more deaths when he was already guilty of so many? It wasn't like anyone would mourn Rivella's passing. Rivella had assured him no one else from the Milanos knew who he was, so no one could possibly connect him to the organization or the assassinations.

One more act of evil and he could try to start his life over, if only for a short while. Being with Brian, even on borrowed time, was worth whatever risk. Once he was simply Alrick Ritter again, he would convince his magazine to speed up their plans to open a branch in the city so he could stay in the country legally. Then he'd send for Rosa and her family so he could watch over them and keep them safe from Privalov. And if he had to kill the bastard and whomever else they sent after him to protect his sister, so be it. He'd do whatever was necessary.

For too long, he'd had no say over his life, but he was a man now. It was high time he took control of his own destiny before he was forced to surrender to the inevitable.

"Come on, you old fart. It's your fault we're late. I told you to check that damn tire before you came to pick me up."

Counting on the shadows to conceal his presence, Alrick watched from his place in the corner of the hallway as Rivella and his henchman finally appeared.

"Sorry, Gio. Maybe we beat him here?"

"No, I am afraid not."

Gio jumped, clearly started by the voice that seemed to float out of thin air. "Shit, man. I swear I'm going to put a bell around your neck."

"I'm a busy man," Alrick said. Rivella and his companion stood beneath an overhead light, and Alrick moved forward just enough that the newcomers could see his silhouette, allowing the darkness of his clothing to blend with the dimness beyond the circle of illumination. "I do not appreciate being kept waiting."

"Yeah, sorry about that. We had some car trouble."

"Your problems are irrelevant." Alrick held out his gloved hand. "I believe you have something for me."

Rivella grinned cockily at his abruptness. He retrieved an envelope from inside his coat and handed it to Alrick. "I like a man who's all about business. Here ya go, your next target, delivery set for tomorrow night." His smile widened until it was all teeth. "I hope you get a kick out of it."

Alrick glared at him in disgust. "I will be expecting payment within the usual time." Without another word, he moved past them and left the building, melting into the night. Rivella's carelessly loud voice drifted out of to him.

"Cocky fuck. I bet this next job will get his rocks off."

"What do you mean?" Rivella's companion asked. "Who's the target?"

"You'll see," Rivella answered, his tone dripping with perverse excitement. "And so will everyone else."

CHAPTER 22

"Damn. This is pointless." Brian let out a gusty sigh as he sat back in the uncomfortable, rickety wooden chair. The library wasn't the biggest in the area, but surely they could afford some better furniture than the scarred, faded pieces that sat scattered about the room. Brian tried to ignore the ominous creak that sounded beneath him as he stared impatiently at the computer screen.

The German Army kept their service records locked up tight. There was no way a lowly American policeman could expect to get his hands on information about someone who may or may not have served beyond the regulation period. It had taken him nearly a full day's worth of research to realize he was following a dead end. If Alrick had been in the Army for longer than was mandated, Brian wouldn't be able to find out for certain without exercising far more clout than he had.

Brian checked the library's computer clock. Only thirty more minutes before closing time. If he didn't come up with something useful today, he didn't know when he'd get another opportunity. Angela had covered for him not going in to work today, but he couldn't ask her to do it again. No matter how crazy all of this uncertainty was making him, it wasn't fair to drag her into his problems.

So just who was Alrick Ritter? Brian didn't have any better answer to that question than he'd had that morning. All he knew for certain was that Alrick really did work for a magazine called *Musikgeschmack.* Trying to decipher the foreign language had been difficult, but perusing the publication's website, he'd managed to find

Alrick's name under the heading *Feuilletonisten*, which meant "feature writers" according to the handy online Deutsch-English dictionary he'd pulled up. And it had definitely been Alrick's name in the byline of that article he'd read in his hotel room. Not that that meant anything. It could easily be a cover, even if it was a legitimate one.

There was, of course, another option. He could meet with Alrick, look him in the eye, and demand to know the truth. Brian had spent much of his career questioning suspects, and even the hardest cases gave something away with sufficient persuasion. Even if the man had been lying to him from the moment they'd met, Brian was confident Alrick wouldn't be able to hide the truth if he questioned him directly.

But that was the problem. Brian couldn't be certain he'd be the one doing the persuading. He was deathly afraid that once those gorgeous blue eyes were fixed on him he would cave, that he'd be willing to accept any bullshit Alrick threw at him just because he'd be so desperate to believe it. Love made him vulnerable, and even though he recognized his weakness, there was no guarantee he'd be able to stand firm against it.

Brian glanced at his cell phone, which was sitting on the computer table next to the keyboard. The message light was still blinking. He'd turned off the ringer after the first two times Alrick had called before he gave in to the temptation to answer. Brian wasn't certain why Alrick hadn't just come to his apartment, demanding to know why Brian was avoiding him. Maybe that was the answer to all of his questions right there. Maybe Alrick didn't give enough of a damn to even be angry at his disappearing act.

Ten messages, Brian thought after checking his call log, and all of them from Alrick. Brian cleared the message indicator. Well, maybe he cared at little, or at least as much as he needed to in order to keep up his cover.

He loves me, he loves me not.

Shaking his head in disgust, Brian decided he'd done all he could for today. Spinning around in circles wasn't getting him anything except a crushing headache. The web browser was still displaying the popular search engine he had been using. For no apparent reason, his gaze wandered away from the computer and over to his phone. Some sort of idea was trying to form, but he was too tired and wrung out to realize what it was.

The message light came on again as he picked up his phone off the table. He glanced at the call log. Alrick again. Damn, the man was persistent, a quality he usually admired, but at the moment, it was a royal pain in the ass. The last thing he wanted to do was talk to anyone named Ritter.

Brian gasped as the thought finally gelled into something coherent. "Hell," he mumbled softly, "it just might work." He glanced at the computer clock again. Only twenty minutes until he'd be kicked out by the prickly old man who was in charge of the computer resource room. It was a long shot, but what did he have to lose at this point?

Rosamunde Ritter.

Alrick had told him that his sister was married, but maybe she still had some records online under her maiden name. Brian entered her name into the search dialogue box and let his finger hover over the Enter key.

"Here goes nothing." There were a lot of results, but only one stood out. Brian clicked on the link for a global White Pages site. "Rosamunde Meier, née Ritter, Potsdam, Germany. Well, fuck me."

"Sir."

Brian jumped when a wheezy voice spoke directly behind him. Crap, had the old man heard him cuss?

"We're closing now. Please turn the computer off before you leave."

"Okay, thanks." Brian turned and watched the librarian shuffle away. He printed out the webpage and shut the computer down. Grabbing the paper from the ancient printer, he folded it and stuck it in his back pocket. It was only a short walk to where he'd left his car in the library's parking lot. Once he was in the driver's seat with the car door closed, he sat motionlessly for a long moment.

Should he do this? Should he even try it? What if he'd found some other Rosamunde Ritter, not Alrick's sister? He could be bothering some poor woman for nothing while earning one hell of a phone bill. But what if it was her? What if he called her and ended up outing her brother to her? Even if he was innocent of everything else Brian suspected him of, Alrick might never forgive him for telling his sister that he was gay. Of course, it was possible she already knew that and a whole lot else about her brother.

Brian forced himself to admit the real source of his fear. He didn't want to call her and have her tell him that her brother had being playing him for a total fool.

It was seven o'clock, meaning it was already the middle of the night in Germany. He might as well take the time to sleep on his decision. Brian chuckled humorlessly, knowing what he was really going to do. He was going to stay up until it was a decent hour in Western Europe and call her at the first opportunity. He'd acted like a pussy for so much of his life, letting people walk all over him. Even becoming a cop hadn't completely cured him of the gutlessness that was such a debilitating part of his character. It was time to man up and figure out once and for all just where things stood between him and Alrick.

After grabbing a quick dinner of greasy take-out, Brian went back to his apartment, all the while keeping an eye out for a familiar car. But Alrick wasn't lying in wait. Brian tried to ignore his aching disappointment at Alrick's continued absence. He exchanged his sweater and jeans for a T-shirt and pajama bottoms and settled on the couch, setting his phone and the printout on the coffee table within easy reach. The pajamas were the same pair he'd packed but never gotten around to wearing during their idyllic weekend in the country. Had that only been a few days ago? It seemed like another lifetime. He turned on the TV while he ate and chugged down a liter of pop, hoping the caffeine would keep him awake.

It was hard going. The abrupt shift from the intoxicating high of admitting he'd fallen in love to the excruciating pain of finding out the man he loved might be a cold-blooded assassin had left him exhausted. Shaking his head sharply, Brian rubbed both hands over his face, trying to keep awake. His eyes ached with a burning dryness that clouded his vision. The show on TV wasn't holding his interest, and soon, not even his swirling thoughts were enough to overcome his need to sleep.

Brian heard a loud snort as he jerked. He started to sit up but stopped abruptly, wincing in pain at the crick in his neck. *Damn*, he thought, so much for staying up. Something black and white from the early days of moving pictures was showing on the television. Stretching to wake up, he reached toward the coffee table for his cell phone. He glanced at the time and did some quick math, realizing that it was shortly after ten in the morning in Germany.

He only allowed himself one deep breath before reaching for the printout. If he took the time to think about it too hard, he would just chicken out. It took two tries to dial the number correctly, the extra digits for the international call tripping him up. The line started ringing before he was completely ready, but he tried to relax and not focus on the dozens of possible ways that this could go.

"*Hallo?*"

It was a woman's voice. Brian panicked. *Shit, of course she's speaking German.* "Um, hi. Er, I mean hello. Do you speak English, by any chance?"

There was a long pause on the line. Brian almost hung up before the woman spoke again. "Is this a joking?"

Good, he thought, *she speaks English. Sort of.* "No, uh, *Fräulein.*" He remembered Alrick calling Angela that and figured it meant something like "Miss." Or at least he hoped it did. "My name is Brian Macon. I'm an American police officer—"

"*Mein Gott*! You say your name is Brian Macon?"

"Um, yeah?" Completely taken aback by her reaction, he sat motionless, eyebrows raised up to his hairline as he waited for her to continue.

"It is you who *mein Bruder*, Alrick, has come to love, *ja*?"

All of his niggling doubts instantly fell away. She could have been lying, but he had called her completely out of the blue. There was no way she could have been expecting him to contact her. Her response was simply too spontaneous, too unrehearsed to be anything less than genuine. Brian sagged in the cushion as relief flooded his body, making him feel weak.

"I hope so."

"You love him too?"

Brian held his breath and took the plunge. "Yeah, I do."

"This is very good. I am very happy you call. Alrick is, um, how to say, he has trouble."

"He's in trouble?"

"*Ja*, in trouble. You help him?"

His relief at learning definitively that everything he felt for Alrick hadn't been a lie began to fade. It appeared there was still more he needed to hear. "If I can. How is he in trouble?"

"*Ach du Scheiße*! My English is no good."

Brian laughed, trying to sound reassuring. "Your English is a lot better than my German." His attempt at humor didn't ease her frustration.

"You are nice, but this is hard to say."

He heard another voice in the background, a male voice. Rosamunde turned away to speak to whomever was in the room with her. A minute or so passed before she came back on the line, accompanied by the sound of another receiver clattering off the hook.

"You are there still?" she asked.

"Yes, I'm here."

"*Gut. Mein Mann*, er, my husband is on the phone now. He speaks good English. He will help me."

"*Hallo*? I am Heinz, Rosa's husband." The man's accent was thicker than Alrick's, but he spoke confidently.

"I'm Brian, um, Alrick's—"

"Yes, I know who you are. Rosa has told me all about the man her brother has fallen in love with."

"Heinz." Rosamunde's tone held a note of warning. There was some conversation exchanged between them that Brian couldn't follow. He stomach twisted as he guessed that Alrick's brother-in-law was none too thrilled with the fact that he was gay.

"No, do not misunderstand me," Heinz said, as though he had read Brian's mind. "I do not care about his love life. It is only that I am worried about my family."

Rosamunde said something else to her husband, sounding very upset and reluctant. A shaft of ice ran down Brian's back, but he forced himself to speak.

"Why? Is there something wrong? Is something wrong with Alrick? Please, Heinz, that's why I called." Brian took a deep breath and pressed forward before he lost his nerve. "I know about his tattoo. It's identical to the symbol on your Army's sharpshooter medals. He told me he was only in for the required nine months, but he served longer than that, didn't he? He was a marksman?"

The line was completely silent for a long moment, neither Rosamunde nor her husband making a sound. Brian looked at his phone, but it was still counting up the minutes of his call. He was just about to ask if they were still there when Heinz spoke.

"Yes, he was," Heinz said cautiously, apparently understanding what he'd nearly revealed.

But it was too late. The equivocal answer told Brian everything he needed to know. He almost ended the call right then. He didn't want to hear anything else. *Shit*, he thought, his chest heaving as he began to hyperventilate. His heart was beating so hard his ribs ached. He wanted to tear it out of his chest to stop it from beating, to stop it from hurting. But this was why he had tried to reach Alrick's sister in the first place. He needed to know the truth. There was no use turning back now.

"I know he's an assassin, that he's the hit man I've been hunting for weeks. But heaven help me, I need to know why." Brian's voice cracked, his ragged tone grating even to his own ears. "I've only known him for a short time, but I know that I didn't fall in love with a goddamn killer."

Rosamunde broke into sobs. Her husband said something soothing to her. Through the unintelligible jumble, Brian caught one word. *Liebling*. He felt like he was going to be sick all over again.

"Alrick is good man!" Between her thickly accented, broken English and her tear-filled voice, Brian could barely understand her.

"Yes, he is a good man." Heinz was calmer, but his words were clipped like he was trying to control himself but was finding it difficult. "My wife loves him very much, and he has always been good to me and our son. But he has fallen into something terrible, and we do not know how to make him stop."

"Why?" That was the question that threatened to rip him apart. "Why is he doing this? He's not a murderer." Brian repeated the conviction like a mantra.

"My father-in-law, rest his soul, was a very stubborn and proud man. I knew him only a short time before he died, but I know that he loved his children and was determined to give them a good life. He was a carpenter and owned his own business, something he intended to pass on to Alrick. But after the Wall fell, the economy became very skewed toward the West. My father-in-law's business began to fare poorly, and he went into terrible debt."

Rosamunde interrupted, her voice dripping with anger. Heinz murmured something reassuring before continuing. "She wants you to know who owns her father's debt."

"Who?"

"The Russians."

Brian's jaw dropped. "The Russians? You mean like the Russian mafia?"

"*Ja*, that is it exactly. When Alrick was a young man, he was offered a scholarship to attend a very prestigious music conservatory after he completed his commitment to the military. But his father ordered him to enlist past the end of the usual period. Rosa was vehemently opposed, wanting Alrick to fulfill their mother's dreams for him. But their father was adamant that Alrick give up his scholarship. He was in the Army for ten years before he was finally discharged."

Brian's head was swimming with an odd mixture of excitement at learning more about the man he loved and sadness that Alrick had been forced to abandon his music. But mostly, he was afraid what else they might tell him.

"Why did he leave?"

"Because of an evil man!" Rosamunde broke in with a shout and followed it with a curse and what sounded like a spit.

"Alrick's superior tried to rape him one night in his barracks."

"What?" Shock spread through Brian, filling his veins with ice. "He was raped?"

"No, but only because some of the other men in his unit stopped it before it got that far. Alrick fought the man off, but his attacker somehow managed to get his gun."

Brian gasped. "He shot him?"

"*Nein*, though what he did was in many ways much worse. He smashed Alrick's left hand with his own gun, crushing his fingers almost beyond the doctors' abilities to heal."

I was in a car accident several years ago and broke several fingers on my left hand. It has made playing... rather difficult.

Another lie, but Brian understood why Alrick had told it. He remembered how distraught Alrick had been at not being able to play for him that night in his hotel. The pain and the memories of what had caused it must have been equally horrendous.

"That's why he couldn't play for long."

"He play for you?" Rosamunde's tone was hushed with surprise.

"Yes, though it caused him a lot of pain." He heard her begin to cry again. "What? What did I say?"

"Alrick has not played for us since he was injured," Heinz explained. "We thought he had given it up entirely."

"It is because he love you, Brian."

Rosamunde sounded utterly certain, but Brian was still trying to process everything. He wasn't ready to give her the answer he knew she was waiting for.

"What happened after the attack?" He tried to pretend this was just like any other investigation, hoping the familiar process would keep him grounded long enough to finish hearing what Heinz and Rosamunde had to say.

"There was an inquiry, of course, but Alrick's superior lied at the hearing and said that it was Alrick who had tried to seduce him. It was his word against Alrick's."

Brian could guess at what happened. He'd never witnessed anything as egregious as this, but he remembered a young female recruit from his class at the Academy who'd had an affair with one of their instructors. When they got caught with their pants down, the instructor had thrown her to the wolves. She'd accepted a disciplinary remand to keep from being thrown out, but he'd heard that, even all these years later, her career hadn't moved much beyond traffic and parking enforcement.

"That is when Russians get to him."

"What do you mean, Rosa?" Brian instinctively used the diminutive her husband and brother called her by. Alrick had been right. She reminded him a lot of Angela, and he knew he could come to like her very much.

"After he recovered, Alrick drifted for a time. He could not work at his father's store because his motor skills had not recovered enough, and he could not play the cello. He had no aim, no purpose. I do not know exactly how they approached him, but the man who gave him his first job, Viktor Privalov, is the same man who is in charge of the debt. This Privalov came to visit my wife while I was away from home." Heinz's voice dripped with rage. "He told her he had turned her brother into a hired killer so Alrick could make money more quickly to pay off his obligation."

Brian understood the man's anger. He could only imagine how he'd feel if one of his loved ones were put in such a dangerous and upsetting situation. "Did their father know about this?"

"No. He went to his grave never knowing a thing. He was a lucky bastard, I think."

Brian expected Rosamunde to jump to her father's defense, but she said nothing. He didn't blame her. How could you defend a man who had forced his son into a life of crime?

"But now, Alrick, he want to stop. He want to stop the killing." Rosamunde's urgent tone reflected her anxiety. "You will help him do this, Brian."

"How can I help? Hell, it's my job to arrest him!" Brian thrust his hand roughly into his hair, frustrated with his own uncertainty.

Heinz murmured something to his wife. She was silent for a moment, but when she spoke, her words were the clearest Brian had ever heard them. "That is how you help. You make him stop. Because of you, he want to stop. He tell me this." Rosamunde took a deep breath. "You make him go to jail. Then he will find *Frieden*."

"*Frieden*?"

"It means 'peace.'" Heinz's tone was heavy.

"Please, you help him. He love you. You love him." Rosamunde sniffed, but her voice remained strong, her determination to free her brother from his terrible burden unshakable. "Only you can save him."

Brian wanted to reassure her, to promise her he would do as she asked. He knew what he should do, what he had sworn an oath to do. He just didn't know if he could. Confronting Alrick with what he knew would be hard enough. If he was really a victim of such fucked-up circumstances, was it right that he spend the rest of his life behind bars? Because that was what bringing him in would mean. Brian didn't know if Rosamunde realized just what she was asking him to do. He would be doing his job, but he would be ruining both of their lives.

There had to be another way.

"Um, thank you both for speaking with me. Let me give you my phone number." He waited until Heinz said that he was ready before rattling it off. "Please call me anytime."

"*Möge Gott Sie segnen*, Brian. *Auf Wiedersehen.*"

He sat in the dark for a long time after ending the call, his cell phone warm in his hand from the long usage. He didn't know what Rosamunde had said before telling him good-bye, but whatever it was, she was putting a lot of faith in him. He didn't know if he deserved it.

CHAPTER 23

"I NEED to talk to you."

Angela looked up to see Brian standing over her. She had just gotten into the precinct herself and honestly hadn't expected to see him so soon. It didn't look like his day off had done him any good. He was peaked beneath his brown complexion, and the dark smudges under his eyes told her he hadn't gotten much sleep. She stood and grabbed her coat. "Sure. Let's talk in the car."

The parking lot was mostly deserted. Angela led Brian to their unmarked vehicle and got into the driver's seat so he could stretch out his longer legs without the pedals getting in his way.

"Alrick is the sniper," Brian said without preamble as soon as they had closed their doors. His gaze was absent as he looked out the front window.

Angela gaped at him. "What?"

"Along with that information you found about the German Army, you also had something about sharpshooters."

"Yeah, because that's what we're dealing with." Angela didn't really know what she was saying. She was just making noise to supplant the confusion in her head.

"You were dead on. There was a picture of a medal that's given to exceptional marksmen. Alrick has a tattoo that's identical to the image on the medal."

"Oh my God." Angela felt her heartbeat skip in her chest from the shock. She wanted to give Brian a hug, but he seemed so distant, she didn't know how to reach him. "Is that what's been wrong with you these last couple of days? Sweetie, why didn't you tell me?"

"I didn't want to believe it at first, but it was all too much just to be a coincidence. The weapon used in the hits just happens to be commonly used by German Army sharpshooters, and he just happens to have a tattoo of a marksmen's medal?" Brian laughed humorlessly, ruefully shaking his head. "So of course I tried my damnedest to deny it. But then my suspicions were confirmed beyond a doubt."

"How?" Her stomach clenched as she swallowed past the lump in her throat. "Did you talk to Alrick?"

"No." Brian shook his head, a sharp laugh jerking his shoulders. "I didn't have the balls to do that. I tried to find out something about his time in the service, but as you might have guessed, all of the records are confidential. Then I had the bright idea to try and contact his sister."

"Alrick's sister? She lives in the States?"

"No, in Potsdam. It was amazingly easy to find her phone number. That should probably be a scary thought, huh?"

Angela ignored his attempt to distract her. "So you spoke to her?"

"Yeah. I called early this morning. Fortunately, her husband speaks fluent English, and between the two of them, they told me everything. Alrick was, indeed, a sharpshooter when he was in the Army. He enlisted because his father needed help to pay off some heavy debts he'd gotten under. And you'll never believe who he borrowed money from. The goddamn Russian mafia."

Angela's eyes went wide as she blinked at him. "Holy shit."

"No kidding. Alrick served for a long time, but then he got into an altercation with his superior officer and was dishonorably discharged. The mafia approached him to do a hit to earn some money, and apparently it just snowballed from there."

"So he's doing it to help his father?"

"Kind of." Brian shifted in his seat as though trying to ease his discomfort with the topic. "His father died some years ago, but the debt remains. If the Russian mafia operates anything like the loan sharks around here, the obligation passes on to the original debtor's relatives. Alrick probably figured it was the only way he could earn enough money to pay them back and keep his sister from having to shoulder any of the burden."

Angela shook her head. "Brian, you have to take a lot on faith to believe all that."

He finally turned to look at her, his green-hazel gaze stormy, pleading with her to understand. "His sister wasn't lying, Angie. She wants me to take him into custody, to stop him before he gets in any deeper. Her English wasn't great, but I could tell she meant every word." His face was haggard, his inner conflict heartbreaking to see. "And it makes sense. I have to believe Alrick wouldn't do something so terrible without a really good reason." He reached out and grabbed her hand in an almost painful grip. "I just have to."

Angela's heart squeezed in her chest when Brian inhaled unsteadily, clearly fighting to maintain self-control.

"I don't know what to do, Angie. Even knowing the truth, I still love him."

She looked at him steadily, holding his hand tightly as she tried to hide her distress for his sake. "Sweetie, what do you want to do?"

Brian's eyes were bright with barely restrained tears. "What do you mean, what do I want to do? I have to arrest him."

"That's not your only option, and you know it." She returned his shocked stare evenly. "Whatever you decide, I'll support you."

"Angela, you can't. Even if I'm ready to trash my career, I can't let you throw away yours."

"Don't you dare tell me what I can and can't do, Brian Macon." She held up a finger and pointed it close to his face. "I care about you just as much as I do anyone else in my family. I won't stand by and watch you give up on something that means so much to you. And Alrick loves you just as much. After watching you two together that night at my house, after seeing how he looks at you, I have absolutely no doubts about that." She bit her lip, considering the practicalities of committing such a grievous breach of duty. "But obviously, he can't keep this up. Maybe if you talk to him—" She broke off when he squeezed her hand even tighter, silent gratitude etched on his face.

"His sister said he's ready to walk away from it all, even without my asking." Brian placed his other hand on top of the one he already held, as though drawing as much strength from the contact as from her unconditional show of support. "And God help me," he whispered, "I'd let him. I want to be with him, Angie." He raised his troubled gaze to hers. "I need him."

Angela reached across and pulled him awkwardly into her arms. "Then we'll figure out a way to make it work."

He slumped against her and released all of the pent up emotion that had been building up over the last two days. Patting his back as if she were comforting one of her sons, she just held him and let him cry. She swore to herself that somehow, she would keep her promise.

"FUCKING SON of a bitch!"

The receiver slammed against the dashboard as Hayley ripped the earphone out of her ear and sent it flying. "You have got to be fucking kidding me!"

She couldn't believe what she'd just overheard. She'd planted the bug in Macon and Lovell's car the first day she'd taken command of Homicide, the opportunity too good to leave unexploited. When she'd noticed them heading out of the office looking grim and serious, she'd hurried to follow. She'd seen that distressed look on Macon's face too many times over the centuries not to know what it meant. She'd guessed they were going somewhere private to talk and was eager to hear how betrayed Macon felt upon learning the German's true identity.

Only now events were no longer unfolding quite as she had predicted. She'd held up the ballistics reports long enough to keep Macon off track until he and the German had thoroughly fallen for each other. Although she took great pleasure in disparaging their abilities, Macon and his partner were two of her best detectives. Once they had the report, it was only a matter of time before they put the pieces together. She'd watched with barely disguised glee when Macon fell apart after reading the information Lovell had found.

The game was almost finished. She'd figured it wouldn't be long until he went after the German and one of them ended up killing the other. Her part in their passion play would be over, and she'd be free to live the rest of this incarnation as she pleased.

Only now, it appeared Macon wasn't quite ready to give up on his blond fuck buddy. Oh, she knew their souls were destined for each other and all that trite bullshit, but she'd never really believed in such airy-fairy sentiments. No, it had to be the sex that Macon was so reluctant to let go. Was the German really so incredible in bed that Macon was willing to overlook the fact the man was a killer and potentially ruin his own life in the process?

"Unbelievable. Damn you, Shai, and your twisted sense of humor."

It seemed the god of fate wasn't quite finished with her yet, but no matter. He hadn't beaten her in three thousand years, and she'd be damned if she lost to him now. Her features resembled a beautiful yet lifeless statue as she reached for her cell phone. She dialed the number by hand, as it would have been the height of stupidity to keep it stored in her phone.

"Yo, whatdaya want?"

"Remember when you said you'd do anything for me, lover?"

"Hayley?" She could almost see the cocky grin spread across Gio's face. "Yeah, anything you need, babe."

"Well, listen carefully."

She sat back in her seat and explained what she wanted. When she glanced out through the front windshield, her back stiffened as she saw Matt Roddy watching her. *Creepy little bastard.* Telling Gio to hold on, she rolled down her window as he approached her car.

"Roddy," she said abruptly, tacitly urging him to get to the point of his intrusion.

"Morning, Captain. Something the matter?"

"No, everything's fine," she answered, a bit perplexed as to why he'd asked. Then she noticed that, unlike usual, he wasn't looking at her. Rather, he was looking down at the broken remote listening device that lay at her feet. Annoyed at his sudden perceptiveness, she turned on her car, the sound of the engine drawing his attention back up to her face. "I have to run an errand, but I'll be back in a little while."

"Okay, Captain. See you."

Fuck again, she thought darkly. He'd tried to act nonchalant, but his homely mug clearly broadcast his suspicion. Hayley wondered if she'd made a mistake having him help her delay the ballistics report. She'd assumed he was so enamored of her he'd do whatever she asked without question. A miscalculation, but not one that couldn't be fixed.

"Hayley, you still there?" Gio sounded impatient and out of breath, the whoosh of the treadmill he was running on audible in the background.

"Yes." She pulled off, watching Matt as he headed toward the precinct building. He paused at the entrance and turned around to stare after her car as she drove away. "Now, about that favor."

"MACON, IN my office."

Brian's confusion was reflected in Angela's curious gaze as they watched the captain disappear back into her office. It was decidedly unusual for her to call him in alone.

"You might as well go and see what she wants."

"As if I have a choice?" The quirky grin he threw her was only vaguely reminiscent of his normal demeanor. Brian held his partner's gaze for another minute. He would never be able to pay her back for the faith she was showing in him.

As if she knew what he was trying to say, she smiled back at him and lifted her chin toward the captain's office. "Go on. Don't keep her ladyship waiting."

"You wanted to see me, Captain?" Brian stopped just inside the doorway of Preston's office, not all that anxious to enter the lioness's den without Angela's comforting presence.

"Yes, come in and close the door. Have a seat," Hayley instructed after he complied. She leaned forward, propping her folded arms on her desk blotter.

Disliking the implied intimacy of her posture, Brian sat back as far as his chair allowed. He'd always found it uncomfortable being the subject of her dark, piercing gaze. Still trying to figure out what she wanted, he struggled to keep his face as blank as possible.

"Oh, relax, Macon. I'm not about to fire you or anything." She pursed her lips attractively as her expression suddenly became uncharacteristically open. "Dispatch received an anonymous call from someone who claims to have information about our sniper."

"Oh, really?" Brian's heart skipped a beat. He forced himself to remain slouched in his chair, projecting disinterest even though something panicked was trying to break out of his chest.

"So they said. It's probably a complete waste of time, but the taxpayers expect us to be thorough, right?"

He nodded, forcing a corner of his mouth up into a smile. He couldn't speak past the anxiety that was threatening to choke him.

"Anyway, I want you to check it out. Talk to the caller. See if they really know anything useful."

"Just me? What about Angela?"

Hayley shook her head dismissively. "No. It's almost the end of shift, and it might take you a while to track the lead down." She slid a sheet of paper across her desk toward him. "As you can see, the caller was rather sketchy about their location."

"In the club district," he read before frowning at her. "That's all we've got to go on?"

"That and the fact that the caller was male. Like I said, I'm sure you won't mind letting Lovell get home to her family while you run down this lead. No point in both of you going. Consider yourself off-duty once you've found them, but don't spend too much time looking. If you haven't had any luck after a few hours, just leave it. Okay?"

Brian cursed under his breath. He'd been planning to confront Alrick after he got off work, hoping to settle things between them for better or worse. Now he had to deal with this crap. "Yeah, sure." He folded the paper and stuffed it in his back pocket. He got to his feet before realizing that she hadn't said he could go. "Is there anything else?"

Hayley smirked at him. "So eager to get away from me, Macon? I'm starting to think you don't like me." She laughed as he struggled to come up with an answer to that landmine. "Don't bother. We don't have to be bosom buddies for you to do your job. Get out of here."

She didn't have to tell him twice. Angela's questioning gaze was on him the minute he stepped out of the captain's office. He headed toward their paired desks, ignoring the dirty look Matt was shooting him.

"So what's up?"

"Hopefully nothing." He shut down his computer and grabbed his coat. "Someone called in with an anonymous tip about the mob shootings."

Angela's eyes narrow searchingly as she looked up at him. "Are you okay?"

"Yeah. It's probably just some whack job, but I have to know for sure. If it really is a legitimate tip—"

Angela kept her voice low so they wouldn't be overheard. "Should I go with you?"

He shook his head. "No. They didn't say exactly where I could find them, so this might take a while. Go on home. I'll give you a call if something comes up."

"You were planning on seeing him tonight, weren't you?"

Nodding, Brian groaned in defeat. "I swear, it's like that bitch has ESP for figuring out the best way to screw me over."

"Nah. She's probably a witch." She smiled at her partner when he shot her a confused look. "You know, black magic."

Her fingers wiggled in the manner that had probably done much to amuse her kids when they were little. He chuckled despite his unease at what the tipster might reveal. No matter what he wanted, he couldn't just ignore a potential lead, especially not since the captain already knew about it.

"Nice one. I'll catch you later, Angie."

"Okay. Good luck."

CHAPTER 24

ANGELA SIGHED as her partner vanished through the door leading to the main hallway. She hoped that either Brian didn't find the caller or it turned out to be a dead end. It had taken him such a long time to open his heart, and he had fallen for Alrick in a big way. She would hate to see their relationship jeopardized before they could figure out what was possible.

"What a mess," she mumbled. Her cell phone rang, startling her out of her thoughts. She frowned when she saw that the number showed up as a blocked ID. "This is Lovell."

"Detective, how nice to hear your sexy voice again."

Angela froze as she recognized the caller. After a moment's thought, she was on her feet, running toward the captain's office. Without bothering to knock, she burst in, earning herself a glare from the startled woman sitting at her desk. "Giovanni Rivella? Is that you?"

Hayley stared at her in shock. *Seriously?* she mouthed. Angela nodded furiously. This was the perfect opportunity to put the focus of this investigation on Rivella and away from the shooter. She held her phone away from her ear and put it on speaker.

"You've got it, gorgeous. I was thinking about the generous offer you and your partner made me the other day. I don't know all of the details about the guy who's been taking out the Cosminos, but if you can promise me immunity from prosecution for whatever small involvement I may have had, I could be persuaded to talk to you."

"I can't promise you anything, Gio, without knowing what you have to offer." Angela kept her eyes on Preston. The captain was gesturing with both hands, telling Angela to keep him talking. "Why don't you throw me a bone, and I'll let you know if we'll be willing to bite."

"Yeah right," Rivella scoffed. "I talk and you drag my ass to jail."

"No, like I said, we're just going to talk. Let me know where my partner and I can meet you." Angela's forehead wrinkled in confusion when Hayley glowered and shook her head sharply. She furiously mouthed a silent question. *You don't want us to go meet him?*

Can't wait for him, Hayley mouthed back. The captain rounded her desk silently and went out her door. Angela wondered for a second how she was able to walk so quietly, but a quick glance toward her feet revealed that she had removed her Italian heels.

"Hmmm. Okay, Detective, I guess I have to take you at your word. But at the first sign of anyone else but you and your partner, I walk."

Hayley came back into her office with Matt Roddy in tow. She jerked her thumb toward him and stared at Angela meaningfully. Angela wanted desperately to refuse the tacit order, but she just nodded in acknowledgement. "Sounds good, Gio. My usual partner, the one you saw with me the other day, isn't around right now, so I'll be with another colleague. Is that okay? It will still just be the two of us."

"Yeah, whatever. You pigs all look the same to me, anyway." Rivella guffawed at his own pitiful attempt at a joke. "Meet me in an hour at the abandoned warehouse where you found poor old Tony Conti. Don't be late, beautiful."

The three police officers stared at each other after Rivella ended the call.

"So, what do you think, Captain?" Angela asked. "Is he for real?"

Hayley shrugged. "Who knows how that little prick's twisted excuse for a brain works? But if there's any chance he's actually ready to roll over on one of the Milano bigwigs, we can't just look the other way."

Angela made a skeptical face even though Preston had gone precisely in the direction she'd hoped. "You do realize he's probably just using us to get rid of his competition within the organization for him."

The captain nodded. "Agreed. Still, these murders have to stop. If Rivella's willing to give us something, then we'll just have to deal with him." She turned back toward her desk and slipped into her chair. "Roddy, go with her. Macon is tied up for the evening following another lead."

Angela glanced sideways at Matt. "You up for this, Roddy?"

"Calling me by my real name, Lovell? Guess you're willing to be civil now that your precious partner has left you hanging, huh?"

Angela rolled her eyes. "Whatever."

"Enough, you two." Hayley glared darkly at both of them. "I'm not running a fucking preschool. I want you to check in when you get there and the second you leave. And be careful. I don't trust Rivella any farther than I can drop-kick him."

Angela suppressed a chuckle. Privately, she thought that would probably be pretty damned far.

"WHAT A dump."

Angela shook her head, following Matt's gaze as he stared out of the car window. "You said it."

The warehouse had once been a bustling center of industry. Now, apparently, it was the place to be to meet with mobsters or to get your head blown off. She shivered at that morbid thought. A glance at her watch told her they only had a few more minutes before the time Rivella had indicated. She waited impatiently while Matt finished calling in their position. Her respect for him ticked up a notch when he notified dispatch to keep any units that might be in the area on alert just in case something bad went down. Not that Rivella could possibly be stupid enough to try assaulting a cop, not when he was under such close scrutiny.

"Come on," she said when he'd signed off. "Either he'll be here soon or not. I say let's give him fifteen minutes, and if he doesn't show, we're out of here."

"Fine by me."

Matt's tone was just this side of civil. Angela sighed as she opened the passenger's side door and got out of the car. He'd insisted on driving, saying that he didn't trust a woman behind the wheel. More interested in focusing on the job at hand than in getting into it with him, she'd let the chauvinistic remark slide rather than show him just how hard she could punch him in the mouth. She just had to get through the next half hour, and then she could gladly put this temporary partnership behind her, hopefully forever.

They both kept their hands near their guns as they approached the main loading door. The structure was a rusted out, double-paneled behemoth that stretched several feet above their heads and half a block in either direction. Fortunately, one of the doors was wide open, so they didn't have to try to force their way in. The warehouse floor was littered with garbage that had been dropped by vagrants or blown in off the street, and three dark stains indicated where Conti and his goons had met their maker. The only sound was the crunch of the broken glass that lay everywhere beneath their feet.

Angela coughed as dust went up her nose. "Shit, this place is awful." She glanced at her watch again. It was two minutes past time. "So I guess we wait." She exhaled sharply, expelling the dust and trying to find the patience to see what the next twelve minutes would bring.

"Do you really think he's going to show?" Matt kept his attention on the warehouse door. "The captain didn't seem too sure."

Angela resisted the urge to mock his hero worship. She supposed she couldn't blame him for being enamored of Preston. Angela could freely admit that she was stunning. But being beautiful wasn't a cure for being a raging bitch. Matt really needed to assess his priorities, not that it was any of her business.

"He probably won't. But like the captain said, we have to at least go through the motions."

"So, is your partner okay?"

Angela turned to look at him. "Why do you ask?"

"He nearly mowed me down as I was coming out of the bathroom the other day. He looked pretty sick."

"Yeah, he had a stomach bug. He's all right now, though."

Angela glanced toward the door to give herself a moment to think. She hadn't realized Roddy paid that much attention to them. If Brian was really going to try to keep Alrick's identity a secret, he would need to be extremely careful. All the more reason to nip this bud at the top and go after Rivella and whoever else in Milano was responsible for this aggravating mob war. She looked toward the front of the warehouse again, but the doorway remained empty as the minutes ticked away. No further conversation passed between them, and after seven more unproductive minutes, she shook her head, deciding it had been long enough.

"Hell, he's not coming. We might as well just leave."

"Wait, I think I saw something moving outside." Matt was squinting as he stared out of the dirty panes of glass fronting the warehouse. Angela guessed they had once been windows. She joined him and tried to focus, but visibility was nil.

"Are you sure? I don't see anything."

A shock of adrenaline went through her as she heard the shatter of breaking glass.

And then she felt nothing.

THE BOOM of the second shot faded into the cold night air. Gio grinned as he lowered the rifle. It had been a long time since he'd gotten to use the skills he'd learned as a kid back when his uncle used to take him out to the country to practice targeting birds.

Gio, a real man needs to learn to handle a gun.

Shooting at birds wasn't nearly as rewarding as offing cops. So what if he'd had to position himself only a dozen yards from the window? It had still been a really sweet kill. The warehouse glass was disgusting, and he'd barely been able to see who he was aiming at. *Let's see that German bastard top that!*

Gio was hiding in the shadows cast by the building situated directly across from the warehouse where he'd told the lady detective to meet him. *Stupid bitch.* Like he'd really have told them anything. It was too bad her partner hadn't been there too, but Hayley had given him the okay to take out the guy she was with. He didn't know why Hayley had such a hard-on for her own people, but he wasn't going to complain. She was one scary broad, and it was that sense of danger he found so exciting. Well, that and her exceptionally fine ass. Whistling, Gio pulled out his cell phone and dialed.

"9-1-1. What is your emergency?"

"Um, hello? Hello?!" Gio pitched his voice as high as he could manage and pinched his nose closed to make himself sound more nasal.

"Yes. What's your emergency?"

"Oh my God, I just saw two people get shot!"

"Where are you?"

"I think they might have been cops!"

"Ma'am, please calm down and tell me where you are."

Gio pulled the phone away from his mouth as he laughed silently. The dispatcher thought he was a chick? That was just perfect.

"Ma'am?"

"Uh, yeah. I was walking past that big warehouse down in the old industrial district. Please hurry!" The phone beeped as he ended the call. "Give that man an Oscar, baby."

Gio started to break down the rifle to return it to its case. It hadn't been difficult to get the Arctic Warfare from a black market dealer. He'd even managed to procure the exact ammo that Hayley told him he had to use. He wondered if he'd get a chance to take out the dead woman's partner. All of that firepower jerking in his hands could easily become addictive. No wonder the German did what he did for a living. It was a hell of a rush. Gio whistled louder as he thought about how he might convince his girlfriend to let him do another one of her guys.

"Heh. Hayley won't mind."

"What won't I mind?"

Gio fumbled the pieces of the rifle he still held as his heart leapt into his throat. He spun around and stared at the woman standing behind him. "Fucking hell, babe! You scared the shit outta me." He stared at her as she gave him an inscrutable smile.

"Is it done?"

"Yeah. They're good and dead, just like you asked." Gio rolled his eyes, annoyed, as he turned his back on her. She could have at least mentioned what a kick-ass job he'd done. Grousing and feeling unappreciated, he knelt down to put the last of the rifle pieces in the case.

"Thank you, Gio."

Ah, he thought, *that's more like it.* "Don't sweat it, gorgeous." He grinned as he shut the gun case, the latches snapping closed with a snick. "I enjoyed it."

"I'm glad to hear it."

Gio froze as something hard and cold pressed into the back of his skull. He started to turn around but hesitated as the object dug painfully into his head. "Hayley?" he said uncertainly. "Babe, what's going on?"

"Don't call me 'babe,' you dumb piece of shit."

HAYLEY'S EYES were cold as she pulled the trigger, the silencer on the gun muffling the sound into a soft pop. Gio fell face-first onto the concrete, blood pooling rapidly beneath his head. Her gloved hand squeezed around the grip in silent satisfaction before she holstered the gun and backed away from the spreading circle of dark, steaming red. The weapon had been bought anonymously and would be disposed of the same way, along with the Arctic Warfare. She picked up the rifle's case and swung it over her shoulder. Without a glance at the dead man lying on the ground, she walked across the street to the warehouse.

Just as Gio had promised, Lovell and Roddy were lying motionless near the broken window. The woman's head was a mess, bits of gray showing among the blood and shards of broken skull. Hayley regarded the carnage dispassionately. She'd seen a lot worse during the more violent eras of the past. Roddy's body didn't have as much damage, but he appeared just as dead.

Satisfied, Hayley reached into her pocket and pulled out a folded piece of paper. Careful not to step in any gore, she bent over the woman's body and tucked the note into the collar of her shirt. Even those idiots who worked for her shouldn't have any trouble finding it. The sound of approaching sirens caught her attention. They had arrived far sooner than she'd expected given the time Gio placed his 9-1-1 call. Apparently, Lovell and Roddy had arranged to have patrol units in the area as backup.

Smart move, but it was too little too late to do them any good.

Standing up, Hayley backed away and took in the scene. "Nice work, Detectives. Consider yourselves on permanent vacation." She spun and headed for the door, leaving the bodies behind as she turned her thoughts toward her next task. The crunch of glass beneath her shoes masked the soft groan that rose from the warehouse floor.

CHAPTER 25

"YOU HAVE taken everything from me." The boy's whisper was harsh with grief, his brown gaze cold with the madness of unbearable pain. "All that you have done, I visit upon you, and you will know my suffering."

"GODDAMN WASTE of time."

Brian gritted his teeth as he walked toward his unmarked car. The wild goose chase the captain had sent him on had turned out to be just that. He'd hit practically every club in the party district, but no one knew anything about an anonymous tipster. He didn't know if the caller had really seen something and had been taken out by the people who'd hired Alrick, or whether the person had been too high to remember that he'd contacted the police. Or maybe he'd never existed in the first place.

After the tenth club had turned out to be a bust, Brian decided to call it a night. He had far more important things to do besides chasing after a phantom, such as going to see Alrick and figuring out where things stood between them. He was anxious and nervous all at the same time, hoping they could find some way out of this mess they were in and terrified of what would happen if they did.

Brian knew that if he simply let Alrick walk, he'd be endangering his own future. He might be making a huge mistake, but he wouldn't know for certain unless he talked to Alrick face-to-face. He was just getting into his car when his cell phone rang.

"Brian, it's Brad."

"What's up, man," Brian replied. "I was just on my way home."

"Angela's been shot. Brian? Brian!"

Brad called his name several times when he didn't respond, but he couldn't have if he'd wanted to. The other detective's abrupt statement hit him like a punch to the gut. The world seemed to tilt, and his stomach flipped as though the ground had suddenly fallen out from under him. The sudden sense of vertigo was so intense he had to grab hold of the armrest on his door to keep from falling over into the passenger's seat. Sweat broke out over his entire body, drenching his shirt as his heart hammered painfully in his chest.

"Where is she?" he finally managed, his voice so raspy he could barely understand himself. "Brad, where is she?" He started the engine and peeled out of his parking spot, not even sure where he was going. He hit the switch for the siren out of habit more than conscious thought.

"She's at that warehouse where Tony Conti and his crew were hit. She and Matt Roddy were both shot."

"Matt Roddy? Why was he there?" Brian asked the question without really thinking about what he was saying. He was operating on automatic as he turned his car in the direction of the warehouse. Holding his phone in a tight grip, he struggled to keep control of the car with one hand as it fishtailed after he took a turn far too quickly.

"The captain sent them out on a job together after you left. I don't know what for. I'm already down here. I'll keep an eye out for you."

Brian ended the call and blindly tossed his phone into the seat next to him. He couldn't look at the empty spot where Angela sat on those rare occasions she let him drive. She should be there at his side like she always was. Growling, he slammed his hand against the wheel. His partner had needed him, and he wasn't there.

Angela's been shot.

That one sentence kept echoing through his head as he drove like a madman through the streets of the city.

Angela's been shot.

He shook his head, rejecting Brad's words as he tried to focus on nothing but the road in front of him. If he could just get to the place where his partner was, everything would be okay. It had to be okay.

"Damn it!" His throat ached as fear clawed at him. "Please be okay," he whispered.

The rest of the drive to the industrial district passed in a blur. He was pretty certain he almost caused several accidents, but he didn't give a shit. If people didn't stop and make way when they heard an emergency vehicle coming through, it was their own damn fault. One unmarked and two marked cars were sitting outside of the warehouse when he arrived. Three patrolmen stood by the door, ostensibly to keep the scene secure, not that there was anyone else around. The place was a ghost town.

Brian scrambled out of his car, his badge already in hand. He held it up and hurried past the patrolmen without a word. A large figure appeared in front of him just as he went through the rusted door.

"Brian, hold up a minute, man."

"Brad, get out of my way."

The other detective was built like an out-of-shape linebacker. The breadth of his shoulders blocked Brian's view of whatever was going on behind him. A large hand landed on his shoulder, holding him in place.

"Just, wait a sec. It's pretty grisly. You might want to prepare yourself."

Brian looked up at him. "How is she?" His stomach knotted as he read the answer in Brad's mournful expression.

"She's gone, man. I'm so sorry."

Brian moved so quickly Brad didn't have time to react. He slid past the larger man and homed in on the place where another patrolman and Brad's partner, Phil Stanley, were standing over two figures lying on the ground. They were gathered around the rightmost body, and Phil had his fingers pressed to the man's neck.

"Matt's still alive," Phil shouted toward his partner. "Where the fuck is that ambulance?"

Brian ignored them, his gaze fixed on the smaller form. She was lying completely still, drying blood matting her hair and speckled over her suit jacket. She was faceup, but the hole in her head was so large it had made a complete mess of her features. Brian fell to his knees and emptied his stomach onto the grimy floor.

A dozen images rushed through his head in an instant. Years worth of memories, of pizza nights and school sports games, of moments of shared camaraderie and moments of shared terror. Everything she had been to her husband and her children, everything she had been to him, gone in an instant.

He couldn't make sense of the buzzing in his head. The realization that Angie was dead was too much for him to process all at once. He told himself it was a joke, just a sick prank someone was playing on him. He stared at his partner's still figure, half expecting her to get up and laugh at him for being such an easy mark. It had to be some sort of crazy Halloween makeup she was wearing. How else could he explain the fact that her beloved face had all but disappeared?

Brad waited silently until he had finished retching up everything that he'd eaten since lunchtime. The detective came over to him while he coughed and gagged. Brad wrinkled his nose as the smell hit him but said nothing about Brian's loss of control. "Macon, I'm sorry. Forensics and the ME are on their way. We'll find out who did this, I promise you that."

"Holy shit. What in the hell happened here?"

Brian looked up at the sound of the newcomer's familiar voice. The medical examiner walked over to them, shaking his head as he looked down at the bodies. His hound dog face looked even sadder than usual.

"That's what we were hoping you could tell us, Jeremy." Brad was interrupted by the sound of a loud siren and squealing breaks. A few seconds later, a couple of EMTs rushed in carrying a stretcher between them. Brad jogged over to them and led them to Matt.

"This one's still breathing," Phil explained urgently.

The EMTs examined Matt quickly. "His pulse is weak, but it's still there." The older paramedic wrapped a pressure strap around the gaping wound in the fallen detective's head. "Frankly I'm amazed. He should be dead."

Brad clenched his teeth as he glanced over at Brian, who was still kneeling at his partner's side. "Just take care of him."

"We'll take him to St. Mary's." The younger EMT set up an IV drip before he and his partner carefully transferred the unconscious man to the stretcher. They rushed him out of the warehouse to their waiting ambulance, trying not to jiggle him too much as the gurney rolled over the litter-strewn floor.

Brian ignored Jeremy's glance of sympathy as he lowered himself next to Angela's body. He grew queasy when the medical examiner pulled a probe out of his bag and started to poke around in the hole in her head but resisted the urge to look away.

"Single bullet. I doubt she felt anything." Jeremy didn't look up from what he was doing to see if his words of comfort had any effect. "Hmmm, what have we here?"

Jeremy reached into his medical bag and traded the probe for a pair of slender forceps before turning back to the body. Brian's vision seemed to narrow until all he could see was the bullet the medical examiner slowly extracted from inside Angela's skull. The familiar contours of the projectile held his attention with grim fascination as every other thought faded away.

"Well, I'll be damned. The sniper's targeting cops now? I thought this was just supposed to be a mob war." Jeremy looked over at Brian and frowned as he saw him shake his head. "What, it's not?"

Brian didn't answer. He just kept shaking his head in silent answer to the question that was ringing in his head with a deafening echo.

"But something about this is odd," Jeremy murmured, turning back to his task when he realized that he'd get nothing from Brian. "There's too much damage compared to the sniper's other victims. Their craniums were left mostly intact, the only trauma being the entrance and exit wounds. It's like the gunman was a lot closer this time. And see how the bullet didn't pass clean through? Like the weapon wasn't as powerful. Hey, kid? What are you doing?"

Jeremy sat back on his heels when Brian suddenly moved toward him, or more precisely, toward the dead woman lying between them. The medical examiner saw what Brian had noticed the moment his hand went toward it. "Wait," he cautioned, "you should put on some gloves first."

Brian ignored him, reaching into her blood-soaked collar, and pulled out a piece of folded paper.

"WHAT IN the hell is that?" Jeremy saw every ounce of color that wasn't embedded into Brian's skin leech away as he read whatever was written on the paper. In a flash, Brian was on his feet and was heading toward the door at a dead run. Everyone watched in shock as he disappeared out into the darkness. The sound of a car engine starting broke the stunned silence, and they heard tires spin against the asphalt with a tortured squeal before the roar of the motor faded to nothingness.

Brad closed his mouth with an audible click after realizing that his mouth was hanging open. "What was that about?"

Phil looked over at his partner and shook his head. "No idea." He scratched at the back of his head and sighed as he watched the medical examiner place the bullet into an evidence bag. "You about done there, doc?"

"Yeah." Jeremy wasn't sure if he should mention that Brian had just taken a piece of evidence from the scene. "Not too much question about the cause of death, but I'll do a full workup on her. And the lab needs to do an analysis on the bullet." Jeremy shook his head sadly as he looked down at Angela's lifeless body. "Damn shame. She was a beautiful woman."

"Detective!"

Both partners looked toward the door as one of the patrolmen who'd been positioned outside rushed in. He looked toward Brad. "Sir, we found something."

Jeremy hesitated for a moment but decided to follow the detectives, leaving the other patrolman to stand guard over Angela. The young officer walked quickly across the street to where his fellows were standing, looking down at something on the ground.

Brad was right on the patrolman's heels, but Jeremy saw him pull up short when he saw what they were staring at.

"Son of a bitch," Brad rasped. "Giovanni Rivella?"

Jeremy's brow wrinkled in confusion as he reached the others. He noticed that a gaping Phil seemed just as perplexed as the younger man came to a stop next to his partner. The dead mobster was lying face-down on the ground, the back of his head blown apart.

"What the fuck is going on around here?"

No one had a ready answer to the old ME's question.

THE ARCTIC Warfare lay at Alrick's feet, still in its case, waiting to be assembled. There was no rush. He could put it together in less than a minute. The wind ruffled his hair as he stood back from the edge of the roof, looking toward a hotel half a mile away. The air was already noticeably warmer as spring approached in earnest. He'd let his hair grow out some, having noticed that Brian enjoyed running his fingers through it. Anyway, it was past time he abandoned the quasi-military cut he'd worn for so long. It would be the perfect symbolic gesture to usher in his new life.

He'd checked out of his hotel that morning. After this was over, he planned to collect his final payment from Rivella to send to his sister, and then he would find Brian and confess to everything. He'd decided that selfishly waiting would serve little purpose and was completely comfortable with the knowledge that he would be putting his fate in Brian's hands. Brian already had his heart. What was handing him his freedom in comparison to that? If Brian accepted his promise that he was finished with this life, that was all he could ask. And if Brian rejected him, he wasn't sure he wanted to continue on anyway.

Alrick held the PM II telescopic lens to his eye and aimed it at a specific hotel window. Rivella had been as precise as usual. Alrick's intended target was exactly where Rivella had said she'd be. But when Alrick focused the scope and examined the scene, he froze in shock.

It seemed that, for once, Rivella had been less than forthcoming with the information concerning his target. Kaitlyn Cosmino, the youngest daughter of Antonio Cosmino, the head of the Cosmino organization. Rivella obviously meant this to be the last salvo in his gambit to wipe out the Cosminos. Alrick had to admit it was a smart move no matter how appalling. Losing his youngest child was sure to destroy Antonio, who was apparently quite the family man, judging by the broad grin on his face as he hugged his daughter to his side. It would be kinder just to kill him, but that wouldn't have satisfied Giovanni's twisted sense of humor.

Too bad Rivella had neglected to inform him Kaitlyn was only a little girl.

The scene through the window was a party, and not just any party. It was a birthday party. Alrick ground his teeth together as he saw the balloons and streamers. A child's party. A huge banner was strung across the longest wall of the hotel's hospitality suite.

Happy 13th Birthday, Kaitlyn!

"Verdammte Scheiße."

Alrick shook his head. He would rather spend the rest of his life doing the most disgusting menial labor he could imagine to earn money than kill a child. If he was really planning to offer himself up to Brian, how could he go to him with such a hideous stain on his conscience? It was already as filthy as he cared to let it get. Rivella had offered him an obscene amount of money for this job, but he felt nothing but serene acceptance as he packed the rifle away. After slinging the gun case over his shoulder, he turned away from the edge of the roof and headed toward the access door. The happy celebration continued on behind him undisturbed.

Alrick's step faltered as the door unexpectedly swung open. Confused, he started to reach for the Glock nestled securely in the shoulder holster beneath his coat but could only stare as an attractive brunette stepped out onto the roof, a silencer-equipped gun pointed in his direction. He could tell by the way she held it that she knew what she was doing. Alrick opened his mouth to ask her to identify herself when she sent him a chilling smile.

"Long time no see."

CHAPTER 26

BRIAN SLAMMED through the manual glass door, too impatient to wait for the automatic sliding door to open. The people milling around the hotel lobby stopped and stared as he rushed past them, his flapping coat revealing his service revolver. He headed straight for the elevators and jammed his finger on the call button.

An elevator opened immediately, but the ride up seemed interminable. Brian could feel the note burning a hole in his pocket, but he ignored it and the damning words written on it. Alrick would be in his room. He would greet Brian with that beautiful smile, and Alrick would hold him while he grieved for his partner. They would laugh and cry over the craziness that had happened that day, and tomorrow they would talk and figure out what to do about this impossible situation.

"Come on. Come on."

Brian tapped his hands against his legs as the numbers on the elevator's display panel counted upward. By the time Alrick's floor number lit up, Brian was ready to tear out his hair. He was out of the elevator before the doors could even finish opening. His gaze fixed on Alrick's door, he fumbled for his wallet as he ran toward it, his heart pounding in a deafening cadence. Not content to wait for an answer to his knock, he pulled out the key card Alrick had given him a lifetime ago. When he slid it into the lock, the indicator light turned red.

"No! Work, damn you!" He tried it again, but the red light still blinked at him mockingly. He kicked the door viciously. "Alrick!" The noise prompted more than one curious guest to stick their head out into the hallway. "Police! Go back inside your rooms." Slamming doors indicated their compliance. He hammered his fist against the painted metal until his hand stung. "Alrick! Open the door!"

Brian's chest heaved as he struggled to breathe. He stared at the door, but despite his mental urging, it remained shut. Slumping forward, he bumped his head against the cool surface. His body felt strange, insubstantial, like it wasn't his own anymore. Not surprising considering he'd have done anything to be anywhere else right at that moment. The note in his pocket crinkled as he turned to rest his back against the door. He pulled it out and unfolded it with a growing sense of fatalism.

> *My dear Brian. Rest assured that your partner*
> *did not suffer. I am very good at what I do. But*
> *the time has come to end our little game of*
> *pretend. I will stage my final performance on*
> *the rooftop across from the Hotel La Rue.*
> *Please come quickly, my love. I do so want to*
> *see you one last time.*

Brian stared at the note for a long moment, struggling to nurse the tiny shred of hope that lingered stubbornly in his heart. Forcing himself to put one foot in front of the other, he walked back down the hall to the elevators. It took a little longer to arrive this time, but it wasn't nearly long enough. Perversely, the elevator seemed to descend to the lobby at lightning speed. Brian hesitated when the doors slid open, but when they began to close again, he made himself exit.

The young woman at the desk stared at him nervously as he held up his badge.

"Alrick Ritter. Is he still staying here?"

Her gaze dropped to her computer screen as she typed, fingers flying across the keyboard. "No, sir. He checked out this morning." She looked up at him uncertainly. "Um, do you need anything else, Detective?"

A slow, burning anger rose up from deep within, searing his heart like acid. Lies whispered so sweetly they had intoxicated him. Deceit cloaked behind soul-stirring caresses. And here he was, the biggest fool on the fucking planet.

"No, I don't need anything else." He turned and headed for the hotel entrance, his hand clenched into a fist as though it were already wrapped around the barrel of his gun.

LONG TIME no see?

Alrick narrowed his eyes in confusion as he stared at the woman. "Who are you? Have we met before?"

She laughed humorlessly. "Now that is an interesting question and a very, very long story. This time, I'm Captain Hayley Preston, Brian Macon's superior." She gestured with her gun. "Keep those hands where I can see them, gorgeous."

He didn't understand everything she'd said, but her identity was crystal clear. Alrick's stomach dropped as he raised his hands to shoulder height. If this woman was a police officer, then he had a problem. He wouldn't fight her, though. If she'd come to take him into custody, then he'd go peacefully.

"How did you find me?" It seemed a simple enough question, but something flashed in the woman's eyes that set his teeth on edge.

"How did I find you? Why do you think you're even here in the first place?"

Alrick tried to make sense of her words. "What do you mean?"

"Come on, do you really think that Giovanni Rivella was smart enough to plan all of this on his own? Do you think he would have thought to hire you without a little prodding?" She smirked as though his naïveté amused her.

"You helped him?" He shook his head in confusion. "But you're a police officer, *ja*?"

"Oh, *ja*." She snorted, mocking his accent. "And do you know what cops make in this town? Hell, it's not enough to pay for my manicures. But I didn't work alone. This would have been far too much for me to arrange without help, especially since I have such a high profile position. No, I needed someone who could move around without drawing too much attention to himself. Macon fit the bill quite nicely."

Alrick started as he heard Brian's name. What was she saying? That Brian was working for the mob and had played a part in Rivella hiring him? He remained silent, but the woman smirked as she read the incredulousness on his face.

"And now that you've outlived your usefulness, Gio has instructed us to get rid of you so you can't be traced back to him." She lifted her chin toward the distant hotel. "Were you trying to leave without doing the girl? I never pegged you for a sentimental little bitch." She shook her head in mock disappointment. "After botching this job, Gio will be glad to see you gone."

Alrick shifted his attention toward the gun in her hand. He didn't know if he could reach his own weapon in time if she really planned to shoot him. She chuckled as she saw his body tense.

"Oh, don't worry. I'm not going to hurt you. There's someone else far more suited to clean up this mess."

His eyes stretched wide as he caught her meaning.

"That's right. He'll be here any minute." The cruel anticipation on her face was sickening.

"I don't believe you."

The woman cocked her head as though she'd heard something. A dark grin twisted her face, and she moved cautiously away from the door. Keeping her gun leveled at him and plenty of distance between them, she made her way around toward the edge of the roof. She risked a quick glance downward, her smile growing at whatever she saw. She jerked her head, beckoning him toward her.

"Here, come see for yourself."

He didn't want to cooperate in whatever game she was playing, but a nasty whisper in the back of his mind urged him forward. Wiping all emotion from his expression, Alrick kept his gaze steady on her gun as he walked toward the roof's edge. Looking downward, he saw a tiny, flashing light far below and realized that it was on top of a car. The faint wail of a siren finally reached his ears.

"See? I told you so."

"*Nein.*" Alrick shook his head, refusing to accept what his eyes were telling him. "You are lying." He watched her closely, struggling to maintain an air of calm as he backed away toward the access door. "I'm leaving to find Brian. Shoot me if you must. That's the only way you'll stop me."

She just smiled. "Oh, I won't have to stop you."

Ignoring her, Alrick turned toward the access door. He was reaching for the handle when the door suddenly burst open. Alrick stumbled back before it could hit him. The figure in the doorway was hidden in the shadows, but when the person stepped out onto the roof, Alrick could only gape in shock.

Brian's face was a mask of rage. The revolver in his hand was steady, aimed directly at Alrick's heart. Alrick wanted to deny what he was seeing, but the reality of Brian's presence was unavoidable. Had this insane woman told him the truth? Had Brian been playing such a deep game of subterfuge and betrayal that he'd fallen for it like some gullible fool?

"Brian," he rasped, "what are you doing here?"

"Shut up!" Spittle flew from Brian's lips as he snarled. "Don't speak to me. Don't you dare speak to me!" His face was mottled, his eyes a swirling pool of fury. "You killed her, you fucking bastard!"

"What? Killed who?" Alrick shook his head. "You are making no sense." His grasp of English began to falter as his emotions got the better of him.

"Angela! My partner. The woman who let you into her home. The woman you stole from her husband and her children." Brian bared his teeth in a grim parody of a smile. "She liked you. She thought you were a good guy, even after I told her who you really were. And you shot her through the head like she was a goddamn dog!"

"Angela?" Alrick's blood ran cold. He didn't know what had shocked him the most, the fact that Angela was dead or Brian's other revelation. "You know about me? How?"

"Your tattoo." Brian's laugh was utterly devoid of humor. "Boy, I'll bet you made your unit proud when you got that deadeye medal. Did they talk you into inking it on your shoulder, or did you just want to have permanent bragging rights?"

Idiot. Alrick exhaled sharply, cursing himself. He'd never imagined that his tattoo would give him away. Perversely, he felt something akin to pride at Brian's cleverness. "Brian—"

"Even then I didn't want to believe it. I convinced myself that I was mistaken, that you couldn't possibly be the sniper. I was so desperate to be proven wrong, I even called your sister."

"Rosamunde?"

"Did you two set the whole thing up? I mean, her story was perfect. Her husband was even in on it. You all played me for a real idiot, didn't you?" The muscle in Brian's jaw bunched as he clenched his teeth. "And I fell for every fucking word," he spat.

Alrick could see the woman out of the corner of his eye. She was still standing near the edge of the roof, well away from their confrontation, as though she was content to merely watch the show. Nothing about this added up. If what she'd told him about Brian was true, then why did he seem so genuinely distraught? And who had killed Angela? It must have been done in such a way as to make Brian suspect him. His head hurt as he tried to make sense of it.

"Brian, I don't understand what all is going on here, but please listen to me."

"No. No more. I don't want to hear any more of your lies." Brian's hand began to tremble slightly as he raised his gun toward Alrick's head. "Screw taking you in. I should just kill you right here."

"*Mery.*"

The word fell from Alrick's tongue as though someone else was speaking through him. Though the sound was utterly foreign, somehow he instantly knew the meaning of the ancient endearment. Suddenly his body felt different, his bones seeming to shrink, his frame becoming smaller and lighter. He knew that he wasn't actually changing, but the illusion was as real as anything he'd ever experienced. Brian froze, staring at him. But it wasn't confusion reflecting from his startled green-hazel eyes. It was recognition.

"What's happening?"

Brian's uncertain whisper tore at Alrick's heart, but he had no answer. He held out his hand, reaching for Brian as the building seemed to shift beneath their feet. Suddenly, everything around them disappeared, leaving only the two of them behind to behold the unraveling of an inconceivable truth.

Untold scores of years flashed through their minds as buried memories were unlocked. Time that should have been lost to them was at long last revealed. They staggered beneath the full weight of their lives, beneath thousands of moments of laughter and sadness, beneath the days of love and the nights of blistering passion. But darkening it all was the inescapable remembrance of heart-crushing betrayal.

CHAPTER 27

Tiye sped toward the pharaoh's audience chamber, his lungs aching with effort as he followed the shouts of soldiers rushing to their liege's aid. He prayed he would be in time to make his brother see reason and to stay the prince's hand. But when he burst into the hall, the only thing Tiye could see was his brother's body as it slid from Rahotep's sword and fell bonelessly to the ground. Nakhti's knife, covered with the blood of his wrath, clattered loudly against the stone floor as it landed beside him.

Time seemed to slow, turning Nakhti's fall into a macabre dance. Tiye could not scream, for all breath had abandoned him. He raised his bewildered stare toward Rahotep, needing to see the denial in his lover's eyes. But it was not his "mery" who stood over his brother so fiercely, his hand clutched around the instrument of Nakhti's death. In the prince, he saw only a stranger. Rahotep looked down with disgust and pity at the wretch who had dared raise his hand against the pharaoh. Somewhere deep inside, Tiye understood that his lover could not have known the identity of the man he had just killed. He and Nakhti were nearly ten years apart and, as they had been fathered by different men, did not much resemble each other. How could Rahotep have known that he had just destroyed the only family Tiye had left?

Yet logic proved futile in the face of his grief. Memories of his life before coming into the prince's service assailed him. Years of want and fear, of violence and rape by some of the very soldiers who stood protectively near the pharaoh. An uncontrollable rage coursed through him, and the bitterness of injustice lay sourly on his tongue.

"Nakhti," he murmured, drawing Rahotep's surprised gaze. He walked slowly to his brother's body and stopped only when the prince grabbed his arm with his free hand.

"Tiye! Why are you here? I told you to wait for me in my chambers." Rahotep shivered as the young slave looked at him with empty, soulless eyes. The pharaoh, who had been hiding behind his capable son, favored Tiye with a glare.

"Who is this boy? Why is he walking about freely when he should be in chains like the rest of this ungrateful filth?"

"Quiet, father!" Rahotep snarled.

The pharaoh stared at his son in shock, but his courage failed him in the face of the prince's black glare.

Rahotep's gaze latched on to his lover's face. Tiye's eerie calm disquieted him. "What is it, pa'sheri?" He glanced down at the dead slave at his feet. "Did you know this man?"

Tiye remained indifferent to the endearment. His gaze fell again to his brother, whose handsome features were twisted with his final moments of pain. He could not look at the prince. He could not accept that the man he loved had just killed the last of his kin. Pulling free from Rahotep's grasp, he bent down and retrieved Nakhti's stained blade.

"Guards!"

The soldiers moved to stop Tiye at the pharaoh's shout of alarm but were stalled by a sharp gesture from the prince. Ignoring his distressed father, Rahotep held up a pleading hand to the silent youth who walked slowly toward him.

"Tiye, give me the dagger." He flinched as those vacant eyes looked past him and gazed fixedly at his father. "Tiye, please—"

"He was my only brother." Tiye's voice was eerily hollow. "He was no traitor."

Rahotep's face drained of all color. "Your brother? By the gods."

He stared at Tiye, his heart stopping at the revelation of the crime he had just committed. He felt chilled, his very blood turning to ice in his veins. He wanted to take his lover into his arms and tell him that they would both soon wake from this nightmare, but then the rest of Tiye's words pierced through the shroud of disbelief that had dulled his senses.

"Traitor?" Rahotep echoed, confused by Tiye's words. "What do you mean?" he asked, but Tiye spoke only to the pharaoh.

"He was loyal to you, though you treated us like garbage. Even when your soldiers raped both me and my mother when I was but a child, we did not try to run away. We stayed because that was our duty. My mother and brother never harmed anyone in their entire lives, and now they are dead." Tiye's voice rose louder and louder until the accusations flew from his lips. "Because of you, my family is dead!"

"Tiye," Rahotep whispered. He gazed helplessly at Tiye, mortified at what he had just learned of his lover's past. Hatred warped the boy's soft voice, and Rahotep felt Tiye's torment in his very being. But beneath his agony was an undeniable hurt. Was not he a part of Tiye's family? Had not they named each other as such in their hearts? Every word Tiye spoke felt as though Nakhti's knife had found its mark.

"You have taken everything from me," Tiye whispered, gaze cold as he stared at the pharaoh. His body coiled with tension like an asp before it struck. "All that you have done, I visit upon you, and you will know my suffering."

The oath was made, and mercy held no sway. Shock at the vicious promise made Rahotep slow to react when Tiye suddenly rushed past him with a snarl twisting his full lips, his brother's dagger raised to strike at the pharaoh's heart. The boy was unbelievably quick, and his swiftness caught the soldiers likewise unprepared. The pharaoh shouted in alarm as Tiye reached him. He caught the boy's arm just before the boy's blade found its target.

"Tiye!"

Rahotep cried his lover's name as several of the soldiers rushed to their king's aid with drawn swords. His heart was tight with pain that his gentle pa'sheri had been driven to such violent desperation. He grabbed at Tiye, fearing the boy would be skewered on the soldier's weapons, but the pharaoh was strong in his fear and pushed the young slave away with a mighty shove just as his son reached them. Tiye spun from him, propelled by the force of the old man's panic.

Time itself lengthened and stretched as Rahotep watched his lover fall toward him, Nakhti's dagger clutched tightly in his small *hand. Their gazes met and Rahotep's heart wept, seeing no end to the demented hatred that blazed in Tiye's beautiful eyes. In that instant, the boy's thoughts became clear. He would avenge his family by taking the life of their killer's son, and not even memories of their love could overcome his need for revenge.*

Rahotep raised no hand in his own defense. If his sweet pa'sheri wished to kill him, then he had no further desire to live. Death would be a welcome escape from the bludgeon of Tiye's anguished fury. Rahotep gazed kindly at his lover as he patiently awaited his end.

"Sire!" The guard standing nearest the prince shouted out a warning and rushed to protect him. The man jostled his arm so the sword still clutched in his hand lifted, its point aimed straight at Tiye. Rahotep tried to turn it away, desperate to avoid the cruel onslaught of destiny that rushed forward to crush them. But in the end, he was just a man, powerless against the whims of the gods.

We are of one body and share one soul.

His own words, spoken to Tiye in the darkness of a passion-filled night, haunted him as the sharp blade of his sword buried itself within his lover's belly. Rahotep felt the bite of unbearable pain as he ran the boy through, the sound of his father's shout distant and faint against the roar from his soul. Tiye collapsed against him, blood covering their white garments in a vivid, ghastly red stain. It was a long moment before the prince realized that the pain spreading through him was not merely grief.

Rahotep looked into his lover's eyes and saw only sorrow and devastating regret.

Forgive me.

His heart heard the words Tiye could not speak. The slave had kept his vow, destroying his enemy even as he destroyed himself. But in Tiye's triumph, they were both defeated. Rahotep glanced down, but only the dagger's hilt could be seen. The length of it was buried deep in his chest. Blood spread beneath their feet as the failing beats of their hearts added to the steaming pool.

The prince gazed toward his lover one last time. His strength failing, he graced the boy with a gentle smile.

"Mery," Tiye gasped, his final breath cooling the blood that bubbled from his lips.

Prince and slave fell to the ground as the pharaoh cried out in horror, their lives sacrificed to tragedy. Yet even as they died, their bodies remained entwined, the prince holding his lover tightly to his ruined heart as they embarked on their next journey....

"Pa'sheri?"

Brian gasped as though awaking from a dream, only this one had been undeniably real. Blinking in shock at the word that had come unbidden to his lips, he stared at Alrick, seeing the tall blond imposed over a slighter, darker figure.

"Mery, I have found you again." Alrick's voice was suddenly light with the tones of youth and a lilt that held no traces of his Germanic roots. His posture was one of uncertain eagerness and unbearable longing, and his entire body inclined toward Brian.

"Pa'sheri, is it really you?"

The question, spoken in a low, commanding voice Brian hardly recognized as his own, was pregnant with cautious hope. He anxiously awaited the answer as he felt his body assume an athletic grace he'd never before experienced.

For the first time in untold ages, they saw each other, man and boy, soldier and priest, and countless other visages that they had borne over the vast expanse of time. Their reunion was as glorious as it was unexpected, for floating above all their other perplexed emotions, they felt the endless stirrings of a love so intense that the gods bowed before it.

"Is this real?" His voice abruptly reverting to normal, Brian's tone was shaky with the fear that the answer would be no.

"I do not know." Alrick's voice grew thicker as the situation overwhelmed him. "I think so." He took a step toward Brian, his intense gaze reflecting his helpless longing. "It all makes sense now. My inexplicable lack of caution where you were concerned. I couldn't understand it, but now I see. Everything about our relationship—from our meeting to how quickly we connected—was fated from the moment of our births." Alrick's stare made Brian's blood sing with heat. "I can see you clearly now, the beautiful, princely figure you once claimed. How can this be anything but real?" he breathed.

Brian gazed at Alrick longingly, his expression shifting between confusion and hope. Then, all of a sudden, he shook his head, closing his eyes as though trying to clear his vision. He backed away as he opened them again and glared at Alrick, his gun lifting back toward its target.

"No. If this is real, then was everything we felt for each other just a lie? Some false memory?"

"Felt?" Alrick shouted. "I'm still feeling it! Brian, *Mery*, this is us. These memories are ours, they belong to our souls. Can't you sense it?" Alrick walked toward Brian until the tip of the wavering barrel dug into his chest. "I should have told you who I was as soon as I found out you were a policeman, but I was a coward." He looked steadily into Brian's uncertain gaze. "But do not doubt that I love you. If you believe nothing else, believe that."

"Back away," Brian whispered, trying not to listen even as he hated himself for wanting to do as Alrick asked.

"This last job Rivella gave me, I wasn't going to do it. He ordered me to kill a child, but I refused. I no longer wish to be a monster," Alrick growled. "Since meeting you, all I've wanted is to be the man you fell in love with. I was on my way to find you, to leave my fate up to you, because I understand now. I am nothing without you." He took hold of the gun barrel, sliding it across his chest until it was pointed at his heart. "And I want nothing but you."

A tear slid slowly down Brian's cheek, his eyes filled with the desperate need to believe what he was hearing. Alrick was standing right in front of him, but it wasn't only him that Brian saw. A myriad of other faces flitted across Alrick's features, each more precious than the last and each looking back at him with the same expression of love that colored the brilliant blue gaze he'd come to adore. A shudder of surrender rippled through him. The gun fell from his hand, landing on the rooftop with a clatter.

"God help me, I love you so much." Brian slumped forward, acceptance leeching the strength from his legs. Ready arms caught him securely, pulling him forward into a powerful embrace. The force that drew them together was far stronger than any nature could wield. It was the strength of destiny, and they had no desire to fight it.

"No!"

The wretched scream rang in their ears, breaking them apart almost before they had the chance to connect. They spun toward the source of the terrible shriek, and Brian felt Alrick tense alongside him as they finally recognized the face of their enemy.

"Hebeny." Brian stared at her in disbelief. "Why are you here? How is this possible?"

Hayley's features were twisted into a deranged snarl, hatred stealing any beauty from her face. "Because you were supposed to be mine, Rahotep, before this disease-ridden little slut stole you from me!" She wrenched her gun around to point accusingly at Alrick.

"Hebeny, stop." Instinctively, Brian stepped protectively in front of his lover, his hands held up placatingly. "I can't believe that you're still holding a grudge after so long. I would have married you, but what happened the night we died was beyond my control."

"You lying bastard!" she screamed, the gun never wavering even as she lost control. "We might have wed, but would you really have let him go?" A bark of laughter spilled from her lips when Brian flinched. "You never could lie worth a damn, Macon. You would have married me, and then humiliated me every damn night by sleeping with him." Her eyes were wild, her hair flying as she jerked her head violently. "I was the daughter of a king! I refused to accept such an insult."

Brian's chest squeezed, leaving him short of breath as he began to understand. "Hebeny, what did you do?"

She threw back her head and laughed, but the sound was tinged with madness. "What else could I do? I called down the god Set to enact my vengeance! I was his high priestess, and he dared not refuse me."

Blinding rage swept through him as he realized that everything that had happened to them was due to nothing more than her petty jealousy. His jaw clenched so tightly he feared his teeth would shatter. "You're insane," he growled.

Hayley glared over at Alrick, who was staring at her in abject disgust. "You were the only one of us who was supposed to die that night. I engineered that slave revolt and turned them loose on the Pharaoh to be slaughtered by his guards. And I am the one who implicated your mother and brother in the scheme so you would have no choice but to avenge them. I knew you would go after his father, and I knew Rahotep would protect him. My prince should have killed you that night, and once you were dead, he would be mine to torture as I pleased.

"But Shai himself has blessed your perverted union." Spittle flew from her lips as she snarled. "Set told me that even killing you wouldn't be enough to separate you. You would just continue to find each other life after wretched life. I couldn't have that." Her hair whipped into a tangled mass as she shook her head. "How could I let you be happy when you had caused me such offense? I allowed Set to curse me so I could follow you throughout all of your pathetic lives. Every time you came together I waited until you fell in love, and then, when you were at the heights of joy, I turned you against each other."

Her manic grin lacked any trace of sanity. A chill ran down Brian's spine as he suffered the weight of her wild-eyed gaze.

"I had Gio kill your precious partner using the same type of gun and ammo as this bastard so even your little pea brain could figure it out." She laughed when Brian gaped at her in horror, but in an instant, her demeanor changed as her eyes blazed with hatred. "For three millennia I have fulfilled my contract with Set. Just because you've somehow remembered the past doesn't mean this time will be any different." She shifted her aim away from Alrick and pointed her gun at Brian. "Now pick up your weapon and shoot him, or I swear by every god that has ever existed, I will kill you."

"No." Brian's face was expressionless as he looked at her. "I am sorry for you, Hebeny, sorry that you've thrown away your existence for such a stupid reason."

"You can end this here and now," Alrick interjected. Staring at her intently, he stepped farther away from Brian, moving slowly so as though not to spook her. "Just give me the gun," he said, holding out his hand, "and this will all be over."

"Don't move!" Hayley backed away from him, growling with frustrated rage. "Do you think Set would just let me walk away? If one of you doesn't die by the other's hand, then my soul is forfeit!"

Alrick eased closer to her, ignoring her shrieks as nothing more than the ranting of a madwoman. "I promise you, it will be all right."

"I said stop!" Her eyes were wild with anger and growing fear as her control of the situation slipped away. "I will not let you beat me. Do you hear?" She shot a wild-eyed glance toward Brian, finally realizing Alrick's maneuver had made it impossible for her to cover both of them. Apparently deciding that the German was the bigger threat, she kept her gun on him as she screamed at Brian. "Now shoot him, you son of a bitch!" Her entire body shook, and Brian saw her finger began to tighten on the trigger.

"Hayley!"

Terrified that she would shoot Alrick, Brian went for his gun. The sound of her current name startled Hayley and drew her attention away from Alrick. When she saw Brian she immediately recognized the danger and whipped her weapon around toward him. Time slowed to a crawl, the motion of her gun tracing a path through the air as she aimed at Brian, his own movements similarly dilated as he fumbled for his service revolver.

Brian managed to wrap his hand around the handle of his gun just as a large body slammed into him. He heard Hayley's weapon go off as the impact knocked the gun from his hand and sent it skittering across the asphalt surface. He hit the rooftop hard, his lungs heaving as the air was knocked out of him. Struggling to breathe, he rolled the heavy weight off him and stared past it to see Hayley aiming for a second shot.

He searched frantically for his gun, finally seeing that it was lying just beyond his reach. The click of a bullet falling into the chamber sounded loudly in his ears as he scrambled toward it, but he kept his focus on the weapon, stretching until his arm felt like it would pop out of its socket.

Just a little farther. His breath was loud in his ears, sweat beading on his face as it finally came to hand. He flipped over and fired blindly, not stopping until every bullet had been spent.

Blinking away the stinging moisture that dripped into his eyes, Brian sat up, his chest heaving as he struggled to catch his breath. His ears were ringing from the explosive sounds of multiple gunshots, but his gaze was steady as he stared at Hayley's body lying motionlessly several feet away. There were several holes in her shirt at the level of her chest and stomach, the fabric around the tears was already darkening with blood.

"Brian, are you all right?"

The ragged whisper made Brian realize precisely what had knocked him over. Alrick was lying on his side, and when Brian crawled quickly over to him and looked down at his face, his heart stopped at the sight of dark blood glistening on his lips. Alrick coughed and more blood bubbled from his mouth.

"Alrick! Shit, where are you hit?" Brian frantically pulled back the coat, his gaze honing in on the round tear in the left side of Alrick's shirt. He stared at the wound in horror. The bullet had pierced Alrick's lung.

"Brian—"

"No, it's okay. Just hold on. It's okay." He knew he was babbling, but he couldn't stop as he knelt over Alrick and tore off his own coat. Ignoring the cold, he wadded it up and pressed it hard against Alrick's chest. Alrick moaned in pain, but Brian didn't let up. He risked removing one hand so he could fumble for his cell phone. He pressed a number that was stored in his speed dial.

"Special dispatch."

"This is Macon, Homicide. GPS code five-six-four-three. Send an ambulance to my signal right away. I'm on the roof."

"Yes, sir."

Brian dropped his phone onto the roof, leaving it powered on so it could be traced. Alrick coughed again, wheezing as he struggled to draw breath.

"Where—"

"Don't try to talk. Lie still."

"Where is she?"

Brian risked a glance toward the body. "She's dead."

The words were barely out of his mouth when the air behind Hayley began to shimmer, the undulations increasing until the darkness rippled like a curtain. Suddenly, a line of light traced an arch from the disturbance. The space within the arch began to glow, growing brighter and brighter until Brian had to shield his eyes.

"What the hell...?" he rasped.

With a loud crack, the disturbance ripped apart, revealing an arched doorway. Brian couldn't see what lay beyond it, but a crackle in the air made every strand of hair on his body stand on end. He gaped as a tall, unspeakably beautiful man with pitch black skin walked through the rent and stepped out onto the roof. His hair and eyes were as red as blood, and his tall, muscular form was bare save for the shadows draped around his waist like cloth. Brian felt his body go hot, then cold, then hot again. He wanted to run away, but even if he could have left Alrick, he doubted his legs would have worked. The man glanced toward them, a cruelly amused smile curving his full lips before he looked down at Hayley's body. A single red eyebrow lifted with interest.

"And what have we here?" The ground vibrated from the awesome depth of his voice. He spoke softly, yet his tone commanded untold power. The man reached down and yanked Hayley's head up by her hair, but incredibly, her body remained where it was. Instead, something else came away in his hand, stretching painfully as he ripped it away from its physical form.

Brian stared in frozen disbelief at what he was seeing. The form resolved itself into the image of a woman, but it wasn't Hayley. The woman was young, her face dark with vicious beauty. Her ancient clothing was instantly recognizable. "Hebeny?" he whispered.

The woman opened her eyes and blinked, her expression disoriented. She looked confused as she saw him and Alrick, but when she looked down at the body lying below her, her face twisted with abject horror.

"Hello, my love."

The spirit shook as the god spoke to her. Her eyes moved to the side as though she wanted to look behind her but dared not.

"It is time, Hebeny."

"No!" She reached up and grabbed the hand wrapped in her hair, futilely trying to pull it away. "Please, my Lord Set! Please let me go!" She cried out as the god shook her, whipping her around effortlessly as she begged for mercy.

"Come, come, little girl, let us have none of that. I have enjoyed your antics more than I can express, but now your time is done. You must pay your debt to me, and I have come to collect." He turned toward the glowing opening and drew back his arm.

"Arggghhh!!!" Hebeny's scream vanished along with her spirit as the god tossed her into the glowing light. Wiping his hands in satisfaction, he turned back toward the two dumbstruck men staring at him in bewildered astonishment.

"I must congratulate you. Watching all of you and your little dramas these long centuries has proved most diverting." The air grew chill as he smiled, the unbearable perfection of his features promising unspeakable cruelty. "I wish you both the best. Well, at least for the short time you have left." His laugh seemed to echo even after he disappeared through the rip. It vanished in a flash of light, leaving nothing behind but the unbroken darkness of the night sky.

Alrick's cough broke Brian from his frozen state. Even through his shock, he'd never relaxed his pressure on Alrick's chest, but the blood kept coming, seeping from the wound and flecking Alrick's lips as his lungs filled with blood. The god's parting words began to make horrifying sense.

"Brian," Alrick wheezed.

"Shh, be quiet."

"No, Brian. It's over."

Brian shook his head, scowling in rejection of Alrick's words. He choked as something painful lodged in his throat. "I feel like such an idiot. I should have known you didn't write that damn note." He was unable to stop the tears that spilled down his cheeks. "*Liebling*? Isn't that what you always call me? Not 'my dear,' like something out of a bad movie."

"I am sorry, Brian. I didn't mean for any of this to happen. Angela—"

"That wasn't your fault." Brian dashed away his tears impatiently, quickly returning both hands to the task of staunching the unceasing flow of blood from Alrick's wound. He bore down as hard as he could, but he couldn't stop the internal bleeding. "It was that bitch. She did this. She did all of it."

"Because of me. She hurt you because of me, just like she did so long ago." A tear ran unchecked down Alrick's cheek, but he didn't have the strength to wipe it away. "I promise that I'll be better next time, that I'll be worthy of you."

Brian shook his head. "No, not next time. Now." His voice dropped to a hoarse whisper as he closed his eyes, unable to bear the sight of Alrick's pain. "I can't lose you again."

"You can't give up now. If I can't be with you in this life, I swear I'll be waiting for you in the next."

Brian felt a hand cradle his face, and he forced himself to open his eyes. The effort of raising his hand made Alrick break out in a sweat, but his gaze was confident through the pain.

"It's just as she said. We will be together again, and there won't be anyone to stop us."

Brian ignored the salty wetness that bathed his cheeks. "But how will we find each other?"

Blue-tinged lips curved up in a small smile. "We always do. But until then, you have to live, Brian. Live for both of us. All I want is for you to be happy."

Brian didn't know if he could keep such a cruel promise. "I'll try," he said for Alrick's sake.

"And I don't want you to be afraid anymore. Don't be afraid to love."

Brian didn't answer, knowing he'd be lying if he agreed. He couldn't swear to that, not now when his heart was breaking into a million pieces. He bent down and pressed his lips against Alrick's. The taste of blood was strong, but he kissed him deeply, pouring out everything that was in his heart. "I love you." The sound was muffled against Alrick's lips, but the truth of it rang out like a clarion call. "Now and forever."

Far below, the blare of sirens split through the night. It was only a minute later that the stairwell echoed with the pounding of boots as the paramedics rushed up to the roof. They burst out through the access door but paused when they took in the scene. The taller EMT started forward, but his partner grabbed his arm and held him back. He looked over at the short man, who shook his head grimly.

Brian knelt on the roof, sobbing as he held Alrick's lifeless body in his arms.

CHAPTER 28

THE BIRD flew low over the lake, hoping to catch a damselfly as a tasty snack. The warm spring sun shone down on Brian's shoulders, glinting off the rippling surface, the brightness occasionally hiding the bird from view. Suddenly, a trill sounded out over the water, heralding the hunter's success.

Brian sat on the shore of the lake, looking out over the water, trying to enjoy the peaceful scenery. Mrs. O'Malley had been pleased to see him, but when she'd asked why he'd come alone, he'd told her simply that Alrick was busy and couldn't make it. He hadn't had the heart to say anything more.

Three weeks after Alrick's death, Brian was still struggling to accept that he was gone. He'd only known Alrick for such a short time, but there were no rules governing love. It had been difficult at first, trying to figure out how to go on. He'd fought with the paramedics when they finally took Alrick's body away, needing to hold on to him as long as he could. When his arms were finally empty, the temptation of the roof's edge had beckoned seductively. But he'd made Alrick a promise, and he would keep it, no matter how much it hurt.

The detectives who'd arrived first on the scene didn't know what to make of what they found. A police captain was dead and a fellow detective was covered in the blood of a suspicious foreigner. They took possession of the discarded Arctic Warfare rifle, and forensics easily matched it to the gang hits. Brian had been placed on administrative leave pending an investigation into his involvement in the shooting death of Captain Preston and a German national. The confusion surrounding the situation had only increased once it was determined that his superior officer had been shot with his own service revolver.

No one knew quite what to think. Ballistics matched the gun that had been found near Captain Preston's body to the bullet that had killed Giovanni Rivella. Gunpowder residue tests revealed that she had, in fact, been the shooter. Suspicions mounted as the story spread of how Brian had been found cradling the body of Rivella's hired assassin. Suspension and possible criminal charges became a real possibility, not that Brian had cared.

He'd been invited to explain the situation to Internal Affairs but declined, making an official statement that he would let the evidence speak for itself. If he was charged for murdering Captain Preston, then so be it. Spending the rest of his life in jail wouldn't have been any great change to his current existence.

He'd hidden in his apartment for days afterward, unwilling to deal with the world and unable to face Angela's family. Deep down, he couldn't shake his belief that her death was his fault. If not for Hayley—Hebeny—and her irrational, undying hatred of him and Alrick, Angela would still be alive. Once the medical examiner had completed the autopsy on her body, her husband had begun making arrangements for her burial. Todd had called him, but Brian didn't answer. He unplugged his landline and let his cell phone battery drain to nothing.

It was Brad who finally came banging on his door four days after Alrick and Angela's deaths. Matt Roddy had woken up in the hospital and had revealed everything he'd learned about Hayley and her relationship with Giovanni Rivella. Once their involvement had been exposed, it hadn't taken long to dig up the rest of the sordid truth. Hayley's fall from grace sent shockwaves throughout the entire department. The official investigation concluded that Brian's part in her death was related to his confronting her about her crimes. With no one around to contradict the theory, Internal Affairs quickly and eagerly closed the case, exonerating him of all culpability.

Brian had his life back, but he didn't want it. His guilt about Angela continued to eat at him, but he began to regret his cowardice for abandoning Todd and the boys. When he finally dragged himself out of his apartment and over to their house a day before the funeral, he'd had no clue what sort of reception to expect, but they had welcomed him with open arms. Brian had begged Todd for forgiveness, but the large man simply wrapped him in a bear hug and told him that he'd always be family. Todd tried to stay strong for his boys, and Sam was manfully hiding his sorrow, but as for Jonathan….

It had taken Brian a long time and a lot of talking to pull the young man out of his depression. A gentle soul, Jon had always been closest to his mother, and her death had hit him particularly hard. Brian had sat with him for hours, letting him cry and rage and indulge his pain until the teen at last found a small measure of solace.

Eventually, Brian told Todd everything about Alrick, Hayley, and himself, about their tragic past and the madness that had driven Hayley to commit so many crimes. He didn't know if Todd believed him. Hell, he could hardly believe it himself. But he knew that Angela's family would always be a part of his life, and he owed them nothing less than the truth.

The funeral was a somber occasion. The entire department turned out for it, and the sound of bagpipes and the twenty-one shots fired in her honor pulled tears from the eyes of more than one hard-bitten cop. The rest of the day had passed in a blur, well-wishers coming and going from the Lovell home into the early evening. Todd had invited Brian to stay with them that night so he wouldn't have to be alone, but he'd needed some time to put everything into perspective.

The voice mail that was waiting for him when he returned home had been a shock to say the least. His bank had called to notify him about unusual activity on his account. Unusual to the tune of an $800 million deposit. Confused and annoyed about having to deal with this on top of everything else, Brian had just been about to call the bank when his phone rang before he could pick up the receiver.

"Ah, this modern technology of yours is rather useful when the occasion demands."

Brian had stared at nothing as his hand cramped around the receiver from holding it so tightly. The voice was one that he would never forget as long as he lived.

"You know, Detective, it is amazing what treasure one can amass over thirty centuries. That Hebeny had quite the financial head on her shoulders, even if in all other ways, she was nothing but a foolish girl. Enjoy your reward for a game well played. After all, she won't be needing it anymore."

He listened to Set's inexplicable message several more times before it made any sense. All of the wealth Hayley had gathered over her long years, investing it and adding to it with every life she lived, all of it was his to do with as he saw fit. Once he'd seen the bank's records and was finally able to accept that he was suddenly disgustingly rich, he acted quickly.

He sent half of the money to Rosamunde, enough to wipe out her debt to the Russians with plenty left over to set her family up for life. The call to her had been a difficult one. She'd been frantic for news about her brother, but of course, no one had known to contact her. Brian felt her loss keenly, guilt piling on top of guilt. Rosa had been distraught to learn of Alrick's death, but the story of what precipitated it had fascinated her. That her brother had fallen victim to such a tragic romance saddened her even as the knowledge that he would be reborn gave her comfort. She made Brian promise that he would come to Germany to visit so her son might know the man who had been so important to his beloved *Onkel*.

Nearly all the rest went to Todd and his sons. Dumbstruck at the generous gift, Todd had tried to refuse, but Brian wouldn't hear it. "I have to believe that something good came out of all of this."

Todd had accepted his explanation but had begged him to stay with him and the boys for a while. Brian knew Todd was afraid of what he might do if they didn't keep a close eye on him, but he'd assured Todd that he was all right. He just needed to spend some time alone so he could get his head on straight.

He turned his administrative leave into an extended vacation, the small amount of Hayley's money he kept more than enough to hold him for a long time. He'd considered just staying at home, but then the memory of O'Malley's Folly had caught hold and refused to let go.

Brian took a deep breath of the pollution-free air, enjoying the warmth of the sun on his face. The water beckoned, but he was nervous about going in without Alrick at his side. The days he'd spent there with Alrick had been some of the most wonderful of his life. It was a comforting setting as he tried to decide what to do with himself.

He didn't have to work again if he didn't want to. He could just live off Hayley's money if he was careful. But somehow, he didn't think either Angela or Alrick would approve. He'd become a cop for a reason, and he knew they'd want him to continue his efforts to help those whose voice had been stolen from them. Still, it was hard to even think about going back to the city.

I don't want you to be afraid anymore. Don't be afraid to love.

Alrick's words kept coming back to him. He hadn't been able to answer when his lover had lain dying in his arms. The pain had been far too fresh. But maybe one day he'd be able to fulfill Alrick's final request—to exist outside of the shell his partner and his lover had worked so hard to break.

He knew, though, that he would never love again. If it were true that everyone had a soul mate, then he'd found his. He'd enjoyed his few short moments of perfect bliss, and the place in his heart where he'd buried Alrick could never be filled by another. Watching over his family would be enough. He swore that Sam, Jonathan, and little Gerry would grow up happy and healthy, and that Todd, Rosa, and Heinz would never want for anything for the rest of their lives. And when he finally passed on and met his lover once more, he would know that he'd kept his promise.

"Mind if I join you?"

Brian shielded his eyes with his hand as he glanced up. The man standing next to him looked down at him with a friendly smile. He read the interest in the man's eyes, but it didn't make him anxious like it would have in the past. They weren't alone on the lakeshore, but Brian didn't feel the need to hide from the obvious pick-up attempt. He smiled up at the man in return but shook his head.

"Sorry, I just want to be alone for a little bit."

The man shrugged, his expression pleasant but disappointed. "Oh, well. My loss."

"Wait." Brian didn't know what he was doing, but he felt bad for being so dismissive. "You're not staying up at the Folly by any chance?"

"In fact, I am."

"So am I. Maybe I'll see you later?"

The man's grin returned. "Count on it."

Brian watched the man walk away for a minute before turning his gaze back toward the lake. "Okay, lover," he murmured. "This is me, living my life."

Alrick had given him this one last gift, the ability to open his heart without fear. He refused to waste it. Brian closed his eyes as a soft breeze brushed across his lips like a phantom caress.

"Until next time, *pa'sheri*. Sweet dreams."

EPILOGUE

Tokyo, 21xx

YOSHI brushed away the sakura blossom that had drifted down to land on his sketch pad. The ground around him was littered with the classic sign of a Japanese spring. He'd been at his new high school for over a week, but he was still spending his break time alone. His mother had urged him to make new friends, but he'd never been good at talking to strangers. It was far easier to just find a quiet place during lunchtime so he could practice his drawing.

Applying his stylus to the pad, he glanced purposefully up at the group of boys who were playing an impromptu game of soccer on the other side of the field. Drawing objects in motion was always difficult, but he was determined to master the technique. If he wanted to be a professional manga artist some day, he would need to be able to pull off difficult action scenes.

One of the figures in particular kept drawing his eye. The young man was tall for a Japanese, his slim figure standing out clearly among his friends as he executed a difficult maneuver. The soccer ball landed in the goal with a solid swish, and the boy jumped up and down, arms pumping in the air. His joy was palpable even across the field. Yoshi found himself concentrating on the player, adding line after line to his sketch pad as he brought the boy's figure to life. His stylus flew across the pad as he looked down to enhance a certain bit of shading.

The object that landed near his feet startled him as it sent up a shower of pink blossoms. His hand jerked, the stylus skipping uncontrolled across the pad. Yoshi sighed as he saw the errant line marring his picture. A double tap to the electronic pad put it in edit mode, and he ran his finger over the mark to erase it. Another tap brought him back to drawing mode. He didn't bother to see what it was that had disturbed him, nor did he look up at the sound of running that was getting ever closer.

"*Oi*! I'm so sorry! Did the ball hit you? Are you okay?"

Yoshi pressed his lips together, annoyed at the disturbance. "Yes," he replied, glancing up just far enough to see that the thing lying near his feet was a soccer ball.

"Oh good. I told Tanaka he has to watch his aim. Hi, I'm Inoue Kaori."

Yoshi had ignored the speaker up to that point, but at the unexpected sharing of a first name, he looked up in surprise. He blinked at the hand that was mere inches away, absently recognizing the Western gesture before raising his gaze beyond it to its owner's face. Yoshi gasped, blinking in flustered uncertainty as a bright smile beamed down at him.

It was the same boy he'd been admiring. Up close he seemed even taller, and he was extremely handsome. Yoshi hugged his sketch pad to his chest as though it would help muffle the sudden pounding of his heart. Taking a deep breath, he returned the familiar greeting. "F-Fujiwara… Yoshi."

Inoue smiled at him, and Yoshi felt his heart beat even faster. His face quickly warmed, and he prayed he wasn't blushing.

"Nice to meet you, Fujiwara Yoshi. Are you a first-year? I don't remember you from last term."

"Um, yes, *senpai*," he answered respectfully. "And you?"

"I'm a second-year."

"*Oi*, Inoue! Bring back the ball! Lunch is almost over."

Inoue looked around at his friends, who were waiting impatiently for him to return. He turned back toward Yoshi and winked. "Gotta go, but I'll see you around?"

"Um, okay." Yoshi thought he must look like one of those bobble-head figurines as he nodded.

With another blinding smile, Inoue was gone. Yoshi gazed after him entranced, admiring the athleticism that was apparent as he ran back to his friends. He was nice for an upperclassman, but Yoshi knew that he had probably been humoring him. Why would he bother to socialize with a shy, awkward first-year?

Inoue was halfway across the field when he suddenly turned around and waved, running backward until Yoshi raised his hand in acknowledgement. Yoshi felt a smile spread across his face.

Maybe high school wouldn't be so bad after all.

Pearl Love has been writing since she was a kid, but it was the pretty boys who frolic around in her head who finally convinced her to pursue it seriously. She's a Midwest transplant who current thrives in the hustle and bustle of the nation's capital. She especially enjoys stories with guns, swords, and massive explosions. Pearl is a Marvel fan girl and owns a ridiculous stash of knitting supplies.

E-mail: pearllove925@gmail.com
Website: http://pearllovebooks.com
Facebook: Pearl Love (pearllove925@gmail.com)
Twitter: @pearllovebooks

Also from DSP Publications

Desert World Allegiances

Desert World: Book One

By Lyn Gala

Livre once offered Planetary Alliance miners and workers a small fortune if they helped terraform the mineral rich planet. People flocked to the world, but then a civil war cut the desert planet off from all resources. Half-terraformed and clinging to the edge of existence, Livre devolved into a world where death was accepted as part of life, water resources were scarce and constantly dwindling, and neighbors tried to help each other hold off the inevitable as the desert fought to take back the few terraformed spaces.

Temar Gazer claims to be the victim of water theft. His claims could be a simple misdirection intended to help him escape a term of labor after his criminal prank caused irreparable damage to a watering system. However as the only member of the council arguing against a short-term slavery sentence for Temar, Shan Polli can't escape the fear that something darker is happening. The more he investigates Temar's story, the more he finds that his world is not as free of politics or danger as he had assumed. Together, Shan and Temar must get to the bottom of the conspiracy before time runs out for the entire planet.

http://www.dsppublications.com

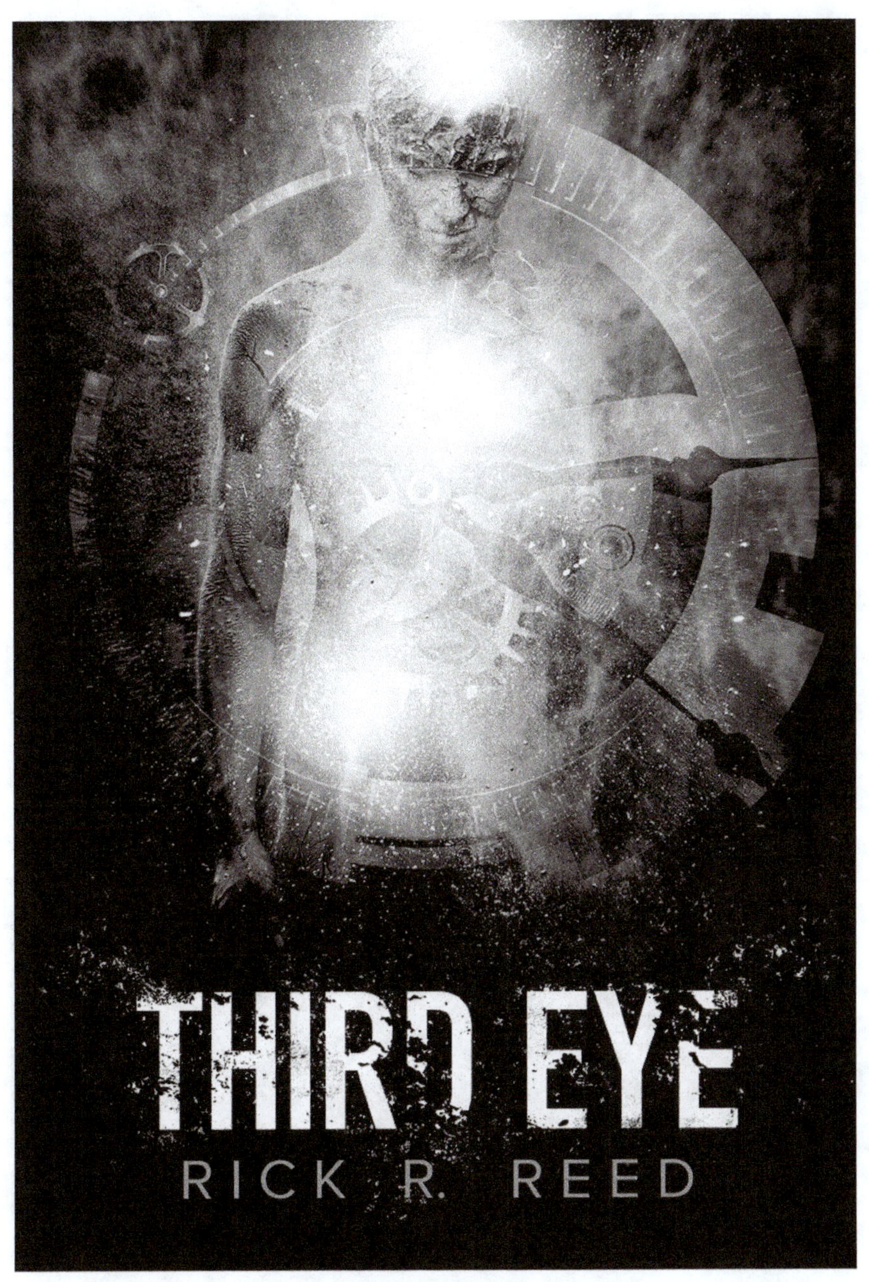

http://www.dsppublications.com

http://www.dsppublications.com

http://www.dsppublications.com

http://www.dsppublications.com

http://www.dsppublications.com

www.ingramcontent.com/pod-product-compliance
Lightning Source LLC
Chambersburg PA
CBHW060936120726
47910CB00002B/358

9 781634 760560